HIRED HIT

ON

JESSAMIN ISLAND

a novel by

Andi Thomas Peters

Hired Hit on Jessamin Island

ISBN Paperback: 978-1-955032-03-2
ISBN Kindle: 978-1-955032-04-9
ISBN Hardback: 978-1-955032-05-6

www.andithomaspeters.com

Dedication

For Laura Leak Cavagnaro, my indefatigable editor, and her sister, Beth Leak Baird. Beth was taken from us way too early by breast cancer, but the memory of her mesmerizing smile still lights up a room. And, to CP and BN whose real stories about our prison system sparked the fictional plot and characters for this book. I am indebted to you for your heartfelt honesty.

PART I

Chapter One

Cray Abbott, the artist

My lawyer advised me that it didn't matter that I was a nonviolent first offender. The Federal Sentencing Guidelines mandated imprisonment. If we fought the charge and lost, my sentence could be up to seven years. Accepting the favorable plea offer of one year at a minimum-security facility was his strong recommendation. Apparently, my innocence was not a consideration. My predicament was even harder to accept since I had never experimented with any narcotic.

"Don't look at it as incarceration but as an extended summer camp paid for by United States' taxpayers," my lawyer said. "The facility is ranked every year as the Best Place to Go to Prison. It's referred to as Club Fed."

I never heard of any publication that ranked federal penitentiaries, a new twist on *Fodor's Travel.* I reviewed the prison guidebook provided by my lawyer. He may be right. The federal correctional facility in Somerset, South Carolina, offered a gym, music room, movie nights, stress reduction classes, and the opportunity to take various courses, including art on hobby day. The humid climate was the only drawback.

I was a struggling artist determined to make it on my own, though I could barely pay my bills despite working two jobs. Not even one amenity offered at the correctional facility was within reach on my limited budget. Still, prison seemed so unfair; but after learning that Somerset was within thirty miles of Beaufort, the hometown of my grandmother, I thought that perhaps this happenstance was twisted fate.

Mom always abhorred Kentucky, my birthplace. When marrying Josh Abbott, my father, she traded views of grassy marshes, sea oats, majestic birds, and grand oak trees draped in moss for endless stretches of tobacco plants. Mom would visit me often, I thought. My grandmother had never gotten over her daughter choosing Kentucky over her Lowcountry roots. And, as I had grown older, I began to think my mother hadn't either. I was starting to come to terms with my limited period of confinement.

After my arrest, Dad confessed the truth to his father, who had driven from the North Carolina Outer Banks to bail me out and help secure a lawyer. My own father couldn't help with these tasks since he, too, was behind bars at the Kentucky Federal Penitentiary. He would soon be transferred to a minimum-security prison —or pre-release transition, as he liked to call it. A reward for exemplary behavior, he boasted. Papa Walt learned the real reason for his son's expedited transfer during his recent visit with Dad. Dad slipped Papa Walt a letter detailing the foiled plan, and said, "Warn Cray to trust NO ONE!"

No one, unfortunately, included my Dad. Dad had been in cahoots with the warden to secure his preferred transfer. All Dad had to do was to help arrange the transport of "only a small amount of cocaine," skimmed from a major drug bust.

Little did I know, Dad would involve me in this scheme. With the warden planning the move, there was no downside, my father was assured. The load would be placed in my trunk during my scheduled visit with my father. A roadblock, searching for a fake escapee, would require a search of all vehicles. I would never know anything about the stash or the participating officers securing it from my trunk. I would proceed on my route home without a clue of the plot.

The masterminds of the scheme didn't foresee my stop for gas before reaching the roadblock nor the TSA agent who was giving his trained sniffer dog a bathroom break. I had no clue about the cocaine in the back of my trunk, but the dog sniffed if out, and the TSA agent arrested me.

I'm sure that Dad thinks my decision to plead guilty for his crime was the ultimate act of father–son loyalty. But that wasn't the reason I took the blame.

My mother's once twinkling, aqua-blue eyes, like the water that surrounded her homeplace, had already taken on the color of the parched earth of the harvested Kentucky tobacco fields. I couldn't bear the further heartache in my mother's weary eyes if she were to learn that Dad caused my downfall, using his only son for personal gain. It was hard enough for me to accept. I couldn't imagine the further burden this would place on her.

Dad's tenure in prison had apparently hardened his once altruistic soul. But worse than my father's transformation, I feared that if I had exposed the real criminals, my mother might be targeted in a plan of retribution. The most dangerous criminals, in fact, could be the ones least expected, like the prison warden and others with law enforcement on their side.

So, I pled guilty to save my mother. I had to protect her from revenge. Though I would be forever scarred with a felony conviction for drug possession, it was my own version of a Purple Heart, the military decoration bestowed upon my paternal grandfather. Thankfully, Papa Walt understood. There was really no alternative but to make the best of Club Fed.

Chapter Two

Josh Abbott, tobacco farmer, Cray's father

I am proud of Cray for chasing his dream of making a living as an artist. I'd questioned him about whether he could make enough money selling his paintings. He said he would get other jobs to help pay the bills, if necessary, but he wouldn't be happy doing anything else.

Cray had a silent swagger that came, I thought, from the confidence of knowing your intended direction in life and the drive to succeed on your own. In retrospect, I had neither.

We did have one thing in common. Cray described his calling as a burning craving, an unquenchable thirst, an unrelenting desire. I experienced these feelings when I first laid eyes on Savannah, Cray's mother. The fire and passion between Savannah and me that created Cray was powerful and intense. It must have permeated Cray's DNA.

I wondered if this overpowering passion had been inherited from my mother, Maude. After all, her one indiscretion had created me. Now, sitting in my cell, I had lots of time to revisit the past.

My whole life, I had worked for Abbott Tobacco Farm, the largest grower of burley tobacco in central Kentucky. I had been destined to step into the shoes of my father, Adam, and the preceding Abbott ancestors. I hadn't been permitted to explore other interests, hobbies, or even possible future vocations.

I could never understand why I hated farming. It was, after all, in my bloodline. Yet, I did hate it — all of it. I hated the long hours in the grueling sun, the orange-brown stain on my skin from handling the tobacco leaves, and the stressful reliance on Mother Nature. I even hated the smell of the fresh tobacco harvest.

My disdain made even more sense when I learned that Adam Abbott wasn't my birth father. I was eighteen years old in 1999 when a tractor accident left me bloody and severely wounded. It also led to my discovery of the truth.

I needed blood. Mom and Dad had type O positive blood; I had type B negative.

"B negative is rare; the local blood bank doesn't have that type. Is Josh's father local?" I overheard the doctor ask my parents.

If not for my near-fatal accident, I probably never would have met the man from whom I inherited this rare blood type. Ultimately, they found the blood that I needed at a regional hospital, and Mom found the courage to answer my questions honestly.

Dad? Walt? Colonel? I didn't even know how to address him, I thought, as I departed on the bus headed toward the Marine Air Station in Beaufort, South Carolina, to meet my father, Colonel Walt Benton.

On the long bus ride, I kept replaying my mother's explanation. Adam Abbott was the first and only man she had ever loved. He was her childhood sweetheart. She always knew she would marry Adam. It had all been decided. She couldn't explain her shameful, one indiscretion, as she called it.

It happened the summer of 1981 when she and her sister visited her Aunt Mildred in Nags Head, a beach town in the North Carolina Outer Banks. It was the longest time she had ever been away from Adam. Her weepy eyes and cracking voice validated her mortification. I didn't know if she was more ashamed of her indiscretion or that she and Adam were sexually active before they tied the knot. "It never occurred to me that Adam wasn't your father," she said.

At birth, Mom said that I resembled her father, Everett Joshua Carter, so they named me after him. As the long-standing manager of the Abbott Tobacco Farm, Grandpa Everett seemed part of the Abbott family.

In my pubescent years, Mom noticed there was more changing than my voice. I was beginning to look eerily similar to the aspiring, young Marine she met on the Outer Banks.

She thought it was her imagination. Other than his name, Walt Benton, her recall was hazy. If she pursued her doubts, what would happen to her marriage? How would Adam react upon discovering that another man could be my father? Her father, my namesake, idolized the Abbott family, and managing the Abbott Tobacco Farm was the only job he ever had. They provided his livelihood and hers. She was overthinking things. There was no way she could have become pregnant after one time. She buried her suspicions. "Please forgive me," she pleaded with me.

I didn't forgive her then because I was consumed with anger. I felt betrayed. I felt an immeasurable void in my identity. Time has a way of providing clarity— and with clarity, forgiveness. I couldn't see it then, but now, I realize that my conception probably wasn't much different from my son, Cray's. History does have a way of repeating itself. But, that's another story.

Upon boarding the bus, my initial excitement in meeting my birth father, Walt Benton, flipped to anxiety when I saw the "Welcome to South Carolina" sign. I was scared, confused, and lost.

My father, Walt, was waiting for me at the bus stop. Even without the Marine uniform, I would have been able to distinguish him from the other locals around the bus station. He looked like he belonged to me—same build, same hair, same eyes.

Walt ran to me and bear-hugged me. His embrace felt like a death grip. "My boy, my boy," he stammered. When he finally released his hold, tears were streaming from his green eyes.

"I bet you're starved," he said, brushing the tears from his face. "How about I treat you to the best seafood in the world? Can't get that in Kentucky now, can you? What will it be—shrimp, oysters, crabs, or flounder?"

"I don't know. I've never eaten any seafood," I said.

"What? Really?" he asked, with a tone of astonishment. "Maudie couldn't get enough of it that summer. Boiled shrimp was her favorite. We couldn't find cocktail sauce hot enough for her. I never met a girl that added a heap of Texas Pete onto everything. You like things spicy?"

In less than five minutes, I learned things about my mother that the past eighteen years hadn't revealed—her love of seafood and Texas Pete. I'd never seen her use any type of hot sauce or eat anything spicy. And, I had never heard anyone refer to her as "Maudie." I had a feeling that I was going to get to know not only my father but also my mother.

On my very first day, I learned more about Walt than I knew about the father who raised me. The second day, Walt was tied up with station duty. He gave me the keys to his car, some spending money, a fishing pole, a tackle box, and a cooler with iced down water and beer. Next, he pointed me toward the Broad River Fishing Pier and the beach.

"You should get to know the area," he said. "I took the liberty of getting you a fishing license. If the fish aren't biting and you're like me, you can be happy as a clam staring at the water all day. Here's a list of my other favorite spots. You can check them out if you get bored or if the heat is too severe."

It must have been at least ninety degrees that day, but the last thing I was worried about was the temperature. Every previous summer, I had withstood fourteen-hour days working in the tobacco fields with the scorching sun but no ocean breeze.

Walt was right. I was happy sitting and soaking in the water views of the barrier islands that surrounded Beaufort. It beat laboring in the tobacco fields. After a couple of hours, the fish started biting. I didn't know if any of my catch was edible, but I placed them in the cooler to proudly display to Walt.

As I headed back to the Marine Air Station, I decided to make a quick detour through the historic downtown. The Port Royal Ice Castle piqued my curiosity— voted #1 every year for the best ice cream and snow cones, according to the sign on the window. While standing in line, I spotted Savannah behind the counter. My mouth dropped open. I had never seen anything like her in Kentucky. Her blue eyes sparkled as she delivered my rainbow snow cone. She flipped her blonde braid over her shoulder and said, "$2.00."

"How much extra for a date?" I uncharacteristically blurted. "I'm from Kentucky. I don't know anything about Beaufort."

My first mistake was mispronouncing the name of the town. I said "Bo-fert."

"Well, for starters, you need to say it right. Down here in South Carolina, it's pronounced "Bew-fert," as in beautiful! I'm Savannah," she said, as she reached over the counter and extended her hand.

"I'm Josh," I replied, shaking her hand and instantly aware of how rough, dry, and bristly my hands were compared to those of the "Bew-fert" bombshell.

For some reason, Savannah Hart accepted the date. She became my private summer tour guide to her captivating town. She introduced me to the hidden gems, as she called her special places. She later introduced me to her wilder side, when she untied her bright-red string bikini on the banks of the Coosawhatchie River.

"It's called skinny dipping," she shouted back at me as she jumped into the water. "You ever heard of it? Or y'all too busy picking tobacco?"

I didn't have time to answer before she dove under the surface. I threw off my swim trunks and rushed in after her. I couldn't imagine anything topping that culmination of desire and raging hormones. I was wrong. It was just the beginning of our summer love affair.

I'd never thought about the exact place where we created Cray. We had sex more times and places that summer than anyone could keep count—the observation deck of the Hunting Island Lighthouse, a secluded bench at Waterfront Park, off the beaten path on the Spanish Moss Trail, and the Highway 21 Drive-In Theater. But, based on percentages alone, a betting man would say Cray was conceived on the beach. Now that I had lots of time to relive those carefree times, the location of Cray's conception was as transparent as Savannah's blue eyes.

We had three hours between Savannah's job as a docent at the Beaufort History Museum and when she reported to The Port Royal Ice Castle, her evening gig during tourist season. It was enough time for an excursion to the Cypress Wetlands, a birdwatcher's wonderland. She pointed out the painted buntings, oystercatchers, terns, cranes, herons, egrets, and sandpipers. I had never met anyone who knew so much about birds. But, her knowledge of nature was part of her beauty. To me, Savannah was one of the wonders of what I now understood was the Lowcountry.

Savannah led me to a secluded spot amongst all the cypress trees. We nestled on a soft, mossy patch. She explained that the rookery was the nesting place and breeding grounds for the egrets. The sex that ensued was truly inspired. Thinking back on the beauty of that spot as I sat in my barren cell, I am now completely confident that the rookery in the Cypress Wetlands was the spot where Cray was conceived. His name was fitting—after the variety of cranes I witnessed on that unforgettable day.

I've made many mistakes. The biggest one, however, was encouraging Savannah to leave her natural haven and plop her down in middle-of-nowhere Kentucky. She was pregnant. I was eighteen years old and now had a family to support. I felt that I had no choice but to return to the security of the Abbott Farm. I had tobacco fields to harvest. I was a tobacco farmer. That was my livelihood then. Now, I'm only known as Inmate #233.

Chapter Three

Hannah Anne Hart, Savannah's mother

Savannah was all I had. She was my everything, my pillar of strength, my rock. We had always been a team, and she was the captain. She was wise beyond her years. I suppose that's what happens when your father abandons you at the age of four. Savannah was the only reason that I hadn't sunk into a deeper depression over the years. I wouldn't quit on her too.

I knew my pleas for her to stay in Beaufort were selfish. What was I going to do without my girl? I knew that the time would come when Savannah would move into a place of her own, fall in love, get married, and have a family. However, I never envisioned her leaving Beaufort, much less the Lowcountry altogether. It was part of her blood, her soul, her essence. She was a walking advertisement of the natural and captivating beauty of our paradise. However, my pleas fell on deaf ears.

I had to set her free. What was it Bo had said when he left? He couldn't be fenced in?

From the minute Savannah was born, she traveled through life with her father's free spirit, always catching a wave. She had his aquamarine eyes, the color of the tidal creeks, rivers, and ocean that surrounded us. While similar, there was also a sharp contrast between Savannah's eyes and those of her father. Savannah's eyes twinkled. They radiated a simplistic happiness and bubbly energy and yet, could be still and calming. Bo Hart's blue eyes were icy cold and flickered with a burning intensity. His eyes reminded me of the eyes of those Siberian Husky dogs that I had seen on TV pulling sleds in the snow.

Perhaps Bo's eyes had always revealed his untamable wildness. Of course, I didn't think of them that way when he rambled into my homeroom class the first day of 7th grade.

"You must be Beauregard Hart," Mrs. Caldwell remarked, "our new student."

"Yes, ma'am. But I go by Bo—never could spell Beauregard."

The class giggled. Bo instantly won Mrs. Caldwell's heart as well as every girl's in the class.

"Well, welcome to Beaufort, Bo," Mrs. Caldwell said. "Are you related to Hannah Anne?" she asked.

It seemed like the whole class turned and looked at me. I could feel heat rising from my face as I looked down at the floor to deflect the stares from my classmates.

"No, ma'am, or I don't think so," Bo said.

"Hannah Anne Hart," she said, pointing at me.

I thought I was going to die.

"There aren't many Harts around here; so, who knows? You two may be related."

"My family just moved here from Texas, and I haven't heard of any relatives here," Bo Hart said, as he made his way to an empty desk on the front row.

"Well, we're glad to have you. Do you have your complete class schedule?" Mrs. Caldwell asked.

It was like no one else in the class mattered. As 7th graders, we were all new to Palmetto Middle School and in the same boat as this Texan who strutted like a cowboy. Bo pulled his printed schedule from his jean jacket pocket.

"Yes, ma'am," Bo said. "It says my first period is algebra, Mr. Rivers, in Room 305. I went there first. That's why I was late, so I apologize."

"No need for apologies. Obviously, no one told you that on the first day, you were report to homeroom before heading to your first period class. Does anyone else have any questions?"

No one spoke up.

Bo raised his hand. I thought that he sure had a lot of confidence being new. Even if I had questions, I wasn't going to announce them to the class for fear of being accused of "sucking up." Bo Hart sure didn't seem to care about any backlash.

"Do we come back to homeroom again today or go straight to lunch?" Bo asked.

"You will come back here during 4th period. We find it helpful on the first day to meet here first so you can get your locker assignments. Any other questions?"

Everyone was quiet. Bo turned around in his front row desk and surveyed his homeroom class. I looked down at the floor to avoid making eye contact, worried that I would blush again.

"Alrighty then. I have a list with your assigned locker numbers. Your lockers are right outside. If you can form a line, behind Bo, I will show you to your locker. Bo, your locker is #12."

"How about that?" Bo said, as he stood to follow Mrs. Caldwell. "That's my football number."

I heard Mrs. Caldwell ask him what position he played but couldn't hear his response as they entered the hallway. By the time I made it through the line, Bo Hart had disappeared.

"Hannah Anne Hart," Mrs. Caldwell said, scanning the list.

If the lockers were assigned alphabetically, mine had to be right beside Bo's, I mean we had the same last name.

"Locker #27."

Typical, I thought. I wouldn't be so lucky. I proceeded down the hallway covered with lockers to about as far away from Bo Hart's locker as I thought I could get. Then, I noticed that the lockers on top were numbers 1-15, and number 16 started the bottom row. My heart jumped when I saw that my assigned Locker #27 was directly below Bo's #12.

The morning classes seemed to drag on forever. I couldn't concentrate on anything but Bo Hart and trying to summon the courage to talk to him at our lockers. What would I say? "Welcome to Beaufort." Nope. That sounded dorky. "Hey, I'm Hannah Anne Hart, your long-lost cousin." Nope, even dorkier, but I was a dork pure and simple. No way Bo Hart would look twice at me.

My heart was beating out of my chest when the bell rang for 4th period. I gathered my books and headed quickly to locker #27. I didn't want to miss an encounter with Beauregard Hart, the Texan who was easy on the eyes.

As rapidly as my heart began beating, it sank just as fast. Bo came walking up with Tina Baker, the most popular girl at Palmetto Middle and the only 7th grader who had made the cheerleading squad. Try-outs had been last May, and I hadn't thought twice about subjecting myself to that process. Entering a different school with new faces was daunting enough.

Tina was different. She seemed to embrace the new opportunities of middle school and the awkward transition into adolescence. I attributed her confidence to her accelerated and rapid pace through puberty. She was taller than most of the boys in our class, who only reached her chest. Their height was probably fine with them since it gave them a great view of her C-cups. She knew she could have any boy she chose in the 7th grade or 8th grade, for that matter.

Before Bo Hart had come onto the scene, Tina had been hanging out with Randy Hubbard, a rising 9th grader at Somerset High School. I had seen them together several times over the summer. One day, I spotted her with the older, hip group. Tina definitely could have passed for sixteen in her skimpy bikini exposing her well-endowed shape. She was more than comfortable in this clique.

For me, summer meant alone time at the beach with only my school reading assignments for company. I don't think I read one word that day. Instead, I jealously watched her applying suntan oil to Randy's chest and back, throwing a football with him on the beach, and making out with him in the water. She never acknowledged my existence. Hannah Anne Hart was simply not in her league.

I was a little curious as to how Tina Baker had already encountered Bo Hart. He had mentioned his football number. Tina must have sniffed out this piece of fresh meat during cheerleading practice, which, like football, started several weeks before the first day of school.

When I approached Mrs. Caldwell's classroom, Tina was leaning in a flirtatious stance against the lockers talking to Bo and blocking access to my locker. I was hypnotized by her moves as she flipped her hair and gave a musical laugh. How did some girls get blessed with the flirt gene, totally absent in my DNA? I mustered the courage to interrupt, anxious to avoid being tardy for homeroom.

"Excuse me, Tina," I said. "I need to get to my locker."

"Oh! Sorry," Tina said, laughing. "This is Bo, he just moved here."

"Yeah, we met," Bo said. "Well kind of. We are in the same homeroom. Hannah Hart, right?"

"Hannah Anne," I said, not finding anything else to offer.

"Our teacher thought we were related," Bo said.

"Well, I'm glad we're not related, that would be weird, wouldn't it?" Tina asked, smiling and flipping her hair.

"Very," Bo said, laughing.

"See you after practice?" she asked.

"Sure thing."

I tried to hold back tears. I could never measure up to the Tina Bakers of the world. Boys like Bo Hart would never give me a second thought, and I would never feel anything but self-conscious in their presence, especially with my tortoise pace through puberty.

Heck, I had purchased my first bra over the summer even though I still didn't need one, according to the insensitive store clerk. My eyes filled with tears staring at the reflection of my skin-and-bones self in the dressing room's long mirror. I failed to fill out the training bra the clerk had offered as a consolation prize. My mother attempted to console me and to "keep my eye on the prize. I should focus on my straight-A record instead of my A-cup. Your boobs will eventually come," she said, trying to reassure me.

My boobs did arrive a couple years later, during the spring of my sophomore year, and my virginity was still intact, unlike Tina Baker and the other girls in town. By that time, Bo had apparently grown tired of them. He finally asked me, Hannah Anne Hart, if I wanted to hang out on the beach at Port Royal.

That day, I finally experienced my first kiss. I mean "finally," but not for the reason one would think—that I no longer had to practice on my mirror or pillow or wonder what real lips would feel like. I thought I was going to find out really fast though when Bo leaned into me after spreading out the beach towel. I worried my heart may explode first. But, it didn't. In fact, it sank like a rock when he didn't even try to kiss me.

After riding the waves on our boogie boards for an hour, I had settled down and was enjoying his company. I was at ease in my element. The ocean and salt air always calmed and centered me.

I thought it was going to happen, and I was more ready when he paddled over close to me. Then, a swell ascended quickly and began to break unexpectedly. He grabbed my hand.

"Hold on, close your eyes," he said, trying to pull me close.

I suppose his touch distracted me, and I relaxed my grip on the board. The wave ripped my board out from under me. It shot up into the air and was riding the current into shore. I was treading water, laughing. I wasn't even embarrassed that saltwater was spewing out of my nose.

"Here comes another one. Hold on," he yelled, grabbing me around the waist.

We rode the wave together. Beads of water rested on his long eyelashes that shaded his blue eyes. His sandy-blonde curls were drenched. He shook his head at me, and water sprayed all over me. With the saltwater dripping from my face, he leaned in. This time, my heart wasn't racing from inexperience but from desire. I wanted him to kiss me so badly. I was ready. The incoming tide and yet another rowdy wave interrupted our first kiss, pushing us closer to shore. The errant boogie board crashed into my face.

"You OK?" he asked, panicked, tossing the board onto the sand.

"Yeah," I laughed. My hair, encrusted in sand, was plastered to my face.

"You look so funny right now," he said, grabbing my hand.

With his other hand, he pushed my hair from my face. I closed my eyes waiting for his lips. Instead, he jerked me forward and started running. I couldn't feel my legs. They were still weak from the anticipation of my first kiss. But, they took over.

With the arrival of my boobs, my nickname, "Board," as in "flat as a board," had been replaced with "Giraffe" and "Spider." I had never grown into my legs, which were disproportionate to the rest of me. My long, tooth-pick legs, that I had always been embarrassed of, redeemed themselves that day. My strides were keeping up with the star wide receiver's. He had dropped my hand when he realized my speed as we ran down the beach.

"Race you to that pink house," as he began sprinting.

That was his first mistake. He sprinted too soon. My momma always told me, "Slow and steady wins the race." If he had chosen the bright, yellow house he would have won. But, he had taken off too quickly. By the time we reached the yellow house, Bo was huffing and puffing. I dashed by him and beat him by ten yards.

He placed his hands on his knees gasping for breath.

"You OK?" It was my turn to ask.

"Damn, girl," was all I could interpret between his rapid breaths.

When he finally caught his breath, he flung both his arms over my shoulders, bending over panting. His head merely flopped down, resting close to my neck. I put my arms around him waiting for him to catch his breath, for his head to emerge, for him to stand up straight, look down into my eyes, grab my cheeks, and kiss me. I had practiced; I was ready.

Instead, he simply said, "Race you back," and off he went.

At that moment, I felt like my breath had been knocked out of me, not from the winning the race but the opportunity—the chance for my first kiss. He was fifty yards down the beach before I began jogging. What an idiot, I thought. I should have let him win. The star wide receiver on the football team doesn't want to be beaten by a girl in a foot race. Why had I not had that clarity at the yellow house? He was ahead of me then, why didn't I hang back? Why did I have to sprint by him?

When I made it back to the beach towel, he was stretched out, like he had been waiting on me for hours.

"Cute," I said. "I almost caught you, but you were too fast. You didn't have to let me win the first time, you know," I said, hoping to placate his ego.

"I didn't let you win. I think it was the other way around, you let me win on the way back. Why don't you run track?" he asked.

"I don't know. Guess I never thought I was good enough," impressed by the fact that he actually acknowledged that I was faster.

"Oh, you're good enough," he said, stroking my hair.

I knew it was going to happen then. Inside my head, I was screaming, kiss me, kiss me now, you fool. Kiss me hard and wild. But he didn't. Instead, he sat up and touched my neck.

"You have a mark," he said. "That boogie board must have scraped you. Does it hurt?"

"No, I don't feel anything," I said, referring to my neck. My insides were feeling all kinds of things.

"Can I tell you something if you promise you won't think I'm weird?"

"You are anything but weird. Shoot," I said, but wanting to say that I think it's weird you haven't attempted to kiss me yet.

"You probably don't remember this, but you and me were in the same homeroom when I started at Palmetto Middle."

"I do remember that. Mrs. Caldwell thought we were related because we were both Harts."

"Exactly. Tina and I were standing at our lockers that day, and she was blocking yours."

"I remember that too."

"You stood there with your head sort of tilted staring at us. I wondered what you were doing until you said that you needed get to your locker. Right then, I knew there was no way we were related."

"Because I was trying to get to my locker? That is weird."

"You already called me weird so no way I'm telling you the rest," he said, laying back on the beach towel.

I knew that I didn't have a flirt gene, but now that this hunk was with me, I thought I didn't even have one potential girlfriend gene. I just kept doing and saying the wrong things.

"Sorry, I shouldn't have said that. Nothing you could say would be weird. Tell me."

He cocked his head and looked me in the eyes. I held his stare.

"That day, it was the way you tilted your head. It was your neck, I noticed your long neck. I thought to myself, yeah, there is no way we're related."

"Long neck? I have a long neck?" as I involuntarily began rubbing the area on my neck scraped by the boogie board.

He removed my hand and placed his on the spot.

"The Texas Harts have no neck. We are all shoulders. Our heads literally rest on our shoulders. My nickname in my last school was "Turtle." Like I said, it's weird, but you have the prettiest, longest, and sexiest neck."

I decided not to disclose my nicknames Giraffe and Spider. He may never kiss me. But, right then, when I least expected it, he did. It was not what I had expected. It was a lingering, gentle peck. I tasted the salt water on his lips. I wanted more.

"You have a great neck, a strong neck," I said, kissing it and even sucking on it a bit. I had never received a hickey or given one. I certainly didn't want to leave a mark on his neck on our first date, but I didn't want to stop. I wanted more of him.

"Kiss me, again," I blurted out of nowhere.

This time, his lips parted, and our tongues touched. It was like nothing I had imagined or practiced.

After that day, we became an item. We became inseparable. And, we finally became intimate. I mean finally because I had been wrong in my opinion of him—that he was a player, that he had probably gone all the way with all his girlfriends. And, there had been a lot of girlfriends between Tina and me.

We advanced beyond just kissing, and with every date, I thought this would be the time—the time where we surrendered ourselves to each other completely. Every time when I thought this was it, he would retreat saying it wasn't the right time. He loved me, and the place and time had to be perfect. Though frustrated, it made me love him more.

"I love you, Hannah Anne Hart," he said the night we first made love on the banks of the Savannah River. It was the first day of our Christmas break, and it was the day he told me he was moving to Mississippi.

Bo's father who had bounced from oil rigs to shrimp boats to boat yards was going to deal blackjack at a new casino opening in Biloxi. I begged Bo to stay. He could live with my family. Why start another new school in the middle of senior year? But, Bo had inherited the rambling gene from his father. He liked new cities and new adventures—he even relished being the new guy at a new school. "Part of who he was," he said. He promised to visit.

Our daughter was conceived that day. When I suspected as much, I called Bo. I needed to come visit. I had to see him. I recall he sounded indifferent. I insisted. I had a bus ticket. I would leave after lunch on Friday. I would arrive at the Biloxi bus station late that night.

"Ok, but I have a basketball game. I'll come get you as soon as I can. It will be nice to see you," he said.

Admittedly, the timing was not the best. I sprung this trip on him, I justified, as I was waiting at the bus station until his basketball game was over. However, I couldn't justify his choice of words, "it will be nice to see you." I would have preferred adjectives like fantastic, wonderful, amazing. Regardless of his comment, on the bus ride down, I pictured his excitement when I broke the news. We were having a baby and would be together for the rest of our lives.

"God, Hannah Anne. Are you sure?" he questioned, over and over.

His reaction was the opposite of what I had anticipated. I certainly hadn't planned for any of this. Now what?

"I haven't been in Biloxi long enough to know who can take care of it. But, I definitely know someone in Beaufort," Bo said.

"What does that mean?" I asked.

Had he gotten someone else pregnant in Beaufort? Tina? Tammy? Darlene? I went through the list of his past girlfriends. How would he have contacts?

He flatly denied every inquisition. He couldn't believe I could even think such a thing.

"Look, I just know, and I promise that you won't be the first girl at Somerset High who has been pregnant. You need to think hard about this Hannah Anne. This could change our lives forever," Bo said.

I didn't need to think hard or even twice about my decision, though I agonized over my mother's anticipated disappointment. I had worked so hard for my straight A's and my number one class rank. How could this happen?? In addition to disappointment, her embarrassment would be significant. I would be the first in the history of Somerset High to hide a bump underneath a commencement cap and gown while delivering the Valedictorian address.

His hesitance aside, Bo and I were married. Hannah Anne Hart Hart—I liked the ring of it. Savannah Harper Hart was born four months later. College could wait; I was in heaven.

Four years later, Bo left $5000 and a note.

Hannah Anne, I am so sorry. But, I am suffocating. Blame it on my upbringing. I can't stay in one place for very long. I am afraid of what I will become being fenced in. You and Savannah deserve better. I don't know where I am headed but will send more money wherever I land. Take care of our beautiful daughter and yourself. I love you both very much but know that this is the right thing. You will know too, hopefully sooner rather than later. Bo

I made progress. I went from reading his beautiful penmanship in that note every day to now only once every month. My therapist constantly reminded me that Savannah should be my focus. Children are miraculous blessings.

Savannah was my focus. When I felt like I was slipping into the quicksand of despair, she rescued me. When Savannah followed in my footsteps with an early and unexpected pregnancy, I begged her and Josh to stay in Beaufort to raise their child. I could help. I knew the difficulty of having a baby at eighteen. They could live with me. Despite my pleas, she chose to support Josh and move to Kentucky with him. He promised her a good life living on his family's farm.

Savannah inherited her father's free spirit, so I knew I couldn't clip her wings. Her spirit, however, was fed by water, salt air, and the birds of the Lowcountry. I prayed that her light wouldn't be snuffed out in Kentucky and that her heart wouldn't be broken, like her momma's.

Chapter Four

Maude Abbott, Josh's mother

I lied to Josh. I knowingly withheld his father's identity all those years. The secret of Walt Benton not only to Josh but also to Adam tormented me every single day.

I justified my silence because Adam was a good father. In my mind, a father was more than a creator; a true father was a protector, caregiver, and provider. Indeed, Adam was all those things.

Now, Josh knows the truth. Most of it, anyway. He knew the most important part—that his birth father was Walt Benton. He didn't need to know all the details. The devil had tested me that summer, and I had failed. I continued to pray for forgiveness for my carnal thoughts every time I reminisced about that treasured summer.

Walt was my true love, the man to whom I had willingly surrendered my virginity. That, alone, made him impossible to forget. Josh was the twist of the knife. He was the mirror image of his father: blonde, curly locks, fit physique, strong hands, and tender heart. The nails in the proverbial coffin were his stunning eyes— emerald green, the color of my birthstone and Walt Benton's eyes. I couldn't help but believe that Josh's incarceration was God's way of punishing me for my sin and my perpetual longing for Walt.

After that summer, I realized the difference between loving someone and being in love with them. I was in love with Walt, but I stifled the emotion. I chose the safest path, the path that was mapped out by my father. I became the wife of

Adam Abbott. I couldn't let Dad down. My sister Hazel had always excelled in that.

I quietly observed and, at times, coveted my sister's ability to push Dad's buttons. She was bequeathed every rebellious, spirited, unfettered gene from our parents' lineage. She constantly wreaked havoc in our household. The final straw came when Boss Man Abbott caught Hazel with Jesse, a sharecropper, in one of the Abbott's tobacco barns. Enraged is a mild description of my father's reaction.

My father idolized Kyle Abbott, or "Cash Abbott," as Dad referred to his boss under our roof. Kyle "Cash" Abbott owned 5,000 acres of land dedicated to harvesting tobacco. My father was Mr. Abbott's trusted farm manager.

"Hideous sin, white trash," he yelled, in between strokes of his belt. The reason that it was the worst beating yet was that Hazel had "stained his good name." The red welts on her legs lasted for days. During her beating, she didn't cry, not once. Her stubborn defiance was mind-blowing.

In our shared bedroom, as I was applying salve to the wounds across her legs, I garnered the courage to question her.

"Why are you out for Daddy?" as big crocodile tears built in my eyes.

"What do you mean 'out for' him?" Hazel asked.

"It's like you intentionally do things to make him mad and rub his nose in the wreckage," I said.

"Seriously, Maude? You really think I wanted Cash Abbott to catch me with Jesse? You know as well as I do that if I had been caught with Adam, ol' Pops would have celebrated with champagne!"

Hazel was right. Daddy had made it quite clear numerous times that Adam was a catch. There was nothing that would make Daddy happier than one of his daughters to become an Abbott. This would provide financial freedom to his offspring and precipitate a move out of the "servant quarters," as Hazel called our home. In retrospect, it seemed that Hazel's revolution started after Dad's disclosure that he thought Adam Abbott was sweet on me.

Even after her beating, Hazel continued her late night escapades, before she learned of her ultimate punishment. Hazel's posse, as she called them, included her best friend, Louise, and in addition to Jesse, several other boys. "About Jesse," Hazel said, though her legs still evidenced the consequences from her last visit with him. The red welts had turned into purple bruises. "I am meeting him in ten minutes."

"Do you think that is a good idea?" I felt compelled to ask.

The roll of her eyes confirmed what I already knew—that I exerted absolutely no influence over her.

"You know the drill," was her only response.

I knew the drill indeed. I would tip-toe down the hall to our parent's bedroom and make sure the light was out. Daddy was always up before the sun, so he crashed early. If by chance, I was caught lurking in the hallway, my mother wouldn't give it a second thought. I was the consummate rule follower. Of course, Hazel was a different story. If I gave the all clear signal, Hazel would slip out our bedroom window.

It was during one of those pre-checks, as Hazel called them, that I first heard my parents having sex. I heard the headboard knocking against the wall in rhythm to my father's guttural grunts. I pictured my petite mother lying there. It didn't sound passionate or loving. It sounded painful, like an animal in distress. It made my stomach hurt. I thought it was disgusting.

Before Hazel was caught with Jesse, I assumed she was cigarette smoking and drinking bourbon with her posse. Now, I wondered if she was having sex with more than just Jesse. I couldn't understand how Hazel could disrespect herself and her body like that. In my view, it was taking rebellion to an extreme.

When Adam first tried to go beyond kissing, I cringed. We had similar moral values. We were saving ourselves for marriage. That's what was drilled into us at church, home, and the sex education classes at school. If you crossed one line, wouldn't others become blurry? When did more become sinful? Adam would try and convince me it was okay. We loved each other; we were going to get married one day. He "wanted me." That comment made me feel dirty, like I was an object. My dad's grunts and the banging headboard would echo in my head. Was something wrong with me? I simply had no desire to go any further.

Hired Hit on Jessamin Island

Two weeks after Cash Abbott ratted out Hazel, my father announced that she would be spending the summer with our Aunt Mildred—his way of showing his boss man that he ran his household with the same firm hand that he ran Cash Abbott's farm. There were severe consequences for any breach of the rules.

Dad thought that a foreign environment was needed. Aunt Mildred, Momma's older sister, would help "straighten out" Hazel. She was a teetotaler and a more devoted churchgoer than Momma. I believe Momma only agreed to Hazel's banishment because it would also be good for Aunt Mildred. She needed the company since Uncle Cletus walked out six months earlier with a member of their Sunday school class. It was a win–win in Momma's mind.

I offered to accompany Hazel that summer. Adam's unstated pressure to get more intimate had escalated. It seemed like every time we were together, I was constantly removing his hand from trying to get in my shorts. He was getting frustrated; I was getting more confused. Time away from him would do us both good. My offer was flatly rejected by my father. His reasons certainly weren't comforting.

"Maude, think about Adam," he said. "When the cat's away, the mice will play."

He laughed when I countered, "Distance makes the heart grow fonder."

"Whoever said that doesn't know how it works."

Daddy finally relented to Momma's compromise. After all, I was the rule abider and the daughter that was going to deliver Cash Abbott's son. Plus, Aunt Mildred hadn't seen me in years. I could educate my aunt about all the tricks up Hazel's sleeves (or dresses). I knew more about Hazel's exploits than my parents did. Mildred needed to be armed with the appropriate weapons in the rehabilitation of the unruly daughter.

It was decided that I would escort Hazel to the North Carolina Outer Banks and stay for two weeks. That should be sufficient time to help get Hazel off on the right foot.

Unfamiliar territory didn't alter Hazel's compass. She picked up right where she left off. Unbeknownst to my parents, there were much bigger fish in the Nags Head pond, and Hazel rapidly attracted a substantial following. My intended positive influence backfired. My inhibited spirit and conformance to society's rules, or at least those that were engrained in us in Kentucky, took flight in the salty wind—much like the Wright Brothers' plane did years ago in nearby Kitty Hawk. Must have been something in the air.

Chapter Five

Walt Benton, Josh's father

After I picked up Josh at the bus station, I took him to my favorite seafood dive. Tourists swarmed Beaufort this time of year. My favorite spot, Ralphie's at Pier 33, looked crusty enough to frighten away our summer visitors. Ralphie's stood the test of time, so I thought it was a symbolic locale for our introduction to each other.

Josh quickly picked up on how to peel the shell from a fresh shrimp. When first watching him, my emotions were conflicted. How in the hell could a son of mine never have eaten any seafood or peeled a shrimp? The coast, and everything associated with it, was intrinsically linked to my soul.

The feeling was fleeting, because Josh instantly fell in love with all of it, even cleaning a fish. I swelled with pride when his preferred crabbing method was the old-fashioned way and the only way in my book—tying a chicken neck to the end of a string. He was a natural—slowly and carefully pulling in the line after feeling the tug. He instinctively knew that the prize would abandon the bait if the line was pulled too quickly. He even enjoyed the messy and tedious work required in getting to the divine morsels of crabmeat. Too many times to count, I witnessed novices abandon the process—too much work for little reward. Josh was different. "Worth the effort," he said.

That summer, I think he personally encountered every creature in the Beaufort tidal creeks and waters. And, he found a pearl in an oyster—the pearl being sweet, beautiful Savannah Hart. She reminded me of Maudie. Ironically, Josh met Savannah on his second day in Beaufort. I had met Maudie on her second day in Nags Head. Like father, like son.

The memories of that glorious summer with Maudie, which had taken many, many years to suppress, came crashing back. My buddy, Kip, had met Maudie's sister, Hazel, the day before. She was walking on the beach with a bottle of bourbon—Kentucky bourbon. She was different from any girl he'd ever met—no flirtatious game playing. "She's like the wild horses on Corolla," he said. "And she has a sister."

Maudie, I learned, was quite different from her sister. She was standoffish, reserved, cautious, guarded, and bordered on prudish. The salt air must have begun to slowly deteriorate her uptight façade. After a full day on the beach and her first tastes of bluegrass bourbon, she revealed a different layer of her personality. She was vulnerable, sincere, down-to-earth, and playful.

When I leaned in to kiss her as the sun was setting, Maudie disclosed that she had a boyfriend or, more appropriately, a "chosen life partner." Her father reluctantly allowed Maudie to accompany Hazel, who was serving a summer penance for her errant ways. Maudie was responsible for relaying all the sordid details about her sister's antics to her summer watchdog, their Aunt Mildred. Maudie was staying two weeks, long enough to ensure all was on course. That was the plan anyway.

On day thirteen, when it became clear where things were headed, Maudie told me that she was a virgin. I didn't want that burden and any resulting remorse on her part, especially with the knowledge of a boyfriend back home.

I retreated, and she looked confused.

"What's wrong?" she asked with hurt in her voice. "Did I do something wrong?"

"No, babe," I said. "I really like you but don't want you to have any regrets."

She answered that concern by helping my bathing suit trunks find their way into the sand.

"You may need to help me a little bit," she said.

She didn't need any help at all, and the thousand stars on the beach that night seem to flicker with their approval. Admittedly, I had extensive experience with girls, but with Maudie, I first understood what "making love" meant. It was natural, yet magical. It was tender, yet intense.

Maudie's two-week stay was extended for two more, then an additional four, then four more. Thanks to her Aunt Mildred, Maudie stayed in Nags Head the entire summer. Her aunt had witnessed our connection and confided in me that she disapproved of the arranged wedding between Maudie and Adam Abbott. She had traveled that path, and it led to misery.

After that night on the beach, like her Aunt Mildred's own metamorphosis, something was unlocked inside of Maudie. For me, I knew she was the one. I was smitten. And, I thought the feeling was mutual. We spent every day together after that. Given that Maudie was mostly unsupervised, we made love every day, often numerous times.

Maudie's parents were under the impression that the girls were under the scrutinizing eye of Aunt Mildred—the austere aunt, the intended taskmaster, Mother Superior. However, this plan had a major flaw.

Six months ago, Aunt Mildred's husband had abandoned her after twenty years of marriage for a church friend. Her aunt had an awakening. All her clean living had left her bewildered, alone, and depressed. Then she met Darryl, the fisherman, who "rocked her world," Mildred proclaimed. Hazel and Maude had never heard Mildred talk like that or seen her so animated. Before her intermittent disappearances, she counseled them "don't judge," "be true to yourself," "you're not promised tomorrow," and "unshackle the chains." She wanted a different outcome for her niece.

I wanted a different outcome for us too. But, I was joining the Marines. Maudie was returning to Kentucky to start community college. On our last night together, I took her to the place where Orville and Wilbur Wright first took flight. After our most intimate of moments, she cried and whispered in my ear, "Thanks for giving me my wings."

After Maudie returned to Kentucky, the "Dear John" letter soon arrived. It announced her engagement. I gave Josh the abridged version from my memory while fighting back a wave of emotion.

"I never knew about you, Josh," I said. "I loved your mother deeply. Truth is, I never got over her, but I don't think I will ever forgive her for keeping you from me all these years."

Chapter Six

Maude Abbott, Josh's mother

At eighteen years old, the summer of '81 with Walt provided more than steamy, intimate moments. There were long walks on the beach searching for sea glass and seashells, riding the Atlantic Ocean waves, and fishing on the surf. I loved how he patiently taught me to hook bait securely on a fishing line.

I wasn't the only one who loved Walt. His sheer presence had a way of elevating everyone's mood. Wherever we went, the locals excitedly hollered: "How's it goin' Walt?" or "Look who's here!" "Where you been hiding, Walt?" And, "My man, Walt!" I was proud to be the girl on his arm.

The most magical times with him were the simplest—holding hands on Aunt Mildred's porch swing, talking about our dreams, or sipping Kentucky bourbon. Hazel had smuggled into North Carolina a load of Wild Turkey bottles in her Samsonite suitcase. She kept the suitcase key hidden. I was so preoccupied with Walt that I never thought to ask her the source of her seemingly buried treasure.

Due to Walt's popularity, it wasn't long before Hazel and I were equally well-known. We were referred to as the "Bluegrass sisters." Hazel ran the show. I continued to be amazed at her versatility and knowledge. I had never heard of the band ABBA, but as their hit song *Waterloo* blasted from the juke box, she sang along word-for-word in her bikini while expertly and nonchalantly flipping her wrists and smashing goals in foosball. It didn't take long before she held foosball and skeet ball championship titles at the local pavilion.

When I wasn't alone with Walt, we were with Hazel and Kip. For the time being, Hazel had buried her resentment of my pairing with Adam Abbott. She was happy; she had finally connected with someone and some place.

The day of our scheduled departure, she informed me that she wasn't going back. Aunt Mildred agreed to let her stay and to provide the necessary cover. Aunt Mildred told my parents that she had made "significant progress" with this delinquent, which would be undone if Hazel returned to Kentucky. Truth be told, I think my parents were relieved. My father didn't want any more incidents that would tarnish the family name, jeopardizing his standing with my future in-laws.

On the way to the bus station, for once in my life, I wanted to be more like Hazel. I wanted to take flight on the wings Walt had given me, have the strength to forge my own path, and turn from the one that Daddy wanted. Unfortunately, I wasn't strong enough.

Walt and I exchanged addresses and promised to keep in touch. After his initial training in Cherry Point, North Carolina, he didn't know where he would land. I promised to visit. I had a light class schedule in the fall at the nearby community college. My father quashed my desire to attend the University of Kentucky—we couldn't afford it, and "if I didn't mess things up with Adam, I wouldn't need any daggum degree."

When it was time to board, Walt hugged me so tightly that I thought he may have punctured a rib. He whispered in my ear Glenn Campbell's line from Walt's favorite song, "Wichita Lineman"—I want you more than I need you, and I need you for all time.

I bawled all the way back to Kentucky as I replayed my fairy-tale summer, with his last words echoing over and over in my head. My recollection of the lyrics wasn't precise; the real lyrics were even better. We wanted each other for all time.

It wasn't long before my queasy stomach and sore breasts foretold what was happening. I was pregnant. We had been careful. But on our last night, I begged him to ditch the protection. I wanted to feel more connected. Then, I naively thought that one time couldn't get you pregnant. Frankly, I didn't care. Now, I was terrified. God's punishment, I thought, for cheating on Adam. I force myself to write a letter that tore me to pieces.

Dear Walt,

After returning home, I realized how much I missed Adam. We are engaged. I will always remember you for many things but, most importantly, my wings. They will be with me the rest of my life. I wish you nothing but the best.

Fondly,
Your Maudie

I sealed the envelope with my tears.

I pleaded for forgiveness daily for breaking Walt's heart and leaving him in the dark about his son. I also pleaded for forgiveness for the trap I set for Adam.

"While I was gone, I missed you terribly. I am ready for the next step. I want you, all of you," I said.

As Adam and I were melded together, I closed my eyes and fantasized that he was Walt. I don't know which made Daddy happier—Adam and my wedding or the birth of an Abbott heir, his grandson, Joshua Carter Abbott. More than his name, Joshua was now blood bound to the Abbott tobacco kings, or so he thought.

PART II

Chapter Seven

Josh Abbott, the young tobacco farmer

Each day I spent with Walt, my resentment toward my mother grew. Savannah was more empathetic, likely due to her plight in life.

"You probably will never know all the facts," Savannah said. "The important thing is that you know about Walt now. He is here, and he loves you. Don't let your past interfere with your present. Let bygones be bygones."

It wasn't until I returned to Kentucky with a pregnant wife that I began forgiving my mother. I was beginning to see first-hand her teenage predicament. I quickly learned that you do what you believe is best for your child, unlike Savannah's father who just up and left one day.

Farming was all I knew. It was all I had ever done. My father, Adam Abbott, owned 5,000 acres of land that harvested the best burley tobacco in Kentucky. My relationship with Adam didn't change a bit after the discovery that he wasn't my biological father. But then again, Adam and I had never been close. We were more like business partners. I was being groomed to take over the Abbott Tobacco Farm from Adam just as he had been primed by his father, Kyle Abbott, and just like Kyle had from his father and so on and so on.

As the only Abbott heir, I was the only hope to ensure my family's heritage and preserve its lifeline. How could I abandon them? Walt understood. Savannah's mother was a different story. Savannah was all she had.

If there were do-overs in life, I would have followed my heart and soul, stayed in Beaufort, and rejected my predestined role to keep the cash machine humming along. I would have done it my way instead of accepting the Abbott Tobacco Farm path chosen for me, like the one chosen for my mother—the one that appeared safe, secure, and full of promise.

My time at the helm, however, presented unparalleled challenges. It was more than just the steep decline in smokers. Sixty years of federal tobacco quotas had been eliminated, and ten years of tobacco buy-out payments had ceased. Cheap labor costs overseas had lured big tobacco to Brazil, Africa, and even Turkey, diminishing contracts for the state's tobacco crop.

Despite these uncontrollable events, the Abbott Tobacco Farm was one of the lucky ones. We retained our contracts with the big cigarette manufacturers, though each year, a record low was established for the number of tobacco acres harvested in Kentucky. Other farmers were throwing in the towel, replacing tobacco with soybeans, corn, and wheat.

The year after Adam ironically died of lung cancer, even though he never smoked a day in his life, our once reliable cash cow was barely breaking even, and returns were unpredictable. The pressure, a kind that my predecessors had never experienced, weighed heavily on me. I blamed myself for failure to stand up to big tobacco when our contracts were renegotiated, and the purchase of 100 percent of our commodity was no longer guaranteed at top prices. The previous guarantees were renegotiated using conditional, subjective terms like "demand" and "quality." I blamed myself for failing to diversify like the other farmers who had seen the coming of Armageddon.

When it was apparent that tobacco was no longer king, Savannah insisted on getting a job. She had always worked during her childhood to help her mother. Her job as a teller at the local bank enabled us to cover our day-to-day expenses, but it wasn't enough to subsidize the farm operations. Asking Walt to bail out the Abbott Tobacco Farm didn't seem right. After all, the farm had robbed him of his true love and his only son.

I was forced to employ illegal immigrants—no federal withholding taxes, no social security, no health insurance, just cash under the table. I ignored other uses being made of our land. When the DEA discovered five acres of marijuana plants, I took the fall. I wasn't going to betray my loyal workers. I knew what was going on and had turned a blind eye. The consequences for illegal employees, my lawyer advised, was much worse than my sentence for permitting their marijuana crop.

My prison warden, William Wilson, knew I wanted nothing more than to be reunited with Savannah.

"I have connections with law enforcement and judges," he told me. "Blow the whistle on your marijuana network, and I will work out a deal for leniency."

I didn't budge. There was no "marijuana network" just my dedicated, hard-working employees who were loyal to Abbott Tobacco Farm. My unwavering silence and resolute disinterest in any "deal for leniency" must have resonated. He knew everything about me, Savannah, Cray, Adam, and Walt. He knew I had no prior offenses, unlike my fellow inmates. The crooked warden became convinced that I could be trusted.

Initially, I assumed the warden's nickname, Wormie Willie, spawned from his looks. He was tall, with a thin, tube-like frame. He was soft, unlike the deputy wardens and guards who took advantage of the prison's weight room. I was certain that Warden William Wilson had never raised a barbell.

In addition to the Wormie Willie, apparently Benji, my cellmate, had grown to trust me too. He shared information that he shouldn't have. This was the kind of place where you needed to keep your ears open, but lips closed.

Benji began confiding lots of scoop establishing that Wormie Willie was a bad dude. Specifically, he was a drug dealer and partner-in-crime with the DEA Special Agent in Charge of the Kentucky Division and the local sheriff, Sheriff Buchanan.

Before his election as sheriff of Person County, Buchanan was a protégé of the DEA special agent. Person County ranked first among the one hundred and twenty Kentucky counties for the number of methamphetamine laboratories seized. The money that poured into Buchanan's campaign from outside sources enabled him to publicize his DEA experience and broadcast his commitment to clean up the county. Buchanan's victory was a landslide. His rapid onslaught on the meth labs propelled his popularity and secured his position.

Benji said that Sheriff Buchanan's meth cleanup was a cover for his participation in the cocaine and marijuana distribution circles. And, he overheard a conversation between Wormie Willie and the sheriff identifying a source for oxycodone.

"It's messed up, ain't it!" Benji said, resentfully. "They put their competition behind bars. After I blow this popsicle stand, I'm gonna blow this place up in *The National Enquirer*. I am going to pocket some serious coin."

If Benji had revealed this information prior to Wormie Willie's pitch for my early release, I wouldn't have fallen for it. I would have known that the sheriff and the DEA agent were in cahoots with our warden in the scheme involving Cray—the scheme guaranteeing my transfer to minimum security followed by early release.

Wormie Willie assured me that the plan was a no-brainer. As required by the rules, Cray turned over his keys and wallet when checking in at the visitation desk. When he left the facility with his returned keys, Cray would never know that a load of cocaine had been placed in his trunk.

My visits with Cray usually lasted a couple of hours. They only needed ten minutes. I took the bait.

During Cray's visits, I would peruse his recent paintings as best I could from behind the glass partition that separated us. The birds of the Lowcountry were his specialty. The way he captured the egrets and blue herons in the marsh brought tears to my eyes. And that day, it was especially difficult to control my emotions. I couldn't concentrate on Cray's paintings because all I could see were images of Wormie Willie's cronies loading the goods in the trunk of his car. God, forgive me, I prayed.

Later, Wormie Willie delivered the news. There had been "an unanticipated glitch." A glitch hardly described the circumstances that would irreparably and radically change my innocent son's life. The next thing I remember was a light shining in my eyes.

"You blacked out, but you'll be fine. Get some rest," the prison medic said.

Warden Wilson excused the medic saying that he would monitor my lucidness. Of course, he didn't care about my health, only my frame of mind.

"If you love your wife and son, don't do anything stupid," he instructed. "We will make this right. Trust me."

I knew Cray may never understand why I sold him out—his words. He didn't have a farm to plow. He didn't have a family to support. He didn't understand the desperate circumstances that led to my confinement nor the burden of failure and disappointment. He didn't understand my resentment. Had I known my real father in my formative years, I could have chosen a different path before it was too late to alter my course.

I did my best to feign ignorance when Savannah visited me the next day. Cray had been arrested for trafficking cocaine, she informed me. The sadness in her eyes and voice left me defeated. Worse yet, my only hope was to trust Wormie Willie.

Chapter Eight

Cray Abbott, the artist, Josh's son

After my arrest for trafficking cocaine, Papa Walt, my grandfather, posted a bond for my release. He drove over ten hours from Duck, in the North Carolina Outer Banks, the place he had retired after his honorable discharge. The Marines awarded him a Purple Heart for the debilitating injuries he sustained while protecting his squadron. The details remained confidential, but he was clearly a hero. I couldn't shake the stark contrast in the outcomes between my grandfather and his offspring.

Papa Walt promised he would retain the best lawyer. He believed my vehement denial. The exculpatory facts were my visit to the prison and confiscation of my keys just an hour prior to my arrest near the prison grounds.

When Papa Walt visited Dad to report the news of my arrest, he learned the true details. At first, he didn't understand how Dad already knew of my arrest. Then it became clear. Papa Walt showed me the letter Dad slipped him during visitation.

Papa Walt spoke to a lawyer he knew in South Carolina.

"He's tough, no-nonsense. He handles matters at the Marine base. I trust him," Papa Walt said.

"You are in a precarious position," the no-nonsense attorney opined.

Hired Hit on Jessamin Island

After discussing his opinion, Papa Walt and I consumed a fifth of Kentucky bourbon. The alcohol prompted a Catholic confession from my grandfather, a desire to absolve all past sins.

"You are old enough to know the truth," Papa Walt said. "I should have been more responsible, more careful. Young love has a way of skewing your judgment. I was madly in love with Maude."

He blamed himself for everything. His lack of discipline and restraint had set off a chain of life events that had burdened him with infinite guilt. He couldn't say he regretted it. Otherwise, neither Josh nor I would exist.

"You and your father are my two most precious blessings," he said, fighting back tears.

He hugged me so tightly, I thought he may have broken my ribs.

We repeated the attorney's assessment of the case. It would be an uphill battle to convince a judge and jury that drugs had been placed in my trunk by prison officials. Dad would have to testify, which presented several challenges. First, he would have no credibility through a jury's eyes. He was a convicted felon serving time for cultivating marijuana. Second, he would be a biased witness. After all, I was his son. Finally, a backlash was inevitable. No one accuses prison officials of such allegations without retaliation.

We talked through every possible scenario and wept. He promised to protect me, Savannah, and even Maude, as best he could.

PART III

Chapter Nine

Charles Walker, the banker

Tightass, stingy, cheapskate, are just some of the names my wife called me too many times to count. While true, I preferred the term fiscally conservative.

Admittedly, my frugality took a toll on my marriage. We, however, can't control our genetic predispositions, which are exacerbated by life experiences. My thriftiness gene came from my mother and my father. I guess you would say that I was doomed to be a penny-pincher.

Scrimping and saving was part of my DNA and had served me well in following my dad's footsteps into the banking industry. But things had changed dramatically since my dad's tenure as president of the Somerset Savings & Loan.

Bankers in my dad's day had modest salaries—no bonus potential for new accounts opened, acquisitions financed, or jumbo mortgages brokered. My family had a simple lifestyle. I was taught that strict budgets and saving for retirement was the American way. I attributed my ability to withstand the South Carolina smoldering summer days in my required banker's suit to the only air-conditioning I ever knew—an open window. The box fans were turned on only when the mercury level on our outside weather thermometer hit one-hundred degrees.

My mother was a consummate coupon clipper, deal seeker, and queen of leftovers. I'm pretty sure that I heard "you don't need that" more than "I love you."

Despite my parents' prudent and economical lifestyle, my father lost everything. His pension was solely dependent upon the performance of his only employer for fifty years. When the Somerset Savings & Loan failed, as many did in the late 1980s, my stable homelife changed. We buried my father a month after his S&L accounts and pension were deemed worthless.

At the time, I believed my mother's account of the cause of death—a massive heart attack. However, the coroner's report concluded suicide. My mother was diagnosed with dementia, shortly thereafter. Her dementia rapidly progressed. I am financially responsible for her round-the-clock care, and for now, I can certainly afford it.

After the S&L crisis, I vowed to always diversify investments, never take anything for granted, to live simply, and to avoid debt. Typical bankers believe in extensions of credit, not debt avoidance, but I am, after all, a product of my parents' genes and their environment.

Time has a way of providing perspective. I never considered it at the time, but I know my father appreciated my mother's spendthrift qualities. My spouse, a polar opposite, had shopping habits that I constantly had to monitor and reign in. The percentage of fights with Alice over the years that had NOT been provoked by money was very low, but my tightfistedness eventually even found a way into those arguments too. But for our social outings, always with other couples, our communications and activities evolved around Tara, our only child. When Alice's disdain for me peaked, I would ask, "If you are so unhappy, why don't we separate?"

Her responses weren't reassuring.

My two favorites were: "I'll be excluded from all social events and lose the annual invitation to the Robinson's New York penthouse," and "The debutante committee frowns upon divorced parents." But the one that solidified my inertia was Tara.

"Tara will be scarred emotionally. Tara will be humiliated. Tara will lose her friends," my wife would add with the upmost certainty.

Admittedly, no one seeks to put their child through a divorce. I knew it wasn't going to be easy. But, shouldn't my child want me to be happy in the same way I wanted happiness for her? I thought if she lost her friends over a divorce, then she needed to find new friends. But Alice knew how to go for the jugular. I wholeheartedly believed her threats that she would see to it that Tara wouldn't have anything to do with me ever again.

"You won't escort her on graduation day, walk her down the aisle at her wedding, or ever hold her baby in your arms. I will see to it. And, you can deposit that in your damn bank."

Tara's fatal accident was the match in the powder keg. The resentment we felt toward one another hardened to the point of no return. We began sleeping in separate bedrooms, and we rarely uttered a word to each other. There was no reason to pretend to be a happy couple anymore, at least under our roof.

Chapter Ten

Alice Walker, the banker's wife

"The pool needs cleaning," I texted to Johnny.

This phrase was code for "all's clear for a romp in the sack." Since Charles meticulously adhered to his own adaptation of banker's hours—7:00 a.m. until at least 7:00 p.m.—Charles wasn't an issue. The code was initiated after Tara began driving.

High school class schedules had changed significantly over the years. I can't ever recall one of my classes being cancelled, but Johnny and I squeaked out a close encounter when Tara arrived home early due to such a cancellation. The unpredictability of the class schedule was bad enough. But the administrators too? They had gotten lax about students leaving the school grounds for lunch period. We instituted the code after Johnny got stuck hiding in the master bath shower for over an hour because Tara unexpectedly popped in for lunch.

A cheating spouse was not something I had aspired to be. But, Charles had driven me to it, and my temporary lovers made me feel desired and worthy. The rendezvous served a dual purpose: intrinsic satisfaction and sticking it to Charles.

If "cheap bastard" was in *Webster's Dictionary*, no definition would be necessary, simply a picture of Charles Walker. The saying "deep pockets but short arms" fit him to a tee.

Our home was a shack compared to others in our affluent neighborhood. Our saltwater infinity pool was the only asset coveted in our zip code. This top-of-the-line pool existed solely because swimming was Charles' exercise of choice. Unless it was pouring rain, he was swimming laps every morning by 5:00 a.m. He was a creature of habit.

He never took a vacation, logged seventy or more hours per week, and his loyalty (which really pissed me off) was foremost to the bank. He was rewarded handsomely for his loyalty and long hours. His paycheck was almost six figures, and I'm talking A MONTH, not a year.

His ultimate pay was disguised in stock options, guaranteed bonuses, and other such nonsense, clearly orchestrated by the bank's lawyers to confuse the middle-class depositors. As the ignorant, dutiful spouse, I had no idea of our net worth. My limited skills, according to Charles, couldn't unravel all the hidden pay or perks. However, I had excellent surfing skills, as in surfing the internet.

According to Google, my husband was worth millions. Given his aversion to debt, we were extremely flush. I was a multi-millionaire, because Google said so. Under South Carolina law, I was entitled to at least half. Charles would never part with half; hell, he wouldn't part with a third. Though I suspected he knew of my various trysts, he wouldn't rock the boat. Worse than losing his spouse, he would lose half of his bank and investment accounts. He monitored them daily.

On the rare occasions Charles spoke to me, he always had this condescending tone. He treated me like an underling. However, I was smart enough to know that neither "union" nor "jointly" were words in his magnanimous vocabulary. (Yes, I used a Thesaurus to find the right word.)

Early in our marriage, I tolerated his absenteeism in our lives. I would benefit from his intellect and his ambition. Over the years, it became clear that he loved his status more than me and even Tara. Titles and the number of zeros in his paycheck identified him. Those things had ripped our marriage to shreds. He didn't appreciate anything I brought to the partnership. Worthless were my accomplishments as homemaker and mother—grocery shopping; scheduling Tara's appointments to the doctor, dentist, and dermatologist; carpooling to dance, guitar and voice lessons; making sure dinner was on the table; supervising homework and school projects; and over-seeing household repairs and upkeep. My contributions couldn't be monetized on a spreadsheet.

Charles had me on a strict weekly budget. From my viewpoint, it was an allowance, and I resented the shit out of it and him. I wasn't his child but his life partner. Wasn't a marriage supposed to be a union? Union, to me, meant cooperation, collaboration, and jointly working together toward common goals. But, what did I know?

Charles deposited my weekly allowance in a separate bank account. Of course, he kept tabs on my expenditures. Speaking of expenditures, Johnny was a budgetary find. He had an array of talents—electrician, plumber, mechanic, and landscape aficionado. He was my handyman, my pool boy, my boy toy, and the fixer of all things. Like my other dalliances, he appreciated my skills.

Johnny was the best and my first choice. Like me, all the neighborhood women frothed at his body. I loved his hands the most—calloused, rugged, and large. They felt like sandpaper but that added to the roughness of our heated interludes. The only negative thing about Johnny was that he wasn't always available when I needed servicing. Seems like Cecily, my neighbor, was always finding some project for Johnny. She had an unlimited allowance.

Johnny assured me that their relationship was only professional, as well as the other women in our gated community who admired Johnny's range of capabilities. None of our husbands even knew how to change a tire. We all agreed that a man with a large toolbox was a turn-on.

A lot more died when we buried Tara. Tara was my purpose in life, the reason I continued to wake up every morning beside my real-life Scrooge. Charles had annihilated my confidence, my spirit, and my zest for life many years ago. If not for Norris, I would have thrown myself into Tara's grave with her.

I mention Norris because he would have blamed himself for two deaths. He was too fine of a man to carry that burden. The emptiness I felt every waking morning was the reason I first called Norris. Johnny was tied up with Cecily who was hosting a dinner party for her husband's clients. "Sorry babe. Cecily has a list a mile long," he responded to my text about requesting an urgent pool cleaning. So, I reached out to Norris.

Norris, a technology geek, ran his business out of his home. His wife, Naomi, was in sales and always traveling. This meant that Norris was tasked with the day-to-day, household chores and childcare duties. Norris Nichols was the only man in the carpool rotation. The multiple schedules he juggled never seemed to rattle him. I admired Norris' dedication to his girls and devoted fulfillment of his honey-do list. I found his hands-on involvement refreshing. But, the other women in our neighborhood clique joked about how Naomi wore the pants in the family. Cecily and my other neighbors found Norris and Naomi weird.

"What kind of man works from home?" "How can a mother 'abandon' her children like that?" "Who has six children?" "Obviously, Norris was trying for a boy; bet his girls feel inferior." Admittedly, I agreed with one comment: "Who names their children with the same letter, especially an 'N'?"

The Nichols' girls were Natalie, Natasha, Nadine, Nancy, Nannette, and my personal favorite, Nature. They had definitely run out of normal names by number six! But, I bit my tongue because Nancy Nichols, the #4 "NN," was Tara's best friend.

Over the years, I sensed Norris' loneliness. I understood how it felt to be taken for granted. Charles was clueless about what it took to keep things humming along—a job he thought was overcompensated when he doled out my monthly allowance.

Norris sensed my situation too. Our platonic relationship changed the night Tara had a project deadline, and the computer decided to go on the blink. I used to resent dealing alone with her dramatic explosions. "Freaking out" was my description of Tara's outbursts to minor blips. But freaking out didn't come close to describing her antics that night. I would give anything for them now. Perspective.

Of course, Charles wasn't around to help that evening. "Client dinner, home late," he had texted. I called Norris, desperate, and he was Johnny on the spot, no pun intended.

"Please send me a bill for your time," I said, after Norris worked his technological wizardry.

"I don't send bills to friends—just expect like-kind returns," he said, with a devilish smile that I had never seen before.

Is Norris flirting with me? I wondered. I went with the flow.

"What do you mean by 'like-kind'?" I asked, rather provocatively.

"Only that you can take a carpool rotation for me some day," he said, playfully.

"Boring! I can certainly do that but, for now, how about a beer or a glass of wine?"

"Actually, a glass of wine sounds great. Naomi just returned from an extended trip. It seems only fair that she deals with the girls tonight."

Tara had frantically resumed her project in her room. Our one glass turned into three. In the past, our conversations evolved around our daughters, but I learned a lot about the man Norris, not the father Norris, that night. As I walked him to the door, he kissed me on the cheek. At the time, I thought it was more than a friendly peck. His lips had lingered; it excited me. I thought that I would test the waters later.

It wasn't too much later, in fact, that Norris was added to the rotation. Other than Johnny, I met the others in their hotels of choice. But since Norris worked from home, he only had limited windows of opportunity, so we always met at my house. He called them his "smoke breaks," because I was "smoking hot, especially in bed." He made me laugh. I made him feel appreciated. We became really good friends—friends with benefits.

We were both excited about the chance to spend an entire weekend together. Norris had begged off from a trip to his in-laws. "He was up to his ears in work deadlines," he explained. He could use the quiet time to catch up while Naomi and their six girls were visiting her parents for the weekend. Charles was out of town. Tara was at a church retreat.

"I am becoming addicted," Norris said. "Numerous smoke breaks will be required over the weekend."

And they were. We had time to explore each other and try new things. No one would have foreseen bedbugs in the cabin at the church retreat. Tara, who definitely had inherited Charles' OCD gene, freaked out and left.

I later learned that the youth minister blamed himself for her accident. She couldn't ride in the church bus with the others to the cabin. She explained that she needed her car. She had a school project, he recalled, for which she would have to leave early Sunday to finish. After the bedbug discovery in the cabin, Tara left immediately that Saturday night.

She didn't knock on my bedroom door. She just came busting in. She definitely freaked out with her discovery. Her screams continued until the front door slammed. I couldn't run after her. Norris had me handcuffed to the bedposts— my idea, not his. Guess it was my father's vocation that provoked that fantasy.

Tara's time of death, fifteen minutes from the time she sprinted from the house.

The policemen arrived shortly after Norris' departure. They said that she crossed the center line, and after seeing the oncoming truck, they believe that she swerved abruptly and lost control. She hit a tree. Her airbag didn't deploy. She wasn't wearing a seatbelt. And, she was speeding. She died upon impact.

Norris later revealed that his daughter, Nancy, had received a text immediately prior to the accident.

"You are not going to fucking believe it," it said.

The neighborhood gossip updated me on Norris. "He was clinically depressed. He cracked, pure and simple. Men are not capable of dealing with children alone, much less six and DAUGHTERS! What was Naomi thinking??" These were only a few of the comments from the grapevine.

None of my neighbors knew the underlying reason for Norris' withdrawal and his mental state. I did feel horrible that Norris blamed himself. I was the only one that knew the source of his suffering. It hadn't come from a wife that was constantly out of town or raising six girls on his own.

Tara had to sense the tension between Charles and me. Any agony sustained from catching Norris and me could have been soothed with a shopping trip. Tara's blood was only on Charles' hands. He relented to my pleas of buying her a car only after he located a deal. If our only child had been given what he easily could have afforded, reliable airbags and the new safety features, her life would have been spared.

That piece of shit her daddy surprised her with on her sixteenth birthday killed my daughter. Not Norris. Not me. But Charles. I would never forgive him. I hated him now more than ever.

Chapter Eleven

Charles Walker, the banker,
Tara's father, Alice's husband

I knew that Alice blamed me. If she had said it once, she had said it a 1000 times.

"Was the money you saved in buying that piece of shit worth our daughter's life?"

For the first time in a long time, we agreed on something. I couldn't take it back. I couldn't make it right. I accepted the blame. I would live with the failure to protect my daughter for the rest of my life.

I tried to comfort the poor youth minister. He was being sensitive to Tara's schedule, her obsession with deadlines.

"She got that from me," I told him.

I wanted to tell him that the bedbugs in the cabin didn't have anything to do with her accident. There were lots of questions. Neither the timing nor the location of the accident made sense. The winding road Tara had been on wasn't even close to the route to our house from the church retreat. In fact, it was in the opposite direction.

Like me, Tara was a fastidious rule follower. Oddly, she wasn't wearing a seat belt, and she had been speeding and texting her best friend, Nancy Nichols. "You are not going to fucking believe it" were the last thoughts of my daughter memorialized in Nancy's phone.

The text alone raised many questions. Tara never used inappropriate language, even during her frequent meltdowns. What happened? Was it something at the church retreat? Had the youth minister hit on her? Is that why he was so upset?

I pushed these lingering questions from my mind and focused on my work. I couldn't let my colleagues down. They were the ones who kept me going. Everyone has their own battle scars. Everyone was dealing with something, like the administrative assistant I recently interviewed. A more extensive background check revealed her son and husband were both in prison. The results were in the stack of mail that had mounted on my desk while I was grieving Tara.

Prior to Tara's death, I would have summarily rejected any candidate with these affiliations. My personal tragedy made me more empathetic.

I liked Savannah Abbott. While personal questions were off-limits in interviews, as instructed by our lawyers, I inferred that there was more to her leaving Kentucky than just her desire to return to her roots, as she explained. Her mother was ill, her husband's job was relocating, her only child was nearby—all could have been plausible reasons. She only offered that she always wanted to return home. It was the uneasy tone in her delivery, the diversion of her eyes, the tightness in her posture, and the change of expression that made me think there was another reason—that reason was on my desk.

Savannah was running away from whatever landed her husband and son in prison. I would have done anything to save my daughter. I failed. I sensed that Savannah Abbott needed to be saved, and I was the vehicle for that salvation. Her salvation would also be my salvation—an opportunity to help me heal. She deserved a fresh start, and so did I.

I shredded the information and directed that an offer be extended to Savannah Abbott. Add $10,000 for moving expenses, I instructed. I was indeed a different man.

Chapter Twelve

Nancy Nichols, Tara's best friend

I couldn't even mourn the death of my best friend. I was burdened with an overbearing weight of guilt. Word quickly spread throughout school that Tara texted me right before she crashed. One of the mean girls, who was infinitely jealous of Tara's and my bestie status, had the gall to ask me if I texted Tara first! Of course, she was implying that I was somehow responsible. But, I hadn't texted Tara. I thought she was at her church retreat without access to a cell phone. The fact that she had texted me was disturbing enough, but the message was even more bizarre.

Tara never uttered any profanity. And, she NEVER texted while driving. She was the DMV's favorite kind of teenager or driver, for that matter. Tara always wore a seat belt and strictly obeyed the speed limit. She never played music and always silenced her phone. Instead of accelerating through a stop light upon its turn to yellow, she would slam on the brakes. She even counted to three at a stop sign. "It ensures that you have come to a complete stop," she explained. Tara was the ultimate defensive driver. All our friends joked about her. I can't remember who pegged her driving habits, "Tara from another era," but it stuck.

Tara was more than my best friend; I loved her like a sister. I certainly had more than my share of sisters, but Tara knew more about me than any of my siblings. We instantly bonded in third grade.

I was the only one in our circle of friends whose father was in the carpool rotation. Even more embarrassing was when Dad volunteered to be the class mom of my third-grade class. But, Tara never teased me like everyone else did about any of those things. She even said it was cool. Her father never helped with carpool or volunteered at the school. He didn't even know her teachers' names.

She used to love to spend time at my house. As an only child, I thought she was intrigued by the commotion and the drama in a house full of girls. As we got older and her OCD tendency bloomed, we spent most of the time at her house, which I preferred.

I was so envious of Tara's room, the room that she didn't have to share with a single soul. It was always immaculate. Her stuffed animals were always neatly arranged on her meticulously made bed. There were no dirty clothes strewn on the floor. Her clothes were carefully organized in her closets. Yes, she had not one, but two closets, and they didn't hold a single hand-me-down.

The best part of her room was the connected bathroom with dual sinks. My five sisters and I shared a bathroom with one sink. Our bathroom was so messy, it seemed ironic to me that it was the place to get clean. I thought Tara's OCD must be rubbing off on me when I could no longer share a dwindled bar of soap, a mangled tube of toothpaste, or even a messy hairbrush with my sisters. I never gave any of those things a second thought, until I experienced Tara's spick-and-span bathroom. Now, I felt dirty AFTER taking a shower at my house.

At Tara's, I had my own sink with my own pristine hairbrush and a dedicated hair dryer that worked continuously until my hair was completely dry. At my house, with all the hair dryers, hot rollers, and flat irons going at once, we blew more fuses than an ice storm. Dad finally implemented the staggered schedule, according to seniority. By the time it was my turn, no hot water remained, and the hair dryer needed cooling down before it was operational.

I loved the calmness, the neatness, and the orderly way of the Walker household. The smell of lemon-scented furniture polish enveloped you the minute you walked in the front door. The only downside to Tara's was the food. According to Mrs. Walker, she was given a pittance of an allowance for groceries, and she only splurged on items for Tara and her. She purchased Mr. Walker's things from the "Quick Sale" carts, which contained items with pending expiration dates or generic brands.

I had picked up on the generic brand purchases pretty quickly. In lieu of Dr. Pepper and Mountain Dew, there was Dr. Perky and Mountain Roar. Apparently,

Mr. Walker was the only one in the family who drank sodas or ate cereal for breakfast.

I was certainly used to generic cereal brands. In our house, our selections ranged from Captain Munchy and Lots of Charms. At Tara's, it was Toasted Wheat and Flakes of Corn. I about gagged the first time I had powdered milk with the knock-off cereal. Who used powdered milk? Mrs. Walker was clearly embarrassed the first time she saw me eating cereal. She explained that neither she nor Tara liked milk—only Mr. Walker. He traveled so much that the expiration date would pass before it was consumed, and she was constantly dumping sour milk down the drain.

These were minor objectionable features that Mrs. Walker more than made up for by doting over Tara and me. My mother was rarely home due to her work schedule. Even when home, she was out of touch. She couldn't deal with the chaos surrounding her. So, I could tolerate the powdered milk and the generics.

I became a fixture there. Over the years, I observed that Mrs. Walker's payback for her small allowance ran far deeper than just milk, soda, and cereal. Mr. and Mrs. Walker seemed to merely coexist. I never saw them exchange any type of loving gesture or engage in any conversation.

The nonexistence of loving gestures, I understood, because those were absent under my roof too. But my parents did converse—mostly Mom yelling at Dad that she was "sick of coming home to a filthy house," and she wished he could at least find the time "to run a brush through Nature's hair."

With Tara's death, I lost more than just a best friend, I lost a second family. At the funeral, Mrs. Walker told me to not be a stranger—that she needed me. I suppose her comment weirded me out a little. I didn't want to be a fill-in daughter. She just needed time, I thought. And, so did I.

PART IV

Chapter Thirteen

Savannah Hart Abbott, the tobacco farmer's wife

After Cray's arrest, I decided to move back to my childhood home in Beaufort, South Carolina. Nothing was keeping me in our town or state, for that matter. The walls were closing in. What had I gained from my blind willingness to follow my husband to Kentucky instead of pursuing my own dreams? When I felt sorry for myself and disappointed in my failure to advocate for raising our child in Beaufort, my supportive side would resoundingly argue—*you were pregnant. You did what you thought was best for your family.*

As it turned out, my best wasn't good enough. My husband and son were now in prison. Worse was that neither had a criminal bone in his body. Both were hard workers, honest as the farming days were long, loyal to a fault, and tenderhearted. None of it made sense. I couldn't help but blame Maude.

Josh was a lost soul when I met him. What made me think I could save him that summer? I failed him and myself at the same time. But, I wasn't going to fail my innocent son.

I was getting the hell out of Kentucky and returning to the place where I could visit Cray often—my beautiful hometown, where peace flowed through my veins, where joy bloomed as I watched my Lowcountry birds, where my soul was comforted by the piercing sunsets, and where my playful spirit emerged with each dolphin's leap. It was the place where I could feel God's hand on my shoulder as each mighty wave crashed onto the surf.

Hired Hit on Jessamin Island

Certainly, there would be a bank that needed a teller. I searched the job postings at every bank within a thirty-mile radius of Beaufort. I don't know what possessed me to apply for a position at the largest financial institution in the area. Did I really think I would be hired as the administrative assistant to the president? Perhaps, the positive energy from the Lowcountry forces was returning to my heart.

I shouldn't have questioned my qualifications for the job. I was smart. I was efficient and organized. I had outstanding reviews from my work as a teller. The interview went well, I thought. I established a comfortable rapport with my potential new boss and eloquently highlighted my abilities. I kept the strong possibility of a new job to myself during my visit with Cray the day after my interview. I didn't want either Mom or Cray to get excited prematurely.

Problem was, I let my heart influence my head, and I was the one getting ahead of the situation. Anticipating a job offer from the bank, I tied up loose ends of my Kentucky life and even started packing.

Now, the high wave I was riding was beginning to crash. I should have heard something by this point. My interview was six weeks ago. Unless my once-keen instincts had totally withered in landlocked Kentucky, I would have sworn the job was in the bag. I was relieved that I hadn't broken the news to Maude yet. But mentally, I had checked out of the Abbott Tobacco Farm. In my mind, I was already in Beaufort. I was more than ready to start my next chapter, so I started researching other job postings. Then, the call came.

"Savannah, I apologize for the delay in contacting you. Our president has been dealing with a family tragedy. We hope you are still interested, because we want you to join our team."

I immediately sent Cray an email and planned a visit. Then, I called Mom to deliver the good news. "Your baby is coming home!"

But, as I hit the road southward, I first visited Josh to relay my news. His excitement was initially tempered because he was already in the know. His warden, of all people, had told him the previous day. Josh delivered this information matter-of-factly, but I found it unsettling. How did the warden learn about my job offer? Was I being stalked? If so, why?

These questions didn't seem to occur to Josh. He had been too focused on the other information the warden shared.

"Cray will love having you close by. It is time to do something for you," he had said. "I can't wait to join you. The warden believes that he can make a better case for a transfer now that my family is in South Carolina."

I didn't want him to get his hopes up.

"You are eligible for parole soon. Stay strong and focus on the new life we will have upon your release, transfer or no transfer. We have the rest of our lives together, and we will not take one minute of it for granted," I said.

Josh made one request before I left.

"When you get to Beaufort, if the Port Royal Ice Castle still exists, will you buy a rainbow snow cone?" he asked.

Even through the thick partition separating us, I could see his eyes glistening.

"The biggest one they have, baby. The biggest one they have," as I hung up the prison phone.

Chapter Fourteen

Cray Abbott, the artist, son of Savannah & Josh

Momma's excitement about her new job and move to Beaufort was evident even over email. I was worried that during our upcoming visit she was going to break the news that she was leaving Dad. Otherwise, why would she abandon Abbott Tobacco Farm?

I wouldn't have blamed her three months ago when Dad took away my freedom—though we weren't exactly in shackles at Club Fed. Heck, the computer I had access to was much nicer than my used, refurbished one from the Discount Computer Emporium. And the Wi-Fi was fast and free.

I thought Walt must have finally told her about Dad and the botched plan. Such news would have certainly prompted her move back to South Carolina. Despite Kentucky's lush, rolling hills, there was something special about the powerful pull of Beaufort County's islands. Mom's temperament changed during those visits to her homeplace. She couldn't hide the sparkle in her eyes when she was there.

I knew she missed Beaufort and Gannah terribly. Gannah is what I call my grandmother, who had vehemently vetoed Granny, Grandma, Mammaw, and other variations. She preferred Hannah Anne. That was a mouthful for a toddler, so I had shortened it to Gannah. It stuck.

I loved everything about Gannah, especially her accent and the way she carried on about mundane things, like the welcome baskets she prepared for newcomers to Beaufort. Gannah should have run for Mayor of Beaufort because her baskets promoted her city's merchants. She included fresh bread from the Beaufort Bakery and Café on Lady Island, chocolate chip walnut cookies from Magnolia's on the Beaufort River, and cocktail napkins or dish towels, that she referred to as "tea towels," from one of her two favorite downtown gift shops, LuLu's and Tabby Shore. And no basket was complete without Chile Lime Sea Salt from the Beaufort Spice and Tea Exchange near the Richard Woods Memorial swing bridge. She insisted that mixed with yogurt, it was much better with fresh shrimp than ketchup-based cocktail sauce. She also readily informed recipients of her treats that the Beaufort swing bridge was the one featured in *Forrest Gump*, not one in Mississippi!

In addition to her welcome baskets, Gannah was also known for the multitude of hydrangeas growing in her back yard. In addition to white, she was especially proud of her blue and purple blooms—a result from manipulating the pH in the soil, she explained. Her homespun concoctions for changing the acidity included vinegar, lemon juice, coffee grounds, eggshells, buried copper pennies, and rusty nails.

Along with the baskets and hydrangea clippings, Gannah's letters detailed the home-cooked meals she provided: she-crab soup, fried green tomatoes, tomato pie, or her famous shrimp and grits. I'm sure there were others but those are the ones I remember. Though the dishes varied, the dessert was always the same— banana pudding. Gannah was famous for that too.

In addition to her letters and pictures, she sent us packages. I vividly remember the last package we received. Gannah enclosed funny, printed cocktail napkins: "My therapist told me to cut back on wine. Then we laughed and laughed." Momma smiled at those but when she unwrapped the candle and tea towels, I could have sworn I saw her tearing up. The soy candle was labeled, "Sand in my Shorts." The aroma was described as "Reminiscent of a relaxing day at the beach, a fusion of fresh coconut, lime, and invigorating verbena soothed by luscious vanilla." The enclosed tea towels said: "Vitamin Sea Recommended Daily," and "May You Always Have a Shell in Your Pocket and Sand Between Your Toes."

I found the stories of her flowers, her baskets, and homemade meals endearing, and her packages filled with local treasures, sweet. She was so far away from us. It was her way of keeping in touch. Momma's interpretation was very different.

"It's her way of meddling—classic southern, passive-aggressive behavior. She wants us in Beaufort. She doesn't seem to understand that your father can't just pick up and move 5,000 acres of tobacco plants. And she doesn't understand how anyone could possibly live anywhere else. The woman would shrivel like a slug in salt if she ever had to leave the Lowcountry."

When you grow up surrounded by tobacco plants and your father is consumed with the 24/7 responsibilities of a farm, your view of the world is skewed. I could count on one hand the number of times we had visited Beaufort. And those times had only included Momma and me since the Abbott Tobacco Farm consumed all of Dad's time. When I was old enough to appreciate my family history, I understood Dad's comment every time he shut the car door for our eight-plus hour trip. "Give Hannah Anne a hug for me, whether she likes it or not," he would say.

I silently took Gannah's side about the Lowcountry. Her letters, pictures, and gifts always took me back. I had always been mesmerized by Beaufort—the salty air, seafood, sweet tea, and huge oak trees draped in Spanish moss. Most of all, I loved the Lowcountry birds. I never told Momma that it was those trips to Beaufort that confirmed my vocation as an artist. After I gave her a painting including all the birds representing her homeplace—terns, herons, buntings, oystercatchers, sandpipers, cranes, and egrets—I think she knew. She wept.

Admittedly, when I first arrived at the Somerset Federal Correctional Institute, the contempt I held for Dad was insurmountable. But, in the short amount of time here, I had acquired empathy for Dad because I, too, was surrounded by professional criminals. And unlike those in the Kentucky Federal Pen, the professionals at Club Fed weren't violent types. Most of them couldn't even win a bar fight. I mean professionals as in doctors, lawyers, corporate executives, and even preachers.

Howard, or "How Weird," was a highly successful lawyer. Despite his success, his family's extravagant expenses grew larger than his receivables. He began dipping into his clients' trust accounts—the special bank accounts where funds were earmarked for real estate closings, estate settlements, insurance payments, and court costs. As such, legal ethics prohibited commingling them with payments for legal services. A pretty basic concept, if you ask me—don't spend money that doesn't belong to you. But, "trust account" was an oxymoron in How Weird's law practice. He rationalized that he would put back the cash when his outstanding invoices were paid. His house of cards began crumbling when a real estate closing was bumped up on the calendar. To pay off the mortgage balance required for the property transfer, he used insurance proceeds received in a client's disability settlement. It was easy at first, movement of funds from one trust account to another. His shell game was ultimately discovered in an audit by the state law examiners.

The stories associated with my professional new neighbors sounded like a broken record. They all centered around the same thing—stealing. In these confines, however, the theft didn't require a stocking cap or pistol, simply access to money that belonged to someone else.

Alton Johnston, MD, or "Doc," one of the lesser original nicknames, had defrauded the government from millions in Medicare reimbursements. Roger Simpson, or "Red," a former national leader of a charitable organization, pocketed significant contributions donated by bleeding hearts. Then, there was "Lucifer," whose given name was Reverend Calvin Baker, a televangelist who suckered his devout followers by offering sham, miraculous healings in exchange for generous gifts in his collection plate.

Each day, I discovered varying levels of bad. The endings were the same. All were tempted, and all succumbed to temptation.

I kept silent about the circumstances surrounding my membership in the club. Like all clubs, the goal was to fit in, be accepted, to go along to get along. None of my fellow inmates would believe that I was innocent and had never broken any law. Hell, the worst thing that I had ever done was come to a rolling pause at a stop sign.

Although I tried to conceal my grounds for membership, every member intimately knew each other's rap sheet. Embezzlement, preying on human kindness, or taking advantage of trusting followers were considered run-of-the-mill offenses. In the eyes of my professional neighbors, I was a real criminal. I had transported cocaine. Even the other real criminals, those with similar drug offenses, ostracized me. To them, I was a rookie and inept—getting caught the very first time.

Let's just say that when I arrived at Club Fed, I wasn't presented with a "Welcome to the Club" basket, like the ones Gannah made. And who would have ever believed that my memories of visits to Gannah's cherished hometown would ultimately provide my acceptance into Club Fed—the prison's version of a welcoming basket.

I was called "Birdman," which was fitting since I was named for one of the beautiful, Lowcountry cranes. However, within Club Fed, my sketches and paintings of these creatures were the inspiration for my nickname. It wasn't long before I built quite a tattoo enterprise.

Tattoos within these walls, at least initially, were inked with supplies from my art classes offered by the community college, my favorite Club Fed amenity. Since I could only apply the inks to the skin's surface, the designs quickly wore off. The fleeting nature of my masterpieces, as they became known, only seemed to stimulate the slew of my repeat customers. Frankly, I was impressed with their requested designs. These dudes had an eye for art and were creative in how to pay for it.

My now loyal customers offered me marijuana, pills, cigarettes, whiskey—any vice of my choice for a priority appointment. I wouldn't accept any form of payment for my temporary tattoos. I was living the consequences of fruit from the poisonous tree that had been promised to my father. When Papa Walt first explained the botched plan described by Dad that resulted in my arrest, I didn't believe him. I do now. I had experienced first-hand the corruption, the bribes, and the extortion. If my resolve wasn't sufficient, I could fall back on Gannah's strong words: "When you lie down with dogs, you wake up with fleas." These guys were junkyard dogs, to say the least.

When sketching a bald eagle for the third time on Guard Wayman's arm, he asked me why I didn't have a real tattoo machine.

"Certainly, you can get one of the boys to get you a tattoo gun," Wayman said. "Hell, real guns are traded in here every day, along with everything else," he said laughing. "It just takes a little cash to make it happen, or you could make some trades with other compensation, if you will, that you get for your work."

"I don't accept any type of compensation for the tattoos," I said. "And, I haven't seen any ATMs, so I don't know how to get cash," I responded in jest.

"Well, then you need a middleman. Anyone hooked you up yet?" Guard Wayman asked.

"I have no idea what you are talking about."

"A middleman is the way cash makes its way in here. You have to be careful, though—there are bad ones who take the money and run. But, I can definitely arrange one for you. My guy is reliable. My contact only charges a small fee. I'll even give up my commission."

"Thanks," I said to Guard Wayman. "But, I don't have anyone on the outside who I can ask for cash, especially for me to buy tattoo equipment. I don't have any use for a middleman."

"I'll float you a loan, and you could repay me with some of the candy you get from the others."

"Candy" was weed, pills, or other illegal substances bartered amongst the inmates.

"I don't like candy," I said. "I simply like to paint; it keeps my sanity."

"Dude, you could be right up there with The Donald," Wayman said. "That is some serious wasted talent."

I didn't know yet how Donald Furr had risen to his status among us jailbirds. He worked in Shipping and Receiving, but he was the man. He ran the show. You didn't want to get on his bad side, and thus, his nickname "The Donald."

"You aren't going to be in here long, and I really want a permanent tattoo of your bald eagles and a painting for my mother. She loves cardinals," Wayman continued. "How 'bout I put in a word for you on a new job assignment in Shipping and Receiving. That would be the easiest place for you to get some tattoo equipment mailed to you directly. The Donald will teach you the ropes on how it's done."

Scarred by Dad's experience, I was suspicious of Wayman's offers. I liked Wayman, but a sinking feeling warned that he had ulterior motives. I suspected he was angling for more than a permanent tattoo and cardinal painting. When I was assigned to Shipping and Receiving the next day, I was convinced he was motivated by something. Whatever his intent, I was happy to be leaving the road-trash cleanup crew, my assignment since arriving. And, I was a little curious about how all the candy I had been offered for my tattoos made it into the prison. I never inquired about the origins of the proffered payments, especially the drugs. The less I knew, the better.

70

Hired Hit on Jessamin Island

Franklin Newton, known as "Fig" at Club Fed, was the prison guard who oversaw the operations of Shipping and Receiving. Fig was Wayman's boss, so I assumed Wayman had put in a good word to him for my transfer off the road-trash crew into my new job. Fig explained that my duties included logging in and carefully inspecting any letter or package mailed to a prison resident. If anything was addressed to "unknowns," they had to be placed in a separate holding area. Unknowns were names that didn't match any current member at the club or bore an incorrect identification number. Those packages were opened by The Donald.

It didn't take long to observe that Fig and The Donald were taking a substantial cut from the cash sent by the middlemen that Wayman had referred to. But, the contents in the unknown stack that were the most troubling were the narcotics. I didn't know what happened to those.

The Donald not only confiscated all sorts of goods from the unknowns but also had the goods on our watchdogs. And then there was Blackbeard. During my time on the road crew, I learned that if Blackbeard shared with our guards the booty hidden for him along the highways, all was forgiven.

"Bobby Flay" sold food that he would steal during kitchen duty. On fried chicken day, he'd make a killing during the nightly card games. Of course, his profits were shared with the guards, just like those of "Wal-Mart." Wal-Mart was the head honcho in the Commissary. He shared the cash he pocketed with the guards while distributing lifted items such as Old Spice, Cheese Whiz, headphones, scissors (yes, scissors), and pornographic magazines.

Before entering these walls, I would never have imagined that an inmate could rise to power. However, in this short time, I quietly observed the steps and devices used to excel in this hierarchy. If you are thinking that the rungs of the success ladder included following the rules, you would be wrong. Serving as a pawn or puppet for the superiors was the path to authority within these ranks. The low-class convicts had nothing to lose. We had already lost our independence.

Things were getting easier for me because I offered something of value to the inmates and the guards and took nothing in return. Ironically, my lack of interest in the various forms of payments instilled some trust. It didn't take long before my tattoo devotees became quite chatty. Perhaps, they needed a reliable sounding board, a listening ear, and no judgment. I practiced the same techniques that psychiatrists, psychologists, priests, and even hairdressers used with their faithful followers.

"Bull," a former high-powered New York investment banker, became a devoted follower and bared his soul to me. Bull had taken the fall on an insider-trading transaction, netting his cohorts millions. They were living lavishly thanks to his refusal to identify them to the prosecutors in exchange for his immunity.

Bull requested a row of piping plovers. They were his daughter's favorite bird among all those frequenting his second home in Palm Beach, Florida. During my etching on his back, Bull divulged more than the details of the insider stock trades. He revealed the participation of my boss, Fig Newton, in the scheme. According to Bull, Fig was "recharging his batteries on a much-needed vacation" with Bull's former partners. They were being wined, dined, and entertained by an escort service on a private island.

Before Bull's revelations about Fig Newton, I agreed with Bull's daughter. The piping plover was a beautiful shorebird. I loved the contrast between its sand-colored body and its yellow, orange, and red legs and black-tipped, orange bill.

As I was sketching the bird's trademark—the black band across the forehead and black ring running around its neck—the markings now on Bull's back took on a different meaning. The black ring around this small, sparrow-like bird suddenly resembled a noose, a warning that Fig Newton would figure out a way to silence Bull and anyone else on the receiving end of Bull's information.

I found it interesting that prison bars, locks, and guards with guns were intended to protect the public from us thugs. We were the lowlifes who couldn't be trusted. We were menaces to society. However, the ones guarding us wayward sons were as bad or worse. Yet, these law-abiding citizens had the privilege to go home each night, while we remained caged and denied all freedom.

I was afraid of what else I was going to hear during my tattoo sessions. If I turned a deaf ear, would this protect me or seal my fate—guilt by association? Was I being set up yet again and for what?

I prayed that Dad received my letters. I gleaned more about criminal behavior inside these walls than I ever knew on the outside. And this was Club Fed. I couldn't even imagine what it was like inside my father's prison. I forgave him for trying to escape.

Oddly, Dad's largest fault was also his most endearing strength. He loved purely. He put family first, which included his employees on the Abbott Tobacco Farm. Duty and loyalty were his guiding principles—the traits that he inherited from Papa Walt, my blood grandfather.

Unfortunately, Dad wasn't tough like Papa Walt. He was weak like Adam Abbott. His weakness had been acquired during his formative years from watching him. Adam was scared to death of his own father, Kyle. Adam had no spine, especially when the patriarch of Abbott Tobacco Farm was anywhere around.

Dad's last letter made me nervous.

Dear Cray,

First, I want to tell you that I love you. I think about you every day and pray that you are OK. I have been doing well. My faith is stronger than ever. I finally see the light at the end of the tunnel. Stay strong. My strength comes from knowing I will be reunited with you, your mother, and Walt real soon. I know I don't have to tell you to be honest and do the right thing because you have done that your entire life. I am so proud of you.

Love,

Dad

Dad didn't know about my new assignment in Shipping and Receiving. But, he did know my mail would be reviewed by someone before being delivered to me. Based on my limited period in Shipping and Receiving, the postmark wouldn't be examined. And, based on the postmark, our reunion could be very soon. The letter was mailed from North Carolina, not Kentucky.

I stuffed the letter in my pocket. I prayed that Dad hadn't fallen for another one of his warden's rotten schemes. As Gannah would say, "The road to hell is paved with good intentions."

Chapter Fifteen

Savannah Abbott, Cray's mother, now banker's assistant

I couldn't hide my news when Cray called to confirm my upcoming visit with him. I was simply beside myself. I had landed a good job on my own. I was returning to the place I belonged. I knew he would understand because he had always followed his passion. But now, his mother was showing the gumption and strength to begin living her life.

My husband and only child were confined, but my soul felt free. The Lowcountry birds that I envisioned every night were welcoming me home. The past was in the past. Everything going forward was going to be righted.

My optimism, however, waned during my call with Cray. He was surprisingly indifferent when I conveyed my exciting news.

"Did Dad know? Did Maude know? What would happen to Abbott Tobacco Farm?" he questioned.

When did Cray start worrying about the farm? Josh had never burdened Cray with an expectation to continue the Abbott farming path. Josh consistently encouraged Cray to pursue his dreams. His artistic talent shouldn't be wasted on a tobacco farm. Cray's creativity would be suffocated by the stress of farming life, Josh continually preached.

I no longer cared about the future of Abbott Tobacco Farm. From my point of view, Josh had sacrificed enough for Maude and the Abbott family.

Maude was cold, at best, when I broke my news. She knew that none of us will ever return.

En route to my new life in South Carolina, I visited Josh. When I stepped outside the Kentucky prison door, I ran to my car and embraced my ten-hour drive to Beaufort with a full heart. I know that sounds selfish and even callous. I loved my husband, but I couldn't get out of Kentucky fast enough. I was optimistic for new beginnings. I didn't know what lay ahead of me, but as Momma would say, I was "as confident as a Bible salesman at a church lock-in" that I was never leaving Beaufort again.

With the North Carolina border behind me, the butterflies in my stomach settled. A flood of memories were resurrected by the sight of the crescent and sabal palmetto symbols on the "Welcome to South Carolina" sign. I recalled my fifth grade teacher, Miss Shelton, and her explanation of the origin of our state flag.

Fort Moultrie on Sullivan's Island was constructed of palmetto logs. The strong, sturdy trunk of a palmetto isn't solid wood but consists of tough, fibrous strands. The composition enables the tree to withstand salty sea spray, hurricane gusts, and even cannon balls, like the ones of the British Royal Navy on June 28, 1776. The palmetto helped defeat the British fleet. It represents courage and strength.

I could feel the protection of the palmetto's indestructibility. I could feel the calm of the sea breezes rustling through its fan-shaped leaves. To me, the tree's foliage looked like fireworks bursting in the sky and represented not only courage and strength but also liberation. I could feel my once confident, lively spirit being restored by a unique connection to a very special place.

Chapter Sixteen

Maude Abbott, the tobacco farmer's mother

Savannah and I were always uncomfortable around each other. We never exchanged harsh words, but there was a coolness between us. After Josh's arrest, Savannah retreated into a deep freeze. I knew she blamed me. I knew the resentment she harbored for me, the farm, and Kentucky. She never knew I shared that resentment.

Growing up, Hazel never would have predicted for one skinny minute that I would trade my life for hers. Envy consumed me. She chose to stay in Nags Head. I had returned home. She blossomed; I withered.

I thought about Walt Benton often—the children we would have had and the adventures we would have shared—a life like Hazel and Kip. There are certainly ironic twists in life.

Though he never said anything, Adam knew long before Josh's accident that he wasn't his birth father. We had a difficult time conceiving a child. I visited the best fertility doctors in Louisville and endured numerous tests. When nothing could be found, the doctors recommended that Adam be tested. Adam suffered from a double whammy—low sperm count and lacking motility, or sperm that didn't swim. Josh had been a miracle, the doctor declared.

Josh had blonde, curly locks and piercing, green eyes and looked nothing like an Abbott. At birth, some of his other features resembled my father, hence his name. And as I predicted, Dad was elated over the combination of his name with the Abbotts. Adam never questioned the origin of Josh's blonde hair or green eyes, not even after the discovery of Josh's rare blood type.

When Savannah relayed the news that she was moving back to Beaufort, I tried to suppress my true feelings of happiness. She would either not believe me or resent that I hadn't expressed them long before now. The latter, in my opinion, was worse because she would blame me even more for the current state of affairs.

So, I kept my elation to myself. But, my insides were singing and dancing. I was bursting with pride and a sense of purpose. The wings that Walt Benton had given me never took flight, but I was relieved and elated that Savannah found her own wings. And, she would fly. Indeed, she would soar!

Chapter Seventeen

Josh Abbott, former tobacco farmer, Inmate #233

I didn't question Walt's advice to keep Savannah in the dark about the sour deal with Warden Wilson that landed Cray in prison. Despite being a decorated, tough-ass Marine, he was perceptive and caring, with an impeccable seventh, emotional sense. He believed that the truth surrounding Cray's arrest would have completely rocked Savannah's world. She never would have forgiven me. To be honest, I haven't forgiven myself.

It had seemed like a perfect plan. When a prison warden, DEA Special Agent and local Sheriff are behind a scheme, how could there be a downside? Cray wasn't supposed to know anything about it, much less end up like me.

From Cray's letters, I knew Walt had told Cray the real reason for his incarceration. Obviously, Cray was aware that nothing was sacred within our concrete walls. Every letter and email was not only opened but also read and every phone call monitored. I read between the lines written in Cray's letters. He knew the truth, and he had forgiven me.

"Being here, I understand the things that I took for granted or didn't appreciate. One, you have always put our family first. Papa Walt shared some examples. We will survive and be stronger on the other side. I love you."

"I have really benefitted from my art classes. Can't wait to show you my recent drawings of Mom's favorite birds. My nickname is

Birdman because of my sketches. I kind of like it. What do you think? Love you, Dad."

Life presents unpredictable challenges. The support and love of those who matter give you the will to fight. Cray's letters, Savannah's new job in her Utopia, and Walt's unconditional love combined to make me want to live to see another day. Without them, I would have long surrendered to the depression. I wouldn't have been able to endure having been cheated out of a different life. What could have been was never given a chance. Any alternative path had been stolen from me by keeping me in the dark about my birth father. I had been offered only one course, and that was toward farming. But my faith and hope were growing stronger now that Savannah was back in Beaufort.

And, I would join her soon. Wormie Willie promised me.

PART V

Chapter Eighteen

Warden Willie "Wormie" Wilson

My daughter deserved so much better. I never trusted banks or bankers. Evil sons of bitches. In my opinion, the practices of lending institutions were despicable. They would hold themselves out as some trusted entity where your money was safe, and your nest egg could grow. In reality, the fine print in every loan document was a gotcha. The hard-earned money of the depositors was used only to line the pockets of the investors and executives.

I had been a loyal customer of Community Bank & Trust since it opened its doors. Hell, I held the scissors at the ribbon-cutting ceremony. "We're your neighbor. We're your friend. We ARE your Community." The slogan was plastered on local billboards and little league baseball jerseys. "Community, my ass" was a more fitting slogan.

My buddies, who previously ran the show, had been displaced for young'uns with shiny MBAs. They clamped down on personal loans made to the community leaders. "Terms and interest rates are now being reviewed more closely by state regulators," my know-it-all, banking executive son-in-law said at my granddaughter's wake, attempting to defend the actions taken against me.

The certified letter informed me that my loans were being called. A payoff was required, or new loan terms needed to be negotiated. My indebtedness exceeded the value of my assets. I could no longer just keep paying the minimum low-interest, monthly payment. I had lost more than half of everything to Alice's mother in my first divorce, then the other half to my second wife. And now this.

That so-called connected son-in-law of mine had been no help. I thought the guilt he had to feel over Tara's death would have softened his cold, cheap heart. He probably had enough cash stuffed under his mattress to pay off my loans. But when I mentioned my dilemma, that arrogant, selfish bastard's only advice was filing for bankruptcy.

There was no way that I would allow my financial situation to be analyzed. I certainly couldn't use the cash that I had accumulated from my recent partnership with Sherriff Buchanan and his DEA buddy. Such a lump sum payoff could come back to haunt me. It would raise a red flag for sure. A bankruptcy filing would jeopardize this new enterprise. I knew that court filings were public records and closely scrutinized. My new partners wouldn't like that exposure. Nope, bankruptcy was not for me.

When I learned that Josh Abbott's wife was interviewing for a job at my son-in-law's bank, I tried to nix it. My partners and I may need Savannah one day. The Abbott Tobacco Farm would eventually need to diversify, and this time we could provide Josh with the necessary cover for harvesting marijuana among his tobacco plants. So, I anonymously mailed the rap sheets on her husband and son to my worthless son-in-law.

I learned that he hired her anyway—totally out of character for the man who avoided the slightest taint to his pristine reputation. According to Alice, he even ran a criminal background check on their pool cleaner.

Then it hit me. Charles had set a trap for himself. I celebrated with a bottle of Jim Beam Black label and a cigar. My plot was foolproof. I had Josh Abbott in my back pocket. That weak man would do anything to be reunited with his family. I was going to make that happen, and I would be rewarded handsomely. The only tricky part of my plan was how to convey this to my daughter, Alice. But I was counting on my instincts. If her marriage was as shitty as I thought it was, this would be a no-brainer.

Chapter Nineteen

Alice Wilson Walker, the banker's wife, the warden's daughter

I was upset that Dad left. I needed him now more than ever. He had originally planned to stay several days after Tara's funeral, but he disappeared soon after her wake. Apparently, he and Charles had a disagreement. I only knew this from Johnny, who was more than my pool boy that day. His presence comforted me, something that my husband had never done and where he continued to fail.

Since Tara's accident, Charles and I had barely spoken, so he wasn't forthcoming about Dad's abrupt departure. Neither was Dad. His text: "Sorry to leave before the funeral. Will call later."

Johnny had seen them talking briefly. "From your dad's body language, he looked really pissed after Charles' quick exit from their conversation," Johnny said.

I missed Dad's call. His voicemail message only said that he was sorry and that he needed to discuss a business proposition with me. He would try me later. I wondered if he had discussed his business idea with Charles, who would have rejected any business association with my father. That may explain what Johnny observed.

Charles had never viewed Dad's position with any respect. But, I admired my father and his commitment to help rehabilitate the underbelly of society, as Charles referred to the inmates under my dad's watch. You certainly don't make it to the top job in a prison without doing something right.

Not that I would ever agree with any position of Charles, but Dad's bad luck and poor decisions had tainted his personal life.

Given my limited vocabulary, according to the book of Charles, I didn't know the right word or words to describe my childhood home life, but three phrases came to mind: getting into fights, getting drunk, and getting screwed. The latter depended on the circumstances and your perspective.

When my parents weren't at each other's throats, they were numbing their misery with alcohol. Dad could handle it better than Mom, who had to sleep off her binges. He finally kicked her out and paid her off when I was ten. Since I chose to stay with Dad, she wrote me off as well. I hadn't seen her since. I thought she would show up for Tara's funeral, to bury the past as we were burying the granddaughter she never met. But she didn't show and neither did Brenda, my stepmother, who, in retrospect, had more motherly qualities than the woman who birthed me.

I suppose Dad married Brenda because he needed help. He couldn't go it alone with a daughter going through puberty. They seemed happy at first. For some time, I experienced a normal household. Supper was on the table. Laundry was washed, folded, and even ironed. Brenda loved to iron while watching her soap operas. I had to give it to her in one category. She was never idle.

Brenda helped me with my homework, taught me how to apply makeup, and gave me fashion advice. I'm confident I would have never made the cheerleading squad without Brenda's pointers. She had patiently worked with me in perfecting the dance moves for the fight song.

While Brenda excelled in her role as stepmother and housewife, she, at some point, started enjoying the "ho" in housewife more than the wife. I guess she got bored or tired of Dad's long hours, mood swings, and being in charge of a daughter that wasn't hers.

Admittedly, Dad was temperamental, but I always defended him. Guarding criminals all day certainly couldn't be easy-breezy. I made excuses for his short fuse.

But for his volatility, he wouldn't have had to pay Brenda a dime. Her black eyes and broken nose cost him dearly. He also had to compensate Danny, the high school football coach, who Dad had beaten to a pulp after catching him with

Brenda. Danny's assault charge and Brenda's domestic violence charge jeopardized his job. So, he paid off wife number two and her lover. Double whammy.

When we finally talked, he told me about his most recent financial setback. Loans were being called, and he sought my cheap-ass husband for advice.

"We both know the man is tighter than bark on a tree, but I thought that Tara's death may have softened his heart of stone," Dad said. "But ya know what the miser said to me?"

"Get a second job?" I guessed.

"Ha. Nope. He told me to file for bankruptcy. Talk about humiliation!" he said. "I think I have had my share of that between your mother and Brenda. I was actually proud of myself for walking away before I punched him."

"I'm really sorry, Dad," I said. "I would help you if I could, but the only money that I have access to is my pithy allowance and Charles keeps close tabs on it."

He then told me his idea. I loved it. The sooner, the better.

I relayed to Dad the dates of the upcoming Southeastern Annual Banking Conference, where Charles had been invited to speak. Before Tara's death, we had planned to go as a family to the Ritz Carlton on Amelia Island. Charles kindly accepted the invitation to be the Keynote Speaker, after all, this engagement was honored with a two-bedroom suite during the entire conference. Charles loved to combine these opportunities with a family vacation because the hotel room and his expenses were covered. As an added bonus, the location was drivable so no airfare expense.

I actually enjoyed these work vacations because Charles was tied up all day and even most evenings with business dinners. A win–win for me as well.

The conference was still several weeks away. Now that it would be just the two of us, there was no way I was going. I was planning a thorough pool cleaning.

The timing was perfect for Dad's plan. I told him to set things in motion for that weekend. I reminded him that the less I knew about the details, the better. An indescribable feeling rushed through my body. Thank you, Mr. Thesaurus, for helping me find the right word—emancipated. I was feeling emancipated.

Chapter Twenty

Josh Abbott, Inmate #233

Guard Ronald Griffin or "Shorty," a sidekick of our beloved warden, whose nickname was the least creative since he stood about five feet small, escorted me into Wormie Willie's office after Sunday morning worship service. My warden was definitely in one of his better moods. He apologized again for the unpredictable mishap that landed Cray in prison. But, "he was a man of his word." He was working on a new arrangement that could not only set me free but also Cray.

"This conversation cannot leave this office," Warden Wilson advised. "An opportunity has come up that can get you out of here. Based on the unfortunate outcome of our last deal, I am not going to say that it's risk free. But, I have thought through every detail. I am working on a car, a fake ID, and an early parole release. I need three weeks. You will be reunited with your family soon," he concluded.

It seemed fitting that on the day when I was offered an opportunity for my freedom, the worship service ended with a hymn by Thomas Chisholm, a Kentucky native.

"Great is thy faithfulness, Great is thy faithlessness, morning by morning, new mercies I see. All I have needed thy hand hath provided; Great is thy faithfulness, Lord unto me."

If this plan actually worked, I would be singing that hymn all the way from Kentucky to Beaufort and for the rest of my life.

PART VI

Chapter Twenty-One

Savannah Abbott,
the banker's assistant

My first day as the administrative assistant to the bank president, Charles Walker, went surprisingly well. Mr. Walker had this comforting, calm aura that immediately put me at ease. If my first day was any indication of what to expect going forward, my tasks were far less challenging than being a bank teller. In fact, it seemed my duties were unrelated to banking procedures and rules. I hadn't given myself enough credit. I was already feeling more confident that I was indeed qualified for this job.

My first day primarily involved word processing, which I could do in my sleep. In addition to my previous full-time, 8-5:00 day job, I spent evenings typing tobacco reports and spreadsheets and handling pay roll and most of the business matters of the farm. Josh was exhausted after fifteen-plus hours in the field. With the dwindling demand for our crop, Josh had eliminated a number of positions, including our bookkeeper. So, I "wore numerous hats," as my mother used to describe my job.

Mr. Walker explained that he was the Keynote Speaker in an upcoming conference to be held on Amelia Island. His speech had to be submitted electronically for inclusion into the conference materials.

"I hope you can read my scribble, and the speech isn't too boring," he said, handing me a legal pad that contained his first draft.

His scribble looked as if it had been typed. I had never seen neater penmanship, a lost art for sure. His remarks focused on the unprecedented challenges with consumer expectations in the new world of digitalization and the accompanying hackers and fraud. In typing his speech, my eyes were opened to the complexity of his job—maximizing efficiencies while maintaining the security of customer accounts. I was realizing that following the strict rules and procedures required as a bank teller, though numerous as they were, were quite simple compared to envisioning the future and creating innovative strategies to stay competitive.

My previous opinion that the top dogs at the bank had cushy jobs shifted after only my first day. Mr. Walker's daily itinerary was enough to make anyone's head spin. Even though his appointments were synchronized to his desktop, laptop, and phone, he instructed that he was still old school and preferred a printout of his daily schedule.

"Ironic," he said, requesting his printed schedule. "I'll soon be speaking to hundreds of bankers throughout the southeast on the importance of technology, but I still like my paper. We'll keep that between us," he said, laughing.

I began thinking the man must never sleep. There was not a free minute in his day. I didn't know where he found the time to craft any speech, much less one that he would present to competitors. Public speaking in front of hundreds of very smart people made my stomach hurt just thinking about it.

My new boss was not only tireless but also a perfectionist. I had worked on at least six revisions to the upcoming presentation. He apologized for all the changes, which flabbergasted me. It was my job after all; I had the easy task, just memorializing his thoughts.

Between revisions, his mail was delivered by the mail room. I thought it was odd that it had been opened. He explained that this step was required for security. In addition to security protocol, there was extensive legal protocol. The mail room electronically logged the sender, the subject matter, and stamped the date the document was received. This itemization was then printed and attached to the daily stack. One of my jobs was to verify the printed list with each item before delivery to Mr. Walker.

A reservation confirmation at the Amelia Island Ritz Carlton was in the stack and a brochure about the array of spa services. For participation in the conference, apparently, he and his wife received complimentary spa treatments. The letter encouraged scheduling as soon as possible to ensure availability. After validating the mail room's log, I delivered the stack to my boss.

"Looks like you have complimentary spa treatments at the Ritz," I said. "I will call and reserve them when you decide how you want to be pampered."

"Ha. I don't think I'll have any time for that," he said.

"Well, I'm sure your wife would enjoy it. I don't mind coordinating with her, if you don't have time," I offered. "Free spa treatments at the Ritz seem too good to go to waste."

"Sounds like you've been there," he said.

"No, but I understand that it's spectacular. Hopefully, you'll have some free time to enjoy it. Let me know if you change your mind. I'm happy to book something for your wife. I really don't mind."

"I'll let you know, but for now, there is something you can help me with. I think my speech is too boring," he said, handing me another revision. "I kick off the entire conference. I don't want to put everyone to sleep from the outset. I need to interject some humor, but joke delivery is not my forté. If you don't mind, see if you can find some humorous cartoons that I could incorporate to keep the audience engaged."

Cartoon or not, I couldn't believe Mr. Walker was relying on me for information to be used in this important event. I took this assignment to heart thinking this would be a momentous task. Who draws cartoons about such a mundane topic as digitalization?

I quickly learned that there must be a cartoon for everything. There were hundreds of cartoons running the spectrum from political issues to even technology and digitalization. One sticking point, they were licensed. I couldn't expose my boss to a copyright infringement claim.

I gave Mom a rundown of my first day and my newfound respect for bank executives.

"He's a really big deal beyond just our bank. He is the keynote speaker for a big conference at the Amelia Island Ritz. Despite his status, he seems respectful, at least what I have seen so far. Get this, he asked me to help with his speech."

"See there! I told you that were qualified. You can do anything. And, you wear all your hats beautifully," Mom gushed.

"I don't want to bomb on my first substantive assignment. Can you help me? I need a funny cartoon about technology, and there is no one funnier than you!"

"Ha! You know I am a technological dinosaur. Get Cray to help you. He has the creative brain. I bet he could draw something. At least, it'd give him something to do. Idle hands are the devil's workshop."

"You're right. The problem is the conference is coming up. I don't have any time to visit him this week."

"How about I go see him tomorrow?" Mom offered. "Write down what I need to tell him about the subject matter. I don't trust myself to get it right."

"Oh, Mom, thank you. But, don't make him feel obligated. He needs to understand that there isn't much time."

I loved the idea of engaging Cray because I feared his new surroundings, though only temporary, would jade him. Prison might torch his creativity. I had no doubt he would come up with something outstanding. But, the more I thought about getting Cray involved, the more uneasy I felt. The challenge would be presenting Cray's ideas to my new boss. It could open the proverbial can of worms about what he did for a living, where he was living, etc.

I wasn't naïve. At some point details about the new executive assistant would percolate throughout the bank. Every office setting has one of those tricky, affable types whose primary goal is to lure you into a seemingly friendly conversation and goad you into unloading family secrets. Phyllis was the chief interrogator here. She quickly tried to befriend me with an offer to lunch and drinks after work. She was already sharing tidbits of inside, confidential information.

Women like Phyllis were masterful at their skill. She politely, and in her plastic authenticity, inquired about my personal life—where I lived, was I married, did I have children, and my previous work experience. She wanted to know whether I was on Facebook, Instagram, or Twitter, a way for those like Phyllis to stalk you. I provided as little detail as I could and attempted to cut off every inquisition. I knew that she would eventually view my invisible wall of silence as standoffish or speculate that I was hiding something. People like Phyllis didn't give up easily, but when they did, beware of the consequences. I decided that it was better for Mr. Walker to hear about my personal situation from me than someone else, i.e., Phyllis.

The next morning, I decided to get it over with first thing, as I delivered his itinerary for the day. He had a small window of time between 8:00–8:30. There was no time for delay or cold feet.

"Mr. Walker, I know you have another busy day," as I handed him his printed schedule, "but I would like to talk you about something. It will only take a couple of minutes, if that is OK."

"Why sure, Savannah, but call me Charles. We're all family here. Is everything OK?"

"Yes, everything is great. I just wanted to discuss a personal matter with you," as I shut his door.

Mr. Walker had an open-door policy, so closing his door indicated the confidential nature of my request. I tried to maintain my composure as I began my rehearsed speech.

"The questions on my job application had only inquired into my criminal background, not my family's. I answered every item honestly. But, to avoid any potential surprises, I want to air a private matter with you."

I recounted growing up in Beaufort to leaving for Kentucky, Josh's expected path at Abbott Tobacco Farm, his arrest and incarceration and then Cray's. After I finished, I was relieved that he seemed saddened, instead of disappointed or angry. A million things rambled through my brain as I tried to interpret his reaction.

"If you need to terminate me, I understand," I concluded.

He paused for what seemed like an eternity.

"Savannah, to say that I am sorry sounds trite and empty. Life can throw curveballs, for sure. If I've learned anything over the years, it is that no one is immune to them. We can only control ourselves, and that can be a struggle on its own. We're excited that you are on our team. I hope that you don't hesitate to let me know whenever you need some personal time. With all this technology at our fingertips, we have flexibility to accommodate."

"Thank you, Mr. Walker."

"Charles," he said.

I smiled. As I exited his office, I felt a renewed sense of freedom. Transparency was liberating. A heavy burden had been lifted. The day only got better. Mom's report on her visit with Cray was great. When she read the assignment from the note cards I had prepared, Mom said his eyes lit up—the way mine used to when I spotted dolphins playing in the Beaufort River.

"He said to give him three days, and he'll have some choices for you. He is so proud of you! He seems really good. He has a new assignment in Shipping and Receiving that he is looking forward to. Got to be better than the road-trash job."

In the short amount of time that I had been home, I realized how much I had truly missed my mother. I had taken so many things for granted growing up. She had my back. It was a type of security that I never felt in Kentucky.

I had also missed her "Hannah-isms," what I called her frank, odd-ball expressions. I told her that I had come clean with my boss about Josh and Cray. He appeared supportive and sympathetic. I assumed she would have agreed with my approach. "Lay your cards on the table" and "deliver the unvarnished truth," she often said. Then again, she often surprised me.

"You don't always need to air your dirty laundry. But, I'm not walking in your shoes, and I trust your judgment."

"Thanks, Mom," I said. "That means a lot. I have missed you, your strength, and practical advice. You are so wise."

"Well, I don't know about that," she said, chuckling. "I know neither of our lives turned out like we dreamed. On the bright side, these difficulties may be a blessing in disguise. They brought you back to the place where you belong, where you radiate, where you flourish. Perhaps Josh and Cray will be stronger and wiser when this is all behind us. Every cloud has a silver lining."

I prayed that this particular "Hannah-ism" would prove true.

Chapter Twenty-Two

Hannah Anne Hart, Cray's Grandmother, Savannah's mother

That Guard Wayman was so nice and cute. Most of the guards had faces only a mother could love, and they weren't friendly at all. I wondered why Wayman chose the path of a prison guard.

When he checked me in earlier in the week, he had gone on and on about Cray's artistic abilities. He showed me the bald eagles that Cray had tattooed on his arms. I agreed with him about Cray's abilities.

"Between us, Cray fell on the sword for someone," I told Wayman. "Cray Abbott would give you the shirt off his back; he wouldn't hurt a flea, and he has never even run a red light. I hope you're looking out for him, Wayman."

"Yes, ma'am. I just got him a new assignment in Shipping and Receiving. Better than the road cleanup crew."

"That's awfully kind of you," I said. "Today, I am hoping to persuade him to use his creative talent to come up with some sketches for his mother. She has a new job and wants to impress her boss with some of Cray's work, some kind of presentation about technology. It's beyond my pay grade, so his mother gave me some notes. Can I take these with me?"

"I'm sure it's OK, but you know, rules are rules. Let me take a look."

Guard Wayman read the notes.

"I don't see any problem but can't say I really understand it. Go for it."

"Greek to me, too. But not to Cray. He will understand this stuff. And, this project will be like a shot in the arm."

By the confused look on his face and the fact that Cray was linked to drugs, I got nervous and clarified my remark.

"You know—like a ray of light, a spark of hope, something to encourage him to keep the faith, a light at the end of the tunnel," I added.

"Aw, yes, of course. I bet Cray can help. He's a smart kid."

I refrained from telling Wayman that he didn't look much older than Cray. I wanted to ask him how or why he chose to be a prison guard but kept that to myself too.

Cray seemed energized by the favor for his mother. I emphasized the short timeline.

"Savannah doesn't want you to fret about it," I told Cray.

"I already have some ideas. This will be fun and better than painting temporary tattoos. I will get right on it. I have a new work assignment and am not really sure about my schedule. But I'm sure I can get it done by the time you are allowed to visit again," Cray said.

I thought that visitation restriction was ridiculous. I would write a complaint about that later.

"And, you won't be able to take anything with you, but I can show them to you," Cray said.

"How ridiculous!" I said. "How could anyone in prison have access to anything illegal to give a visitor?"

"It's just a rule, Gannah," he said, shrugging his shoulders. "If you think Mom will like them, I think I can mail them to her. I work in the mail department now."

"That nice Guard Wayman told me about his help in getting your new assignment. He thinks you are really talented."

"Ha. I guess. He likes free tattoos, though they are only temporary. But, he did ask me to paint a picture for his mother. She apparently loves cardinals."

"I like him. He's very polite and friendly," I said. "Most of the other guards are plain rude and have faces like a bulldog chewing on a wasp. They'd make a freight train take a dirt road."

"You have a way with words, Gannah. I'm sure Mom loves being with you. I'm so happy she is back in Beaufort. Tell her that I am proud of her."

Savannah was tickled to death with the report of my visit with Cray. She had been ridden with guilt that her new job consumed her time and prevented her from visiting him the last two weeks. "That's what I am here for," I preached, in my attempts to ease her conflicted emotions.

"Once you develop a routine and demonstrate your value with your boss, the world is your oyster. For now, it is good for me to spend time with Cray. I am making up for lost time—the days, months, and years that I surrendered to the Abbotts."

So, I anxiously awaited my three-day hiatus before I could return to Somerset. I couldn't wait to see what Cray had drawn. I hoped that cute Wayman checked me in again.

My cheery disposition took a nosedive when I saw the prison guard who was waiting for me. He hadn't just been hit with the ugly stick, he got whopped with the whole forest! His coyote looks made my skin curl.

"I understand that Cray Abbott is your grandson," he snarled.

"Yes, sir. I'm here to visit that fine, young man."

"Well, he's still on duty, so let's chat a little until he's free," he said. "I'm Franklin Newton, Wayman Ritchie's boss."

You could cut the tension in the air with a Ginsu knife. I wondered what happened to Guard Wayman.

"I don't mind waiting. I know you have more important things to do," I said, hoping this snake would slither away. This man gave me the heebie-jeebies.

"I need to understand why you are here. You brought in some papers on your last visit. That's against the rules. I need to know what you took into the visitation area," he demanded.

Hells bells. I didn't like the tone of his Frankenstein voice, his beady eyes that you could barely see underneath his bushy eyebrows, or his authoritative puffed-out chest. I would have preferred swimming with sharks.

"I was cleared by your numerous check points," I said, authoritatively.

"I'm the ultimate check point so I need an explanation what you brought with you during your last visitation."

"Being Wayman's boss and all, I assume you know that Cray is a very talented artist," I said, thinking this man was a real dilly. "His mother wants him to create some cartoons for a conference. Something about technology. I am old school and don't know about all these things so I asked her to write it down so that I could ask Cray if he could help. That's all I had—notes about what she wanted."

"What type of conference?" he asked.

"A banking conference on Amelia Island. Cray's mother is the assistant to the bank president," I offered, proudly.

"When is this conference?"

I couldn't figure out what the big deal was and wondered if this guard gave everyone the third degree. Wayman had looked at the notes and had given me the green light. I wasn't about to throw Wayman under the bus to his boss.

"I'm not exactly sure, but soon."

"I will need that information."

"No problem. We certainly weren't trying to break any rule. We thought that it would be encouraging for Cray to use his artistic talent to help his mother," I said, trying to sound positive and confident in the presence of this intimidating brute.

With that, Guard Newton ceased interrogating me and left me sitting in the waiting area.

Chapter Twenty-Three

Cray Abbott, the artist

According to Gannah, Mom really liked her job and respected her new boss. I hoped she liked my cartoons, and that her boss would use them in his presentation about data digitalization.

Of course, I had to explain them to Gannah. She had never heard of the cloud. In the simplest way I could, I told her that it was like a storage device that you could access through the Internet instead of filling up space on your computer hard drive. One cartoon depicted birds avoiding certain clouds because they contained too much data. I thought the sketch was quite clever. Gannah still didn't seem to get it.

She liked my next one better, primarily because of the colorful bird wearing jewelry. I placed a string of dull, monochromic starlings on a telephone wire with the words "birds of a feather." On a different, larger wire, a colorful, bejeweled, avant-garde bird perched on a wire labeled "digitalization."

I had to enlighten my grandmother on the message.

"To be successful in this rapidly advancing technological world, you have to risk being different and take chances. The opposite of being birds of a feather."

"Over my head," she said. "I'm sure Savannah will understand these. You are so talented, Cray. Your ability doesn't come from me. My stick figures don't even look like stick figures."

Gannah communicated that Wayman's boss had scolded and questioned her about the notes she brought on her previous visit. She was so startled by his inquisition that she couldn't recall his name. He told her that he would only release the drawings after he verified every detail about the conference.

"Was it Franklin Newton?"

"Yes, that's his name. He wasn't very friendly. Actually, he was downright rude. He makes a cold, dead fish look like Prince Charming. Mud wouldn't even let him put a stick in it!"

It took all my willpower to keep from laughing. I knew that Fig Newton was listening to our conversation.

"He's just doing his job, Gannah. And, speaking of the rules, I can't let you take these, but, hopefully, you can remember enough about the cartoons to see if Mom is interested. If she is, you can bring the details about the conference next week, and Guard Newton will help me get them to her."

My comment was all for show, for "Prince Charming." The last thing I wanted was to involve Fig Newton. I didn't trust him one bit. And, I sure didn't want to owe that man any favor in return. By next week, I hoped to figure out how to mail my sketches to Mom, especially with my new assignment in Shipping and Receiving. Wayman already told me he would help. He really liked the cartoons. Hopefully, his offer wasn't just buttering me up for another tattoo.

PART VII

Chapter Twenty-Four

Savannah Abbott

When I received the package with Cray's cartoons, I marveled at his ability and continued to question where this creative gift originated. I sent copies to Josh. I wish I could have been with Josh when he saw them. The picture I imagined of his beaming smile wouldn't scratch the surface of his amazement. Along with a copy of his sketches, I included some photographs that I had taken of the rookery and the river at sunset. I began crying as I sealed the letter.

Dear Josh,

> Things are going well here. Thank you again for your understanding on why I had to leave. I realize I should have taken this step earlier. Mom is happy that I am back home.
>
> Do you have any updates on your parole? I am enclosing some sketches. I am also enclosing some photos. I will explain them further when we talk. I trust that you receive everything.
>
> Savannah

I had so many conflicting emotions. I couldn't discern if my tears were triggered by sweet memories with Josh in our favorite places or my maternal awe of Cray's talent.

My tears were also likely due to relief. I had come clean to my boss about my son's address—the Somerset Federal Correctional Institute and my husband's—the Kentucky Federal Penitentiary.

It was likely a combination of all those things, but I realized I had bottled up so many feelings. Once the tears started, the floodgates opened. I was due a good hard cry.

After I regained my composure, I took Cray's sketches into Mr. Walker's office. I detailed my search for some cartoons for his speech, and my concern about using licensed content. I relayed that Cray was an artist and that I asked him for ideas, hoping it would help his fortitude. I handed him Cray's work.

"Admittedly, I'm just a tad biased, but I think these are better than any I've seen. I've reviewed enough cartoons about technology to last me a lifetime," I said.

He put on his reading glasses and smiled as he surveyed them.

"These are indeed excellent. There is only one problem," he said, removing his glasses and placing them on his desk. "My topic has been changed."

"I emailed your speech last week to the program chair. How can they change the topic after you already turned in your remarks?"

"Seems as if another speaker has included the impact of digitalization in the banking industry in his comments. Now, the course planners want me to focus less on digitalization and more on the challenges of attracting young talent and customer service. I guess I am back to square one on my speech, but I'll figure out how to include the cartoons. I like them."

"Doesn't the conference start on Tuesday?" I asked, wondering how he could start all over given the time we had spent on the first one.

"Yes, Tuesday evening with a cocktail reception. I open the meeting sessions first thing Wednesday morning."

"You have a packed schedule this week," I said. "And the management retreat this weekend. So much for getting your speech in early."

"I was thinking the same thing," he said. "If we hadn't submitted the electronic draft ahead of the deadline, they wouldn't have noticed the duplication of content."

"I'm happy to work over the weekend," I offered.

"Thanks, but that's unnecessary. I won't have time to focus on the speech until Monday. I do have an idea. If I am going to pull this off, I need to lock myself in a room away from the office and all the interruptions. You mentioned that you had never been to the Ritz. What do you think about working from there on Monday and Tuesday instead of the office? I was thinking that you could invite your mother, and you two can enjoy the amenities while I prepare my remarks. Then you can type them up when I'm done."

"Well, the Ritz sounds better than my cubical. If you are serious, I will talk to Mom and see if she can swing that," I said, but knowing that even one night at the Ritz was not in our budget.

"I certainly don't need the two-bedroom suite that is reserved. Go ahead and call the organizers and inform them of my scheduling conflicts. Let them know that I am willing to prepare different remarks but cannot submit the speech before Tuesday afternoon. And ask them to exchange the suite for two individual rooms for Sunday–Wednesday instead of Monday–Friday."

"What a generous offer. I'll call and see if they can make that change before I get Mom too excited," I said.

After I confirmed the change in the reservations, I called Mom. She was ecstatic but a little wary.

"Four days at the Ritz Carlton on Amelia Island?" she asked. "Make sure you understand the arrangements. You know there is no such thing as a free lunch. We can't get stuck with the bill."

"OK. But his accommodations are comped for participation in the conference. He requested that I change his suite to two rooms and for one less night, so I don't think he would have had me make those changes if the room wasn't covered," I explained.

"Our lives have been nothing close to a fairy tale," Mom responded. "Even Cinderella's coach turned into a pumpkin, ya know. Your father has gone dark the past several months, so I am down to my last pennies. I never know how much he will send on the best of days, and I never know when!"

Her comment hit me hard. I had been an indentured servant to Abbott Tobacco Farm, like Josh, I thought. If I had managed the grind of farm life better, I could have talked to her more and visited her more often.

"I thought he paid you alimony on a regular basis," I said, realizing that I never understood or appreciated my mother's dilemma all these years. With her propensity for gift baskets, it never occurred to me that she experienced any financial angst.

"No alimony and that ship has sailed," Momma said. "If I could turn back the hands of time, I would have hired a lawyer."

"You are divorced, right?" I asked.

"I was eighteen and pregnant. That word was the last thing on my mind."

"So, you're still married?" I asked, incredulous.

"Unless he has taken care of it. Look, I know it sounds foolish, but I never had the strength to rock the boat. Hindsight is 20/20. Your father has been a good provider over the years, just never consistent. I never know when he may resurface from who knows where and send a check. For now, though, even one night at the Ritz would put a serious dent in my budget. So, find out about the deal, better to be safe than sorry," she said.

I didn't want to sound cheap or unappreciative of an offer to trade working out of my padded cube to a room at the Ritz, but Mom was right. We couldn't risk getting stuck with the bill.

"I confirmed that the room request change can be made," I communicated to Charles the next day.

"Great," Charles said.

"They were actually very nice about it and apologized again for any inconvenience. Mom is excited too." I paused before continuing, "I don't know how to ask this, so I'll just get to the point."

Before I could finish, Charles interrupted me.

"Savannah, you will be working. All charges are covered. If not, I will take care of the difference. This is really helping me out. No need for further discussion."

"Yes, sir." I said, graciously. If the number of revisions on his second speech was anything like the first, I would indeed be working most of the time. I welcomed the dramatic change of scenery in my workspace. I was looking forward to my first glimpse inside the Ritz and my mother feeling like a princess.

Chapter Twenty-Five

Josh Abbott, former Inmate #233

The days, minutes, and hours that proceeded my meeting with Wormie Willie passed so slowly. I tried to focus on my daily tasks and keep my emotions in check. Some days, my heart would race with excitement in anticipation of holding Savannah again. Other days, panic would consume me, causing my entire body to shake and every pore to perspire. Could Savannah and I pick up where we left off? Or would she view me differently? Would I ever be truly free or forever shackled by shame, guilt, and failure?

As the third week approached since my meeting with the warden, the competing feelings between panic and excitement were replaced with doubt. I had not heard one iota from him since he proposed the sketchy plan. I recalled the meeting vividly. I had been leaving the chapel at the conclusion of the Sunday lesson on faith when I was called into the warden's office. As I left the church, I was filled with the spirit and thought faith would lead me home.

This Sunday's service was on the power of prayer. The visiting pastor asked, "How do we consistently incorporate prayer into our daily schedule? Prayer should not be a matter of convenience. No shotgun prayers where we beg for something and then don't talk to God for weeks."

This message hit home because, admittedly, prior to my arrest, my prayers were limited to the supper table when I would spout off a rote blessing. My relationship with God had definitely taken on new meaning since my confinement. My daily meditations always ended in prayer.

Hired Hit on Jessamin Island

Now, I talked with God multiple times a day. I even learned to listen, and that prayers can be a dialogue. I vowed to be a better man on the other side, to help the less fortunate, and to love deeply.

I skipped the typical Sunday afternoon ritual in the TV room where every NFL game would be available on one of the five flat screens. Funny thing is, before prison, I had access to only one game from my limited cable package. I had then yearned for the extended NFL Sunday Ticket. Now, I couldn't care less if I ever saw another game. I just wanted to absorb Savannah's every move, every blink of her blue eyes.

I sat in my cell hoping that this was the day I would again be summoned into the warden's office. He said he only needed three weeks. If there had been some problem with the plan, wouldn't he have informed me? I jumped from my metal bed every time the large steel door opened and slammed shut. But guard after guard passed my cell, with no order to the warden's office.

Anguish consumed me. I didn't eat a bite at the standard Sunday night dinner offered during football season—fried chicken, potato salad, mac and cheese, green beans, and coleslaw. Even the apple cobbler, my favorite dessert, didn't tempt me. My stomach was tied in knots.

In between tossing and turning that night, I prayed. I prayed for Savannah and Hannah Anne. I prayed for Walt, Mom, and Abbott Tobacco Farm. But mostly, I prayed for Cray—that he was OK, that he would stay strong, that he would stay honest—everything I had written to him in the letters I kept hidden in my pillowcase. I had written several drafts after leaving Wormie Willie's office over three weeks ago. I wanted to convey enough information to signal my anticipated release but with sufficient obscurity. I knew Cray's mail was read. It was my insurance policy, so to speak. If something happened to me, perhaps it could help Cray.

I finally dozed off. I thought I was dreaming that someone was in our cell and shaking me. But, when I felt a hand over my mouth, I realized it wasn't a dream. It was Shorty. He had cleaned out the locker holding my clothes and other belongings that had been confiscated upon my arrival and replaced with my prison uniform. He leaned over and whispered in my ear.

"Change your clothes and verify that your personal items are accounted for. I'll be back in ten minutes."

After changing and confirming that my watch, wedding band, and wallet were in the bag brought by Shortie, I reached into my pillowcase and grabbed the drafts of the letters to Cray. I stuffed them into the side pocket of the duffle bag.

I looked over at Benji, my loyal cellmate for the past five years. This may be the last time I saw him. I whispered under my breath, "Godspeed, Benji."

Shorty returned, unlocked the large steel door, and quietly opened it. We proceeded down the long hallway to the warden's office.

"Good morning, Josh. Hope you are rested. You've got a long trip in front of you," my warden said.

He handed me a set of car keys, a wad of cash, and a driver's license with my picture but the name Thomas Phillips. There was a reservation for Thomas Phillips in a motel, the Jessamin Island Breezeway, in Thurmond County. I knew the selected motel was intentional, meant to keep me focused on my ultimate goal—to be reunited with Savannah. Thurmond County was the county adjacent to Beaufort County.

"You have $5,000," he said, "to be used for the motel room, gas, food, and other incidentals that you will need on the way."

Then he proceeded to give me my instructions.

"When you make it to Jessamin Island, park the truck in the motel parking lot and place the key in the magnetic key box that is on the right rear axle. Don't use the truck again. A third party will retrieve it. After it's gone, you are free to go. I assume that, in the short term, you will be in Beaufort."

"Yes, sir. My mother-in-law's."

"The motel is within walking distance to the bus station. You can purchase a ticket for Beaufort. Here's the contact information for your parole officer. Make sure you check in immediately after you get there."

"What about Cray, sir?"

"Let's take this one step at a time. Just follow the exact route provided, strictly follow speed limits, and avoid other customers at gas stops. If all goes as planned, I'll be in touch in a couple of weeks and provide an update on Cray."

"God bless you, warden," I said, extending my hand to William Wilson. As the highest-ranking prison official reluctantly shook my hand, my first handshake with Walt came to mind. Walt's grip was strong, firm, and confident. Wormie Willie's was limp, soft, and clammy. Shorty interrupted the awkward moment.

"Let's go," Shorty said. "I'll escort you to the county line."

I picked up my duffle bag with my limited personal belongings and took a deep breath as we exited the office. My legs suddenly felt like rubber. I felt faint. I tried to keep my focus directly on Shorty, following him to the private parking area belonging to the prison officials. Give me strength, I prayed, as I swallowed the bile surging into my throat. I wiped sweat from my brow and questioned my ability to operate a vehicle at all, much less for the next ten hours.

Skepticism washed over me. Why was Shorty escorting me to the county line? Was someone waiting for me there to put me right back to where I started from and, if so, why? Was there something I was missing? Did the warden have it out for my family? I counseled myself to stay calm and have faith, as I cautiously gripped the steering wheel and followed Shorty.

All the questions whirling in my brain stopped just after I saw Shorty exit the highway. There wasn't another car in sight. I decided to alter the route provided by Wormie Willie in case someone was waiting for me along the way.

After crossing the North Carolina line, the first exit was for Harper's Corner. My body and mind instantly felt at ease. Harper, Savannah's middle name, reassured me that I had done the right thing in ditching Wormie Willie's directions. I took the Harper's Corner exit and found a gas station with multiple pump islands but with the fewest customers. Before removing the pump, I attempted to open the retractable bed cover on the truck. I needed to know what I was transporting. It was locked, and I didn't have the key. It was apparent that I was delivering something to Jessamin Island, and the something was in the truck bed. I suddenly wondered if there was a tracking device on the truck. Was my every move being monitored? Did Wormie Willie know that I had veered off course as soon as Shorty was out of sight? The only other customer was seven pump islands down from me, so I quickly checked underneath the vehicle. I saw no evidence of any type of tracker, but I wasn't going to be a sitting duck while waiting for the tank to fill. I ignored the sign: "Do not leave your vehicle unattended while pumping gas." I clamped the lock for the automatic fuel nozzle, and I hurried inside to get provisions for the remaining five or so hours. If anyone was loitering by the truck when I left the store, I would abort the mission and run.

I was determined not to repeat the unforeseeable complications that led to Cray's arrest. I was keenly aware of anyone and everything around me. All seemed normal, other than the convenience store clerk. I thought I must be hallucinating. She looked like Savannah on the first day I met her at the Royal Ice Castle, down to her side braid and twinkling blue eyes. I paid for my coffee, bottled waters, and various snacks. The clerk was either inherently chatty or in serious need of conversation.

"You must be having a snack attack!" she said, laughing as she was ringing up my supplies. "I will probably gain five pounds from just touching these," she giggled, holding up the package of Little Debbie powdered sugar doughnuts. "You must work out a LOT!"

"Just have a long trip ahead of me and don't have time to stop. This is my lunch and dinner," I said.

"Where you headed?" she asked.

"Jessamin Island, South Carolina."

"You got family there?"

"No but close by in Beaufort. Got to make a stop first. Now that I think about it, let me go grab some beer," I said.

I instinctively started to grab a 12-pack of Budweiser. It had been so long since I had any alcohol, I opted for the 6-pack. I planned to consume all six after checking into my hotel in a solo celebration.

"I need to see your ID," she said, with a flirtatious grin and twirling her braid.

I handed her my fake driver's license. She looked at me, then looked back at my license. I hadn't even looked at the license Wormie Willie had given me. I couldn't even remember my assumed name.

"Thomas Phillips," she said, checking me out. "The DMV sure messed this up."

"What do you mean?" I asked, attempting to conceal my nervousness that she knew the ID was fake.

"It says your eyes are brown. You have the greenest eyes I've ever seen," she said, leaning onto the counter.

It suddenly hit me that the convenience store clerk may be flirting with me. I was overly paranoid for thinking she was examining the validity of my ID.

"Funny. I've never paid any attention to that. But, I'm sure not going to wait in the long lines at the DMV to change my eye color," I said.

"Yeah. I know what you mean."

She offered my license back to me but maintained a firm grip.

"My name is Brandy, Thomas Phillips."

The way Brandy said my fake name while not relinquishing control of the plastic sent chills down my spine. Perhaps, she didn't believe it was my true identity after all.

I left the store and quickly returned to the truck and replaced the fuel nozzle. I opened the passenger door and moved my duffle bag to the floorboard, making room for my purchased items in the seat. The letters that I had written Cray suddenly resurrected in my mind. My heart was beating rapidly as I reached for the duffle bag. Had Shorty searched my bag while I was getting my instructions from Willie? I had been preoccupied and certainly wouldn't have noticed. My hands were visibly shaking as I zipped open the side pocket.

My heart rate began returning to normal when I saw that all the letters were still there. From Cray's letters to me, I knew he, too, had witnessed corrupt behavior. Hopefully, I would be resting in Beaufort to the surprise of Savannah, Hannah Anne, and Walt by the time Cray received my letter. I was still going to be careful in my communication.

Which one of my drafts would be obscure enough that a mail screener wouldn't pick up on the news of my release? Wormie Willie's instructions had been quite clear that I shouldn't relay my news until I arrived in Beaufort.

I thought I selected the safest letter to mail. As I shut the passenger door, a van pulled up to the pump beside me. A man got out and began approaching the truck. He was now standing in front of it.

"Nice truck," he said. "What year?"

"I don't know, it's a rental," I said, turning in the opposite direction. My mind was racing. Should I run? Should I retreat into the store and lock my myself into the bathroom? Brandy would help me, I thought.

"I am trying to convince the wife," he said, nodding his head toward his minivan, "to let me get one of these, you know, practical, safe, and good for hauling. Only problem is video playing screens aren't standard. My wife thinks you can't take a trip without popping in a video for the kids."

He proceeded to the container mounted on the island between our cars and reached for the squeegee and began cleaning his windshield.

I circled around the truck and headed back toward the store. I wasn't leaving until the minivan left. Brandy was preoccupied with something on her phone.

"Sorry, I meant to ask you if you know where the post office is," I asked her.

"You know you can GTS," she said, giggling.

"GTS?" I asked, confused.

"Google that shit," she said.

"Ha! Yeah, my phone died," I said, quickly and proud that I pulled that one out. I certainly couldn't reveal that inmates weren't permitted phones, so I didn't have one and thus no ability to GTS.

"I want to get something in the mail and don't want to stop again. A tight schedule."

"The post office is about seven miles from here. I'm happy to drop something off for you, Thomas Phillips," she said.

"That's a nice offer, but it's important. I need to do it myself."

"Well, I am clocking out in ten minutes, and the post office is close to my next job at the Burger Barn. Pretty glamorous, huh? If you can spare ten minutes, you can follow me."

"Thanks, sounds good. If you are sure it's not out of your way."

"Nope. I drive right by it."

"Well, it must be my lucky day," I said. "I am in the black truck."

"Yes, I know," she said with a playful smirk. "I am the lucky one."

As I waited for Brandy, I was overcome with desire for this stranger—a younger version of my wife. It had been so long. She didn't know me; I didn't know her. I was weak. I tried to suppress the fantasy that began floating in my brain. I may never make it to Jessamin Island, much less to Beaufort. I wanted to trust this road I was on, to freedom, to be reunited with Savannah, but it all seemed surreal. I knew why I chose this particular exit. But why did I choose this station? Why was this cute, and seemingly innocent, woman thrown in my path—a woman who reminded me of my wife? Were my hormones completely out of control? I imagined myself with Brandy in the backseat ripping off our clothes, kissing wildly, and ...

A car horn jolted me back to reality. Brandy pulled up beside the truck in a white Honda and motioned me to follow.

As I left the service station, I reached over and grabbed one of the beers and gulped it while following Brandy in the opposite direction of the interstate.

Chapter Twenty-Six

Savannah Abbott

When I first received the confirmation and accommodation package for Mr. and Mrs. Charles Walker at the Ritz Carlton, I ached with jealously. I perused the enclosed spa brochure and felt like an unworldly, classless hayseed. Luxury spas were foreign in our small town in Kentucky. I never had even one manicure or pedicure at the limited nail salons. Suddenly, a spa experience moved to the top of my bucket list.

One of the Ritz's signature spa treatments jumped out at me. It was called "Heaven in a Hammock." It combined benefits of zero-gravity and touch therapy...a gentle massage, the rocking motion of a hammock, and the ebb of the tide. I experienced that with Josh once during our magical summer in Beaufort, before my world had been turned upside down.

I fantasized about the life of Mrs. Charles Walker. What was it like being married to a successful and powerful man? The list of amenities were likely endless: a large home with a pool; an exclusive, gated community; a landscape and yard service; interior decorators; weekly house cleaners; a country club membership; tennis and golf leagues; clothes from expensive boutiques; and glamorous shoes. Her life included expense-paid trips to lavish resorts, complete with spa treatments and champagne while the charming husband was wowing new admirers to fund her lifestyle. My envy was greener than my husband's eyes.

How do some people skate by in life, I wondered, while others are dealt bad hand after bad hand? I always thought of myself as honest, loyal, and loving. Was there something in my past that I was completely unaware of that merited my punishment? Conceiving a child out of marriage? My God, I thought, was kinder and more compassionate than that. I had always had a strong faith until my world had been rocked. It all seemed so unfair.

Stop feeling sorry for yourself, I thought. Focus on the positive. After all, I had an expense-paid trip to the Ritz with Mom. Even if I had to spend most of the time working, I was going to get a glimpse into the lifestyles of the Mrs. Charles Walkers and share it with my sweet momma.

When we arrived, the hotel was grander than the pictures on its website. Uniformed bellmen immediately encompassed our car.

"Welcome to the Ritz Carlton," one said, opening Mom's door. "I'm Ramsey and you are?"

"Hannah Anne Hart and this is my daughter, Savannah Abbott, but we both feel like Cinderella!"

"Well, our job is to treat you both like princesses. We'll deliver your luggage to your room shortly. Here's your valet parking ticket. Call the number on the ticket if you need your car during your stay. But, if you're like most of our guests, you won't leave the premises."

"I am not planning on leaving this castle, Ramsey," Mom said. "You may have a hard time getting rid of me, period!"

As we approached the check-in desk, another young man greeted us: "Welcome, Ms. Abbott and Ms. Hart. I see that you will be here for three nights and that all of your expenses have been taken care of, so I don't need anything other than a photo ID. Also, I notice that you have complimentary spa treatments. Our spa is quite popular. I recommend that you book your appointments as soon as possible. There is a spa menu in your room. Your luggage should already be there. Do you need assistance finding your room?"

"No, thank you," I said, trying to sound confident that I had navigated my way through luxurious hotels numerous times. I also tried to suppress my excitement over the news of our complimentary spa treatments.

"Well, I am impressed already, and we haven't made it past the lobby," I said to Mom, who was gawking at everything around her.

"I know, these men are hotter than a two-dollar pistol," Mom said.

"I was talking about their service. Wonder how they knew our names?" I asked.

"They are wired, that's how. When Ramsey asked me my name, he radioed it in."

"How do you know that?" I asked her, thinking she had probably read such nonsense in one of her books.

"Because I saw him and heard him," she said. "I told you I was going to absorb everything about this place more than a sponge in a pool of water."

Though I couldn't afford our opulent accommodations, I was overcome with this pride that I had a small part in her sheer wonderment and giddy euphoria.

"Wow," we gasped, simultaneously after I opened the door to our room. It was a weird mother/daughter moment where our voices, intonation, and body language were exactly the same, down to our exclamation.

"Jinx, you owe me a Coke," Mom shouted, which was what we did in Beaufort when two people said the same thing at the same time.

"Instead of a Coke, how about a glass of champagne? I packed several bottles."

"You are always thinking! I would love a glass," as she flung open our balcony doors, displaying our expansive ocean view. "Out here."

By October, the sweltering days were replaced with lower humidity and comfortable temperatures. The muggy nights had given way to crisp, cool nights. I took my champagne and the spa menu and retreated to the balcony.

I excitedly read the options to Mom while the waves accompanied my descriptions of the invigorating spa packages. I booked a facial for me. Momma chose the Heaven in a Hammock massage.

"This night calls for a toast," Mom said. "Here's to crashing waves, salty air, sand in our toes, and being with my daughter. And, here's to Heaven in a Hammock!"

"And to our Lowcountry birds," I added.

We clinked our glasses and soaked up our fairy-tale surroundings knowing the clock would strike midnight soon.

Chapter Twenty-Seven

Brandy, the convenience store clerk

There was something mysterious about Thomas Phillips—the way he surveyed the store before paying cash for gas on Pump #1 and then coming back in and approaching the counter with additional purchases. I had not only been trained to spot potential shoplifters but also those who were after cash from the register. My instincts told me he was neither, but there was definitely something off about him—something secretive.

Typically, I steered clear of conversation and eye contact with the store's customers and attempted to hurry them along. I was numb to the inappropriate comments by the early morning construction workers getting pumped up on caffeine with coffee, Mountain Dew, or energy drinks prior to their shifts. I was immune to the crass behavior from random interstate travelers, ranging from winks and dangling tongues to outright propositions. The community leaders were often the most disturbing. I could write a book on pick-up lines. I was consistently hit on by men, and the occasional female, from all walks of life.

With Thomas Phillips, it was like the tables were turned. I wanted to talk to him, but he was the one in the rush, the one avoiding me. He wasn't interested in chit-chat. He flinched when I asked for his license. Of course, I knew he was old enough to purchase beer. When I was ringing up his items, his arms were fidgety, and he was rocking on his heels. His eyes were moving in every direction, except in mine. He kept looking over his shoulder. He appeared to be on edge.

Before he left the store, he paused at the door and then made a mad dash to his truck. I wondered if he was running from something. He was too well-spoken, handsome, and polite to be on the run, I thought. After all my encounters with a wide range of people between my three jobs, my instincts were excellent. I had seen it all.

I became convinced that he was famous—a TV or movie star, model, singer, or professional athlete. When he got out of his truck and started walking at a fast pace back inside the store, I hoped he hadn't notice that I snapped a picture of him on my phone. I couldn't believe my luck when he asked for directions to the post office. The post office was nowhere near my next job—a small white lie. He'd never know. I just wanted to know more about this man—the most handsome I had ever encountered. I was determined to find out more about Thomas Phillips.

Chapter Twenty-Eight

Thomas Phillips a/k/a Josh Abbott

Brandy was leaning on my driver's side door and smoking a cigarette when I exited the post office. Interesting, I thought. Perhaps she simply needed a smoke before clocking into her next job.

"Thanks for the directions," I said.

She exhaled a plume of smoke.

"What's your real name, Thomas Phillips?"

"What do you mean?" I asked, trying to maintain my composure.

"I mean, I don't think your name is Thomas Phillips."

"What do you think it is?"

"I'm thinking you are famous and traveling incognito."

"Famous, huh? That's funny," I said, feeling more at ease. "I'm about as far from famous as there is. I'm a farmer."

"Seriously? Well, that explains your muscles and strong hands. And coveralls," she said, laughing.

She flicked her burning cigarette in the air and put her hands on my hips. She pulled me into her.

"The kind of farmer that likes a good romp in the hay?"

I closed my eyes and took a deep breath. I lurched when I felt her hand on me.

"Let's get out of here," I said instinctively, without thinking.

I was simply overcome with an intense desire like a wild animal that had been released from captivity. I didn't make it far. A corner spot in the far end of the post office parking lot. We moved to the back seat, and it was better than I had fantasized. It was like she needed me as much as I needed her.

After, I kissed her forehead.

"You better get dressed. What time are you supposed to be at work?"

"I called them on the way over here. I said I would be late. The afternoon shift is slow anyway."

"Well, then, you got an extra cigarette?" I asked. "I'm not a smoker but sure seems like one would be good right now."

She picked her skirt up from the floorboard, reached into the back pocket, and pulled out a pack of Marlboros. She put one in her mouth and lit it, then handed it to me. I took a long draw. She took it from my hand and did the same.

We shared a lot more than that cigarette for the next hour. When we were spent, she wiggled back into her skirt.

"Where's my top?" she asked, laughing.

"Can't be too far."

"I'll never curse the United States Postal Service ever again," she said, kissing me softly on the cheek.

While I was pulling on my pants, she located her top in the front seat, apparently on top of the rejected letters to Cray.

"I thought you mailed your important letter. These were in the seat," as she handed me the other drafts. "Don't want you to have a wasted trip to the post office."

Hired Hit on Jessamin Island

"I don't need those."

"Who's Cray?"

"My son."

"So, I am betting Savannah is Cray's mother?"

"Yes. How do you know about Savannah?" I asked, with remorse sinking in and feeling really paranoid. Was Brandy a setup to test me? Was she a strategically placed mole for information that could be used against me?

Brandy sensed my angst.

"Chill, Thomas Phillips. I don't know anything about Savannah other than you kept repeating her name over and over. If I were the jealous type, I would have left an hour ago. So, what's your deal? You don't strike me as the cheating kind of guy and, trust me, I can sniff those out like a fly on shit."

I tried to choke the tears that began building in my eyes, but it was useless. I hugged the flesh of this naked young woman and cried on her soft skin.

I laid it all out, including my real name. I loved my wife, Savannah, and my son, Cray, with all my heart and soul. But, I had a strong sense that I would never see them again. We shared a beer and smoked more Marlboros.

"I knew you were something special, Thomas Phillips."

Her kiss this time was not passionate or wild but tender.

"I hope Cray gets your letter, and I hope even more that you will be with your true love again. I may not be the most religious person in the world, but I feel that a higher power brought you to me and me to you. Be safe. You will always be in my heart, Josh Abbott."

As I drove back to the interstate and my mandatory route to Jessamin Island, waves of emotion surrounded me. How could have I cheated on Savannah? How could I have been so careless with a total stranger? I prayed out loud for forgiveness. Jumbled between my regret, shame, and guilt, I was comforted, in a cosmic weird way, by my throbbing groin. I had imagined Brandy was Savannah. If I died tomorrow, I had been with my wife one last time.

Chapter Twenty-Nine

Hannah Anne Hart

The Ritz Carlton on Amelia Island must be what heaven is like. I couldn't recall a time when I slept better. But, then again, I never slept in a featherbed with a pillow-top mattress, goose down pillows, and four-hundred-thread-count Egyptian cotton sheets.

Savannah was still sleeping. We were early risers, but she hadn't budged. I quietly made a cup of gourmet coffee from the fancy coffee machine, slipped on the plush robe hanging in the closet, and headed to the balcony to watch the sunrise.

The crash of the ocean's mighty waves sounded angry to me, but it was a wrath that I found comforting. They helped me expel my internal fury. I had always relied upon the water to snap me back into reality. All those years when Savannah was in Kentucky and I was lonely, I'd go to the water to break my waves of depression. Who knows how many miles I had clocked on the beach. It had always done the trick, and it looked like it was working for Savannah as well. Even in the short amount of time she'd been back home, I could sense a change in her spirit and body. Her skin, eyes, smile, and even her hair had brightened.

Savannah's blue eyes had always been her trademark, but when she first arrived, they looked more gray than blue. They were smoky and gloomy. They reminded me of thick storm clouds in the heat of August before a violent storm. And her smile, the one that could once captivate a room, was dead. Her bronze skin had washed away, and even her golden hair was dingy.

Just last night, while we were sitting on the balcony sipping champagne, it hit me that the Beaufort version of Savannah was resurrecting right before my eyes. I attributed the conversion to the return to the place she belonged. The water and the salty air were powerful, healing forces. My praise of the Lowcountry's restorative power was interrupted when the glass door opened. My daughter joined me on the balcony.

"Good morning," I said. "You missed the sunrise. This morning, it seemed to just burst, anxious to start the day."

"I hate I missed it. I can't believe I slept so late," Savannah said. "My bed was so comfortable. Did you sleep well?"

"Like a baby. I love this place. Thanks so much for including me."

"Well, I can't take credit. It was actually Charles' idea for both of us to come."

"When can I meet this nice boss? I want to thank him."

"He had a retreat over the weekend so was planning to arrive late last night. He is going to work this morning on his speech. Depending on the progress he makes, I may have to work this afternoon. But, I'm confident that you can find something to do," Savannah said.

"Right now, I'm looking forward to my massage," I said. "Let's head to the spa after breakfast. I read there is a dry sauna, steam room, and a jacuzzi. I want to have time to try them all."

We were waiting for the spa to open like shoppers on Black Friday. The friendly spa assistant welcomed us with a glass of infused-water made with lemons, strawberries, and basil. She led us to a swanky locker room. After changing into the extra-soft cotton terry robe and velvet slippers, I started rethinking my agenda. I could be as happy as a dog with two tails, simply curled up on one of the chaise lounges in my cozy robe. I was not one to flip through a style magazine, they only depressed me; and my Elliott Gray book was in the room. So, I joined Savannah in the steam room.

We slowly inhaled the eucalyptus steam with chilled cucumber slices over our eyes. Then we switched to the dry sauna while hydrating on blackberry water. After a quick trip to the jacuzzi, we sipped green tea while waiting for our scheduled treatments. The other women in the relaxation area acted like this was just another day in the office, but I felt like a movie star.

I surveyed the room and tried to snap a picture in my brain of every detail, down to the bowl of almonds, cashews, and craisins. My mental photography was interrupted when a handsome, young Argentine with a head full of black curls entered the lounge.

"Ms. Hart," he summoned, canvassing the room.

I had the urge to yell "Bingo!" Instead, I stood up and walked toward him while trying to suppress my grin.

"I'm Santiago. How are you doing today?" he asked.

"Great, Santiago," I said, while under my breath whispering, "especially now."

Heaven in a Hammock with Santiago was the icing on the cake. I hadn't felt this relaxed and excited in more than forty years. The last man who had touched me was Bo Hart. As Santiago's hands applied pressure on my shoulders and then down my back, I closed my eyes and imagined it was Bo's hands rubbing oil all over my body. Afterward, I was tingly from head to toe. I couldn't recall ever feeling this way. Heaven in a Hammock with Santiago had been better than the sex I could recall with Bo Hart, at least in a therapeutic sense.

Savannah's facial seemed to be the ticket for her as well. Her skin was glowing. We culminated our divine morning with tomato bisque, shrimp salad, and mimosas. Savannah was beckoned to work, but my glorious day continued.

I took a long walk on the beach searching for sea glass then lounged by the pool reading *Alibi*. I finally relented to the attentive pool boy, who could have been Santiago's brother, and I ordered a margarita.

"Don't be shy about the salt," I instructed him.

As I was sipping my second afternoon cocktail and listening to the echoes of the waves, the sheer elation of the day dissolved like the white caps rolling onto the surf. Why wasn't my love for Bo enough for him? Would I ever find anyone I could love like Bo? But, someone who would love me in return. The hour with Santiago evidenced that I needed to be touched, and beyond that of professional massage. I needed the sensual caress of a man who loved me.

The effects of my drink began kicking in. I closed my eyes and thought about Bo. I tried to remember what his body felt like next to mine—his skin, his hair, his muscles, and his long fingers. It had been decades ago. Were my recollections accurate or had they been distorted and even enhanced in my mind? Why had I not soaked up and treasured Bo like the Ritz Carlton spa? Had I taken him for granted? What could I have done differently? What could I have done to keep him from walking out on Savannah and me? After my third cocktail, my very tipsy mind flipped to Savannah.

Despite Josh's current situation, he was a good man. He would never abandon Savannah. Over the years, I had forgiven him for taking my daughter away from me. He truly adored her. But what about Savannah? Savannah was blessed with Bo Hart's authentic charm. But, she also inherited his free spirit. I hoped that my grounded and loyal traits would counter those wild genes passed on to her from her father.

Savannah and I had never discussed how she was coping with her needs since Josh's imprisonment. Savannah was still in the prime of her life. Before today, I hadn't thought about whether she was struggling. It had never occurred to me that she might be unfaithful to Josh. But, I suddenly wondered how her natural desires were being addressed? Was I that naïve? Was Savannah really working right now or romancing her boss? Was I included on this trip to be the cover for an affair? Did I really know my daughter after all?

The high that I had been experiencing all day suddenly turned into despair—that not even the crash of the ocean's mighty waves could soothe.

PART VIII

Chapter Thirty

Nancy Nichols, Tara's best friend

Weeks had passed since Tara's funeral. I decided it was time to visit Mrs. Walker. My last class had been cancelled, and to be honest, I wasn't in the mood to go home.

As I was getting ready to ring the doorbell, I spotted Dad at the same time he saw me. He quickly opened the door and began speaking in this high-pitched, jittery voice that I had never heard before.

"Well look who's here! Alice had some computer problems, but we're all done. Alice, Nancy's here," he said with exaggerated emphasis before the new voice launched questions at me. "Why aren't you in school? Are your sisters home too? Was Alice expecting you?"

"Which question do you want me to answer first?" I asked, calmly despite the awkward vibe in the air.

Dad stepped out of the house onto the porch.

"I must have lost track of the time while working here. Isn't it a little early for you to be out of school?" as he shifted his eyes to his left wrist as if to look at his watch.

"My last class was cancelled. I guess Ms. Jones wanted to get an early start to fall break. I thought I'd check and see how Mrs. Walker was doing, you know, and stuff."

"I'm proud of you, honey," he said, avoiding eye contact. "I think that is a great idea. I'm sure she will appreciate that and enjoy seeing you. I'll see you at home," he said, and left me standing on the porch.

As I was trying to process this exchange and the nervous exit, Mrs. Walker came to the door.

"I thought I heard Norris say it was you. Please, come in," giving me a big hug.

Was it my imagination, or did Mrs. Walker seem as rattled as Dad?

"Your dad is a lifesaver. I am such a technological dumbo. It sure is nice to have an expert in the neighborhood. I've been thinking about getting a job. I am going crazy here without Tara. Your dad is helping me navigate these job websites. I had no idea some were targeted to gullible people like me—asking for my social security number and all my personal information. I am apparently an easy target for fraud!"

She was talking a mile a minute. If Dad was legitimately helping her with job sites, why were they both acting so strangely?

"I think it's great you are considering a job," I said, attempting to interrupt her nervous jabbering. "I have been thinking about you and thought I'd stop by. I should have called first."

"Oh, don't be silly, Nancy. You are always welcome. I made some chocolate chip cookies earlier. Would you like one and perhaps a glass of milk?" she asked, laughing.

"Yes, to a cookie, but I'll pass on the milk," I said.

Mrs. Walker seemed to have somewhat regained her composure. We avoided bringing up the elephant in the room, or not in the room, and had a nice visit. She asked me how I was doing and to fill her in on the scoop. The initial awkwardness transformed into our old chitchat.

"I've been going through Tara's things," Mrs. Walker said. "It would mean a lot to me if you would take Tara's clothes. If you don't want them, perhaps some of your sisters would. I just can't imagine your family's clothing expense."

Though Tara had shared her clothes with me on numerous occasions, I knew that I could never wear anything of hers again. But, my sisters would be in shopper's heaven. Deep down, I knew Tara would be smiling if Nature sported one of her outfits. Tara always felt sorry for Nature being the last in the line for hand-me-downs.

"That is so sweet of you. If you are sure it would be okay," I said, wondering if she could really handle seeing anyone in Tara's clothes.

"No, Tara would love it. I would rather someone I know make use of her cute clothes than a stranger. I can't bear to throw her things away. If there is anything that was special between the two of you, I'd love for you to have it. If you want to go up to her room, I'll see if I can find a box."

As I walked up the stairs to Tara's room, I felt sick to my stomach. I didn't know if I could do this. We had spent so many nights in her room, staying up late talking and sharing our innermost secrets about crushes, dreams, and fears.

The Walker's house had as many bedrooms for three people as mine did for eight. The master bedroom was on the main floor, and the other three bedrooms were upstairs. Tara's room was at the end of the hallway past the other guest rooms, as Mrs. Walker called them. But I had never seen any guests at their house other than the rare visits from Mrs. Walker's father. Mr. Wilson had some important job at a prison in Kentucky. I always thought he and his job were equally creepy.

I couldn't recall when Mrs. Walker began sleeping in one of the guest rooms. I do remember she said Mr. Walker snored and got up at the crack of dawn, so it was the only way she could get any rest. At the time, I didn't think anything about it. My father slept on the couch when Mom was home for a number of different reasons—he was working late, she had jet lag, she had a headache, etc.

As I passed Mrs. Walker's sleeping quarters, I noticed that the bed was not only unmade but also disheveled. A pillow was even on the floor. Mrs. Walker's motto was "You can't start your day, until your bed is made." It had rubbed off on me. I was the only one in my family who made their bed.

Something made me take a closer look inside. I surveyed the room and saw a man's watch by the bedside table. I knew that watch. It was Dad's. He must have realized it was missing, too, when he looked at his wrist on the porch before darting away. I stuffed it in my pocket.

"I couldn't find a box," Mrs. Walker said, finally entering Tara's room. "But it hit me that we can use one of Tara's suitcases."

She opened Tara's closet and pulled out a suitcase and began cleaning out my best friend's closet. My stomach was in knots. I just wanted out of the house— the weight of Dad's watch was like a heavy anchor in my pocket.

Mrs. Walker began neatly folding Tara's clothes into the suitcase. She was talking about her memories of each item, but it was like I was in a tunnel. She must have sensed my awkward silence and offered to finish going through the rest of Tara's things later.

Halfway through my walk home with Tara's suitcase full of clothes, Tara's text, her last words, echoed with every step I took. YOU...ARE...NOT...GOING...TO...FUCKING...BELIEVE...IT." I looked up into the sky and said, "I am listening, my friend. I'm listening."

Chapter Thirty-One

Alice Walker, Charles' wife,
Warden Wilson's daughter

I was not looking forward to being holed up by myself on Jessamin Island for the next several days. With Charles heading to his conference at the Ritz, it was the perfect time for a romantic getaway. Per Dad's instructions, I had taken the cottage off the rental market this week, without telling Charles. He would freak about losing a week's rental income. Though it was imperative that I be there, I dreaded being there alone. I now resented that cottage like everything else in my marriage.

The only reason that Charles relented to a vacation home was that he scooped it up for next to nothing in a foreclosure sale when the housing market crashed ten years ago. Tara and I had yearned for a beachfront home. Instead, we got a small cottage on a tidal creek that Charles immediately placed in the rental pool. Though I would never admit it to Charles, "Tara's Cove," the name Tara bestowed on our little abode, was a perfect retreat for us. By us, I mean Tara and me.

Our cottage was secluded and peaceful. Tara and I used to spend hours in kayaks navigating the pathways in the marsh. I didn't even mind the short walk to the beach from the cottage. Tara preferred hanging out at the pool that Charles had installed. Though Johnny maintained the pool at Tara's Cove, even his presence wouldn't erase the memories with Tara there. Jessamin Island would never be the same without her.

With Charles busy at the conference, I had the perfect reason for my trek to Jessamin Island. There were always maintenance projects after the summer rental season ended and before the holiday regulars returned. I begged Johnny to accompany me.

"I'll have to take a rain check," Johnny said, hurriedly pulling up his pants. "With all the leaves falling, I am up to my ears with my yard service clients. I have more to do than I can get to. Plus, there is this really hot customer who needs her pool heater fixed."

"Ha," I said. "I couldn't give a shit about the pool heater, but I guess you need to keep Charles happy so he will keep you on the payroll."

"Let me know when you're back. You can give me your to-do list for Jessamin and anywhere else," he said, dashing out of the bedroom.

"Well you know that satisfying me will be at the top of the list!" I shouted.

I loved being with Johnny, but I wasn't his top priority. His job was. I pulled the covers over my head. Though I had been immensely satisfied only minutes ago, I now felt empty. I wanted to be someone's priority in life.

I called Norris. I had been patient with him and worked hard to dispel his culpability for Tara's death.

"If Tara hadn't caught us, she would still be alive," he had said, repeatedly.

He had either come around to my way of reasoning or was as miserable and lonely as I was. Several weeks after Tara's death, we picked up where we left off. Norris and I connected on so many levels. Our trysts helped us cope. We made each other feel desired, appreciated, and loved.

"Can't you create some business prospect in Bluffton or Hilton Head?" I asked Norris for about the fourth time. "I am going to be all by my lonesome, and the cottage is only available this week."

As usual, Naomi was out of town. He had to work and had daughter duty. He was taking advantage of fall break by catching up on dentist appointments, and some of the girls had birthday parties to attend. Other than Nancy and Nature, I couldn't keep their names or birth order straight. With a name like Nature, that youngest one was hard to forget. I didn't know how Norris juggled their schedules.

"You're a great dad, Norris," I said, rubbing his back. "I know you feel overwhelmed with all your daughters' activities, but I'd trade places with you," as I started tearing up.

He pulled me into him and hugged me tightly, really tightly. He kissed me gently on the forehead and wiped my tears. Then, he wiped his eyes. When I realized that he was crying, I grabbed his head and placed it on my chest. I combed my fingers through his hair. As I held him, I realized that he was such a good lover because he was so sensitive and caring. And then there was our common bond, we were both so damn neglected.

I pulled his face to mine. This time, it was wild and intense. Though we were with each other, we were in other worlds—places where uninhibited sex made you feel better.

Our unanticipated second act lasted a while. We shouldn't have extended his smoke break, but I, for one, wasn't thinking of anything other than feeling desired before leaving for Jessamin Island.

When Norris realized the time, he frantically got dressed and darted for the door. Then Nancy showed up! I thought the job hunt excuse to Nancy was a masterful example of thinking on your feet. I mean Norris was an expert in all things dealing with technology. It was his job, after all, to make house calls. Totally legit why he would be at my house. And it laid the groundwork for any sightings by any of the nosey neighbors.

What was it about schools these days? No wonder our educational system was in the toilet—teenagers coming and going as they pleased. When I was in high school, you never dared to leave the school grounds until the bell rang. No one had cars; no one left campus, and no teacher cancelled classes. Were substitute teachers as antiquated as answering machines? I laughed as I considered my last thought.

We were the only family in our neighborhood that hadn't converted to the automated voicemail feature. It costs a whopping $10 more a month. "Who needs that?" Charles argued. "Waste of money."

Nancy and I had a great visit, but her mood had dramatically changed while we were going through Tara's clothes. I knew she missed her best friend.

"We can finish this up another time," I suggested.

"That would be good," Nancy said.

"I leave tomorrow for Jessamin Island. A renter cancelled at the last minute, so Charles wants me to take care of some maintenance. Other than that, I'm free whenever it's convenient for you."

I started to give her another hug, but she quickly picked up the suitcase.

"Thanks for the clothes," Nancy said. "I'll come by after you get back. Have a good trip."

I would have a good trip, indeed. If all went according to plan, when I returned from Jessamin Island, I would have a new lease on life. A life without Charles Walker in it.

Chapter Thirty-Two

Thomas Phillips

My arrival at the Jessamin Island Breezeway went smoothly. I stuck to Wormie Willie's instructions. I parked the truck, placed the key in the magnetic box on the right rear axle, and checked into the motel. I carefully examined my surroundings as I walked to Room 414 with my duffle bag, snacks, and beverages.

I entered my room, found the TV clicker, popped a beer, and collapsed on the bed. For once, I began thinking that I should give ol' Willie more credit. All had gone according to plan, except for my diversion from his mandated route.

At 5:00 a.m. this morning, I was sleeping on a metal bed in a cell in a Kentucky federal prison. I never thought I would appreciate a two-star motel room. But, I took a deep breath, stacked my pillows, rested my head, closed my eyes, and soaked up my freedom.

The interlude with Brandy in the back seat of the truck came crashing back. It seemed unreal, like a dream. I had experienced one hell of a day. I finished my beer and popped another one, then another. I could feel the tension in my muscles finally beginning to unwind.

Savannah was waiting for me when the bus arrived in Beaufort. It was déjà vu. Her braided hair was hanging over one shoulder, just like it was at the Royal Ice Castle on the first day we met. When the bus stopped, her long, thin, tan legs were running toward me. Her arms were outstretched. The bus doors wouldn't open fast enough. I turned to the bus driver and yelled, "Open the door, open the door!" I beat on it.

I realized it wasn't me yelling or beating on the door. It was someone at the door to Room 414.

Chapter Thirty-Three

Savannah Abbott

Every morning when I awoke, Momma was sitting on our balcony in her Ritz Carlton robe, sipping the gourmet coffee, and waiting for the sunrise.

"Our checkout is not until noon," I said, joining her. "What do you think about catching the sunrise from the beach?"

"That's a great idea," she said. "Otherwise, the poor bellman will have the undesirable task of peeling me off this balcony. This is a glorious place, and I have enjoyed it so much. I'm very sad to leave."

"Me too, but we have one last sunrise to see and hopefully a dolphin or two."

We hit the coffee station in the lobby and headed out to the beach. Momma was unusually quiet as we walked. When the sun peeked out of the water, she sat down.

"I don't want to miss one second of this," patting a spot on the sand for me to sit beside her.

She grabbed my hand and held it tightly as the sun rose.

"The past few days have been an awakening for me," she said. "I have realized that I have not been the mother to you that you deserve," her voice wavering.

"Don't be silly, Momma. What are you talking about? You are the best."

"No. I am not. I've been selfish. I've been wallowing in self-pity for so long. I haven't been able to see past my own troubles. I should have been more attentive to your feelings and all that you've been through."

"Momma, if anyone has been selfish, it's been me. I should have called you more often. And, I definitely should have visited you more. You have always been so strong that it never occurred to me that you were hurting."

"Stop it," she said. "And let me finish. You know that I love having you back in Beaufort. I have wanted this for so long. But you have your own life. You have Josh and Cray. I love Josh. I hope you know that. He's a good man. Though things haven't turned out the way you expected, I know that he adores you and would do anything for you. I never had that. I have always envied your relationship. You know I loved your father so much, but he was never capable of loving me the way that Josh loves you."

She squeezed my hand tightly.

"I know it's been hard and, at times, unbearable," she continued. "But good men aren't a dime a dozen. I know you admire your boss. He seems like a good man too. I just don't want you to start chasing something you can't have."

"Momma, are you suggesting that there is something going on between Charles and me?" I asked, wondering how she could think such a thing.

"I don't know, Savannah. You have spent a lot of time with him in his room working."

"Exactly. Working. That's why we are here. I love Josh, Momma. I know he loves me. I know that we will be together again, and it will be better than ever. This time, we are going to be sharing our life with you. That you can count on. And, for the record, Dad is a fool."

Momma rested her head on my shoulder, and I stroked her hair. She was still beautiful and young at heart. She deserved to find love again, someone like Josh who would love her back unconditionally.

"How about we treat ourselves to the breakfast buffet?" I asked. "Our last hoorah before heading back to reality."

"Reality is a bitch," she said.

She stood and brushed the sand from her pants. We walked hand-in-hand down the beach. I never felt closer to my mother. All these years, I had failed to appreciate her pain and the ache in her heart over her lost true love. It made me realize that, despite my current situation, I was blessed with a wonderful man, and we were going to be fine.

We giggled as we filled our first plate with cantaloupe, pineapple, strawberries, grapes, and yogurt. Cheese grits, bacon strips, sausage links, eggs Benedict, and French toast found their place on our second plate. It was a feast befitting two princesses before the clock struck midnight or, at the Ritz, the noon checkout time.

Chapter Thirty-Four

Charles Walker, the banker

I believe my remarks were well received. However, speeches were not a good return on the investment of time. These speaking gigs, as Alice referred to them, were the least favorite part of my job. I wasn't a natural public speaker. I had improved over the years but continued to overprepare. Alice was all too eager to point out that weakness.

I regretted that Savannah hadn't been able to enjoy more free time during her stay. She didn't seem to mind. She kept saying work was why she was here. Clearly, five-star hotels like the Ritz were foreign in her world. Though they were common in mine, luxurious retreats were not my style. Come to think of it, I didn't have a style. I never had time to pursue one.

During my speech alone, I had missed numerous calls and the emails had mounted. While Savannah was at the conference, I asked Phyllis, the assistant to my vice president, to handle my phone calls. I left my itinerary with her but, apparently not my assigned speaking time. Otherwise, why would she be blowing up my phone? I had fifteen missed calls from Phyllis alone.

As the next speaker was being introduced, I gracefully exited the conference hall to pick up my voicemails.

"Mr. Walker, this is Phyllis. It's urgent. Call me as soon as possible."

"It's me again. Really need to speak to you."

"Trying you again. There is a police officer here, wanting to speak to Savannah."

Phyllis had this way of exaggerating situations. She loved to slyly interject drama behind the scenes to get attention. I had learned a great deal about these drama queens over the years.

Joe, my trusty VP, defended her when I broached the subject of removing her from the executive floor. In his opinion, the quality of her work trumped the complaints continually made to the Human Resources Department. "Jealousy, pure and simple," he said. "We can't capitulate to such nonsense." She didn't work for me, so I deferred to his judgment.

Phyllis was probably overplaying the situation back at the office. But, given Savannah's personal situation coupled with the presence of a police officer, I returned her calls.

"I've been trying to reach you!" she said, theatrically.

"I thought I left you my itinerary. I was giving the keynote address at the conference when you were calling," I said, flatly.

"Oh, yes, but there's a police officer here that needs to speak to Savannah."

"Did you tell him that she was out of the office today?" I asked.

"I knew the conference started today but assumed she would be back. I told him that I would be happy to give her a message."

I bet you did.

"She may have left. I don't know. Have the officer give me a call," I instructed.

"Yes, sir. I'm just worried sick so let me know what you find out."

Not in a million years.

It didn't take long for Phyllis to relay the message to the officer. My cell phone rang immediately from an unidentified caller.

"This is Chief Deputy Jimmy Barbee with the Thurmond County Sheriff's Department. I am trying to reach Savannah Abbott."

"Yes, sir. I understand. We are attending a conference. Is there a message I can give her?"

"Are you a relative?"

"No, sir. I work with her."

"In what capacity?"

"I am her boss."

"Well then you can deliver the news. Her husband, Josh Abbott, is dead. Hung himself."

"I'm sorry. What did you say?"

"Her husband is dead. Hung himself. Found him this morning in his cell."

I was dizzy. I wasn't comprehending this information.

"I'm sorry. Who are you with?"

"The Thurmond County Sheriff's Department."

"Thurmond as in Thurmond, South Carolina?" I asked.

"Yes."

"Sir, I don't think we are talking about the same person. Mrs. Abbott's husband is in Kentucky."

"Was. He was released yesterday from the Kentucky Federal Pen. Didn't check in with his parole officer. He was picked up last night on Jessamin Island in possession of crack cocaine. We would like to speak with Mrs. Abbott as soon as possible."

I tried to sound as calm as possible, but this news was so unsettling on multiple levels. Did he say the Kentucky Federal Pen? I questioned whether it really could be the same prison where my father-in-law was the warden.

"Yes, I am sure she will want to speak to you. She will be in touch."

I sat down in the nearest chair and tried to gather my thoughts. In this job, I was required to deliver bad news many, many times. I've announced layoffs and terminations to employees and poor economic projections to investors. Nothing like this.

The message about Tara's accident began ringing in my ears—the message that kept me up at night. I tried to block it from my memory every waking day. But, it was as clear as the day I first heard it. "She hit a tree. Her airbag didn't deploy. She wasn't wearing a seatbelt. She was speeding and texting. She died upon impact."

I located the nearest men's room and hid in a stall. I didn't even try to fight the tears—the tears fell for Tara, my father, Savannah, and for Josh Abbott. I exited the stall, splashed water on my face, took a deep breath, and went to find Savannah to deliver the news.

Chapter Thirty-Five

Savannah Abbott

Mom and I laughed at our indulgence. We had eaten more in one sitting than we usually did in a week.

"I think I'll enjoy a long bath with these fancy Ritz sea salts before packing up," I said, opening the door to our room for the last time.

"OK, but this one is going to the balcony and gaze at the water," Mom said.

"That's a better idea," I said, tossing the package of sea salts into my suitcase. "I can take a hot bath at home."

Like Mom, I wanted to soak in this bit of paradise a little longer. As I followed her to the balcony, someone knocked on the door.

"Checkout is at noon, right?" Momma asked.

"Yes. Probably just housekeeping trying to get a jump on things."

"Tell them that we won't be leaving one minute before we have to!" as she proceeded to the balcony.

"Still here. Come back, please," I said.

"Savannah, it's Charles."

Charles? Wasn't his speech this morning? Had I messed something up? A million angsts were racing through my head as I opened the door. Charles Walker was as white as a sheet.

"Can I come in?" he asked.

"Of course. Is everything OK?"

He followed me into the room. Momma saw Charles and slid the balcony door open.

"Charles, thank you again for..."

Before she could finish, Charles interrupted her.

"Please, sit down."

Mom and I exchanged nervous looks, as I sat down on the edge of the bed.

"After I finished my remarks, I returned some calls to the office. There was a police officer there."

He sat down on the bed beside me and grabbed my hand.

"It seems that Josh was arrested last night on Jessamin Island," pausing as if to find the right words, "for drug possession."

"What? That's impossible. Josh is in prison."

"He apparently was released yesterday."

"I don't believe that!" I said. "I would know. He would have told me."

I knew that there had to be some mistake. There was no way I wouldn't know about Josh's release. His release was all he ever talked about.

"There is something else," Charles said.

Charles squeezed my hand tightly. Beads of perspiration were forming on his forehead. I had never seen this man so anxious or so distressed. I had never seen him perspire.

"The man who was arrested hung himself in his cell. The officer said it was Josh. The police want to speak to you."

I felt ill. I jumped up and didn't make it to either the sink or the toilet. Every morsel from the Ritz buffet splashed all over the marble bathroom floor. That's the last thing I remember.

Chapter Thirty-Six

Hannah Anne Hart, Savannah's mother

I worried for a second that my breakfast may have the same demise as Savannah's. Instead, my maternal instincts kicked in. Charles and I picked Savannah up. She was so limp. A knot was already bulging on her forehead.

"I'm calling an ambulance," I said.

"Let's get her to the bed first. I think she just fainted," Charles said.

We laid her down on the bed. I ran into the bathroom and threw several of the plush towels over her vomit and doused a washcloth with cold water. I wiped her face. I grabbed a bottle of the artesian spring water that Savannah and I had intentionally avoided due to the $15 price tag. Savannah didn't want Charles to think we were taking advantage of his generosity. But, that was the last thing on my mind as I opened it. She regained consciousness fairly quickly.

"Drink some water," I instructed her, continuing to wipe her face with the washcloth. "Are you OK, honey?" I asked.

She shook her head, but her eyes looked lifeless. I thought she may be in shock.

"I think we need to get her to a hospital," I said, emphatically picking up the phone on the nightstand.

"No, I'm fine," Savannah said, taking several swigs of the water, then taking deep breaths. "Charles, tell me again what you know."

Charles looked at me for approval before proceeding.

"The police officer said Josh had been in the Kentucky Federal Penitentiary," Charles said, his voice shaking.

Savannah was so clammy.

"Yes. That's right."

"I just assumed he was local like Cray. But, he was released in Kentucky and is in the Thurmond County jail for possession of drugs. None of this makes sense."

"Thanks, Captain Obvious," I said, then realized I was talking to Savannah's boss. "Sorry, I'm just a tad upset."

"I understand," he responded, calmly. "I'd like to find out more information before Savannah speaks to the Thurmond police. I have a small cottage on Jessamin Island. It's rented most of the time, but how about I find out if it's available? If it is, you and Savannah could spend a couple of days there while I see what I can learn. What do you think?"

"That's a kind offer," I said. "If any of this is true, I surely don't see any rush for her to subject herself to questioning."

"I'll call the rental agency," Charles said, stepping out of the room.

While he was gone, I located my anxiety medicine. After Bo Hart walked out of my life, my therapist prescribed an antidepressant, later some anxiety supplements. I was ashamed that I needed this crutch. I had become less dependent over the years but always had them at my disposal when the wave of melancholy began seeping in.

"Take this, sweetie," holding the orange pill in the palm of my hand.

"What is it?" Savannah asked.

"Just trust me on this one," I said.

I thought the good Lord must have been looking out for us. This week was the only time Charles Walker's place was available. There was only one important issue—how to get in? He explained that since it was rented most of the time, there was a door code instead of a key. For security purposes, the code changed periodically. He didn't know the code.

"I will find out before you get there," he said. "Leave me your cell number. I'll call you. Here's the address."

Charles likely downplayed the luxury of his second home by referring to it as a "small cottage." It was on an island, after all. But this was no time for cynicism. I was indeed grateful. I was embarrassed as well. He had just presented a speech about technology. I confessed that I still relied on paper maps. I hadn't learned how to use GPS on my phone. He started writing down the directions, and I worried I wouldn't be able to read his writing. Savannah was in no position to be my co-pilot. When he handed me the paper, I did a double take. I couldn't believe his handwriting; it was like a typewriter.

"Do you want me to extend the time for checkout?" he asked.

"I don't think that is necessary. I want to get her out of here. Jessamin Island is only a couple hours, right?"

"If there's no traffic, you could make it in about two and a half."

I knew that my little orange pill would calm Savannah down in the short term.

"Sounds good. And Charles, thanks again for everything."

"I'll call the front desk and send up a bellman for your luggage. You have your valet ticket?"

I handed him the ticket and stuffed the expensive artesian water in my purse along with Charles' directions. Savannah and I headed to our escape on Jessamin Island.

Chapter Thirty-Seven

Charles Walker

I was reeling from delivering the disturbing information to Savannah. But, I withheld that her husband was released from a prison that was likely the prison where my father-in-law was the warden. Before she talked to the police, I wanted to verify that fact and the circumstances surrounding his parole. I had access to the best source, my father-in-law, but I doubted he'd be forthcoming with the information. Our last conversation didn't end well when I advised him to file for bankruptcy. We had never been close and, after his second wife left him, he was even less pleasant to be around. I couldn't remember the last time we had even spoken before Tara's wake.

This seemed to be the day for receiving troubling information. When I placed a call to the management company, I learned that the cottage was available, which was good news, but the reason was rather perplexing. I was told that I had taken it off the rental market this week. I immediately asked for Betsy, who was the most competent employee at the management company. The turnover there was ridiculous. I didn't trust anyone there but her.

"Do you mind checking?" I asked Betsy. "Unless I've lost my mine, I didn't request that the cottage be removed from the rental pool."

"You didn't. Alice did. She said that you wanted it off the rental market this week for maintenance," Betsy said.

"Well, obviously, a miscommunication between Alice and me. I've been out of town a lot," I said but finding Alice's request odd.

"No problem. You know that the door code was changed, right?"

"No. Out of the loop on that as well. It's a good thing I called you."

"Alice has it. You know we change these periodically for our rental houses for your protection."

"Ok, thanks. I'll call Alice."

"While I have you, Tara's Cove is rented next week; the renters arrive on Saturday. It continues to be one the best rentals, such an adorable cottage."

It was probably time to sell Tara's Cove. It brought back too many memories.

"I'm in a conference on Amelia Island. So, on second thought, in case I can't get in touch with Alice, do you mind locating the code? I need it in a couple of hours."

"Sure, but it may take me a bit. We've got a lot of folks checking in. Let me know if you're able to get it from Alice first."

"Thanks, Betsy. I appreciate it."

I hung up and called Alice's cell. It rolled directly to her voicemail, which was full. I sent her a text asking about the code. Then, I called the house. As expected, I got the answering machine. I never knew how Alice occupied her time. It seemed every time I needed to get in touch with her, she wasn't available.

"I am going to Jessamin after the conference is over," I said into the recording.

I didn't see the need to relay any additional information.

"I talked to Betsy, and she says the code has been changed. Can you call me as soon as you get this message and give it to me?"

I became concerned that Alice may be at Jessamin. The conference schedule had aligned with Tara's fall break; we had originally planned to spend it at the Ritz. Since Tara's death, we had avoided the topic of our family vacation. I was literally walking out the door when Alice told me that she wasn't going to Amelia Island. I didn't want her there any more than she wanted to be there. I was relieved and didn't ask any questions.

I wasn't optimistic that Alice would respond timely. I called Harry, our trusted handyman. If Alice arranged for some maintenance this week, he may have the new code. There was a hide-a-key somewhere; Harry probably knew that too. I wasn't having any luck. I got Harry's voicemail.

There was no way I was returning to the conference. The walls were closing in around me. I couldn't shake the possibility that Josh Abbott had been in my father-in-law's prison. My thoughts were interrupted by my phone vibrating. It was the rental agency.

"It's Betsy. I have the code, unless you already have it."

"Great. I left Alice a message but haven't heard back from her yet."

"Well, it's 6290 pound, pound. Remember to enter the pound sign twice. Apparently, the requirement to enter it twice has created confusion."

"Got it. Thanks again, Betsy."

I called Hannah Anne Hart and relayed the message. Given her admitted lack of technological savvy, I worried she may have issues like some of the renters.

"Remember to enter the number first then pound, pound."

"Pound pound?" Hannah Anne asked. "What is that?"

"The number sign on the code box. Savannah will know. Just remember to hit it twice. My rental company warned that the new code has presented some issues. If you don't mind, please call me when you arrive. And, let me know how Savannah is doing."

I started planning next steps. First, I was going to ask my lawyer if it was advisable for Savannah to retain her own lawyer before meeting with the authorities. Then, I had to figure out how to ask my father-in-law, Warden William Wilson, about a possible former inmate Josh Abbott. None of this smelled good.

Chapter Thirty-Eight

Nancy Nichols, Tara's best friend

I was so pissed—another fall break spent babysitting Nannette and Nature. My parents had made it all too clear over the years that they don't get a fall break. It was work as usual. At least, I got to use the car.

I dropped off my sisters and two others at a birthday party. I was Dad's replacement in the first leg of the carpool and only needed to be home by the time they returned. I had at least two hours.

How was I going to spend my free time? I never tortured myself shopping. "You don't need anything. You don't even have room for all the hand-me-downs from Natalie, Natasha, and Nadine," Mom constantly reminded me.

Tara and I had done everything together. Tara got anxious in crowds, so we mostly hung out with each other. As a result, I had only a couple of friends who I would classify as close. And, they were on various trips enjoying the break.

My confinement was depressing for many reasons. I was lonely. I missed Tara. Last fall break, I was with Tara and Mrs. Walker on Jessamin Island. Now, I was bored out of mind.

When my mind was idle, Tara always popped in it. I decided to visit the scene of her accident. It was time to try and piece together why she was on that road. I stopped by the local grocery and bought a bouquet of flowers.

I was thinking about Mrs. Walker. During our last visit, she asked me about Tara's text. "Do you have any idea what she was talking about?" she asked. Of course, she found it odd that Tara had been texting and driving, but the language was equally abnormal. Mrs. Walker also provided me with new information.

Prior to the text to me, there was a call to The Loaded Taco. The Mexican restaurant was one of the hangouts for our class. The food was good and inexpensive. It was within everyone's budget, and the waiters always kept you supplied with free chips and salsa no matter how long you lingered. Unbeknownst to Mrs. Walker, it was where Tara's boyfriend, Jorge Sanchez, was one of the waiters. Mrs. Walker assumed Tara was going to pick up a to-go order, but the road she was traveling wasn't in the direction of the restaurant. "None of it makes sense," Mrs. Walker said.

I placed my fresh flowers among the others under the tree that were now dry and dead. The once colorful ribbons were tattered and faded. I wrapped my arms around the large trunk of the tree. The thick bark scratched my face, but I didn't care. Why did you take my friend? Why didn't you save her? My tears washed down my cheeks.

I sat beneath the tree for a while. In a weird way, Tara was there too. I blankly stared at the passing cars. They all seemed to slow down at the winding bend, especially the ones towing boats. Those seem to approach the curve with the upmost caution. Why was she speeding, especially on this treacherous road? Then it hit me. She was headed to meet Jorge. During one of our late-night talks on her bed, she had revealed her secret.

"Jorge Sanchez and I are going steady," she had said, grinning from ear to ear.

I could see that she was lovesick. And I understood why. We both would burst into giggles when he delivered our chips and salsa at The Loaded Taco. He was hotter than a match.

"Really? Like how? Like where do you see him?" I asked.

"Near his family's seafood market—in a cemetery!" she said, with her eyes widening, anticipating my reaction.

"That's beyond spooky," I said. "You're making all this up!"

"No, I'm not. Cross my heart and hope to die, stick a needle in my eye!" Tara said.

Being reminded of those words, I shivered.

"It's not a cemetery, cemetery...only a few headstones," she had continued. "It's our private sanctuary. And it's not spooky at all. It's actually very romantic," she said, starry-eyed. "There are big oak trees cloaked in Spanish moss with endless views of the river. You have to pinky promise before I tell you the rest," as she held her pinkie finger toward me.

Only Tara From Another Era would still insist on pinky swears at sixteen!

But, like I had done all our lives, I locked my pinkie with hers and followed up with "Pinky promised!"

"There's a marina there. We sit on a blanket and watch the boats and talk about everything under the sun. It's where he first kissed me. He said that the humming of the boat engines was better than any make-out playlist," her voice quivered with excitement.

"TMI, TMI!" I yelled, as she began describing their "petting" there too. "And who says 'petting' anyway! You are truly Tara From Another Era," I said, laughing.

I headed farther down the winding road hoping to find the origination of the boats. Several miles down, I saw a marina. I turned into the gravel parking lot. A number of fishing boats were docked, and there was a flurry of activity at the arrival of the day's fresh catch. This didn't look like the spot she described. I didn't see anything close to a cemetery, and it was far from romantic. The smell of fish permeated the air. Tara would never be caught here; she was too OCD. *Why was she on this road though?* I looked for a place to turnaround thinking I had stopped too soon. Then I saw it. A sign with an arrow "Sanchez Seafood Market straight ahead."

I drove until the road ended on the point—the location of Sanchez Seafood Market. My heart raced as I saw the collection of oak trees Tara had described behind the market. I parked and walked through the lot. The gravel crunched under my feet with each step in rhythm with the swaying of the Spanish moss hanging from the large oak trees. It was like a horror movie scene. It was downright eerie. I took a sandy pathway leading through the trees, and goose bumps stood up on my arms. But, Tara was right. The path emptied into a beautiful setting. The weathered headstones added to the serenity.

Undoubtedly, this was where Tara and Jorge met for their rendezvous. I sat on a mossy mound, providing the perfect spot to view the boats coming and going into the marina. It was so peaceful. It was as if time were standing still. Before her text to me, Mrs. Walker said that Tara had called The Loaded Taco. She wasn't placing a to-go order, she was arranging a meeting. She was upset. She needed comforting. She needed Jorge. She was on her way to this very spot. She never made it. On the way to her boyfriend, she reached out to her best friend as well. And in doing so, she perished.

I sat in silence for a while. I realized that I had discovered my sanctuary too.

When leaving, I stopped to read the headstones. The dates on both were illegible but I could make out the epitaph on one:

> Waste not your time with useless wrath,
> but ease your soul along the path,
> haste to the stream, and cast your fly,
> for one day here you too will lie

I ran my fingers over the words.

"I'll be back to visit you soon," I said aloud to the surrounding air. As I was walking back to the parking lot, I noticed an etching in one of the big oaks shading the headstone—a big heart with JS loves TW.

After my visit to Tara's secret refuge, I was ready to pick up the remainder of her things that Mrs. Walker had offered. I recalled that she was returning from Jessamin Island today. I stopped by the house to ask Dad if I could use the car a little longer. Tara's house was only a couple of blocks away. I had enough time before Nannette and Nature would be home from the party. Dad wasn't there. I wondered if he was at the Walker's...helping Mrs. Walker with her job search.

When I arrived at the Walker's, their electronic gate was open, so I drove up to the back of the house. The pool cover was off. It appeared Johnny, their pool guy, had been working. Oddly, there were tools in the bottom of the pool. I stepped over the toolbox on the walkway and headed to the back door leading into the kitchen. The door was open. Perhaps Johnny was inside working, but where was his truck? I tapped on the screened door.

"Hello? Is anyone home?" I asked. Thoughts of my father and Mrs. Walker getting it on in the upstairs bedroom flashed through my mind. My wobbly legs headed toward the stairs when the ringing phone startled me.

The answering machine clicked on. Mr. Walker's voice echoed throughout the kitchen.

"I am going to Jessamin after the conference is over. I just talked to Betsy. She says the door code changed. Call me as soon as you get this message and give it to me."

"Mrs. Walker?" I said. "Are you here?"

I walked up the stairs. The house was eerily quiet.

"Mrs. Walker?" I asked again, as I approached the guest room. No one was there. The room was as neat and tidy as usual.

I ran down the stairs and out the door. Johnny's truck pulled in, as I was walking at a fast clip down the walkway.

"Hey there, Nancy. I wondered whose car that was. I had to run to the hardware store," Johnny said.

"I dropped by to pick up some things that Mrs. Walker has for me, but she's not here."

"Alice is at Jessamin but should be back soon. I'll let her know you came by. You doin' alright?" he asked.

I knew the intent behind the question. How was I handling the death of my best friend?

"I'm OK. I'll stop by later."

I felt somewhat relieved that I didn't catch Dad and Mrs. Walker in bed. Still, I couldn't shake a weird feeling. Mr. Walker's message didn't make sense. Didn't Mrs. Walker say that a renter cancelled at the last minute and that Mr. Walker wanted her to get some maintenance completed or something like that? Didn't she say that's why she was going to Jessamin? If she was there, why was he calling the house looking for her?

I started thinking how I used to idolize the Walker household, but over the years, I had detected nicks in the pristine façade. Their house was as screwed up as mine.

I spoke to my friend again. I thought about her last words to me: *You are not going to fucking believe it!* But, I did believe it. And, I was also starting to believe in fate.

PART IX

Chapter Thirty-Nine

Charles Walker

I finally heard from Harry. He hadn't heard from Alice about any maintenance, didn't know the code, but the good news was he knew the location of the hide-a-key. The bad news was that he had the key with him and was out of town.

"Since renters are there all the time, I just keep it on my key ring like I do all the others. I'll put it back when I get back to Jessamin, but I'm tellin' ya, y'all need to come up with something better. It's a pain in the ass to open, and that fake rock sticks out like a sore thumb. I mean people aren't stupid."

"No problem, Harry. I've heard from the rental agency and have the code now. You keep the key. There's really no need for a hidden one since the installation of the digital code system. Thanks for calling me back."

If I hadn't received the code from Betsy, I would have been more than irritated that I couldn't access my own house. My keys were at the office. The only helpful news from Harry was that Alice hadn't scheduled any maintenance. The woman wouldn't pick up a finger to do anything herself. Hell, she didn't know the difference between a hammer and a screwdriver. So, I was pretty confident she wasn't at Jessamin. But, then again, I didn't know where she was.

Hannah Anne called. They arrived at the cottage. Savannah was resting.

"Thanks for calling. Glad to hear that you made it OK," I said, relieved that they hadn't run into Alice. Certainly, Hannah Anne would have mentioned it if they had.

"Well, I was worried at first," Hannah Anne reported. "I couldn't get the code to work but then realized I didn't hit that number sign button twice. After that, a piece of cake. You have a lovely home. I love the view of the tidal creek. Savannah is curled up on your porch hammock. This is the perfect medicine for her. We both appreciate it."

"I've got a call into a lawyer; it's most likely not necessary, but it's just engrained in me from my job," I said. "I guess the Thurmond County Sheriff's Department is just doing their jobs as well. However, I don't want Savannah walking into an interrogation blindsided by accusations implying that she had anything to do with a drug distribution."

"Well, of course she didn't!" Hannah Anne said, with stiff authority.

"We both know that, but I'm just crossing all the t's," I said, not really knowing how to explain that I had heard of worse.

When Alice and I were first married, her father's star was rising within the law enforcement ranks in the Thurmond County Sheriff's Department, due to his aggressive tactics if you ask me. He used to brag about his interrogations and the tricks pulled to obtain confessions. I naively asked about "Miranda" rights for the accused—the right to remain silent and to obtain legal representation.

"That's not how it works in the real world, son. These people don't deserve any rights," he responded, laughing derisively.

From Savannah's account of her husband's initial arrest, he didn't sound like a drug runner. The way Savannah spoke about her son, he certainly didn't fit the mold either. But, they both were doing time for drug-related charges. Savannah may not have all the facts. I, for one, knew that things didn't always appear as they seem. My marriage was proof of that.

Alice and I were like strangers in the same house. I couldn't recall the last time we even slept in the same bed. We put on a good front at the mandatory social and school events. I began thinking that sometimes your circumstances push you into doing things that you never thought possible. I wonder if my father felt that sort of pressure when he committed suicide.

I couldn't bear to return to the conference hall. I couldn't endure the hordes of exhibition booth sponsors with artificial handshakes and empty compliments about my speech. It was a charade in hopes of having business tossed their way. I wasn't even interested in the talks that I needed to hear—those about mezzanine loans, packaging debt for the securities market, or cutting-edge ideas. I uncharacteristically decided to take a walk.

I left my shoes and socks by the steps leading down to the beach, rolled up my suit pants, and did something that I had not done in a very long time. I couldn't even recall the last time. How many years had it been? I had truly forgotten the feeling of sand between my toes. I walked closer to the water's edge and felt the coolness of the water trickle over my feet.

I stared into the endless expanse of water before me, reflecting on the color of the sky and how it melded into the ocean. The insignificance of my life hit me harder than the waves tumbling onto the surf. Why was I still here on this earth, trudging along like a robot? How had I failed to appreciate the simplest of wonders, like sand between my toes? Life is fragile, I thought. It's about time that I start living it.

My spiritual awakening quickly passed when my phone rang while I was brushing the sand off my feet and pulling on my socks. I reached into my pocket. It was the office.

"Thank heavens you answered this time," Phyllis said. "The police were here again, and this time there were three of them. They were looking for you. Did you ever get in touch with them?"

"Yes, I did."

"Well, what in the world is going on?"

I wasn't going to give Phyllis any information to create more havoc in the office.

"You informed them that I was out of town, correct?"

"Yes, I told them you were at a conference and that I believed you had already spoken to someone. They asked the location of the conference, so I gave it to them. I hope that was OK, but I didn't know what to do."

"That is certainly fine," I said. "I'll be back in the office tomorrow. See you then."

I hung up abruptly, cutting off any other questions that I wasn't going to answer. Three officers at the office looking for me? I decided to call my lawyer, not about Savannah's dilemma, but apparently mine.

Does anyone answer their phone anymore? I left a message on his voicemail.

I put on my shoes and headed back inside. When I opened the door leading into the expansive lobby, I knew instantly that something was terribly wrong. I observed at least five police officers in the lobby. Blue lights were bouncing off the walls like I was entering a nightclub.

One approached.

"Charles Walker?"

"Yes," I said.

The next thing I recall is my head being smashed against a marble pillar while I was being handcuffed.

"You have the right to remain silent. Anything you say can and will be used against you in a court of law. You have the right to an attorney."

So, the Miranda rights are still alive and well, I thought. But those words were as void and empty as I was feeling. I knew that my life had just been changed forever.

Chapter Forty

Savannah Abbott

I didn't know if it was the peacefulness of this secluded cottage, the cicadas' maraca-like music, the moon's reflection on the tidal creek, the effects of the orange pill, or the combination that had finally calmed me down. My anguish was subsiding. I was ready to go back to Beaufort and face the facts. Mom could continue to coddle me at her house. I couldn't hide from the inevitable confirmation from the police that Josh was dead.

"Mom, I'm glad we came here, but I am ready to go home."

"You mean right now?" Mom asked.

"No, but let's leave in the morning."

"Charles said that we could stay a couple of days, so he's clearly not expecting you at work tomorrow. Don't you think you need some more time to process all of this?" Mom asked.

"No need to 'hope against all hope,' as you would say. I need to talk to the police."

"You are a strong woman, Savannah, but everyone has their breaking point. Trust me on that."

I knew Mom was referring to Dad. In the short time I had been home, she had alluded to him too many times to count. I tossed and turned all night. I thought about Josh. I thought about Cray. I thought about how Mom's life would have been different if Dad had been around. I thought about Josh and Walt. Josh's life would have been different if he had been raised by Walt. Not that the Abbotts weren't good people, they were. But clearly, Josh didn't fit the Abbott mold. His problem was that he did what he was supposed to do. And what he was supposed to do was run the Abbott Tobacco Farm. He never made waves. That's why none of what Charles said made sense. Josh would never sell drugs; he had never used them. He wasn't a smoker even though he had grown up with tobacco all around him. Then, the fact that he was released without telling me was especially troubling.

My faith was rocked. My faith had given me hope that I would be reunited with my family one day. It kept me steady. I knew that my husband and son were gentle souls, good people, and victims of misfortune. I recalled Walt's words after Josh's arrest. "Honorable character stands the test of time. Unfairness isn't fair but serves its purpose; it's a pawn in the game of life. We decide if it will defeat us or if we will use it to empower us. You must keep moving forward."

I had taken Walt's advice to heart and continued to move forward, although after Cray's incarceration, it was more like treading water. I had survived for Josh, Cray, and Mom. Soon after arriving at the cottage, I called Walt to tell him what I knew about Josh. He disclosed information that I had never been told—that the warden from the Kentucky federal prison had framed Cray. I couldn't even comprehend the implications. It was like life's undertow had a hold of me and was pulling me out to sea in a giant riptide.

I thought that once I was back in my childhood home, I would feel more secure— I could picture the moss draped throughout the Spanish oaks lining Momma's street as a blanket of comfort. But, on the drive back to Beaufort, I doubted my resolve. I wanted her to turn the car around, head south, and just keep driving until we couldn't go any farther. I may have hit my breaking point.

And, as we turned down the canopied road, instead of moss, the trees were swathed with intense blue flashes, an omen of bad things to come.

Before we could comprehend the scene, our car was surrounded by police. I was yanked out of the front seat, and a large hand slammed my face into the window. My arms were twisted behind me, and my wrists were handcuffed. "You have the right to remain silent... ."

If life was a game, I felt like I had busted in blackjack, folded in poker, or been checkmated in chess. I was broken. I was done.

PART X

Chapter Forty-One

Hannah Anne Hart

The events of the last twenty-four hours were more than enough to digest for a lifetime. Josh had been released from prison, failed to report to his parole officer, arrested for possession of crack cocaine, thrown in jail, and hung in jail. Then, my sweet angel and Charles Walker were arrested for attempted murder. "Murder for hire" was what they called it.

While on Jessamin Island, Savannah had contacted Josh's parents, Walt Benton and Maude Abbott, and relayed the news about Josh's death and the sketchy facts as she knew them. Walt immediately sprang into action and retained a lawyer. He had not known of Josh's release either. He was going to get to the bottom of all the questionable circumstances. "How in the hell could a man behind bars been able to hang himself?" Walt asked.

Walt had his own unsettling information to share. He said that the warden of the Kentucky federal prison was a living example that "absolute power corrupts absolutely." That man had framed Cray.

Cray and Josh were fearful of the scope of revenge that the warden's well-connected band of law enforcement officials would take against them and the rest of the family if they reported the truth. In addition to the fear of retribution, the cards were significantly stacked against them.

"Who would you believe?" Walt asked. "A convicted felon serving time and his son, who was caught with cocaine in his car, or law enforcement officials whose job it is to protect us? It was a no-win situation, and Cray's decision not to fight the charges was really his only choice," Walt explained. "Cray didn't want to put you in harm's way, Savannah."

I was worried that Savannah may have met her Waterloo with these revelations. Now, her arrest might be her complete undoing. It seemed like a vortex, a spiral worse than those I had experienced over the years when Bo would ask—in his sporadic, unplanned way—to visit Savannah.

This time, I sucked it up and contacted him. I located Bo on an oil rig in the middle of the Gulf. He was immediately wiring money for the best attorney. Once again, he asked to visit. He would honor my decision, like he had in the past. This time, however, the pain in his voice was palpable.

I had flatly rejected Bo's numerous appeals to visit Savannah in the early years. I told him he couldn't have his cake and eat it too. A young child wouldn't be able to process the intermittent and unpredictable pauses from his journeys.

I believed that. It wouldn't have been healthy for Savannah. I would have had to deal with the wreckage after he left. But truth be told, I always worried more about me. My heart couldn't handle it. Any visit would be temporary. He wouldn't have an epiphany. He wouldn't realize that he had make a huge mistake, that he loved me more than anything in the world and couldn't spend another waking day without me. Even his requests to visit would trigger an emotional setback and lead to increased visits with my therapist and dosages of my medication. When I would get back on track, Bo would again resurface and plead to see his daughter, and the spiral would start again.

I knew my refusals were selfish and self-centered. But now, it wasn't about me. My daughter needed all the help she could get. She needed to see her father. I accepted his invitation with open arms and an open heart.

Instead of being unsettling, Bo's quick arrival steadied me. It was as if he knew what the chaotic situation required. And more surprisingly, Bo Hart and Walt Benton hit it off like long-lost friends.

Initially, I found that odd. The differences between the two were patently obvious. One man had been robbed of the opportunity to raise his child. The other had been given that opportunity but fled from it like a car screeching away on two wheels. One man was a disciplined Marine serving his country at all costs. The other was a rambler seeking the next thrill.

Despite those contrasts, I noticed similarities, and they were profound: toughness, confidence, swagger, charm, and charisma. But, most importantly, both men were authentic and had no pretense. Those qualities in these two fathers gave me hope.

Chapter Forty-Two

Walt Benton

I was struggling with so many emotions. I had earned a Purple Heart, the oldest military award recognizing valor and sacrifice. At this moment, however, I felt like a fraud. Hell, I couldn't even save my son. I was a coward, pure and simple.

When first learning about Josh, I should have gone to battle for him like I did for the thousands of faceless souls who didn't share one drop of my DNA. I should have fought for him, just as I should have fought for Maudie years before.

Maudie was arriving tomorrow to bury our son. The love for her I thought I buried many years ago was resurfacing in my tattered, empty heart. Perhaps it was the fifth of Jack Daniel's that Bo Hart and I shared while lamenting the lives we chose. Bo had a chance to mend things with Savannah. I, on the other hand, was getting ready to place my lifeless son under six feet of dirt. Gone. No second chances. Not even the ability to hug him one last time. No goodbyes. Not one last "I love you, son."

I gulped a big glass of water hoping that it would help my splitting head. I adhered to the schedule engrained in me from all my years as a Marine—never sleeping past 5:00 a.m. I drank more water while waiting on the coffee to brew. I had a big day today; I needed a clear head.

Hannah Anne had set out some mugs on a wicker tray with a dainty little sugar bowl and a miniature silver spoon beside linen napkins with an "H" monogram. There was a note with perfect penmanship. "Good morning! Cream is in the fridge." A true Southern lady, I thought, knowing that she took pride in this presentation although I preferred my coffee black.

I retrieved the book that I had just purchased, *Alibi* by Elliott Gray. I retreated to the back porch with my coffee and book to learn something about this author who I would soon be meeting.

Elliott Gray, a criminal defense lawyer, retired from the grind of a law practice when he had hit it big from the sales of his legal thrillers. The author just happened to be one of Charles Walker's best friends since childhood.

As I read the back cover, I learned that *Alibi* was the author's twenty-first book to make *The New York Times* Best Sellers' list.

"Alibi, the newest thriller by Elliott Gray, is yet another gripping adventure in the life of R.J. Barrett, the lawyer who tackles the unwinnable cases. Fans of Elliott Gray's works are prepared to expect the unexpected, and Alibi certainly doesn't disappoint in that regard. A page turner from beginning to end. Another masterpiece."

Bo joined me on the porch.

"Mornin'," he said.

Bo had a fresh bottle of whiskey in one hand and his coffee in the other.

"Hair of the dog," he said, as he dumped a splash in his coffee. He offered the bottle to me.

"Why not?" I said, as Bo shared his hangover cure with me. "You ever heard of this guy?" I held up my new purchase. "Elliott Gray, apparently some popular author."

"Nope. Never been one to curl up with a book. Hannah Anne probably does. She is the bookworm. She never saw a book she didn't like," Bo said.

"Well, you and I are in the minority. Says here he has sold over three hundred million books and they have been translated into forty-three languages. He's apparently a childhood friend of Charles Walker."

"No shit," Bo said.

"Taking time off of his book tour to join the legal team. Meeting with him later today."

"No shit," Bo said again. "What time are you meeting?"

"3:00. I am going to visit Cray first and then drive over to Hilton Head—some big, secure spread of the author friend. The lawyers thought it would be a good place to convene. I understand the man is very private, so let's keep this to ourselves for now. If you want to join me, I'll swing by and pick you up. I'd like your assessment of him."

"Sounds good. I will be climbing the walls by then. You know, all the time I lived here, I never went to Hilton Head."

"Well, you weren't here very long, as I understand things."

"Touché," Bo said. "I'm going to make a grocery store run. Those two must have eaten like birds. There is absolutely nothing in the fridge or pantry worth eating. I am having Pop-Tart withdrawals. Any requests?" Bo asked.

"I haven't had a Pop-Tart in years but used to love the frosted blueberry."

"Now, here's a man with some taste," holding his hand up for a fist pump. "The frosted strawberry is my favorite. You like potato chips?"

"Yep, nothing better than with French onion dip."

"Exactly! Who'd a thought a Marine and Bo Hart would have anything in common? I'll fix us up. And a frozen pizza or two?" Bo asked.

"A bachelor's gourmet dinner—let me get my wallet," I said.

"I got this, bud. I'm not good for much, but I can navigate a grocery store, or at least the cereal, chip, and frozen food aisles. I really appreciate all you've done so far with the lawyers and all. I'm sure Hannah Anne appreciates having a reliable man here."

"We are all in this together, my friend."

I wasn't much for fiction legal thrillers. I preferred historical, non-fiction but quickly found myself entrenched in Elliott Gray's book. If Hannah Anne hadn't interrupted my porch reading, I would have lost all track of time.

"Damn. I've got to get a move on," I said, after she joined me. "This book is pretty good. Have you ever read anything by Elliott Gray?"

"Yes, as in twenty of his books. I see that you have his new release. Are you a fan too?"

"Before yesterday, I'd never heard of him."

"You're kidding, right?"

"No. Guess I'm stuck in a time warp with my reading preferences. I'm partial to World War II. Anyway, Bo has gone to the grocery store for some unhealthy snacks. If you need anything, you could possibly catch him on his cell," I said.

"Or just send him right back. The man's got ants in his pants. Have you noticed that he can't sit still?"

"The thought has crossed my mind, but he's a good man. We all have a shortcoming or two. I've got to hit the road for Somerset. After that, I'm meeting with some lawyers in Hilton Head."

I decided to keep the Elliott Gray addition to the team quiet since I didn't understand his role. I wasn't sure that Hannah Anne would be able to contain the news, being a huge fan and all.

"You need some breakfast. I will scramble you a few eggs."

"Don't worry about me."

"Bacon and toast?" Hannah Anne asked, brushing over my comment.

"Now, don't go to any trouble," I said. "Bo is picking up breakfast stuff."

"No trouble at all. I like having someone to cook for. Savannah doesn't like a hot breakfast. That woman prefers Pop-Tarts. Just like Bo used to. Wonder if that man still eats those things? He could eat a box a day!"

I remained silent on that topic. She'd find out soon enough.

I regretted appeasing Hannah Anne's southern hospitality. The amount of whiskey I had shared with Bo last night wasn't the only problem. It was the angst building about how to inform my grandson that his father is dead. I pulled over and heaved Hannah Anne's breakfast onto the side of the road on the way to the Somerset Federal Correctional Institute.

Chapter Forty-Three

Cray Abbott

I was putting the finishing touches on Wayman's fourth bald eagle. Ever since the tattoo equipment had been delivered into Shipping and Receiving, I didn't have time for anything else. When word circulated that I didn't accept any form of compensation for my work, I had a waiting list of customers. The guards became the managers of my schedule, and I understood why upon learning that the fees I had refused were being pocketed by them for a priority appointment. I kept quiet. After all, they supplied the equipment and the inks.

Wayman knew about Walt's visit so, other than his fourth bald eagle, my morning was free to put the finishing touches on a painting I had been working on for Walt. With my practice on Wayman, I thought I had perfected the bald eagle. The bird's piercing eyes weren't hard. It was the powerful aura and the magnificence of the bird that had been the most difficult to capture. I was proud of my latest effort.

When Wayman returned to escort me to the visitation area, I showed him my painting for Walt.

"I hoped he likes it," I said.

"Wow," Wayman said. "Will you paint one for me too?"

"Don't you have enough of them on your body?" I asked, but adding, "Sure, if you do me a favor."

I wanted to give Walt the painting during his visit and asked Wayman to take a detour through Shipping and Receiving. I needed a padded envelope.

"Sure. No problem," Wayman said.

While Wayman was distracted combing through the container of the incoming mail that had not yet been sorted or approved for delivery, I slipped the letter from Dad with a note to Walt in the envelope with the painting. We then proceeded to the visitation area where Walt was waiting for me.

Walt's patented bear hug was longer and tighter than ever. I sensed something was amiss. When he finally released his grip, I saw tears brimming in his green eyes. What now? I wanted to run. I wanted to flee to the four walls of my confined space. These walls permitted me to paint my birds and momentarily live in the real world that I longed to reenter. But at this moment, I needed those walls to protect me, to shield me from the turmoil on the outside, and to block the words that Walt was trying hard to assemble.

Chapter Forty-Four

Walt Benton

The visitation area in Cray's minimum-security prison resembled a hotel lobby, but I knew the surveillance cameras picked up on more than just our movements. For that reason, I rehearsed my delivery of the news all the way to Somerset. My nerves were so edgy. I should have packed a flask with Bo's whiskey. I needed a swig to calm me.

The sight of Cray being escorted into the visitation area by a guard coupled with the news I was going to report tested my strength. I was thankful for my rehearsals and that there was absolutely nothing in my stomach. If I hadn't left my breakfast on the side of the road, I was confident it would have ended up on the floor of the Somerset prison.

I got off to a shaky start but recovered. I carefully conveyed the facts of Josh's release, his arrest on Jessamin Island, and his death in jail. The look of defeat in Cray's eyes prevented me from telling him that Savannah was now sitting in jail on attempted murder charges. All I could muster was that drugs seem to be involved and that Savannah was being questioned too. I knew I had to put on a false certainty and convince Cray that there was absolutely nothing that could stick against Savannah. She would be fine. I finished without breaking down. We sat in silence for what seemed like an eternity.

"I know this is a lot to take in. I assure you that a team of lawyers and other experts have been retained. Even your grandfather, Bo, appeared and is committed to the mission."

This last bit of news made Cray smile.

"I know that makes Gannah happy. I bet that sounded weird, but she's never gotten over him, you know. Life is certainly unpredictable, isn't it? I just wish…"

Cray paused and took a deep breath. He grabbed my hand and squeezed it hard.

"I painted you a picture. It's a bald eagle. I've gotten a lot of practice from tattoos on one of the guards. I'm up to four of them on his arms and back."

He handed me the envelope. He stopped me when I started to open it.

"You can't leave here with an unsealed package."

"I can't wait to see it. I know it's great. Thank you, Cray. I'll open it at Hannah Anne's. It will raise our spirits."

"I've got to report to my job in Shipping and Receiving. Thanks for the visit."

"I'll be back next week and give you an update on things."

"Thanks, Papa Walt. I love you."

"I love you too, Cray. We will get through this."

"I just wish…," beginning those same words but again pausing.

Cray hugged me and whispered in my ear.

"I just wish I could have said goodbye."

"Me too, son, me too."

Chapter Forty-Five

Bo Hart

"I should have gone with you to Somerset," I told Walt on our way to Hilton Head. "I know I put on this tough cowboy image, but I am not strong enough to do what you did. I appreciate it."

Walt didn't offer words of understanding. Despite his aviator sunglasses, I could see that his eyes didn't flinch.

"I wasn't ready for a baby. Hell, I wasn't ready to be married. You know, so much life to live, so many places to explore. I did try though. For four long years. I was suffocating. I know it sounds selfish. But the way I looked at it, it would have been worse on everyone had I stayed. I would have been a disappointment to Hannah Anne and Savannah."

I felt like I was in a Catholic confessional booth. Walt was the priest behind the barrier, his sunglasses. He just kept staring straight ahead. I was having a heart-to-heart with a rock.

"I have supported them over the years. I have asked Hannah Anne more times than I can count to visit Savannah. She made it quite clear that I was not welcome, that Savannah didn't want to see me, and she didn't either. They were doing fine without my disruption. It would have just confused Savannah. I'm not trying to bad-mouth Hannah Anne. I mean, I get it. But just so you know, I did try."

We rode in silence a bit longer. Enough confessions for one day, especially to a mute priest.

"I don't judge you, Bo," Walt said, when he finally broke the awkward silence. "You're a good man. I like you. I'm certainly not going to tell you what to do, but my son is dead. Savannah is still very much alive. You have time to make amends, not only with Savannah but also with Cray. Your grandson needs you too."

"I'm all ears. How do you think I can do that?"

"Well, for starters, come with me on the next visit. We need to wrap our arms around him more than ever."

"OK, I will if you don't think it will cause more mayhem. All of this is a lot to process."

"No excuses. Cray smiled when I told him you were in town."

"Who does he look like? Hannah Anne stopped sending me photos years ago."

"At times, I thought he looked like Josh and me and then other times, I saw more of a resemblance to Savannah. Today, I was taken back when he came through the door. That young man, your grandson Cray Abbott, looks just like you."

"Shit," I said, choking up. I swallowed hard.

"What's he like?" I asked, after choking back tears.

"Well, he is a talented artist. Lowcountry birds are his passion. He didn't get that from my side. As Jack Daniel's and I told you last night, I was only with Josh's mother for a summer, and we weren't exploring Maudie's artistic talents then. Perhaps the talent came from your side of the family."

"Interesting. I used to doodle a lot—cartoons and stuff like that. I also was pretty good at woodworking. I made Savannah a swing that is still hanging out back. But, I never attempted a painting."

"Now that you mention paintings, Cray gave me a painting today. It's in the envelope in the back seat. Why don't we take a look?"

I opened the envelope and pulled out a remarkable bald eagle. It was if the bird was soaring in the car. So detailed. So real. So imposing. I felt tears building in my eyes again. What a fool you have been, I thought. I was speechless and didn't want to see this Purple-Hearted Marine watch me break down.

Walt raised his sunglasses and glanced at the picture. He quickly lowered his glasses and in a shaky voice announced he needed gas. I knew that he had been moved to tears like me. While he was getting the gas that we didn't need, I noticed some other papers in the envelope. A note from Cray to Walt. I put that one back inside. It didn't seem right for me to read. I pulled out the other papers, an envelope addressed to Cray Abbott, with a letter inside.

While Walt was inside the store to regain his composure, I read the enclosed letter to Cray.

Dear Cray,

First, I want to tell you that I love you. I think about you every day and pray that you are OK. I have been doing well. I see the light at the end of the tunnel. Stay strong. My faith is stronger than ever. My strength comes from knowing that I will be reunited with you, your mother, and Walt soon. I know I don't have to tell you to be honest and do the right thing because you have done that your entire life. I am so proud of you.

Love, Dad

This note was like a sucker punch. I had never met my son-in-law either. My family had needed me. The sporadic influx of cash was not nearly enough. Where had I been? Sure, I had traveled and had a romance or two along the way, but no one had come close to Hannah Anne.

I was so deep in thought that I almost jumped out of my skin when the door opened. Walt resumed his driver's position. He fastened his seat belt and looked at me.

"You alright?" Walt asked.

"Take a look at this. Was in the envelope with the painting."

Walt read the note.

"Oh, and there is a note to you as well. I didn't read it for what's it worth."

I reached into the large envelope and pulled out the note from Cray and handed it to him.

Papa Walt,

In addition to this note, there should be three things in the envelope—my painting, a letter from Dad, and the envelope it came in. I received Dad's letter several days ago. I was able to retrieve it while working in Shipping and Receiving. Otherwise I don't think I would have ever seen it. Sounds like he will be released soon, or that's how I read it. But then I noticed the postmark on the envelope. It was mailed from Harper's Corner, North Carolina. I have a bad feeling about this. If Dad was released, why wouldn't he have told me? Did you know? Does Mom know anything?

If not, I am worried he may have fallen for another one of the warden's scams. I may be paranoid but even in Club Fed, I have personally witnessed corruption and bribery every day. I remember Dad's advice: "Warn him that NO ONE can be trusted." Something is not right. Will you check it out and give me a sign that everything is OK next time you visit?

I love you,

Cray

"Anything else in there?" Walt asked.

"No, well just the envelope."

"Let me see it," Walt said.

I handed it to him wondering why he would want to see Cray's address to the Somerset Federal Correctional Institute on an envelope.

"I'll be damn," he said.

"What is it?" I asked.

"Read this. We have a little detour. I am going to listen to my son's advice. 'Trust no one,'" Walt said.

PART XI

Chapter Forty-Six

Walt Benton

When Bo and I entered the sprawling home of the famous author Elliott Gray, it was evident that Charles Walker had spared no expense in assembling his legal team. We participated in the mandatory handshakes and introductions of Elliott Gray, Charles' childhood friend and author, Charles' trusted corporate attorney, Vincent Ellis, and Rollins Bishop, a criminal defense attorney from Atlanta. I privately advised Bo that his only job was to listen intently. Though the meeting had been pitched as a "united defense," we needed to understand the charges and ensure that Savannah, most importantly, wasn't being thrown to the wolves.

Rollins wasn't shy in letting us know that he was big time. He rattled off a list of famous clients and his successes that ranged from white-collar crimes to first-degree murder charges and from insider trading to campaign finance violations. He had unlimited resources at his disposal—including his team of experienced attorneys, paralegals, and private investigators. I'm sure Rollins Bishop was good. The fluff wasn't what impressed me; his range of resources did.

Earl Dixson, whom I retained for Savannah, was a one-man shop in Beaufort. His office wasn't in a fancy, Atlanta high-rise but an old house on Main Street. I trusted Earl. I had first-hand experience with him on numerous sensitive issues on the Marine base. He was street-smart, tough, and most importantly, honest. And, he had handled as many cases in Thurmond as he had Beaufort. If this case went to a jury, I knew the people in the neighboring county wouldn't take kindly to a big shot from Atlanta. In my experience, residents of Thurmond County made those in Beaufort appear urbanized. They took home cooking to a whole new level.

Rollins Bishop immediately took charge. He summarized the evidence against Charles and Savannah.

"Josh Abbott was released on parole. A prison guard drove him to a bus station and put him on a bus for Beaufort, South Carolina. He was instructed to immediately report to his parole officer. He failed to do so, and after some period of leniency, an APB was circulated. Local law enforcement agencies within a 200-mile radius of Beaufort were contacted and a picture circulated."

From my impression of Rollins Bishop thus far, he wouldn't welcome interruptions. Now was not the time to share my evidence establishing that Josh never boarded any bus to Beaufort. Rollins Bishop continued his recitation of the evidence.

"Following up on a tip of drug-related activities near the Jessamin Island Breezeway, an officer questioned the clerk on duty. The clerk communicated that a man had recently checked in, paying cash, and seemed anxious. The man kept looking out the door. After giving him the key to his room, the man didn't proceed to his room but hid in the parking lot for a while. After showing the clerk the photo of Josh that had accompanied the APB, he said it was the same man."

Why was Josh at the Jessamin Island Breezeway? A sentence in Cray's note began replaying in my mind. "I am worried he may have fallen for another one of the warden's scams."

"The officer decided to question the guest," Royce Bishop continued. "When Josh answered his door, the report is that he was strung out, could barely walk, and was belligerent," Rollins continued. "The officer saw an open duffle bag with drug paraphernalia. The bag contained crack cocaine, photographs of a home on Jessamin Island, named Tara's Cove, and photographs of Alice Walker. Also in the bag was a substantial amount of cash along with instructions providing the address, Alice Walker's schedule, and methods of access into the home."

This rendition was unfortunately believable. But, there was a gaping hole.

"With all due respect, this is my son you are talking about," I said. "He was an honorable man. With that being said, what is the motive here?"

"The motive, sir, is that Charles Walker and Savannah Abbott were having an affair. Mrs. Abbott wanted a divorce due to Josh's drug trafficking business. He needed money to get his network reestablished, and he needed drugs. The hit on Alice Walker helped him fund his large purchase of narcotics."

"That's bullshit and totally fabricated. My son loved his wife deeply, and she adored him. The love they had for each other was beyond compare. For argument's sake, even if the preposterous assertion of the desire for a divorce is true, no way my son was involved in drug trafficking and wasn't desperate for money, period—and definitely not for drugs. He never even smoked a cigarette, though growing tobacco was his livelihood.

"That's why we're here. I'm simply relaying the prosecution's case," Rollins Bishop said with authority. "Don't shoot the messenger. We're in this together."

"Well, it shouldn't take long to get these bogus charges thrown out. My grandson gave me this letter today. I made some copies. Take a look."

I distributed copies of Josh's letter to Cray that I had made at a UPS store on the way to the meeting. For now, I withheld Cray's note to me relaying his worries about Josh. I waited for the team of attorneys to read the contents.

"Note the postmark on the envelope. Josh's letter was mailed from Harper's Corner, North Carolina, on the day that, according to the prosecution's case, Josh was on a bus headed to Beaufort."

"So, you don't believe Josh was on the bus?" Rollins asked.

"How in the hell could he have been two places at the same time?" I asked.

"Obviously, he couldn't. Of course, we will nail down every fact but from my experience in these cases, I will offer a hypothetical counter by the authorities. Anyone could have mailed that letter. There are a range of middlemen out there who, for a fee, will do all kinds of things. They have connections, and they have insiders. The fences around and bars within a prison can't stop these activities."

That could be a plausible explanation for anyone else but not for Josh, unless he had undergone a complete transformation in the place that was supposed to rehabilitate him. None of it made sense. And setting aside any argument about my son's character, the facts didn't support such an outlandish scenario. Josh hadn't escaped. He had been released earlier than anticipated; certainly, the facility officials wouldn't recommend or support an expedited parole for just anyone. I refrained from these comments or further discussion. Rollins Bishop's responses had clearly established that he knew more than I did. He assumed that I was naïve and clueless about the reality of our prison system.

"So, I suppose these so-called middlemen are also how Josh obtained the instructions for the hit?"

"No. That would be Savannah Abbott."

With that he handed me a copy of a different letter.

Dear Josh,

Things are going well here. Thank you again for your understanding why I had to leave. I realized I should have taken this step earlier. Mom is happy that I am back home.

Do you have any updates on your parole? I am enclosing some sketches. I am also enclosing some photos. I will explain them further when we talk. I trust that you receive everything.

Savannah

It was becoming clear that there's black and white and then lots of gray. Speaking of gray, Elliott Gray had been meticulously taking notes and had not uttered a word. Assignments on follow-up items were discussed, and dates were set to reconvene.

There were lots of holes to fill. I had to have faith that this team of experts could plug the holes with credible, solid proof. Circumstantial evidence wasn't going to cut it.

Chapter Forty-Seven

Hannah Anne Hart

As I was unloading the multiple bags of groceries from Bo's run to the store, I couldn't help but laugh at the purchases. It was like a group of teenagers had been turned loose in the Piggly Wiggly. Along with the frozen pizzas now stacked in my freezer, there was an assortment of potato chips and various dips, fried chicken, slaw, and hot dogs. If it weren't for the ten packs of Pop-Tarts, I would have thought we were headed to a football tailgate.

The offerings of Pop-Tarts had certainly expanded since Bo was last here. I was embarrassed to admit that the chocolate chip cookie dough, pumpkin pie, and s'mores flavors were tempting, especially toasted with a slab of vanilla bean ice cream on top. Perhaps for dessert, I thought. I was making shrimp and grits for dinner tonight, Bo's favorite dish, or at least, that's what it was four decades ago.

Dinner tonight would certainly bring back many memories, especially with Maude Abbott to arrive. If she was allergic to shellfish, she could have a frozen pizza or even a Pop-Tart for all I cared. I hadn't seen her in forty years and had never forgiven her for what she did to Josh. I'll never believe that she thought Adam Abbott was that boy's father. Even the dogs in the street knew those green eyes belonged to Walt Benton.

My stock was simmering, and the stone-ground grits were slowly cooking. I was on pins and needles waiting for Walt and Bo to return from that attorney meeting. In addition to the grocery store supplies, Bo had stocked my bar with bourbon. It was "5:00 somewhere," as Bo used to say. I poured myself a glass and went to the porch.

Depending on which way my pendulum was swinging, the memories my porch resurrected either brought comfort or severe distress. My therapist had identified the trigger for these polar-opposite reactions. It was the hobby horse swing that still hung from the large oak tree in my backyard. Bo had spent hours making that horse in his workshop. I recall that he almost broke his neck securing it to the large branch.

Before Savannah's love for the Lowcountry birds blossomed, she had been obsessed with horses. Savannah didn't have dolls or doll houses but plastic horses and a miniature barn, also built by Bo.

Bo was here now, even if temporarily, and I was happy as a clam. Those anxiety demons could just climb that tree or take a ride on "Robbie Hobby," what we had called Savannah's swing. Wherever they went, they knew they were not welcome here—at least for tonight.

I was in one of my happy places, sipping my bourbon and reminiscing about the nights Bo and I had relaxed on the porch swing after finally putting Savannah to bed. I didn't hear them come in and just about jumped out of my skin when the screen porch door slammed.

"Something sure smells good. I know I'm old, but my olfactory senses must still be young—is that your secret roux?" Bo asked.

"It is," I said, taking a sip of my drink to hide my smile.

I was thankful I was sitting because I was weak at the knees by the fact that he not only remembered my roux but also our substitution for the word smell. "Olfactory senses."

One of the books we used to read nightly to Savannah was about senses and had a picture of a skunk under the word "SMELL." Bo would yell, "Shoooo—eeeey." Thereafter, if anyone mentioned the word, "smell," Savannah would start chanting "Shooooo-eeeey" over and over and over. It was cute at first. Our positive reaction had cemented this response. Going forward, we avoided the word "smell" at all costs.

"And young lady, is that a bourbon?"

"It is indeed."

"It's 5:00 somewhere," he said.

"My thoughts exactly!"

"Mind if we join you?" Bo asked.

"Please. Sit. I want to hear about the meeting."

"Walt can fill you in. I'm having a hard time with all of this."

Was detached Bo Hart getting emotional? He jumped up and the screen door slammed behind him. I guess you can't teach an old dog new tricks. Forty years later, the man still left the door wide open. But this time, I didn't scream, "Close the door! You're letting all the good air out."

Bo returned with Walt. It was like those two were long lost friends.

"So, spill the beans," I said.

"If you don't mind, can we wait on Maudie? I thought she'd be here by now," Walt said. "And I need a little liquid courage. It's been a long time."

I hadn't had bourbon before 5:00 for as long as I could remember, and I was already lightheaded.

"You OK?" I asked.

"I will be soon," Walt said. "Two down and one to go."

Walt was uncharacteristically quiet and somber. I clearly understood the emotional trauma of the day for him. He had met with lawyers about the case against Savannah, delivered the news to Cray about the death of his father, and now was about to see Maude for the first time since their summer in the Outer Banks.

"I survived Bo's return, so you'll survive Maude's too," I whispered to Walt and squeezed his hand. "Here's to liquid courage!"

I went inside and began the final preparations for dinner. I wasn't about to hold up dinner for Maude Abbott. I set the table, lit the candles, opened the wine, and was about to add the shrimp to the roux when the doorbell rang. I took a deep breath. Here we go, I thought.

I couldn't even remember what Maude Abbott looked like. I was so sad the day of Josh and Savannah's wedding in Kentucky. That day had been one big blur. The only thing I could clearly recall was it had been hotter than Hades under the large gazebo on their tobacco farm. There was no sea breeze or large oaks with drapes of Spanish moss providing any shade. That landlocked state had a tightening grip around my throat from the moment I had arrived and surrendered my baby into its arms.

When I opened the door, I almost gasped. Maude Abbott was stunning. Her auburn brown hair barely touched her shoulders; her smooth skin didn't look a day over thirty years old, and her 5'9" frame was still slender. How could I have forgotten these traits? She wore blue jeans and cowboy boots. The corduroy collar on her tartan-plaid shirt completed the look of what could have been on the cover of a *Garden and Gun* magazine.

I neglected my Southern manners. Instead of extending my arms and welcoming her with a hug, my hands were tugging on my homely, shift dress attempting to cover my gangly legs. My outdated flats seem to call more attention to them. I could have disguised this irregularity if I owned a pair of stylish boots like Maude. The insecurities I felt watching Tina Baker and Bo while standing at my locker in 7th grade bubbled up. I only hoped that my mouth wasn't gaped open.

"Hannah Anne?" Maude asked, interrupting my gaze and self-centered thoughts.

"I'm sorry. Come in Maude," as I quit pulling on my dress, giving her an obligatory hug. "It's just I haven't seen you in so long. You look wonderful," I said.

And she did. Poor Walt Benton, I thought. Poor, poor Walt.

"You are here just in time for supper. Hope you haven't eaten."

"I haven't and to be honest, I don't think I can eat one bite. I'm a ball of nerves."

I found her honesty refreshing and knew the feeling all too well.

"I understand. Did Walt tell you that Bo is here?"

"No, he pretty much just cut to the chase."

"I don't have the words to tell you how sorry I am," I said. "I loved Josh; I really did, and it wasn't just because he adored my Savannah. He was a great man and an even better father and husband. My heart is aching for you."

"Thank you, Hannah Anne. I know that none of this is easy on you either. But you and I both know that Savannah is not capable of this. If I die fighting this battle, then so be it."

"I have you in Savannah's old room. I hope that's OK."

"Anything is fine."

"Just so you know, Walt and Bo are down the hall from you."

"Well, the way I look at it, we have more important things to worry about. I found a couple of places that I am going to check out tomorrow, down by the river. I only plan to stay here tonight."

Before Maude arrived, this news would have been a welcomed relief. But, I started thinking I had been unfairly nursing a grudge all these years. Maude seemed tenderhearted, like her son.

"Well, I hope you know that you are welcome here, but I understand on all counts. Bo and Walt are on the back porch. We are having bourbon, but I have wine, tea, water—can I get you anything?"

"Actually, a glass of bourbon would be perfect. Where are my manners? I have something for you."

She reached into her large leather tote and pulled out two bottles. The label said: Abbott Farm Single Barrel.

"So, are you making bourbon now?"

"I guess you could say I'm a silent partner. The distillery is in one of our old tobacco barns. It's doing quite well."

"The boys will love this. Let's all have a glass."

Maude followed me to the kitchen. I retrieved a glass for her. She grabbed my arm.

194

"Before we go out, can you pour me a little bit?"

"Need some liquid courage?"

"Yes, I do."

I gave her a heavy pour of the Abbott Farm bourbon. She tossed it back like nobody's business.

"I'm ready," Maude said.

She was so smooth and confident, there was no way Walt sensed any apprehension.

"Hello, Walt," she said, extending her hand with her perfectly, manicured nails.

He stood up and took her hand. Then, it was like any planned response by him went up in flames. He pulled her into him for a big bear hug. He held her for a while, and I saw his shoulders shaking. It broke my heart for so many reasons. I kept my mouth shut for their moment of mutual mourning—for the son that was dead and for the love that was lost.

Chapter Forty-Eight

Walt Benton

If Hannah Anne hadn't gone to so much trouble making supper, I would have been perfectly content with the bourbon on the porch. It was dark enough that I could gaze at Maudie without her or Hannah Anne noticing, or Bo, for that matter. If he could see me, I was confident he would notice that I was smitten all over again.

Hannah Anne wouldn't be surprised. She viewed our situations similarly. But, she didn't know the depth of my anger and contempt toward Maudie all these years. It had about broken me. I thought that my heartache had been dulled by the animosity and resentment. But, when Maudie walked through the back-porch screen door, I was in the North Carolina Outer Banks all over again.

"We can't let Hannah Anne's famous shrimp and grits go to waste. Who's hungry besides me?" Bo asked.

"I am," Hannah Anne said.

Bo followed Hannah Anne into the kitchen to help with the shrimp, but I knew what he was doing. Hannah Anne's wink at me confirmed that they both thought I needed some private time with Maudie.

"You look good Maudie. Kentucky must be treating you well," I said.

"Had to get that Kentucky dig in there, didn't ya?" as she punched me on the shoulder. "Ouch! That hurt me!" she said rubbing her knuckles.

"Never were the strong one," I said. I wanted to take it back as soon as it flew out of my mouth.

"I understand your anger. I really do. But, now's not the time to open old wounds."

I couldn't answer. I was afraid some other dig would jump out. I wanted to bury the hatchet. Maudie was right. This was not the time or place. I didn't want to ruin the evening.

Thankfully, Hannah Anne and Bo reappeared announcing supper was ready. We proceeded inside.

"Walt, will you say grace, and then I'll serve the plates?" Hannah Anne asked.

"Sure," I said, swallowing hard. "Dear Lord, bless this food that we are about to eat. We thank you for our many blessings, and we thank you for Josh. We are thankful for the time we had with him. You created a fine man, and we are forever grateful."

I paused. I simply could not break down, not here, not now. I took a deep breath.

"Son, we know you are with us and will always be with us. We love you. Amen."

"Amen," Bo said. "I would like to make a toast," raising his wine glass.

We followed Bo's lead.

"Here's to Joshua Abbott. I regret that I never knew you," Bo said.

We clinked our glasses.

Bo offered to do the honors of serving the plates and that he did. I could barely see the rim around Hannah Anne's china.

"Bo, we need to save room for dessert," Hannah Anne commented at Bo's generous servings.

"I didn't know that you made a dessert," Bo said, "but nothing is better on this earth than your shrimp and grits."

After I had made enough of a dent in my plate to spare Hannah Anne's feelings, I decided now was a good time to relay the facts of the day.

"Since we are all together, I'd like to share with you what I learned today from my visit with Cray and the meeting with the lawyers."

"Hold on," Hannah Anne said. "We need more wine for this."

"I was thinking the exact same thing," Maude said. "And thanks, by the way, to all of you for what you've done so far."

"Bo is going with me next week to meet Cray. If you are still around, I'm sure he'd like to see you," I said to Maudie.

"Well, I don't know about that," Maude said, "but I sure would love to see him. The last thing I want is for my presence to interfere or cause more pain. I plan on being here as long as I can help."

"That's good because there are limitations on Cray's visitation. I'll find out tomorrow the earliest time we can schedule one," I said.

I summarized my visit with Cray, the sealed envelope containing the picture of the bald eagle, Josh's letter to Cray, the post-marked envelope showing it had been mailed from North Carolina, and Cray's note. I laid out the prosecution's case according to Rollins Bishop and told them that Bishop anticipated that the prosecution would respond that anyone could have mailed the letter.

"Whoa, Whoa," Hannah Anne said. "Why on God's green earth would Josh have someone mail a note that he could have mailed himself?"

"I agree with you, and I didn't argue with the man. I assume he would counter that Josh was on a bus heading to Beaufort when the letter was mailed."

"Hogwash. Tell me this. If Josh were planning a hit, he NEVER would have written his son in some kind of secret code implying that he may be released soon. That would be used against him. He would have made the hit, let a couple of days pass, and then sent a letter that he would be getting out soon."

"You and I are on the same page. Josh wasn't on that bus. I don't know if he hitchhiked or how he got to North Carolina, but he mailed that letter," I said.

"Well I am getting the bus schedule tomorrow for that day and check out the route from Kentucky to Beaufort," Hannah Anne said.

"We should have hired you as our private investigator. You may have missed your calling," Bo said.

"Ha! Like I told you, I've read all of Elliott Gray's books. That's what he would do."

"I think Cray was on target in the note. Now is as good a time as any to give you the real facts behind Cray's arrest. More wine, please," my voice cracking like a teenager going through puberty.

Maudie filled my glass and then squeezed my hand. How could such a small gesture represent an enormous range of feelings? Was it sympathy, empathy, comfort, support, appreciation, admiration or even after all these years, possibly still affection?

Chapter Forty-Nine

Maude Abbott

I was relieved that Hannah Anne decided to forego serving dessert. I couldn't eat another bite. My stomach had been turning flips since I walked through the door in anticipation of seeing Walt for the first time in over forty years. No doubt, the combustible emotions were flickering just below the surface. But, the recap of the lawyer meeting was like throwing gasoline on the simmering flames. It was becoming quite clear that the facts surrounding Savannah's case could be stretched and slanted—like the way I had distorted the facts to Josh when communicating my surprise that Walt Benton was his father.

Hannah Anne explained that the letter from Savannah to Josh enclosed cartoons that Cray had drawn and photos of the rookery she had taken for her photography class. She was so proud of her latest snapshots, she wanted to share them with Josh. Hannah Anne helped her select the best ones to send. Walt presented Rollins Bishop's likely retort about Hannah Anne's explanation: "You're a biased witness and you can't prove it." Everything began sinking in. This was not going to be easy.

Hannah Anne's waning spirits seemed to be temporarily energized by Walt's disclosure that Elliott Gray was a member of the defense team. I must have been living under a rock in Kentucky. In fact, it must have been a massive boulder. I had never heard of this popular author of legal thrillers, but it was like Hannah Anne knew him personally. She had a bookshelf dedicated to his works. She was confident that Elliott Gray would figure out a way to prove that the sketches Savannah referred to in her letter were not related to a hit. Walt agreed that

Hannah Anne should accompany him and Bo on the next meeting. He gratuitously added "if you're still in town, you should come too, Maudie."

Preparation for the meal, or more likely my appearance, coupled with Walt's disclosures seemed to have zapped Hannah Anne. She said she was "worn slap out" and politely excused herself. But, like a gracious Southern hostess, she had set out mugs, along with various teas and honey, for our morning coffee and asked us again if we needed anything before she "hit the hay."

Bo, Walt, and I retired to the porch for a night cap. At Bo's request, I poured the three of us a glass of Abbott Farm Single Barrel Bourbon.

"You know that I don't mind if you prefer something else. You aren't going to hurt my feelings," I said.

"You have those?" Walt asked, dryly.

He just couldn't help himself, but I did lob that one up to be slammed down my throat. Bo abruptly changed the subject.

"Tell us how this fine bourbon is named after your farm," Bo said.

"Well, I've had to change things up a bit. It was either that or go bankrupt. The Abbotts always grew burley tobacco, but with the decline in the smoking population, I diversified into dark air-cured—that's what is used in smokeless tobacco products. Then, one of Cray's friends had an old family bourbon recipe and a desire to get into the business. I had more than one barn that was sitting empty, so it is now the distillery. I converted enough acreage to grow the corn and wheat needed for the production. So, you're looking at a 25 percent owner of the Abbott label."

"You go, girl," Bo said. "Very impressive."

"I wouldn't go that far. It wasn't my idea and really a no-brainer. Kyle Abbott is probably rolling in his grave, as well as Adam. That land produced the finest quality of burley tobacco in the state; but from my point of view, if you can't sell it, it's worthless. I had the freedom to diversify, something that Adam could have never done—too much family pressure, I guess."

"It's strange how we can't just chuck the way we were raised. I'm living proof of that. Part of our blood, I suppose." Bo said.

I knew from Josh about Bo's abandonment and his rambling ways. But, the man sitting here now seemed far different. For Hannah Anne's sake, I hoped he wouldn't take off any time soon.

Before the conversation got any deeper, I thought Bo would enjoy the story about the barn that was now the distillery. I armored myself for any backlash from Walt.

"About the barn...Walt, I can't remember if you knew all the details about why Hazel was shipped off to the Outer Banks that summer," I said.

"Well, it was clear that she was a hellion; I do recall that she and your father didn't see eye to eye."

"That's an understatement. Bo, my sister and I were quite the extremes. I was a goody two-shoes and clearly Dad's favorite. That just made things worse for Hazel. She could push my dad's buttons like nobody's business. Hazel had always been a free spirit. I suppose she began resenting me, Dad, and a lot of other things."

I decided to omit the detail that I was the daughter Dad had chosen for his vehicle into the Abbott family. Dad's boss, Kyle Abbott, had one son who was destined to become "Cash Abbott, Jr.," and I, his wife.

"My father was the farm manager, so our house, or quarters, was on the farm. Hazel was friends with all the workers, which really irritated Dad. It was my job to make sure the coast was clear when she would climb out of our bedroom window at night. I could smell tobacco and bourbon on her breath when she returned. One night, Dad's boss found her in one of the barns with Jesse, one of our sharecroppers. She was 'naked and carrying on,' he reported to Dad. Needless to say, Dad hit the roof."

"Poor Hazel," Bo said, laughing. "I bet she got a nice whooping."

"Yeah. The marks on her legs lasted for days."

"Oh, I'm sorry. I didn't mean to be so crass," Bo said. "I experienced the belt many times as a kid. I'm pretty sure that was the preferred method of punishment back then."

"You're right, but that time it was like my father had gone mad. I just remember hearing the rapid slaps of that belt and Dad yelling, 'This not hurting you, girl? How about this one?' I stood outside the door crying and begging under my breath for Hazel to cry, scream, or anything that would show him that she was in pain. She didn't cry, not once. He only stopped when I ran in. I couldn't stand to hear another strike of that belt. I yelled, 'Stop it! Stop it! You're going to kill her.'"

I paused. That night was becoming clearer than it had in a long time. Walt refilled my empty glass.

"You OK?" he asked, squeezing my hand tightly. I had forgotten about Walt Benton's large hands. I wondered how his encompassing touch had escaped my memory. But, now, I remembered how these hands made me feel that night on the sand, under the stars, while they were touching my entire body. I took a big gulp of my bourbon. The fire in my throat brought me back to the present.

"So, I guess that's when she was booted to the Outer Banks. Not such a bad place, better than military school!" Bo said.

"You're right about that," as I regained my composure. "I think Dad thought she would hate it with my strict Bible-thumping aunt. Funny how things turn out. Hazel flourished there."

"She sure did," Walt said.

I decided to keep quiet that I knew from Hazel that Walt had retired to Duck, North Carolina, a quaint town in the Outer Banks. "No, I haven't seen him," Hazel offered like she had been reading my mind.

Duck was about thirty miles from Manteo, where Hazel and Kip had moved to raise their family. But Kip and Walt had stayed in touch over the years. They would meet in Nags Head and go fishing in the Oregon Inlet. Hazel had always updated me after their fishing trips. She told me that Walt always asked Kip about me. I always thought she either exaggerated that nugget of information or manufactured it altogether.

"Yes. She and Kip have three boys and a girl, Priscilla."

"Named after you." Walt said. "I recall that when Hazel first introduced you as Priscilla Maude, I thought it was such an old, dull name for a girl so cute."

I thought the bourbon must be loosening ol' Walt up.

"Apparently, my niece felt the same way. She prefers Pepper, and from the time that child could talk, she said her name wasn't Priscilla, it was Pepper. So, they finally relented. She gives Hazel a taste of her own medicine for sure."

"So, what about the barn?" Bo asked. "You need to land this plane before I'm too drunk to remember!"

"I guess I did digress a little. Yes, the barn. The barn where Kyle Abbott caught Hazel and Jesse; it's now the distillery. I thought that was the perfect use for it. I created a separate company for the distillery—Hazel's Passage, LLC. That barn changed the course of our lives. Without it, who knows what would have happened to Hazel. Now, she is content. She is a wonderful mother to four adorable children and has a husband who loves her as much today as the day they met. Plus, there was this wonderful young man named Josh who we were blessed with because of it."

It was getting kind of heavy. I suppose Bo felt like an intruder or a third wheel. He politely excused himself and said that he was interested in learning what was so captivating about Elliott Gray. He was going to borrow a book from Hannah Anne's collection and hit the sack. He proceeded inside, with the screen door slamming behind him.

"Well, now there's just two," I said. "I'm going to sit out here a while longer. I love the way this place smells. There is something incredibly calming about the salt air."

"It smells even better over here."

Walt grabbed my hand and led me to the porch swing.

"Listening to you tonight, it hit me like a ton of bricks why you went back, why you married Adam. You were a pleaser, Priscilla Maude. You were your daddy's girl, whether you wanted to be or not. You went back so Hazel could stay. Otherwise, like you said, who knows where that lost soul would have landed," Walt said.

"Yep. But instead our son ended up being the lost soul. I am so sorry."

Although I had lectured myself on the trip down to hold it together, I found myself wiping tears that were streaming from my eyes.

"We all need a good cry. Let it out Maudie," Walt said, putting his arm around me.

I placed my head on his shoulder while we rocked gently on the swing and then later on his bare chest in the bed. It had felt as fresh, real, and tender as it did the first time on the sands of the Outer Banks.

Chapter Fifty

Hannah Anne Hart

I pretended to retire to my bedroom with Elliott Gray's new legal thriller. But, after watching the sexual tension between Walt and Maude and suffering from my pent-up desires every time I laid eyes on Bo Hart, I put *Alibi* aside. I needed a romantic novel, not a legal thriller.

Bo, Walt, and Maude seemed impressed that I had read Elliott Gray's twenty books. Little did they know that my stash of Jacqueline Summers' romance novels far surpassed my Elliott Gray collection. These trash novels had sustained me over the years. Jacqueline Summers consistently portrayed scorned women who had survived. Without her books and my medication, there is no doubt I never would have been able to get out of bed. Obviously, Jacqueline Summers had suffered from lost loves. She was my real hero, not Elliott Gray.

Sadly, Jacqueline Summers was of no help to me tonight. At this moment, her similar plots about the crazy things people do for desire hit a little too close to home. Instead of escaping into her fantasy world, I was stricken with a shame of enormous proportions.

I continued to question the extent of Savannah's relationship with Charles Walker. My thoughts and actions, those that a supportive mother would never do, consumed me with guilt. I may have crossed the line in investigating my suspicions. But, they had spent a lot of time together in his room at the Ritz. I couldn't help but wonder whether they were really working the entire time.

Hired Hit on Jessamin Island

I tried not to pass judgment. I knew Savannah wasn't capable of murder. She was still young; she was beautiful, and she was in the prime of her life. She had needs just like every other woman on the planet. She needed to feel loved and wanted, just like her momma. Ironically, the man of my dreams was sleeping upstairs, and I was hunkered down with a book.

I put my book down and prayed. I prayed that if Savannah had made a grave mistake, there would be no evidence. Otherwise, she was going to jail for attempted murder that I knew from the depths of my soul she was incapable of committing. Illicit sex, maybe. Murder, not in a million years.

Even thinking that Savannah could be unfaithful to Josh kept me up most of the night. I looked at the clock what seemed like every hour. At 6:00 a.m., I finally relented to my sleeplessness and went to get coffee. Odd, I thought. Walt was always up by now. He woke up at 5:00 a.m., a military habit he explained. But, all four mugs were still on the tray.

They must have stayed up late and had too much bourbon, which made me smile. Admittedly, I had dreaded Maude's arrival. I had enjoyed the attention from Walt and Bo and knew that Maude's presence would interject a different dynamic. In fact, I hadn't wanted her here at all. But, I had been wrong about her. I realized that when I saw her standing in the doorway. I had created a false image of her in my mind all these years. Hindsight is 20/20. If only we had do-overs in this life.

I slid "Lost Love," my new Jacqueline Summers' book, under my pillow, dressed, and took Elliott Gray's new book and my coffee to the porch swing. I was quickly enthralled with his perpetual lawyer character, R.J. Barrett. I was reading about the murder when the screen door slammed and sent my coffee flying. The mug hit the floor and shattered.

"Good Lord, woman!" Bo said, as he started picking up the remains of my mug.

"You scared me to death!" I said.

"Me or Elliott Gray?" Bo asked, laughing. "I'll get you another cup."

Bo returned and sat beside me on the swing.

"Guess who didn't come in last night?" he asked, sheepishly.

"What do you mean?"

"Walt, my roommate. His bed is still made."

"Oh no. I knew this wasn't a good idea. Wonder where he went? Poor thing."

"Poor thing, hell. He's with Maude, I'm just sayin'."

"And... what are you waiting on? Do tell it."

"Well, after you left us, we went to the porch for a night cap. Maude started telling us about how her farm came to be on a bourbon label. I'll save that for later because it was a long story. Anyway, she got off track and told about the summer she met Walt. I excused myself because it was getting really deep. The tension in the air was thicker than Beaufort in August. I thought they needed some time alone. I took one of your Elliott Gray books and went to bed. I was actually surprised that I liked it. I was still reading when I heard the stairs creaking. When Walt didn't appear in our room, I did worry that things may have gone south, and he left. But that thought was only temporary. Did you know that Savannah's bed is very squeaky? It needs some serious maintenance."

"Oh, this just makes me so happy! It's as plain as the nose on my face that they are still goo-goo eyed with one another. I think it's so romantic."

Obviously, Bo wasn't interested in discussing Walt and Maude.

"I'm hungry. Can I bring you anything?" Bo asked.

"I think I'll have the dessert from last night," I said.

"What did you make, by the way?"

"Sit tight. I'll be right back."

I toasted the Pumpkin Pie–flavored Pop-Tart, heaped a scoop of vanilla bean ice cream on top and delivered it to Bo on the porch.

"Best breakfast ever!" Bo said.

And it was. I suddenly realized that I had misjudged Pop-Tarts all these years. I had also misjudged Bo Hart. I could never change him. I had to accept him for who he was—a wanderer, an explorer, a man who was an eternal tourist through life. But sadly, I knew that his independence and free spirit, though exhilarating, were also debilitating. There could never be a "happily ever after" for us. And at this moment, that was OK. I had Jacqueline Summers for that. I was just going to soak up every minute with him under my roof before he relented to the irresistible call of the wild.

Chapter Fifty-One

Walt Benton

Maudie was sleeping soundly on my chest. My arm was still around her, and my entire body was numb, especially my arm. But, I wasn't about to move it. I didn't want to wake her. I was afraid that upon awakening, she may have regrets. I worried that I was only a subconscious salve for her profound heartache. She had comforted me as well.

Our shared grief over the death of our son was engulfing, but our sexual reunion meant much more to me than support, more than consolation; it was precious, like her. However, she might view it as a mistake with the clarity of morning light. She may be remorseful.

So, I tried to lie as still as possible. I had been wide awake for over two hours, and now other parts of me were awake as well. Those parts wanted her all over again. I closed my eyes and tried to memorialize last night. I wanted to be able to hit rewind and relive it vividly—no matter where I was, no matter how old I got.

My stomach growled, sounding like an alarm clock. She stirred and lifted her head with a confused, disoriented expression.

"What time is it?" she asked, rolling over and pulling the covers up over her naked chest.

"The clock says 7:15, but it could be 8:15 if Hannah Anne hasn't set this clock back."

"Guess we're busted. Are you prepared for the walk of shame?" Maudie asked.

I felt like a dagger had been plunged into my chest. Is that truly what she felt— shame? I sat up, moved to the edge of the bed and put my feet on the floor with my back to her. I surveyed the room. Shame? Shame was far from what I was feeling right now. Where were my pants?

"Hey, what are you doing?" she asked.

"Getting ready for the walk of shame," I said, curtly.

"Oh Walt, I'm sorry. It's just an expression. I didn't mean it that like."

She wrapped her arms around my waist and planted kisses on my neck.

There was no masking the fact that I had woken up full of desire. In the past, my full erectness in the morning validated my manhood—that I still had it and that my innate cravings hadn't been smothered by my loneliness. But now, it seemed a little unfair that my emotions were right out there in the open. Transparency was an understatement. Her kisses and touching made it even worse.

"About last night..." I began, as I unleashed her arms.

"Perfect?" she asked. She turned my face around, leaned in, and kissed me gently. "Come here."

I moved back into the bed, and she rolled on top of me.

The night before, we reacquainted ourselves and consoled each other. We were intimate, exploring, gentle. This morning, Maude was full of raw desire, and I had been thinking about her for hours. The loud squeaking and knocking of the bed muffled my moans. I was more than embarrassed that our morning reunion ended so quickly.

"Sorry," I said. "Rather selfish of me. This bed probably woke up the entire neighborhood."

"Who cares?" she said, laughing.

"I'm starving," I said. "I want the dessert that we missed last night."

"Oh really?" she said and began kissing me again. "I'd like to serve it to you."

She wrapped her legs over my shoulders and pulled my head toward her stomach. I more than willingly obliged. She placed a pillow over her face to drown out her whimpers. Her body was shaking with excitement.

"Well, you still got it, old man. I don't think I can take the walk of shame. I'm not sure I can walk at all!"

"I'll bring you a cup of coffee and take the hit from the front lines downstairs. Be right back."

Before heading down to face the looks and comments from Bo and Hannah Anne, I stopped into the bathroom and scrubbed my face with soap. Thankfully, Bo was sitting alone at the table reading the newspaper.

"You look like you've been freshly fucked," Bo said. "Guess you've already had dessert, or I'd offer you the dessert Hannah Anne planned for last night—a pumpkin pie Pop-Tart with ice cream. That was what WE had for breakfast," he smirked.

"Interesting, right now I need a cup of Joe," as I headed into the kitchen laughing to myself about Bo's comments and thinking if only he knew.

I fixed two mugs.

"Where's Hannah Anne?" I asked.

"She's taking a shower. We got tired of waiting on you two love birds. We are going to visit Savannah. It's time she gets to know her old man. Afterward, we are making a grocery store run. Hannah Anne is planning another dinner tonight with a homemade dessert, banana pudding, her specialty, unless you've had enough already."

Bo was clearly wanting details or even a hint of what had transpired between Maudie and me. But, I wasn't going to kiss and tell.

"She doesn't need to go to all that trouble," I said. "I can pick up something."

"Oh, I think she is in heaven being able to cook. It lifts her spirit. And, it sounds like we need to hit the hardware store. That bed needs a serious dose of WD-40."

He offered up a fist pump, which I returned. Suddenly, I couldn't suppress the grin from my face.

"I'm proud of ya, bud," Bo said.

"Maybe it's time for you to get your head out of your rambling ass," I said, and proceeded back up the stairs.

"How'd it go?" Maudie asked, still laying in the bed.

"Other than Bo commenting on my 'freshly fucked' appearance, that the bed needs a 'serious dose of WD-40,' and that I had dessert for breakfast, it was fine," handing her the coffee mug.

"Good Lord! Bo seriously said those things in front of Hannah Anne?"

"No, she is taking a shower. She apparently got tired of waiting on the 'love birds' to wake up. They are going to visit Savannah and then shop for dinner supplies."

"How about you and I go shopping for different accommodations? There are a couple of lovely inns downtown that I'd like to check out," Maudie said.

"I like that idea. I think this bed needs more than a little WD-40."

"I'm thinking that it needs you. I need your arms around me again. There, I go back to better times, blissful times."

Her statement reinforced my thoughts that we had needed the comfort of that magical summer before real life sucker punched us in the gut. No parent is supposed to outlive their child. I knew she was especially vulnerable right now. Her pain needed soothing. She needed a distraction. I ached over Josh's death in a profound way, but it wasn't a new pain. It was the pain that I had been suffering daily with what seemed like the death of Maudie over the last forty years. I had finally written off our summer romance as merely the result of youthful exuberance, naïveté, and stimulations of the salt air.

While no longer young or naïve, I hoped the magical influence of sea breezes that had brought us together nearly four decades ago were powerful enough to reunite us. This time for good.

Chapter Fifty-Two

Maude Abbott

While taking a long, hot shower, I questioned my boldness in suggesting that Walt stay with me somewhere else. On the other hand, time was of the essence. Losing Josh made me realize I couldn't take love for granted.

I could only stay a couple of weeks here, and I wasn't going to leave Beaufort without making amends and testing the emotional waters. These waters had traveled many miles since that summer on the Outer Banks. They had weathered us and pulled us apart. I wondered if their gradual corrosive power over the past forty years had eroded any hope of a reunion.

I closed my eyes and let the water beat down on my face. Last night was wonderful, but this morning was just WOW. Our bodies emanated heat and welcomed our uninhibited lovemaking. If last night was any barometer, our waters had finally merged into a peacefully flowing river that could help soothe my incredible grief over the death of our only son.

There was no more perfect place for us to spend time together than on the Beaufort River. Josh had loved his time on the river and the surrounding waters that summer, the summer when he not only met Walt for the first time but also sweet Savannah. From my research, my first choice was The Admiral, an antebellum house that predated the revolution and now a popular bed and breakfast. The inn had undergone a massive update—the large rooms had four-poster beds and marbled baths. It boasted 1,000 square feet of porches, all with river views. Within walking distance, there was a coffee shop and café, tavern, seafood grill, and even an Italian bistro.

Walt agreed. No need to look any further. He booked a waterfront room. We christened it appropriately before strolling down Main Street hand in hand. We were dreading the unavoidable visit to the Cypress Wetlands. Savannah had chosen the location for Josh's memorial service. The service was tomorrow.

Chapter Fifty-Three

Hannah Anne Hart

I had reservations about Bo accompanying me to visit Savannah. Now was not the time for her to become reacquainted with her father, I thought. She was dealing with more than enough. But, the look in his eyes reflected more than a resounding plea, it was a look of desperation. I had said "no" too many times to count. It was time.

Over the years, I had pushed my inner turmoil aside for the sake of my daughter. I suppose I had developed a strength that I didn't recognize or appreciate. But when my daughter was delivered to us with handcuffs around her wrists and in an orange jumpsuit, whatever strength I had mustered over the years flew right out the barred windows. Her aquamarine eyes had returned to the gray abyss when she arrived at my door from Kentucky. Then, she noticed the man standing in the corner, and her demeanor changed. She instantly knew that her father was there. Her expression turned from despair to elation.

Bo and I discussed that he would wait until I introduced him at the appropriate time, but he couldn't help himself. He ran up to the window and with tears rolling down his cheeks, he yelled through the glass, "Baby, baby, my baby."

I allowed the two of them to become reacquainted. Savannah was on an emotional tilt-a-whirl. It hurt not to be able to hug her. I let her sobs and tears subside. I waited for Bo to pull himself together. Then, we began to discuss her case.

"So, what do you think about your lawyer?" I finally asked.

"He's no nonsense. He is not going to rely on Charles' team of lawyers. He has always done his own homework. I really like him."

"What did he say about your letter, honey?" I asked.

"What letter?"

"The letter to Josh where you enclosed the sketches and photos."

"Yeah. What about it?"

"The prosecution says that the photos you sent Josh were of Alice Walker and the Jessamin Island house, and the sketches referred to in your letter were maps detailing how to enter the house—you know, instructions for the hit."

"That's ridiculous. I sent him Cray's cartoons for Charles' presentation. The photos, well Mom, you know those were pictures of the rookery and the sunset for my photography class."

"I know that. But how can we prove it?"

"There must be some record of what I sent. I told Mr. Dixson that if I understood things correctly from Cray and Josh, all incoming mail is reviewed."

If anyone was listening to our conversation, one thing Savannah didn't mind the guards knowing was that her lawyer was a bulldog, and he would get to the bottom of the mail sent into the prison. But, I had already heard of too many ways these so-called law-abiding officials twist the facts.

"Yes. Unless there isn't," I said. "We need to think of another way."

"This is all so crazy. I just keep thinking of all the innocent people whose lives have been turned upside down by our legal system. Look at Cray, for heaven's sake. I am never getting out of here. You need to accept it too."

"Hush your mouth! Can't never could," I said. "You have to focus on your case and think about every teensy fact. Earl Dixson is counting on it. He can't unravel these pieces on his own. He needs for you to be strong; we need you, and, more than ever, Cray needs you."

"Your mother's right, darling," Bo said. "I have let y'all down for many, many years. Now's not the time for apologies, lame excuses, or justifications from me.

I'm here to try to make it right going forward. We've still got a lot of life to live and a lot of lost time to make up. It's time for the Harts to kick some ass. For us to do that, we need you and your spunk on our side. We need you to fight. No daughter of mine would give up. You will get out of here. I won't accept anything else."

The first Hart family reunion was more than memorable. Admittedly, a jail is not the same as a picnic with checkered tablecloths, casseroles, fried chicken, and my famous banana pudding; but it was our reunion, and it was great. We were reunited and united on our mission to save Savannah from injustice.

When we were leaving, Bo promised to visit often, and for the first time, I really believed he may stay in one spot for a while. But, the proof was in the pudding.

I had several missed calls on my phone from Walt. I was happy that there was a diversion from the meeting with Savannah. Bo seemed all out of sorts. I handed Bo the written directions for the grocery.

"You know you can use your phone for that," he said, as he punched in the address.

"Guess I haven't caught up with all the technology. Everything I need is in a five-mile radius of home. That's where we're different."

"Touché," Bo said, clearly getting my uncharacteristic dig.

Walt must be rubbing off on me, I thought. But, it seemed to have served him well. He and Maude had booked a room at The Admiral, only the most elegant and historic B&B on the river.

"I have a message from Walt. He wants to treat us to lunch. He and Maude are at the Salamander Grille drinking Bloody Marys."

"I'm game. I need a drink, a stiff one," Bo said. "It's so hard to see Savannah in that place," his voice cracking.

I wondered how it was that Walt and Maude had already located two of my favorite places in the city. My envy was greener than Walt Benton's eyes.

"You probably don't have written directions there. I'm going to teach you something today," Bo said.

He handed me his phone and gave me a tutorial on how to use the map app and locate the Salamander Grille. Not only did turn-by-turn directions begin booming from his phone, but there were pictures of the specials of the day. The Pop-Tart à la mode had long worn off. As the tensions from our visit with Savannah subsided, I was ready for Lowcountry gumbo and a crab cake.

What I wasn't ready for was the gushy state of Maude and Walt. I was witnessing an abrupt transformation. The anger and resentment that hung in the air last night had evaporated. Now, they stood united leaning on each other for support, physical support. They couldn't keep their hands off each other. I needed more than a Bloody Mary to endure this lunch. It had been enough for me to hear Bo's rendition of the squeaky bed.

The Bloody Mary reigned in my jealousy. I was happy for Walt and Maude. If anyone deserved happiness, it was Walt. He had been such a calming influence over the years. I loved hearing them rave about my town and the shops they visited on Main Street. They also thought that the Cypress Wetlands was perfect for Josh's service. Walt was working out the details. I thanked him again for making the arrangements for the service and retaining Savannah's attorney, Earl Dixson.

"Savannah likes him," I told Walt. "She trusts him. I like the fact that he isn't going to ride on the coattails of Charles Walker's team of suits. He is looking out for Savannah's interest."

"How is Savannah holding up?" Walt asked.

"Well to be honest, she didn't look so hot until she saw Bo. Then, she lit up like a Christmas tree."

"How's Bo doing?" Walt asked, directing his question to Bo.

"Alright, under the circumstances. Savannah's quite special."

"I'd like to visit her," Maude said.

"She'd love that," I said. "I'll add finding out about the visitation rules to my to-do list."

"What else is on your list?" Bo asked.

"Well, I researched the bus route from the supposed bus station where Josh boarded for Beaufort. The stop in Jessamin Island was the stop immediately prior to Beaufort. Unless Rollins Bishop miscommunicated the facts from the prosecution's case, why did Josh get off on Jessamin Island? Why didn't he just proceed on to Beaufort? So, I am making a list of questions for Rollins Bishop and Elliott Gray. I know Josh wasn't on that bus. And, I don't think Charles Walker and his wife are happily married. I know y'all will think it's either the Bloody Mary talking, or all the Elliott Gray books I've read, but my instincts are telling me that this was a setup, pure and simple."

"Setup, by whom?" Walt asked.

"Charles Walker's wife, of course."

"No more Elliott Gray books for you," Walt declared.

"Not so fast. I'm buying this theory," Bo asserted. "Y'all know that Hannah Anne was the Valedictorian of her class. Keep going with your theory. And another round," he said to the bartender.

I decided that I was no longer going to sugarcoat anything. All the facts needed to be on the table. I told them about the conference and Savannah's help with her boss' presentation, the topic being changed at the last minute, Walker's wife bailing on the trip, and his offer of their Jessamin Island home as a place to recover from the shock of learning the news of Josh's purported suicide.

"The house is apparently on the rental market most of the time. He even had to call to see if it was available," I said, as I continued to espouse my theory. "If Savannah was supposed to have anything to do with a murder in that house, there is absolutely no way she would have stayed there, particularly not the night after this supposed hit was to be made. And, she would have never let me step foot in it. No one else had knowledge of the details of that home but Charles Walker and his wife. I only met him briefly, but that man wouldn't have set Savannah up like that. So that leaves his wife."

"I'm going to call Earl and ask him if he knows about any of these details," Walt said and stepped out to call Savannah's lawyer.

"Let me understand this," Bo said. "You think the wife put a hit on herself?"

"Yes, I do."

"Why?" Bo asked.

"Because she wanted her husband to rot in jail. I won't tell you the things I've thought about doing to you all these years," I said.

"Ouch!" Bo said. "I guess that means I better stop eating your cooking, woman."

"I like your theory and don't call me Rollins Bishop, but how would his wife have the connections to pull this off?" Maude asked.

"That's what we need to explore. Who knows? She may have been screwing a police officer on the side for all we know. Y'all need to read more."

"That's just it," Bo said. "You read too much. Those are fiction books, ya know."

"Truth is stranger than fiction, so they say," I said.

Walt returned and reported that Earl was a step ahead of us. He had copies of the purported hit instructions. He was going to bring them to our next meeting. If we want a preview beforehand, he said we could come by his office.

"Let's go," I said to Bo.

"But I'm starving. Can we eat first?" Bo asked.

"Here," I said, dumping the bar nuts in his hand.

"We'll go by the seafood market, pick up dinner, and more wine," Maude said. "We'll meet you back at the house."

I gave her a hug and whispered in her ear, "Don't forget the whipped cream. You'll probably need it later at The Admiral."

"Great idea," Maude said, winking at me.

Bo handed me his phone to test my recall on his map app tutorial. I punched in Earl Dixson and nothing came up.

"Try Dixson law firm," Bo said, laughing.

"Smarty-pants," I said, as the navigation voice directed us to Earl Dixson's office.

"Got any mints?" I asked. "I smell like a Bloody Mary."

"Here's a nut for the nut," Bo said, sharing one peanut from the bar snacks that I had dumped into his hand. "I'm just glad that you're my nut."

Most people wouldn't view Bo's comment as a romantic gesture, but, for some reason, it made my insides quiver. I had no comeback. I looked out the passenger window so Bo couldn't see that I was grinning from ear to ear.

Chapter Fifty-Four

Walt Benton

Maude and I perused the menu, but I wasn't hungry for food.

"How about we pick up some filets and tuna steaks for dinner and bypass lunch? That is, here."

"What do you have in mind?" Maude asked.

When she began stroking my thigh, I knew that she knew exactly what I was thinking. She kissed my neck.

"Let's get out of here. To room 314."

All I can say is that I was relieved that there were no other guests close to Room 314. Maude had unbuckled and unzipped my pants before the elevator doors opened to the third floor. After we entered our room, I was impressed with my dexterity, slowly unbuttoning her shirt and removing her pants while our mouths were glued together. My shirt was still on when we were done.

"That's a first," Maude said. "But now you're all wrinkled. You're going to have to change unless you want to a get another ribbing from Bo."

"It will take more than a new shirt. This calls for a shower, and unless you want a ribbing from Bo, you need one too."

I led Maude into the shower. We washed the lingering smells of wild sex from our bodies, which about ended us back in the bed.

But, we had dinner to buy and an update to hear from the meeting among Hannah Anne, Bo, and Earl.

Chapter Fifty-Five

Bo Hart

Hannah Anne was definitely on her "A" game in Earl Dixson's office. My wife continued to amaze me. Yes, she was still technically my wife. I was in and out of so many states over the years that I never got around to filing for divorce. Hannah Anne hadn't pursued one either.

I began thinking that the house still had to be in the names of Beauregard and Hannah Anne Hart. I had sent enough money to provide for her and Savannah over the years, but I knew that it wasn't money she wanted. It was me. It was a father for Savannah. But, you can't turn back the hands of time, as Hannah Anne would say. She talked like an old lady. It was part of her charm. She was one of a kind, for sure. She was irreplaceable, and I loved her. I just didn't know how to show it.

In fact, the only thing that I did know was how to adapt to new situations. My whole life, my family had hopped from city to city and state to state. I was always the new boy in a new school. I definitely knew how to do that. I never had time to get close enough to anyone to reveal my true colors. Hell, I didn't even know what my true colors were. I just knew how to make a good first impression. I was never around long enough for the second or third one. But Hannah Anne loved me through and through. I did know that. I just couldn't figure out why.

Earl Dixson showed us the photos allegedly found in Josh's duffle bag. Hannah Anne recognized the Walker's home on Jessamin Island—Tara's Cove. Savannah had told her it had been named after the Walker's daughter, who had died tragically in a car accident. There was a shot of the house from the front, the side, the back, and even portions of the yard. There were also several photos of Alice Walker. A red arrow made with a sharpie pointed to a rock in a landscaped area in the backyard. Written instructions, also said to be found in Josh's bag, included the address to the cottage, Alice Walker's arrival and departure times, and methods of access into the home.

> Option #1 is the back door. The entry is hidden from the neighbors. The key to the back door is in the rock (see photo). Option #2 is the front door. It has a keyless entry with a digital combination lock. The code is 6290 ##. The # must be entered 2x. The door will unlock after entering the code.

Upon reading these instructions, Hannah Anne sounded like a drill sergeant issuing orders.

"You need to find out from Charles' attorneys the name of the rental agency. Call them and find out the rental schedule of that house and when the code was changed. And question their maintenance guy about a hide-a-key."

Earl Dixson was taking notes.

"First of all, the vacation home is apparently rented most of the time," Hannah Anne told Dixson. "Charles Walker didn't even know if the house was available when he offered it to Savannah and me. He had to call the rental agency to find out. And when he called, he learned that the door code had been changed," Hannah Anne said, emphatically. "He didn't even know where the hide-a-key was located. So, he is either a really good actor or there is no way he typed those instructions. If he didn't know how to get into his house, there is no way Savannah did. This was planned by Alice Walker, I guarantee you that."

"Anything else?" Earl Dixson asked, looking up from his yellow legal pad.

"Yes, get the bus schedule the day Josh was released. And confirm the passengers. I researched the bus route from the supposed bus station where Josh boarded. There was a stop on Jessamin Island before its final stop in Beaufort. Why did Josh get off the bus? Why did he check into a hotel? And a hotel that is only twenty miles from Beaufort?"

"I need to put you on the payroll," Earl Dixson said, "I like your instincts."

As I was filling in Walt and Maude about the meeting, they agreed that it all sounded suspicious, but it was a little far-fetched that Alice Walker would contrive a hit on herself to frame her husband.

"I don't think a jury will buy it. The prosecution's theory of an affair between Savannah and Charles is a more believable scenario. We all know that the spouse is always the first suspect. But, I am beginning to buy Hannah Anne's theory. If not Charles and Savannah, who else would have a motive other than Alice Walker?" Walt said.

"I know we are supposed to have a united defense, but what about Charles Walker?" I asked.

"I was thinking the same thing," Maude said. "Perhaps he has a mistress or just hates his wife, but I think we need to have Earl explore the Walkers' relationship."

"Or maybe Alice Walker was cheating, and he found out about it," I said. "I know I probably don't deserve an opinion in any of this, but I think we need to be cautious in sharing information with Walker's lawyers. Our sole focus should be on Savannah."

"Are you suggesting that Charles Walker wanted to knock off his wife and used Savannah to help establish his defense?" Hannah Anne asked.

"The thought crossed my mind today when you were spouting off all the details about the key and the door code," I said. "I don't want to sound like the Atlanta big gun or anything, but all of Walker's so-called lack of knowledge about how to get into his own house seems too convenient. It could have been calculated—a charade so he would have a witness that could testify that he didn't know the facts in those hit instructions. Does anyone besides me find it strange that a bank president would invite his assistant and her mother to a posh resort and then offer his vacation home at the time that his wife was supposed to be murdered?"

"All possible scenarios, if someone else was the hit man," Hannah Anne said. "But the evidence is that Josh was the hired gun. Charles Walker didn't know Josh. And even if he did, why on earth would he involve his assistant's husband? That doesn't make sense unless Savannah is involved, which we know she isn't. We are on the same page about that, right?"

"Of course we are," Walt said, with no hesitation.

I would never admit it to Hannah Anne or anyone else. But, I was getting this uneasy feeling about my daughter. I'm not proud of the fact that I knew my daughter the least of those around the dinner table, but this lack of knowledge gave me a clear, open-mindedness lacking from the others. And I had seen worse over the years.

I hoped I was wrong. If I was right, I would lose my wife forever into a darkness that even the water surrounding her utopia couldn't heal.

Chapter Fifty-Six

Hannah Anne Hart

It was so nice of Walt and Maude to bring dinner, but I had lost my appetite for anything but the wine. It had been a long, stressful day starting with the visit with Savannah. I kept telling myself the source of the pit in my stomach was Savannah's situation. I knew in my heart that she had nothing to do with any of this—even if Charles Walker had become more than her boss.

I knew, all too well, the ache of desire. I wanted desperately to be touched, to feel a man's hands on my body, and to feel loved. The yearning for Bo all these years was exacerbated in the present by lovey-dovey Walt and Maude. They may as well have been pouring salt in my wounds.

I barely touched my food. I had no room for food because I had a fire in my belly. Walt and Maude had advanced past bourbon-sipping chatter on the porch swing. They had a waterfront room at The Admiral. They were going to be holding and comforting each other all night long. Walt and Maude were discussing The Admiral's nightly activity—a fire and reading of poetry.

"Please come with us," Maude said. "You've had a long day; this will be relaxing. It will help take your mind off everything."

I tried to fight back tears and lied about a headache, blaming it on the Bloody Mary and lack of lunch. I politely excused myself from the table.

"Don't worry about the dishes. I'll get them later. I don't want you to miss the event," I said. "Bo, poetry may not be your thing, but The Admiral is just lovely. A great bar to boot with a wide selection of bourbons—worth the visit."

"Come with me," Bo said.

"I'm going to bed," I said. "I'll see y'all tomorrow."

Lying was not my forté. When I reached my room, my mind must have willed a sickness because I didn't feel so hot. I needed to focus on the next day's service for Josh. I needed to review the remarks Savannah had given me to read at the service, but I was simply spent. I turned on my noise machine, got in bed, and placed a cold washcloth over my eyes. I listened to my machine simulating the ocean's crashing waves, helping my anxiety float away.

Seconds later, I thought I must be delirious. I felt an arm around my waist. But the wet kisses on my neck made me flinch. The man I had longed for every waking day was now beside me. I felt like a turtle, retracting myself into a hard shell. The hard shell was what had protected me all these years and kept me from cracking. Why couldn't I reciprocate his advances? Perhaps it was my survival instincts kicking in. I froze and was as stiff as a stone, an immovable hard-hearted rock. I didn't move. My room darkened. Bo must have turned off the light when he relented and left my room.

Chapter Fifty-Seven

Hannah Anne Hart

As usual, I woke up at 1:00 a.m. Normally, I would fall back to sleep by 3:00 a.m. Not tonight, I remained wide awake. My noise machine with its calming ocean sounds didn't even come to my rescue. At 4:30 a.m., I gave up hope of falling back to sleep. I got up, fixed a cup of coffee, and took Savannah's remarks for the service to the porch. The service was today. I couldn't put this off any longer.

I nearly fell out of the porch swing when I read that the rookery at the Cypress Wetlands was the location of my grandson's conception. I recalled the day as vividly as if it were yesterday.

Savannah had a three-hour break between her job as a docent at the Beaufort History Museum before reporting to The Port Royal Ice Castle, her evening job during tourist season. For as long as I could remember, she felt responsible for me, instead of the other way. She was astute and wise beyond her years. She didn't know the exact reason that I was under my bed covers that day, but she sensed that an episode was looming. During these episodes, I wouldn't emerge from my bed for days.

My breakdown was precipitated by one of Bo's unpredictable phone calls. He was going to "be in the area."

"Since I am so close, I thought it would be a convenient time to drop by. I need to catch a glimpse of Savannah."

"In the area," "a convenient time," "catch a glimpse," Bo's tactless words sent me into the stratosphere. He thought he could simply "drop by" and check the Father-of-the-Year box. So, when my sweet-to-her-core daughter invited me to Cypress Gardens for bird watching before her second job of the day, I told a little white lie.

"That sounds delightful," I said, "but I took your advice and volunteered at the library."

Savannah knew that I was a book worm and had politely nudged me to get out of the house and do something for myself. "Books give you pleasure. Call the library and see if they have an opening, and if not, ask if you can volunteer in some way. It may lead to something more," Savannah urged.

Like I said, she was wise beyond her years. My daughter was the ultimate cheerleader to boost my insecurities, my failures. I couldn't tell her that her encouragement made me feel worse. It was a role reversal that embarrassed me. I was the mother. I was the one who should be encouraging my daughter.

"That's wonderful!" she said, excitedly. "I am so proud of you. I can't wait to hear about it."

"You should go anyway," I advised. "I know you love bird watching. Can you find another friend?"

"I wanted to ask my best girlfriend first," she said. "But, I'll see if Josh wants to go. I know Kentucky's birds can't hold a candle to our Lowcountry species."

"Of course, they don't. There's only one paradise, and it's right here."

I knew then that my daughter was smitten with Josh Abbott. He was very good-looking, but I knew from experience that looks didn't make a man. I reminded myself that my infatuation with Bo Hart, Savannah's father, and my first and only love was not the same as Savannah's obvious crush on the visitor from Kentucky. I found relief that Josh was only here for the summer. When he returned home, Savannah would move on.

I should have accompanied Savannah to the Cypress Wetlands that day. I didn't go to the library for any volunteer job. I was in the bed with one of my Jacqueline Summers' novels in my attempt to forget Bo's call, his request for a "glimpse" of his daughter.

Now, when reading Savannah's remarks for the memorial service, I felt green around the gills. Her comments were difficult enough to bear. But, it was her revealing the significance of her selected location for the memorial service that took my breath away—the rookery.

If I had gone with her that day, the course of our lives may have turned out differently. But, I had lied about a job, refused her father's request to visit, and curled up in bed with a romance novel. My self-pity had sparked this irreparable chain of events.

I must have drifted off to sleep on the swing. The slam of the porch screen was equivalent to an alarm clock. Bo had a Pop-Tart in one hand and mug of coffee in the other.

"You're up early," I said, sheepishly.

Surprisingly, I didn't feel awkward in Bo's presence, which was part of the reason I was up most of the night. I had fantasized about what could have transpired if I had not pretended to be asleep when he came into my room. I had endeavored to drift off into a deep sleep, a dream state that altered the ending of the previous evening—where I welcomed Bo's touch, where I returned the favor, where we reconnected completely, and where we were like Walt and Maude.

"I couldn't sleep. How about you?" he asked, interrupting my morning fantasy.

"What do you mean?" I asked, in a confused frame of mind and unsure of his previous question. I was still imagining what could have been, what should have been.

"How did you sleep?" he asked.

Perhaps I was paranoid. But, there was something in the tone of his question that intimated a hint of suspicion—like he knew that I faked being asleep when he laid down beside me and kissed my neck.

I wanted to say, I didn't sleep a wink. All I could think about was you. How about we go back to bed and start over? How about we hold each other tightly and ... Bo interrupted my thoughts again.

"Hello? Where did you go? I asked how you slept?"

I took a deep breath and ditched my thoughts.

"Great," I lied. "I think I must have crashed as soon as my head hit the pillow. I guess all this stress finally wore me down. I need some more coffee. Can I get you another cup?"

"It's going to take more than this coffee to get me though the day. Will you grab that Abbott Farm bottle of bourbon?"

"Good idea," I said, hoping the burn from the alcohol would replace the burning of my whole being, the intense desire I had for him.

When I returned to the porch with the bourbon and two glasses, Bo was sitting on the swing reading Savannah's eulogy. He abruptly brushed his face, attempting to eliminate evidence of his tears.

"It's beautifully sad, isn't it?"

"Can I speak at the service? I wish I had known him. I want to tell him that."

"Of course, you can," as I gave us both a generous pour from the bottle.

The glisten in Bo's aquamarine eyes was debilitating. I sat beside him on the swing before my legs buckled from beneath me. I took a healthy gulp from my glass. I needed the sting from its bite. When Bo put his arm around me, my heart felt weak from the intensity of its pounding. I seriously may faint, I thought. I rested my head on his shoulder.

"Savannah's quite a poet," he said, breaking the silence. "I keep a journal when I travel, and it contains a poem or two. Guess we have something in common."

"You have a lot of creativity in you; you made Robbie Hobby," pointing at the swing still hanging from the oak tree. "And her barn, remember that? Instead of a doll house, she wanted a barn for her horses."

"I had forgotten all about the barn."

"You have many talents, Bo. If you stayed in one place for a while, you could put them to use."

These memories triggered my pain from his desertion and squelched my desire for him. I patted him on the leg.

"I've got to shower and finish my remarks for the service."

I stood up without looking at him. My emotions were flip-flopping like a fish out of water. I was afraid that my current resentment would revert to craving him all over again. I let the screen door slam behind me. Later, we rode in silence to the funeral service.

I had asked Walt to start the service and was thankful for that. I didn't want to go first. The memorial needed to start on a strong note from a strong man. I worried that my emotions would get the best of me, and I wouldn't be able to utter a single word through my sobs. My angst had begun this morning with Bo. Now, I was dealing with a bundle of emotions. My faith in Walt was confirmed when he started the service with his strong voice.

We are gathered here today to remember Joshua Carter Abbott, wonderful husband, father, and son," Walt said. The 34th Psalm says, "*The Lord is close to the brokenhearted and saves those who are crushed in spirit.*"

We all are very sad that you are no longer with us, but we have faith that our crushed spirits will be healed with your spirit. Your loving spirit. Your trusting spirit. Your loyal spirit. Everyone you met was touched by all those things. I love you, son. I look forward to the day we will meet again."

Walt then sprinkled some of Josh's ashes on the patch of moss underneath the cypress trees that comprised the rookery in the Cypress Wetlands.

"This is hard. So hard. I love you so much," Maude paused, her voice quivering.

I didn't think she was going to be able to continue. She was struggling to maintain her composure. On second thought, I should have asked Bo to follow Walt. But, I had reasoned that Maude was his mother, and Bo didn't even know Josh. Walt grabbed Maude's hand. His squeeze was so strong, I could see the veins bulging in his hand. Walt's encouragement helped. She took a couple of deep breaths, and thankfully, she regained control. She continued:

Your beautiful green eyes were always so full of life and joy. The innocence and gentleness that rippled through you from the day you were born developed into currents, then swells, as you grew into the man that you were. I failed to tell you how proud I was of you. You spent grueling hours in the hot sun farming land about which you didn't care. It was what you thought was right, what you were supposed to do for your family. You sacrificed so much but didn't load your son with your burdens. You set him free. You always encouraged Cray to pursue his own dreams. You were selfless. And the love you had for Savannah was unparalleled. You taught me so much, and I am forever grateful to you, my son. I love you.

Maude sprinkled some of the ashes in the same soft spot on the green moss. She passed the urn to Bo and clutched Walt's hand. Walt handed her a starched-white handkerchief from the pocket of his equally starched white button-down. Bo passed the urn to me and began unfolding a piece of paper from his shirt pocket. I was surprised that he had prepared written remarks. I also was surprised to see tears glistening on his long eyelashes.

I have lots of regrets in my life, but the biggest is that I never knew you. I do find great comfort in knowing that you loved my daughter from the moment you first saw her. As a father, there is no greater hope for your child than that they find true love. Your love for your family is honorable and powerful. Though we never met, you taught this crusty ol' man a thing or two. I am grateful to Hannah Anne for including me in this remembrance. Rest in peace.

Bo returned his paper to his pocket, took the urn, and sprinkled some more of the ashes on the ground.

At that moment, an egret soared over us. I was overcome with the presence of Josh. I scrapped my prepared remarks. I wanted to talk to him. I began:

Granted, we got off to a rocky start, but you know how much I loved you. You promised me that Savannah would return to her magical homeplace, and she did. That promise gave me strength and great comfort. But, my comfort was based on the belief that you would accompany her. We would create great memories fishing in the creeks, walking on the beach, and watching the birds. But, I will now find a different kind of comfort. When I see an egret soaring over a pond or majestically standing still on the water's edge, I will think of you. You will always be with us.

I sprinkled ashes on the soft patch of moss, handed the urn to Bo, and returned to my script, unfolding the papers.

"Savannah wrote these words for you and I am humbled to read them."

Bo put his arm around my shoulder and gave it a reassuring squeeze.

Dearest Josh: I can recall so clearly the day you appeared at the Royal Ice Castle. You later said you didn't notice that I was blushing when you paid me for the rainbow snow cone and then asked, 'How much more for a date?' That summer, I learned a lot about you. I learned that when you arrived, you were confused and broken. But, your eyes never exhibited your internal pain. You were strong; you were tender; you were you. And you always did what you thought was best for your family. You were so unselfish, so giving. I have been struggling with so many emotions, mostly anger. A resentment that you spent your last days unjustly imprisoned, steel bars restraining you from freedom and from your family. But my fury subsides when I think about the fact that family, your extended family, was what put you there. You always treated your workers with absolute respect. You toiled beside them every day. You were loyal to them. You lived and died because of that loyalty. That is the part of your soul that I loved so much. I requested that some of your ashes be spread in the rookery of the Cypress Wetlands, where I am certain Cray was conceived. I'll never forget the day we spent hours watching the birds. You had never seen buntings, oystercatchers, terns, or herons. Egrets were your favorite. You loved how they would soar and glide so effortlessly through the sky, and in their stillness, how they were graceful and noble. Egrets represent purity. They are caring and nurturing. It's no wonder that the egret is Cray's favorite bird to paint, and with every stroke of his brush, you will be with us. When Cray and I are reunited, we will celebrate you again. Until then, we are keeping the rest of you safe and secure. We love you. We will miss you every single day. I will love you forever and ever.

I noticed the egret again, now resting in the cypress tree. Maude saw it too. She elbowed Walt, cocking her head in the bird's direction. I turned to the magnificent bird and directed my remaining comments to it.

Savannah told me that she has begun writing poetry. The writing is therapeutic and gives her peace. She was hesitant to share her scribbles, as she calls her poems. You all know how modest she is. But she reluctantly shared one that she calls 'Survival.' I want to read it for Josh.

Survival

The sun eventually arrives after a storm, even after a hurricane.
I'm sitting at the edge of the world,
With the wilderness of the marsh surrounding me.
The vastness of nothing but the bluest sky,
With the cypress trees soaring above the wetlands.
The ripples of the water now harmonize with nature.
Before the stillness returned, the waters continued rising,
until they suffocated this estuary.
The tall blades of boundless green must have felt like I do now,
Attempting to keep their tips above the rising flood,
Gasping for air, before drowning.
My future is as murky and bleak as this spot under four feet of water.
But, the marsh survived and returned to its glory.
I am trying to soak up its perseverance and rebirth.
I pray that for me too.
That my heart will recover,
From the storm that took the love of my life.
But the sun always follows a rainbow,
And, you are my forever rainbow.

I had held myself together up to this point, but the tears started flowing. I couldn't finish. I handed the paper to Bo. He handed me a red bandana that was stuffed in his pocket.

He read from my notes.

"Let's close by singing a verse from Josh's favorite hymn," distributing copies of "It is Well With My Soul."

He grasped my hand. As he began singing, I learned something about m husband that I never knew. He had a beautiful singing voice. A hypnotic, strong, and heavenly tune began flowing right out of his mouth.

When peace, like a river, attendeth my way,
When sorrows like sea billows roll;
Whatever my lot, Thou hast taught me to say,
It is well, it is well with my soul.

Chapter Fifty-Eight

Hannah Anne Hart

I promised Savannah that I would visit her after the service. But right now, I couldn't even bear to see my angel, my rock. I needed to be alone. I needed to feel sand between my toes.

I loved the solitude of the beach at this time of year. I didn't have to dodge blankets, frisbees, footballs, bocce balls, or sandcastles. There were no squealing toddlers running in and out of the surf. There were no tantrums from children during a game of beach baseball. Best of all, the hordes of teenagers with their music blasting from all those wireless speakers that had replaced the once gigantic boom boxes were gone. I never understood why beach intruders wanted to drown out the melodic roar of the waves and the squawking of happy birds with their loud music.

Today, this giant mass of blue was mine alone to savor. Just as it had many times in the past, the ocean lifted my spirits. It was the one thing I could always count on. The changing of the tide was as constant as the sunrises and sunsets. Precise, reliable, and steadfast. Abandonment was a foreign word to them.

As I was walking, I noticed the DANGER sign near the jetties. Funny that I had never noticed it before now. But that sign interrupted my zen-like state of mind. It was like a punch in the gut, a foreshadowing of things to come.

And, when I arrived home, Bo was gone.

Chapter Fifty-Nine

Walt Benton

The original plan was a group lunch after the service, before Hannah Anne's visit with Savannah. But, it turned out that we needed our own private time. I took my fishing pole and headed to the Broad River Fishing Pier. It had been one of my favorite spots when I was stationed at the Beaufort Marine Base. I used to relish this quiet time with just me, my tackle box, and the Atlantic. It didn't matter if the fish weren't biting. I would watch the other solitary fishermen and wonder about their life stories. What pressures or worries brought them to this same spot to find a little peace and perspective? But, most of the time, my thoughts would just take a break, allowing me to absorb the relaxing effects of Mother Nature. I could spend hours simply staring at the water.

This reliable escape looked exactly the same, though many years had passed since I was last here. The pier had weathered many storms, and yet it still stood sturdy, steady, and offering solace to the hundreds of lost souls who walked its planks. With each cast, I waited for that mindless space to wash over me. Unfortunately, it wasn't working today.

Later, I was preoccupied with the meeting with the lawyers. Charles Walker's team was there including Rollins Bishop and Elliott Gray. Savannah's lawyer, Earl Dixson, was present as well. They were going to update us on facts uncovered since our last meeting. Maybe there would be a glimpse of hope, a sliver of new evidence that would dent the prosecution's case. Nothing could resurrect my son from his ashes that we had just spread. The best I could hope for was to resuscitate his reputation and save the love of his life.

My thoughts jumped to the love of my life, Maudie. These unfortunate events had brought us back together. Was our connection only fleeting? Was it reignited only due to the situation? Were we grasping for some temporary comfort? Would these feelings stand the test of time, like this ol' fishing pier?

Among all my contemplations, I lost track of time. I called Bo to let him know that I was on my way to pick him up for the lawyer meeting. He didn't answer. I was hoping that he and Hannah Anne had reconnected like Maudie and me. It was obvious he was enamored with her but only in a way a guy could notice. It was also evident that Hannah Anne had built a pretty significant fortress around her feelings.

After several unanswered calls to Bo, I called Hannah Anne. She informed me that Bo was gone. His car, his bags, everything. I had this sinking feeling that the events of the day had triggered a similar response in Maudie. I called her. No answer.

I rushed over to The Admiral, Room 314. As I opened the door, I was preparing myself for the same fate—no luggage, no Maudie. I felt sick.

Chapter Sixty

Maude Abbott

After the service, it was clear that we all were dealing with our individual emotions and needed space. Josh had known his true father for more years than he hadn't, but the fact was that I knew from the beginning. And those eighteen years he hadn't known Walt were gone and could never be recaptured.

Would Walt ever forgive me for keeping the truth from him? And worse was that but for Josh's accident, the truth never would have surfaced. I had tried to justify my decision all those years, but my guilt was like an enormous black cloud that followed me daily. I thought that the cloud would lift, dissipate, even disappear after the discovery, but the cloud just got thicker and heavier.

I loved Adam but not the way that I loved Walt Benton. Marrying Adam seemed the safest thing to do at the time, but that path was shallow and weak. My deceit haunted me from the day Josh's innocent green eyes first looked up at me—for nurturing, for love, and for honesty. From the moment that child was born, I had let him down. My sorrow and regret were choking me.

After walking aimlessly around the downtown hoping to find a diversion from my thoughts, I headed to the bar at The Admiral. I ordered a martini. I could count on one hand the number of martinis that I had drunk. The medicine began to work. My shameful feelings were lifting. Too bad the Abbott's prolific sharecropper and my reliable friend, Jesse, wasn't here.

Jesse and I had spent many a late night reflecting on life. We talked through all of our "what ifs" and "but fors" while smoking cigarettes and drinking bourbon—

his tribute to Hazel. Had it not been for my summer in the Outer Banks, I wouldn't have been caught within a mile from Jesse, much less smoking a cigarette or drinking any form of alcohol with him. But that summer changed me. Nothing was black and white. I had learned a lot about the areas of gray.

Upon my return to Kentucky after delivering Hazel to Aunt Mildred, I learned that my dad's boss, Kyle Abbott, my future father-in-law, had given Dad an ultimatum—Jesse or Hazel had to go. The Abbott's return on Jesse's use of the land was highly profitable. He was indispensable to Abbott Tobacco Farm in Dad's eyes, which trumped his very own flesh and blood. I was relieved that Hazel never learned about either the ultimatum or Dad's choice. Hazel had decided to stay in Nag's Head without knowledge of Dad's willingness to oust his first born child. I couldn't judge Daddy. I, too, had chosen the Abbott Tobacco Farm.

Over many bourbons and smokes over the years, I tried to assure Jesse that his situation had worked out for the best. He had a wife, beautiful children, and had made a good living. Hazel was happily married with children as well. Getting caught with Hazel in the barn was divine intervention, the stars aligning. My situation was the polar opposite of a celestial alignment. It was a jumble of the highest disorder.

After my second martini, I bravely asked the bartender if he had cigarettes for sale. I took the pack and my third martini to the Adirondack chairs by the river. The combination of these vices didn't provide the escape I had desired.

When I was heaving over the toilet wondering if Walt would return, I heard the door to our room open, as I retched again.

Chapter Sixty-One

Walt Benton

I was trying not to panic, forcing myself to maintain positive thoughts that Maudie hadn't left like Bo. As I unlocked the door to Room 314, the last thing I expected to see was her puking in the toilet. An almost empty pack of cigarettes and a completely empty martini glass were on the bathroom sink. Strangely, I smiled. I was just relieved that she hadn't left.

"Babe, what can I do?" I asked, as I grabbed a washcloth and turned on the faucet. I wanted to splash my face with the cold water. Was she still really here? The sound of her insides erupting was certain validation that I wasn't imagining things.

"Please forgive me, please forgive me," she said, between hurls.

I called Hannah Anne. The plan was for all of us to meet with the lawyers. But Bo had fled, and Maudie had her head in a toilet. This was no time for judging. We all had our ways of dealing with grief.

"Maudie is not feeling well. She's actually quite sick. So, she is not coming with us. I will pick you up in about fifteen minutes," I told Hannah Anne.

"That's not necessary. You've done enough. Take care of Maude. I'm going to visit Savannah and then head on from there. Surely, it won't matter if I'm a little late. I will fill you in on all the details."

"But..." I began before she interrupted me.

"But nothing. I know what you are thinking. I am fine, Walt. I really am. I knew it was only a matter of time before Bo ran like a scared rabbit. Stay with Maude. Second chances are a blessing."

"You are a blessing too. Let me know about the meeting. I am confident that we are all in good hands with you on our team."

After a nap, Maudie's color returned to normal. She went on a wild binge, she explained. She tried to drown her sadness and guilt. Guilt that Josh had missed eighteen long years not knowing his real dad, because of her choice. Her pleas for forgiveness weren't due to her overindulgence of martinis and cigarettes. Her remorse was the result of her knowing all along that I was Josh's father. One thing was certain. She never had sex with Adam Abbott before she discovered that she was pregnant.

Chapter Sixty-Two

Hannah Anne Hart

When I arrived, the lawyers were in the midst of reviewing documents that the solicitor had disclosed. Their current focus was on criminal records that Charles Walker received prior to hiring Savannah. Apparently, Charles had ignored information revealing that both the husband and son of a potential employee were in prison.

Rollins Bishop explained that Charles Walker had always taken a very hard line with any new hire in the "C-suite," which was the floor designated for the top executives. The solicitor relayed that in a prior instance, Charles Walker flatly refused to consider a candidate due to a shoplifting charge against her husband. Though the position was mail clerk, the lowest position on the coveted floor, Charles reportedly said, "The entire family has to represent our culture. There is no room for error."

His conservative convictions were attributed to the bank's success. Everyone knew that the man at the top was unyielding in his hiring practices. To offer a position to Savannah, the wife and mother of convicted felons, was totally out of character, a dramatic deviation from his strict, unwavering criteria. The divergence from his pattern of behavior was especially troubling given that Savannah was filling the position of Charles' chief assistant. For all these reasons, Rollins was deeply troubled with this disclosure.

"It certainly looks like Mrs. Abbott's close connections to convicted criminals could have given Charles an idea about the perfect hit man. That will be the solicitor's position anyway," Rollins Bishop surmised.

"Hold your horses! I may be talking out of turn, but this is my family," I said. "Yes, while my son-in-law and grandson are convicted felons, that is not who they are. Josh and Savannah had nothing to do with this. It is obvious that this is an inside job, just like my grandson's setup. You need to focus on the corrupt prison system and Charles Walker's wife. Have you asked your client about his marriage?"

Rollins quickly realized that I was someone who would tell it like it is. I wasn't impressed by his resume, his long list of client representations, his successes, or his seven-figure salary.

"My client has expressed 'tension' in the marriage, which heightened after the death of their daughter," Bishop said, calmly and authoritatively. "Charles Walker is not an impulsive man. He is not one to take extreme measures under any scenario, personal or professional. Setting aside all the exposure to him personally, there are others to consider—bank investors, loyal employees, and customers. There are a host of people to whom he is accountable. He communicated in convincing fashion that he has spent his entire life building his reputation. He would not try to kill his wife under any circumstances. He would have simply asked for a divorce. Charles is quite adamant that his relationship with your daughter is strictly professional. The closest thing he has to a mistress is the bank, his most important and cherished asset," the high-powered lawyer argued as if he were preaching behind a pulpit.

Rollins then asked me to explain my comment about the setup of Cray. I surveyed the room and all eyes were on me. Had Walt not disclosed that fact? Had I slipped up and said something that I shouldn't have? I wished Walt were here now. I had let the cat out of the bag, and there was no retreating. So, I laid it all out.

"Interesting. Alice Walker's father is the warden of the prison where Josh Abbott was incarcerated," Rollins disclosed. "How can this setup be proven now that Josh is no longer with us?"

"Well, Josh told Walt. So, Walt can prove it," I said. "Cray Abbott wouldn't sell drugs any more than the Queen of England would attend a Tupperware party. I'm telling you right now, I am convinced Alice Walker is behind this. This new information about her father makes my hunch more credible. You guys need to investigate that hussy. We need a private investigator to follow her. I would bet your boots that she is the one with someone on the side."

After this last comment, amongst all the stone faces in the room, I noticed a smirk on Elliott Gray's face. After the assignments for further follow-up were discussed, the meeting began to adjourn. I took the liberty to introduce myself to one of my favorite authors.

"Mr. Gray, my daughter and I are huge fans. I have all your books, sir. I brought some from my collection. Do you mind autographing them for Savannah and me?"

Despite all his success and sensational story-telling talents, I found him reserved and modest. He was quite the opposite of the egotistical Rollins Bishop.

"In addition to being a voracious reader, you appear to be a quick study in the law," Elliott Gray complimented me, under his breath, while signing my books. "You must have read too many of my books. I agree with your theory. In fact, I shared the same theory with Rollins earlier."

"What did he say to you?" I asked, incredulous that Elliott Gray agreed with me.

"He told me to save it for my next novel."

Chapter Sixty-Three

Hannah Anne Hart

I didn't have the heart to tell Savannah that Bo had skedaddled yet again. I apologized that our visit would have to be quick because I was already running late for a meeting with the lawyers. My excuse for Bo's absence wasn't completely false; I only intimated that he was at the meeting. I quickly cutoff further questions by informing her that Elliott Gray would be in attendance. I thought I saw a glimpse of the old sparkle in her eyes. Apparently, Savannah was a bigger fan of Mr. Gray than I realized.

I filled her in on the service and how beautiful the rookery was that morning. It seemed like every egret within miles was in attendance, and one, in particular, was very attentive, watching over the service. Savannah was moved by the presence of the egret and the words of Walt, Maude, and Bo. She didn't even mind that I had shared her poem. She had discovered this streak of creativity during her confinement. My daughter was taking advantage of her solitude.

I found her words uplifting. I thought that mother and daughter were both experiencing different levels of introspection. I was proud of myself for my strength. In the past, I wouldn't have been able to handle all the events swirling around me. I would have retreated under the covers for a couple of days, coaxed out by increases in my meds. But, I felt stronger than ever. My mission to save my daughter required courage, energy, and focus.

Walt had warned me again that someone was likely eavesdropping on our conversations, so I was careful not to divulge or ask too much. But, I had to find out what she knew about Charles Walker's marriage. I was building my case against his wife. I couldn't share my suspicions with Savannah yet.

"I have a question before I go. I know you have only worked with Charles for a short time, but have you heard or picked up anything about the state of his marriage?"

"Well, I guess there are a couple of things, but it's nothing more than office gossip. You know he is a very private person."

"Have you told Earl Dixson these things?"

"No, like I said, it's just gossip, and I never participated in any of those discussions."

"Honey, now is not the time to take the high road, despite what I have preached in the past."

"OK. There is one thing. He said that his wife blames him for their daughter's death."

"I will see Earl at the meeting and tell him he needs to see you pronto. Think long and hard about anything you've heard or picked up on. It's all important, Savannah. If there is anything that I have learned from the gospels according to Elliott Gray, every minuscule detail matters."

Chapter Sixty-Four

Earl Dixson

The successful and highly paid barristers like Rollins Bishop were entertaining to say the least. I had known the type since my law school days. They would sell their soul for a high class rank so they could be recruited by the best law firms. I had never played any of those games. All I ever wanted was to return to my hometown and offer top-quality representation to those who couldn't afford it. I wasn't tempted in the least by the firms offering a six-figure starting salary for a totally inexperienced, newly licensed attorney.

I was first in my class at Harvard, a law school more esteemed than where Rollins Bishop graduated. Yes, I admit to looking up his bio, his undergraduate degree, his law school, and all his accolades. I was merely curious. I wasn't trying to out-credential him.

If I had learned anything over the years, it was that these Rollins Bishop–types always snubbed their noses at me. They assumed that their rich salaries, their limitless array of resources, and generous marketing budgets made them better lawyers. What they didn't get was none of those things made me feel inferior. I wasn't threatened, resentful, or jealous of the big firm lawyers, the big firm perks, or the big firm pay. Most of all, I wasn't envious of their braggadocio, big-time trial experience.

Lawyers like Rollins Bishop wouldn't roll the dice on a full-blown jury trial. There were too many variables with uneducated, random citizens to blemish their record of wins and losses. I had to hand it to those types, they had a way of setting the stage in the event that they were unsuccessful.

The Rollins Bishops of the legal community used bad facts to convince their clients to settle—to accept a plea in lieu of risking jail time—simply to save their pristine win–loss records.

The story line was always the same: the solicitor placed a very attractive offer on the table, one that could never have been obtained by any other attorney, they would boast. I silently watched Rollins' theatrics. He countered every argument or fact noted in our favor—yep, setting the stage.

My biased opinion was that there was no bite beyond the bark of these so-called heavy hitters. Rollins Bishop was oblivious to the corruption within the prison system. I had always been a skeptical pragmatist, but my preconceived prejudices were confirmed many years ago after hanging my shingle. Don't get me wrong. There are some really good guys out there trying to seek justice, but there are also a number of really rotten ones. Rotten is probably the wrong word. Maybe it's jaded, tainted, weary, or greedy. Whatever it was, I had seen it firsthand more times than not.

The supposed case against Charles Walker and Savannah Abbott smelled bad from the beginning. Now, with the disclosure that Alice Walker's father was Warden William Wilson, I was convinced that it was a frame job. I had witnessed his schemes from his tenure in the Thurmond County Sheriff's Department, before he climbed the ladder in the federal prison system. I was drawing a blank on his nickname. What was it? Weasel? Whacko? Woolly? I agreed with Hannah Anne Hart's assessment. In fact, she had sold me on more than just her theory.

Since we first met, I hadn't been able to get her off my mind. When she walked into the meeting, I had a difficult time focusing on anyone else. Before then, any feelings for a woman waltzed out the door with Marsha.

Marsha was fed up with my long hours for what she called my "deadbeat" clients. She resented that she needed to work, which I could never understand. On our first date, she told me that nursing school was her lifelong goal. It was her dream career. But she quickly wanted to ditch her ambition right after she said, "I do."

Throughout the years, I had been approached by several large firms in Atlanta to head up their white-collar criminal practice. My guaranteed, annual pay could have been triple that of my best year in solo practice. And, if budgeted projections were exceeded, my salary could be doubled in bonuses. Every time I refused one of these offers, Marsha grew more indignant. In her mind, I had thrown away numerous opportunities for big bucks. And, she was right about that.

Soon after leaving me, she was spotted on a date with a doctor from the hospital. I wasn't all that surprised. When I learned that she and the doc had been seeing each other for years, I can't say that I cared. Since then, the few times I obliged matchmaker friends, the dates were more trouble than they were worth—too much effort for stilted conversation, too much effort to find commonalities, too much effort...period. I didn't want to work at anything in my leisure time. But, Hannah Anne Hart was different. She was vivacious. She was tough. She was spirited. She was beautiful. And, her legs...I kept imagining her long, lean legs wrapped around me. Hannah Anne Hart had exhumed my buried desires. There was only one problem. She was my client's mother.

Chapter Sixty-Five

Savannah Abbott

I was heeding Mom's advice and trying to remember everything Phyllis had told me during my first week on the job. Phyllis was the self-anointed Queen Bee of the support staff on the C-suite floor. I knew the type. The bank where I had previously worked in Kentucky also had someone like Phyllis. They were tricky types. I wondered if there was a school of gossip where these species learned their trade. The similarities were uncanny.

The orientation begins with invites to lunch, offers to show you the ropes, and revelations of inside information about the C-suite executives, including their quirks and secrets. These ploys were like a seductive drug, coaxing you to trust them.

Phyllis had quickly let me know that she was the most tenured assistant on the cherished executive floor. She had been with Joe for twenty years. She also made it clear that Joe was every bit as powerful as my new boss and not nearly as difficult to work for. She had politely declined the position I had accepted, she professed.

"Charles Walker is a hard nut to crack. You have your work cut out for you," she had said.

She attributed his moodiness to his disastrous homelife. The good moods coincided with long business trips. His bad moods, from nights at home.

"We are dying to know if he has a girlfriend out of town, so keep your eyes and ears open," she said.

When Phyllis and her followers learned that I wasn't going to be the source of scoop, they turned on me. I was now an outsider. Phyllis was enjoying the fact that Charles and I were now behind bars. This led the way for Joe to move into Charles' coveted spot, and Phyllis, into the role as chief administrative assistant to the president.

I was going to feel silly relaying this chatter to Mr. Dixson, but I promised Mom that I would. And who knows? Maybe some of it would lead to something that could help. Pushing aside the rumors that had been divulged to me, I tried hard to remember anything else that Charles had shared.

After my tearful disclosure to him that my husband and only child were serving time, I recall that he was so gracious and understanding. I found comfort in his words "life can throw curveballs" and that "no one is immune to heartache." At the time, those words didn't suggest any dark secret. Now, those words coupled with the information that he disclosed at the Ritz, well, it was apparent things weren't so great at home.

While we were at the conference, Charles worked away on his speech at the desk inside his room. I planted myself outside on his balcony with my laptop to soak in the views while working through the numerous changes that he continued to make. He only took one short break and joined me.

Our conversation was coming back to me. He said that he had been participating in this conference for years and not once had ventured onto the oceanfront balcony. I told him that Mom and I watched the sunrises and sunsets from ours and couldn't get enough of the views. I mentioned that he worked too hard.

"I should have taken more time off," he confessed. "You just can't get some things back."

I had heard about his daughter and assumed he was referring to her.

"I understand that you lost your daughter right before I started working for you. I am so sorry. I can't imagine what you are going through. It certainly puts my situation into perspective."

"My wife blames me," he said abruptly, "and she's right."

His disclosure was so out of character. He never had come close to volunteering any information about his wife or daughter. I was taken aback and didn't know what to say.

"I'm sure she doesn't blame you. We all have a unique way of dealing with grief," I said, wondering how he could possibly think he was to blame for a car accident. That is what Phyllis said happened.

"I bought my daughter a used car. Her airbags didn't deploy. Her car didn't have all the bells, whistles, or alerts when crossing out of your lane. I should have been more concerned with safety features than the price. And I should have spent more time with her."

"Don't beat yourself up. When my husband was arrested, my father-in-law shared good advice, 'Unfairness is not fair. We decide if it will defeat us or if we will use it to empower us.' I'm sure you have many great memories."

"I'm sorry for my digression. No wonder I have avoided the balcony all these years. The ocean has a way of making you contemplate life."

After that exchange, he excused me. He said to enjoy some time with my mom. I thought he just needed time alone.

While this was all fresh in my memory, I jotted down some notes. My thoughts actually brought me back to reality for a while. I had spent every waking hour thinking about Josh and worried about Cray's fate. The only thing keeping me sane was my poetry. After finishing my notes for my next meeting with Mr. Dixson, I worked on another poem about my husband.

Emerald

The stone of Venus and queens.
The gem of passion and unconditional love.
A protector of evil; visionary of truth.
Mystical influence; enormous power.
The color that begins carpeting the thawing earth in the spring.
Renaissance. Renewal.
Cleansing. Healing.
The color of the ocean on the day we met.

Hired Hit on Jessamin Island

The color of your eyes.
The color of hope.
Like a deep breath to start anew.
But my hope is waning.
I am finding it hard to breathe.
How could my soul ever be restored, without my rock,
my partner, my precious gem?

Chapter Sixty-Six

Hannah Anne Hart

When I was leaving the meeting with my autographed books, I noticed Earl Dixson. He wasn't far behind me. I am embarrassed to say that I forgot to mention to him what Savannah told me about Charles Walker. Instead of seeking counsel with Savannah's lawyer at the end of the meeting, I made a beeline for Elliott Gray.

"Earl, are you in a hurry? I need to talk to you away from the others."

"How about Port Royal Java? It's on the way back to Beaufort."

"Do you have directions?"

"It's about nine miles from here. Or if you have your phone, you can map it."

"I do, but I'll just follow you," I said.

I didn't want to trust my newly acquired GPS skills. Didn't anyone use old-fashioned directions anymore? And, I wondered if Earl always drove this slowly. When he slowed even more at each traffic light, I realized he was ensuring that I didn't get lost in the traffic. *A gold star in the "attentive" column.*

We took our coffee to a table in the back corner.

"What's on your mind?" Earl asked.

"Well, first, there is something about that highfalutin Rollins Bishop that rubs me the wrong way. I know he is Charles' lawyer, but I don't trust him one bit as far as Savannah's defense is concerned."

"That's my job," he said.

From the tone in his voice, I was afraid that I had offended him.

"Of course, it is, and I didn't mean to imply that you aren't doing your job. I just didn't like the atmosphere in the room when he was talking about those criminal records. He was inferring that my family is crooked to the bone. I didn't feel comfortable sharing any more information. In the future, I'll let you decide what to share and what not to."

"OK, what have you learned?"

"Well, for starters, apparently there is office chatter about Charles Walker and his wife. Savannah hasn't shared this information with you because she says it is only gossip. She's not the type to spread such nonsense. But in this case, I told her she needed to tell you everything, and let you decide whether it's worth any follow-up. You know, the devil is in the details."

"Yes. You are right. What has she heard?"

"We didn't get into the specifics. I was already late for the meeting. Plus, I'm certain those walls have ears. I told her to make sure that she told you everything and think long and hard about anything she has heard—rumor or not. But, Charles Walker told her that his wife blamed him for their daughter's death. You know that his daughter died in a car accident, right?"

"Yes, before you arrived today, Walker's lawyers shared information on the marital front."

"Really? Do tell."

"OK, but with the understanding that what I say to you must not be shared with Savannah. That's my job. My conversations with her are privileged, but yours are not. So, going forward, don't discuss anything about the case with Savannah. If you have any questions or ideas, just relay them to me," he cautioned.

"I have been very careful because I don't trust anyone in that jail."

"Good. Today, Rollins shared that Tara, Charles Walker's daughter, sent a text to her best friend right before she slammed into the tree. The text said, 'You are not going to fucking believe it.' Of course, that could have a hundred different interpretations. She had come home unexpectedly from a church retreat. I am going to follow through with a recommendation you made today and retain a private investigator to keep tabs on Alice Walker."

"Great!"

"I like the way you think. If you have more time, I'd like your ideas about some other things, unless you'd prefer an office visit with Walt and Bo present."

"No, I'm all ears. All I've got is time on my hands."

I bit my tongue before blabbing that Bo had flown the coop and that Walt was distracted with Maude. Earl was Walt's long-time confidante, and his reconnection with Maude was his story to tell, not mine.

Earl told me about Josh's letter to Cray and the postmark from North Carolina. Earl said he had subpoenaed records from the post office.

"What kind of records?" I asked.

"The post office keeps fairly detailed records these days. It has to be the only letter sent from this post office to the Somerset prison. I am hoping to learn the exact time the letter was mailed."

"How do you know it wasn't mailed from one of those blue collection boxes?"

"I don't know, but I will find out. I have also requested copies of video from all the cameras at the post office. We can review video recordings from the day the letter was mailed. We may not learn anything, but I am not leaving any stone unturned."

"Let's say that Josh did mail that letter. How does that help with the case? Walt says that Rollins Bishop finds a way to spin everything in favor of the prosecution."

"I agree. But the prosecution's case has been consistent on the fact that a prison guard took Josh to the bus station and watched him board the bus to Beaufort. Josh was to get in touch with his parole officer immediately upon his arrival. After you first disclosed the bus schedule, I obtained the exact route, all stops along the way and the corresponding times. The bus route went through western North Carolina. If Josh mailed that letter, his route was three hundred miles east of where the bus route entered the state."

"Rollins Bishop would say that Josh got off at a stop and had one of his so-called middlemen pick him up and drive him the rest of the way."

"I thought of that as well," Earl said. "The date and time the letter was mailed will help establish whether Josh could have hopped off at a stop in North Carolina, or any stop for that matter, and caught a ride roughly four hours east in time to mail the letter."

"When do you expect this information?"

"I am hoping to hear something soon."

"Well, let me know when you do. By the way, do we know the name of Tara Walker's best friend—the one that received the text?"

"Yes, we do. Hannah Anne, you need to leave the investigations to the professionals. We don't need you to become a witness, more than you already are. It's getting late. How about I treat you to dinner? There's a great Italian place on the way back into Beaufort. It has fantastic shrimp scampi with linguine. How's that sound?"

"Great. I've been running from one thing to the next and haven't eaten all day. I'll follow you," I said quickly before he assumed I would punch the restaurant into my GPS.

While following Savannah's attorney, it seemed like Josh's memorial service had been a week ago. After I realized that Bo was gone, the thought of food had made me nauseated. Now, I was starving. The return of an appetite was a good sign that I was going to be OK. I enjoyed Earl's company, and he appreciated my ideas. Hiding under my covers due to Bo's departure would have to wait until after dinner.

Chapter Sixty-Seven

Alice Walker

Thank heavens Daddy finally left. He believed it was necessary to spend some time with his daughter, given that she had survived a "hit" ordered by her own husband. Given that he was the prior Sheriff in Thurmond County, he still had lots of contacts there.

"I need to check in at the department and ensure that the case is on track to fry your husband's ass," he said.

As soon as his car was pulling out of the driveway, I poured a glass of champagne and texted Johnny. "The pool has been neglected. After all I have been through, I need a long swim."

He responded immediately, "I've been worried sick about you. I'm glad you reached out. I have an opening at 10:00 tomorrow."

"See you then!" I responded.

But I couldn't wait for tomorrow. So, I texted Norris. "My computer is on the blink."

He responded immediately. "I can take a look in an hour."

"Perfect, it's the one in the downstairs bedroom," I responded.

I was waiting for him. With Charles in jail, I had resumed my residence in the master bedroom, Charles' room. Thinking about sex with Norris in Charles' room added to my excitement. Norris smothered me with kisses as I undressed him.

"I have been thinking about you every day. You OK?"

"Yes, now that you're here," I said, as we became entangled quickly.

It was wilder than usual.

"Thank you. I needed that," I said.

"Do you want to talk about it? I can stay a while longer, if you feel like talking."

"I am really fine. Sorry I have been out of touch. My father has been here. You know, I'm still his little girl."

"Of course, you are," as he stroked my hair. "You know, we have never really talked about our situations. My marriage is lacking in a lot of areas, but I can't imagine what you must be going through. I'm here for you, Alice."

"Thank you, Norris. It's very unsettling to live under the same roof with a man who would prefer you dead. It hasn't all sunk in yet. I hope this doesn't change things between us because I don't know what I'd do without you."

"I don't know what I would do without you either. You make me happy. You make me feel appreciated. I hope that you know that I'm always here for you. But, if you need time, I understand."

"You're such a sweet man, Norris Nichols. You know, I think my computer has another issue. Do you have time to fix it?"

He laughed and rolled on top of me again.

"This issue is going to take a little longer to fix," he said.

He stayed longer than he probably should have. His phone began ringing continuously. He ignored it. He needed me as badly as I needed him. We were in the heat of things for what seemed like an hour.

"We need a weekend together," he said, as he pulled on his pants. "Six missed calls from Naomi. I guess I am going to get a tongue lashing."

"I'll give you a tongue lashing but the good kind," as I kissed him long and hard.

I grabbed one of Charles' shirts from the closet and walked him to the door.

"I've missed you," he said. "I have an opening at 10:00 tomorrow. I need to make sure everything is still working properly. What do you think?"

"Shoot. I have a meeting with a lawyer at 10:00. Should take a couple of hours. But after that, I'm all yours. Can you come over at 2:00?"

"I'll see what I can do," and he kissed me again.

Poor Norris. He was one needy man. I hoped he wouldn't crack when I moved to Florida. Now that Charles was behind bars, my freedom was only weeks away. I would keep Norris satisfied until then.

Chapter Sixty-Eight

Maude Abbott

"I understand if you never want to see me again," I told Walt after coming clean about everything.

And I mean everything. I told him about Adam's increased physical advances, which precipitated my offer to accompany Hazel to Nags Head. It had been engrained in me to save myself for marriage. Adam's aggression and pleas to "do it" had made me feel cheap and dirty. I had needed a break from him. I had convinced my father that I needed to accompany Hazel to make sure she was off to a good start at Aunt Mildred's.

"Everything changed after I met you. I knew what real love felt like. Then, after I learned that I was pregnant, I was scared. I was confused. There were so many people to consider—Dad, Hazel, and you. For some odd reason, I didn't want to disappoint my father. He was counting on me to legitimize our family and follow the path into the Abbott dynasty. Then, there was Hazel. Daddy would have blamed Hazel for leading me astray and would never have forgiven her. I couldn't let her down. Finally, and most importantly, you. I was afraid you might abandon your dream to become a Marine if you had a family to take care of. You would have resented me and possibly even our child. Adam was a good person. He was a known wager; you were a gamble. My future had been planned, and it was secure."

I even confessed that I relented to having sex with Adam for the first time when I returned.

"I needed him to think the baby was his. When Adam and I tried to have more children, we couldn't. He had fertility issues, which prevented us from conceiving a child. He and I both knew that he was not Josh's father. But he never said a word, and neither did I. I thought about you every waking day. How could I not? Josh looked just like you. I am sorry, so sorry. Please forgive me," I said over and over again.

When I had finished spewing everything, I was prepared for a quick exit. Walt was silent.

"Please say something. Please tell me it's not too late for us."

My soulmate hugged me tightly.

"It's never too late. The past is the past. We can only control the future. I have wanted you in my future from the day I met you. I feel the very same way today. I love you, Maudie."

"I love you more," I said, and I meant it from the depths of my soul.

Chapter Sixty-Nine

Hannah Anne Hart

Was it the wine, the best shrimp scampi ever, or just finally being able to relax after a very emotional day? Whatever it was, I was really enjoying Earl Dixson's company. Our conversation was so effortless and natural.

The restaurant was closing. We had overextended our stay for sure. He insisted on picking up the check and making sure I got home safely. *A gold star in the "considerate" column*, I added to my mental tally. When I arrived home, I don't know what came over me.

"Would you like to come in for a nightcap?" I asked. "All my guests have left and with all that has gone on today, I'm not ready to be alone just yet."

"Yes, I would," Earl Dixson said, without hesitation.

I poured him an Abbott Farm bourbon and started giving him the history of the distillery while we were sitting on the porch swing. We talked some more, and I poured more bourbon. I knew it was getting late, but I didn't want to be alone. As I started to launch into another story about Savannah's childhood, he interrupted me.

"Sorry to interrupt, but can I kiss you?"

I didn't know what was happening to me. Too many Jacqueline Summers' books I thought, but I took his glass and placed it on the table beside mine.

"I thought you'd never ask," I said.

I guess kissing is like riding a bike. It had been a long time for me, but Earl Dixson started easy. A soft peck and then an extended one. I hadn't remembered how stimulating such a simple act could be. He must have felt my heart racing.

"You OK?" he asked.

"Yes, more than OK. It's been so long. You took my breath away," finding myself leaning into him. I wanted more, and he delivered.

He called me the next morning to tell me what a great time he had. A dozen roses arrived later with a note: "Just because." He called me that afternoon.

"I've had a productive day. Are you up for a road trip? To North Carolina."

"Sure, but whatever for?" I asked.

I'll explain on the drive. We may need two days. Pick you up at 5:00?"

"That works. And, I love the flowers."

I felt like a giddy schoolgirl. I had a couple of hours, so I rushed to the lingerie boutique downtown. In the past, I had only window shopped. Though I didn't want to get ahead of myself, I was overdue for a makeover.

Earl pulled up at 5:00 on the dot. *A gold star in the "prompt" column*, I added to the list. He kissed my cheek, retrieved my bag, and opened the car door for me. I wasn't used to this kind of treatment. *"Gentlemanly," "mannerly"—two more columns, more gold stars.*

"It's about a five-hour drive, so I packed sandwiches and waters in the cooler. I'm not a fan of fast food when traveling."

A gold star for "prepared." "Me neither," I said, withholding that I rarely ventured beyond the Beaufort County line.

"I'm glad you could come. Aside from the fact that I like your company, I need your help. And, your intuitiveness is a bonus. Before I get to the purpose of this trip, I'll update you on Alice Walker. It seems you were right on target with your suspicions."

Two more gold stars in the "appreciative" and "humble" columns.

"And…" I said. I couldn't wait to hear if what he learned matched what I had seen.

"My private investigator went to survey the residence and attempt to place a tracking device on her car. Apparently, the Walker's garage is behind the house, and they have an electric gate. It's a pretty secure layout."

"Yes, it's a gated community. You need a code unless you can follow someone in," I blurted, without thinking.

"We have that code. My guy has worked there several times. I was referring to the gate at the Walker's house not into the community. Would you like to share how you know about the gate into the neighborhood?"

Busted, I thought.

"A little birdie told me?" I offered.

"Hannah Anne, have you been spying?"

"Can I retain you to be my lawyer?"

"I'm waiting," he said.

"Well, it's clear that Rollins Bishop thinks the sun comes up just hear him crow. Walt says he doesn't appreciate any opinions by simple lay persons like us. No one had instructed me not to poke around. And, I actually started snooping before the arrests."

"Goodness. What am I dealing with here? What on earth prompted you to spy on Charles Walker?"

"I'm not sure I want to say since our communications aren't privileged."

"You got any cash on you?" Earl asked.

"Cash? Are you going to accept a bribe now, counselor?"

"No. But, if you give me a dollar, I'll accept this engagement, and your disclosures will be protected by the attorney–client privilege."

"All I have is five bucks," I said, stuffing it into his shirt pocket.

"So, fill me in on what prompted your surveillance of Charles Walker's home."

For some reason, I trusted Earl Dixson with every ounce of my being. For the next hour, at least, I told my woe-is-me story. When Bo Hart walked out of my life, I turned to romance novels for my pleasure. It was the only outlet I could count on.

I knew Savannah had inherited her mother's love language of touch. It was part of who we were. She was still in the prime of her life, and her sexual needs were still very much intact. With Josh in prison, I wondered about how she was taking care of herself. After she returned to Beaufort and started working for Charles Walker, more than her demeanor changed. Her appearance did as well. She took more time with her hair. She began wearing a touch of makeup. The sparkle in her eyes returned.

"I was suspicious. That's all. I knew that she loved Josh, but we can't fight our natural needs. After weeks of investigating, I gave up. I no longer wondered about Charles Walker and Savannah. Alice Walker, however, is another story. That woman is juggling a number of men. Many at hotels, but she has the nerve to entertain some under her roof. I have the license plate numbers on all except one. He lives in the neighborhood and apparently makes house calls."

"His name is Norris Nichols, Nancy's father."

"Goodness! Nancy? Is she the best friend of Tara Walker?"

"That's the one. Norris Nichols showed up today," Earl said. "He was there quite a while. My PI got photos of Mrs. Walker in nothing but a man's shirt in the doorway when Nichols was leaving. And he left on foot. He lives in the neighborhood. Do you recall Tara's text message to Nancy right before her accident?

"I sure do."

"So, you are probably thinking what I am," Earl said.

"That Tara Walker caught her mother with her best friend's father?"

"Well, you got me on that one," Earl said. "I was thinking in more general terms. She caught her mom cheating and texted her best friend. Your theory is better. Perhaps it's time to have a little visit with Nancy Nichols."

"This may backfire on us. If Charles Walker knew about his wife's extracurricular activities, he had motive. That's what Bo has thought all along—that Charles wanted to knock off his wife and used Savannah to establish his defense. Bo questioned Charles' claim that he didn't know how to get into his house on Jessamin Island. He thought it was weird that a bank president would invite his assistant and her mother to a resort and then offer his vacation home for the same time that his wife was supposed to be murdered. Now that we know that Charles ignored Savannah's background check, Bo's theory makes sense."

"I agree except for the discrepancy about the bus schedule. If Josh was released on parole and was put on a bus by prison officials to Beaufort, how did he make a stop in North Carolina and then end up on Jessamin Island, twenty miles from Beaufort? His bus ticket was in the name of Josh Abbott. His hotel room was for a Thomas Phillips."

"Thomas Phillips? Who is that?" I questioned.

"Josh had a fake ID; they are as easy to come by in prison as a cigarette."

"I'm beginning to think that Rollins is right. All of this evidence can be turned sideways and upside down. There is no smoking gun."

"But, my dear, there may be. That's why we are taking this road trip."

Chapter Seventy

Hannah Anne Hart

We arrived in Harper's Corner, North Carolina, around 10:00 p.m. When I learned the name of our destination, I knew instantly the reason that Josh decided on this location to mail his letter to Cray.

"I don't need any further evidence to know that Josh stopped here," I told Earl.

"Why is that?"

"Harper's Corner—Savannah's middle name is Harper. This is not a coincidence!"

"Interesting. Hopefully, the video from the post office will provide additional proof."

Earl had made reservations at a nice B&B. The proprietor was going on and on about the history of the home, the breakfast schedule, and tea and cookies at four o'clock. Blah, blah, blah. Earl was being too gracious. I grabbed his hand.

"Sorry to interrupt. But we've had a long day," pulling him away from this chatterbox.

"I understand," she said, winking. "Newlyweds?"

"Who? Us?" I asked. "Lord no."

I laughed to myself wanting to throw her for a loop by adding that he was not only my daughter's lawyer but also became my lawyer during the trip. I wanted to add that attorney–client privilege had some very unique privileges. Then, Chatty Cathy burst my bubble.

"Oh, yes, I see that you have two rooms and for two nights," she said, raising an eyebrow. She seemed to imply that we were having a rendezvous, and one room would remain unoccupied.

I should have known that polite Earl wouldn't have been so presumptuous. Earl carried my bag to my room. My bag contained my impulsive, yet hopeful purchase that had put a serious dent in my budget. I had removed the tags, so I probably couldn't return the expensive lingerie. I tried to assuage the dust devil of emotions by assuring myself that Earl was focused on the long day ahead— reviewing the video from the post office on the day that Josh mailed the letter.

"The post office doesn't open until 8:30, so we'll have time to enjoy the breakfast. The options look quite good. I'll see you in the morning."

My expression must have sent him the wrong message.

"That is, unless you want to sleep in. I can get yours to-go, if you prefer."

A gold star in the "thoughtful" column, I mentally added to the growing list of superlatives. My look had nothing to do with the breakfast invitation versus more sleep. I didn't want sleep. I wanted him. I wanted Earl to stay in my room.

"Breakfast sounds good," I said, attempting to disguise my disappointment. "I'm an early riser. You know the early bird catches the worm!"

"Well, I was thinking 7:30. Is that too late for you?"

"No. That's just fine," I said, not wanting him to leave. I wanted to fall asleep in the arms of a man instead of a Jacqueline Summers' novel.

"Sleep well," Earl said, closing my door.

He didn't even kiss me good night. I was left to share my new lingerie purchase with Jacqueline Summers. And to fan the flames of letdown, I had forgotten to pack my book. Obviously, I had gotten way ahead of myself imagining what could unfold on this trip. But, the outcome was as different as chalk to cheese. So, I curled up into the king-sized bed, clutched two pillows tightly against my lacy negligee, and fantasized about Earl.

Surprisingly, I slept like a baby. I didn't even wake up at my usual time of 1:00 a.m., tossing and then turning before eventually drifting back into an unsettled sleep. *Note to self: quit reading romance novels in bed. They only detonate frustration and underscore your loneliness.* Despite the fact that the mangled pillows were the only thing in my bed the next morning, I had a spring in my step as I hit the shower.

The greeting by effervescent Chatty Cathy didn't even damper my spirits. I was excited to spend the entire day with Earl Dixson, even if it only involved pouring over video footage from post office patrons.

"Mr. Dixson must still be enjoying those down pillows. They are dreamlike, right? Is he joining you for breakfast?" she asked, while showing me to a table. "Curious Cathy" was a more appropriate name for the proprietor.

"Yes, he is. He will be here shortly, I'm sure. I'll just have some coffee while I wait, if that's OK."

"Absolutely. Any orange or grapefruit juice? It's all freshly squeezed."

"One of each, please. And some waters as well."

"Here are the breakfast options for this morning. All to die for!" Curious Cathy said, pleased as punch with the offerings on the hand-written menu. "Everything is sourced locally...farm to table, for real."

In addition to the usual breakfast fare of yogurt, fruit, and oatmeal, the more decadent selections made my mouth water. The menu included lemon souffle pancakes with blueberry compote, sweet potato hash with applewood smoked bacon and poached eggs, and Bananas Foster French toast, to boot. But, I was sold on the breakfast bowl. I couldn't go wrong with stone-ground creamy grits topped with sage sausage, fried eggs, jack cheese, and an heirloom tomato. If the execution of these dishes was as good as the descriptions, I could learn to tolerate Curious Chatty Cathy.

Earl arrived at 7:30 on the nose.

"Look who finally woke up!" Chatty Cathy chirped to Earl, as she poured his coffee.

"I hope you haven't been waiting too long," he said.

"Nope, you said 7:30. I just got a little jump start to peruse the menu. And ordered juice. Which do you prefer orange or grapefruit? Both freshly squeezed."

"Ladies first. I'm used to juice out of a carton!"

"Chivalrous," another column, another gold star.

"What have you decided on?" Earl asked, eyeing the menu. "Damn, I left my readers in the room. You can order for me. I've never seen a breakfast that I didn't like."

"Easygoing," another gold star and extra gold stars for liking something other than Pop-Tarts for breakfast!

"I'm having cheese grits with sausage, fried eggs, and tomato. My second choice was the Bananas Foster French toast, so I'll order that for you unless you want pancakes or sweet potato hash."

"I trust you. Go for it! And more juice, please. I'm going to retrieve my glasses— definitely need them to review videotape. And thank you for coming with me. I'm glad you're here."

Gold stars all around! I only hoped the butterflies now fluttering in my stomach would subside before Chatty Cathy delivered my breakfast bowl.

The breakfast had definitely been the highlight of the morning. We were five hours into watching movements in and out of the post office with no sign of Josh. Given our big breakfast, we decided to skip lunch and power through. The helpful government workers brought us a pitcher of water and two paper cups, apologizing for the dysfunctional vending machine.

The sooner this exercise was over, the better for me. I was bleary-eyed and getting claustrophobic in the windowless, cramped space. Who knew that there was so much activity at a post office? It seemed to be a gathering place in this city. All the visitors were running together. Just when I thought I couldn't distinguish Josh from any other human in Harper's Corner, I saw him. I thought my heart stopped beating. I couldn't form a sentence. The only thing I could do was flail my arms and point. I thought I was hyperventilating. Earl stopped the video.

"Are you OK?" he asked.

"It's him," I said, but couldn't form any other words.

The next thing I remember was a blurry Earl and feeling wet. In addition to seeing spots, I thought my mind was playing tricks on me. Earl was shirtless.

"I think you fainted," Earl said, wiping my face with his shirt that was drenched with water from the pitcher that the government workers had provided.

I laid my head on his shoulder and couldn't stop the tears. I suppose the emotions that I had been suppressing since learning of Josh's death, Savannah's arrest, and Bo's departure were too much to hide. The façade of strength that I had outwardly displayed melted on Earl's shoulder. He rocked me gently.

"I'm so sorry. So sorry. I don't know what I was thinking. I should have never subjected you to this," he said, wiping my face with his wet shirt.

I closed my eyes, trying to regain my composure. This was important. My daughter's freedom was on the line. I took a deep breath.

"I'm good now. Let's continue."

"Hannah Anne, don't try to be a martyr. We can finish this tomorrow. I think you need some rest."

"Not a martyr, but a mother. I can't stop now. Not in a million years."

Earl Dixson kissed me on the forehead.

"You are one incredible mother."

I can't describe what my face must have expressed. I had always felt inadequate in the mothering department during Savannah's formative years. I had wasted so much time wallowing in self-pity.

"You have to know that. You're really special."

"Let me go dry your shirt with the hand dryer in the restroom. But, that is Josh. Note the time and load the video from the outdoor cameras."

I didn't know how anyone could dry their hands from the machine in the restroom. The paper alternative wasn't going to help dry Earl's shirt either. I finally relented when it was just a bit damp. I had to get back to that video footage. I was riding a high that was better than any romance novel. We had confirmed that Josh was here! He was here!

"It's still damp. The hand dryer isn't the best. But I couldn't take it any longer. Have you found anything else?"

"Yep. Take a look at this."

The outside cameras showed that Josh exited the post office and began talking to a girl that, if I didn't know better, was my daughter. They appeared to know each other.

"Zoom in. I must be seeing things. That girl looks like Savannah."

"You're not seeing things. I thought the same thing."

Earl zoomed in. If not for the cigarette in her hand, I would have sworn on a stack of Bibles that I was looking at my daughter.

"Take a picture on your phone. Her shirt is embroidered with 'Burger Barn.' See if you can locate that on your GPS."

Earl held his phone up.

"The Burger Barn is seven miles away."

"You hungry for a burger?" I asked Earl.

"I am now."

We easily spotted Brandy Chastain. But for her brown eyes and her curvier figure, she could have easily passed for my daughter. She had escorted Josh to the post office. She knew the story that no one else knew. Her story was the smoking gun.

With Brandy's disclosures, Earl's disposition changed before my eyes. He probably felt the weight of two possible convictions lift from his shoulders. That arrogant, bag-of-hot-air, Rollins Bishop hadn't uncovered any exculpatory evidence even with all his resources. He was about as worthless as a screen door on a submarine.

Earl ordered two beers. I couldn't remember the last time I drank a beer, but it was ice cold and went down way too easy. Brandy brought two more "on the house." We shared the pimento-cheese bacon burger, Brandy's favorite, and an order of fried pickles.

"Sharing is caring" with gold stars abound.

Bo turned his nose up when I wanted to share an entrée at a restaurant. He ignored my arguments that we were on a budget, and the portions were too large for one person. Bo just laughed when I offered that "sharing is caring."

Earl left Brandy a big fat tip and gave her his business card. He'd be in touch about the trial date and to discuss the questions she should expect on the witness stand. "Josh was a good man," she said, her eyes filling with tears.

Chatty Cathy seemed offended that we'd missed the tea and cookie hour.

"I still have some cookies left over—white chocolate macadamia nut. They are to die for! I'll fetch you some for your rooms."

I couldn't eat another bite, but I wasn't going to turn down a homemade cookie. Though the woman got on my last nerve, there was no denying that she could cook.

"Would it be too much trouble to get me a bag of ice?"

"I'm happy to get you a glass of tea."

"The ice is for my neck. It's a little tight. I must have overindulged in those fluffy pillows last night."

"I'm sure your hard work today didn't help," Earl surmised. "You go on up. I'll bring the ice."

"What kind of work have you two been doing today?" Curious Cathy asked.

"I'm a lawyer. We are working on a case. And if we have to come back, we know where to stay. You do a great job here," Earl said.

I left quickly while biting my tongue. I would have told her it was none of her beeswax. She must have bent Earl's ear. It seemed like fifteen minutes passed before he knocked on my door.

He had a small Ziplock baggie in his hand. He held it up apologetically.

"Apparently, most of the ice was used during tea hour. But I know all about the age of her freezer and the slow ice maker, if you're interested. If it's any consolation, we have extra cookies," as he held up another baggie.

"I probably just need a hot shower. I'm not used to down pillows," withholding that I had clutched them too tightly the night before.

"Let me work on your neck. It's the least I can do after making you peer at video footage all day."

I pulled the chair from the desk, plopped down, and dropped my head.

"I'm all yours."

He started gently. I jumped when he hit the sensitive spot.

"Oh, there it is. You have some knot there."

His fingers honed in and added a little more pressure. He moved to my shoulders.

"Good gracious, woman. You are tight as a tick."

His strong hands reminded me of Santiago at the Ritz Carlton spa. I didn't want him to stop.

"I guess I'm not used to sitting all day hunched over a computer screen. I'm sure you're beat too. But boy, this sure feels good. Five more minutes and you can stop. Consider it my pay for the day."

"What if I don't want to stop?"

What happened next was so unexpected and sudden that I couldn't accurately recall how we ended up naked in the bed. All I wanted was to remember every detail because I needed to bottle every single minute. The creaky metal bed frame was providing the accompaniment. The squeaky wheel must get the grease because Earl was very attentive. I told Earl that we needed to be a little quieter. Curious Cathy may be listening. He didn't pay me a bit of attention. And, the louder the noise, the less I cared. I was in another world.

Whatever it was, we both needed each other. I felt desired by a man who wouldn't abscond to another state in the morning. In fact, he was still there when the sun began peeking through the curtains.

"Does attorney–client privilege cover this?" I asked, when he stirred.

"Probably not. South Carolina prohibits attorney–client relations during an attorney-client relationship."

"That's an interesting rule. I'm sure there is a spicy story behind that one. But, I don't care if you fire me. I like our relations," I said, rubbing his chest.

"Me too. But, you know, for once in my legal career, I couldn't give a rat's ass about the rule."

"And, there is this other thing," I said.

"What is that?" he said, stroking my hair.

"We are in North Carolina," I added with a wink.

The noise that morning had to trump Bo's account of Walt and Maude's lovemaking. I loved every minute. When we finally rolled out of bed, I noticed the scuff marks on the hardwood floor.

"Chatty Cathy may assess a damage fee," I said.

"It would be worth every penny. That's what handymen are for, right? Let me go check out and field the questions about why we missed breakfast."

"Good idea. I have many weaknesses, and one is a short fuse with a busybody."

When Earl was checking out, Curious Cathy mentioned to him that I must not have slept well again.

"Sounded like she tossed and turned all night and morning!"

We laughed over her concerns about my neck all the way back to Beaufort. We never heard from Chatty Cathy about any damage to the floor in my room. As it turned out, we were the ones needing a handyman. We needed him for the wobbly wheels on Earl's office chair and the broken leg on his couch. The sex that ensued after the discovery of new evidence was therapeutic on the one hand but equally as hazardous. When the leg collapsed on his old couch and we fell onto the floor, we couldn't stop laughing after ensuring that we hadn't sustained any broken parts of our own. As Savannah's case grew stronger, so did our relationship. The sex was better than I could remember with Bo. And for the first time in forty years, Bo Hart was a distant memory.

PART XII

Chapter Seventy-One

Rollins Bishop

After I hung up from Rick Watson's call, I convened an emergency meeting of the defense team. Once again, Charles' famous childhood friend offered his home in Hilton Head. Charles had demanded the author's inclusion because he was supposedly a legal mastermind. But, I had yet to figure a delicate way to tell Charles the fictional plots and schemes that made Elliott Gray millions were just that—fictional. There was simply no place for the writer's ideas in a real-life, attempted murder case. His last name was even fitting; a box of rocks was more interesting than this dull human. The man sat in all our meetings like a knot on a log. Other than the sweeping views of the Atlantic from our dedicated meeting space in Elliott's home, his contributions to the defense team were worthless.

Surprisingly, the one I ended up having to worry about was the unsophisticated, country bumpkin from Beaufort, Earl Dixson. He was like a bull in a china shop and an itch you couldn't scratch. At times, I felt sorry for him. He didn't have my resources, my staff, or my hourly billing rate. I laughed thinking about his wheels spinning while hopelessly conducting his own investigation—wasted time he could never bill his client. But, unlike the other small-time law practitioners that I had been associated with over the course of my career, Earl Dixson didn't defer to me in the development of our theories, defense strategy, or potential witnesses.

He had filled my voicemail on more than one occasion with his ideas. The homegrown counselor had been more than a thorn in my side. I may have gone too far when I told him that I'd appreciate it if he didn't blow up my voicemail. I was juggling five other cases and had lots of important people that needed to get in touch with me.

Before my scolding abruptly halted his calls and thus his sharing of his amateurish investigatory findings (and what I referred to as local-yocal intel), Earl had communicated that the solicitor was in a hotly contested re-election primary. His opponent's platform called into scrutiny the amount of taxpayer dollars spent on the solicitor's jury trials in comparison to the percentage of convictions. If the propaganda circulated was even close to being accurate, Rick Watson's record was precarious, at best. At worst, it was a "reckless squandering of taxpayer money," and "a poor investment for Thurmond County," as claimed by his opponent's ad blitz.

Rick Watson's previous losses were not newsworthy, so they were easily swept under the rug. The defendants in those cases hadn't been high-profile businessmen, much less the president of one of the most successful banks in the state. Moreover, the underlying motive of the Walker case was salacious— knocking off a wife for a pretty young assistant. The media coverage requests had already created a buzz at the courthouse. Rick Watson's performance would be excruciatingly analyzed. Eyes would be focused on every action from his selection of the jury panel to his examination of every witness. This was the type of trial that could make or break a career. And Rick Watson knew it.

The emergency meeting was to convey a plea offer from the solicitor. Rick Watson proffered a plea of three years to both defendants in the Somerset Federal Correctional Institute, the minimum-security facility that was consistently ranked as the cushiest prison in the country. It was the location of Savannah Hart Abbott's son. She would be able to see him daily. "It's a no-brainer," Rick Watson said, and I agreed. Taking even a strong case to the jury was like playing craps in Vegas—totally unpredictable.

There was only one hurdle, Earl Dixson. I anticipated resistance. But, I was prepared to accept the plea for Charles Walker, with or without Savannah Abbott. The case against my client was tenuous. But, I was certain when the jury laid eyes on Savannah Abbott, there would be no doubt in their mind that Charles Walker hired her for more than the number of words per minute she could type on a keyboard.

Chapter Seventy-Two

Elliott Gray

During the meetings among the defense lawyers, I had quietly watched and taken copious notes. I was not immune to the fact that everyone thought I was only part of the defense team to make them think outside the box. I knew they were waiting for me to offer bizarre or unconventional theories, like the ones in my published legal thrillers. While this was true, Charles expected much more from me.

For as long as I could remember, Charles had been painstakingly meticulous, precise, and well let's just say, down-right persnickety. Growing up, his nickname was Mr. Clean, after the bronzed, bald, muscular, pierced-ear figure that appeared on the all-purpose cleaner.

Charles' nickname certainly didn't derive from the physical characteristics of the branded image. It originated from his spotless room and bathroom. It always had a strong smell of Pine Sol and Clorox. His bathroom had to sparkle. His bed had to be made to military inspection standards. Charles' closet was the first time I had ever seen a clamp hanger for pants.

I always assumed his strict father was behind his shipshape living quarters and neat appearance. His father, a banker, was the ultimate nerd. All the guys used to rib Charles about his father's pocket protector. Honestly, I couldn't recall a time when I had seen old-man Walker without his customary accessory fully loaded with pens.

As we got older, I realized that Charles' neurotic fastidiousness wasn't commanded by his father. It was who he was. Back then, OCD wasn't diagnosed. If so, Charles would have been the poster child. Despite these quirks, Charles Walker was popular with boys and girls in high school and revered by the teachers. He was polite, smart, a consummate rule follower, loyal to a fault, and reliable. For these reasons, none of our childhood friends were a bit surprised at his ascension to the highest position in the largest bank in the state. And, anyone who knew Charles Walker also knew beyond a reasonable doubt that he was incapable of even daydreaming about committing any crime, in particular, murder and especially of his wife.

Charles requested that I provide him with a full report after each attorney meeting. He not only expected my candid assessment of every sliver of evidence against him but also every detail about the attorneys. He wanted to understand their charisma, approachability, nervous twitches, and habits.

In retaining Rollins Bishop, Charles had totally relied on the recommendation of his long-time business lawyer, Vincent Ellis. Rollins had come highly endorsed by Vincent. "Rollins is highly successful and well-known. His clients range from Atlanta's top businessmen to professional athletes."

After reviewing Rollins's impressive resume and client list, Charles only asked a single question of Vincent: "How will he come across to a jury?"

Vincent's clients were banks and large corporations. Vincent spent his time in boardrooms not courtrooms. But, Vincent convinced Charles he was in great hands with Rollins Bishop.

When first meeting Rollins Bishop, admittedly, I was impressed with his confidence and swagger. Over the course of our subsequent meetings, I became less convinced that he was the right man for the job.

Now Earl Dixson was a different story. Earl didn't put on airs. He didn't flaunt the number of successful acquittals he had obtained. He didn't wear $3000 custom-made suits with silk pocket squares. Hell, Earl Dixson's socks didn't even match. He likely paid $10 for his haircuts, instead of $300 like Rollins. I would bet every penny I had earned selling books that the man had never had a manicure. On the other hand, Rollins' nails were evenly filed and glowed the same spick-and-span luster as Charles' childhood bathroom.

Earl Dixson was authentic and raw. Equally important, he was local. He didn't rely upon a host of underlings to do the dirty work. He rolled up the sleeves of his cotton-blend, frayed shirt that had probably never seen the inside of a dry-cleaning operation and got down in the trenches.

I cancelled a book signing to attend an emergency meeting called by Rollins. We learned the urgency was due to a plea offer communicated by Rick Watson, the county solicitor, South Carolina's equivalent to a district attorney. Once the trial started, the offer was off the table. Rollins was going to strongly advise Charles to take it. Though it appeared that the defense had credible witnesses, Rollins gave what I called a CYAS—cover-your-ass spiel. He explained that a courtroom atmosphere was a totally different environment. Despite all the preparations in the world, there were always unknowns that may or may not play in our favor. The plea offer was something you could "take to the bank."

Earl Dixson was incensed.

"Even taking the solicitor's evidence at face value, the case is flimsy," Earl said. "There is no doubt in my mind that the hit instructions originated with William Wilson and his daughter, Alice."

When Hannah Anne Hart had first proclaimed a similar theory weeks ago, I thought she must have read too many of my books because I was thinking the same thing. But, it seemed that with each newly unearthed piece of evidence, that theory gained strength.

I became totally convinced in our theory when Earl told us about his past experiences with William Wilson before he left his position as the Thurmond County Sheriff for the Kentucky warden position.

Earl had seen everything from illegal searches to manufactured evidence. He had similar encounters with Chief Deputy Jimmy Barbee. Barbee's emulation of the former sheriff was the secret to his rapid rise within the police ranks, Earl opined. From Earl's accounts, the Chief Deputy had taken more than a leaf from William Wilson's book. He wasn't sure who was worse. The problem was that the judge would never permit the jury to hear about Earl's discoveries in other cases with these two crooked cops. Without this corroboration, I worried that it may be a reach for a jury to believe that certain law enforcement officials could be so immoral. As Hannah Anne Hart would say, "It was a hard pill to swallow."

Charles was the antithesis of a risk-taker. He wouldn't even take short cuts. Now that his freedom and the career that he had spent his entire life building were at stake, his wariness was off the charts.

"I am going to take it, Elliott, unless you advise otherwise," Charles said, after learning of the plea offer.

The trial was scheduled to start the next week. Time was of the essence. What would I advise? I wanted to hide behind the pages of my new novel where I could control the outcome with a stroke of my pen. But this was the real world, not a world of fiction. It had been years since I tried a case. I didn't have a foolproof answer for my best friend.

Chapter Seventy-Three

Earl Dixson

I'll never forget the call from Walt after his grandson's arrest. It was months ago, but I still got chills recalling his strong voice cracking when he said that he needed help, not for the Marine base but of a personal nature.

Prior to that request, I had only worked with Walt in his professional role. It was no wonder he was a leader in the Marine Corps. His moral characteristics checked all the boxes: courageous, decisive, dependable, ethical, sound judgment, loyal, and tactful. But, upon first meeting him, his other characteristics were what intimidated me.

I guessed his zero-percent-body-fat physique came from knocking out one hundred push-ups daily. Even when he wasn't in uniform, his clothes were impeccable, nary a wrinkle. He probably had a dedicated sock drawer, perfectly folded and arranged by color. I was lucky if I could find two matching socks. Most of the time, I'd locate one inside a pair of shorts due to the static cling caused by my outdated dryer. I never learned how he kept his thick head of hair neatly coiffed.

Though I'd say we had a solid relationship, he kept his personal life close to the vest. However, he had disclosed his son's situation and that he should have involved me when Josh was arrested in Kentucky. He explained that at that time, he thought he needed someone local. Walt blamed himself for Josh's imprisonment believing, that he should have hired better counsel. "I should have hired you," he said. When he asked me to take his grandson's case, I was honored that he trusted me.

Walt conveyed that his twenty-one year old grandson, Cray, had been visiting his father. He stopped for gas en route to home from the Kentucky prison. An off-duty TSA agent accompanied by a trained sniffer dog alerted local authorities that a customer was smuggling drugs. A large amount of cocaine was located in Cray's trunk.

After learning that Cray had visited the prison run by one William Wilson, I suspected something was up. After Josh's confession to Walt about the setup, I alerted Cray and Walt to the dilemma. First, Josh needed to testify for his son to stand a chance. Second, it would be a tremendous hurdle for a jury to believe a convicted felon's story that law enforcement officers were the guilty parties. Josh would not be a sympathetic witness for any defense, much less one involving his own flesh and blood. His testimony basically would be that he sacrificed his son in exchange for an early prison release. Finally, I warned Cray and Walt that there could be serious retribution against Josh for making accusations against those on the inside. In fact, everyone in the family could be at risk.

I obtained a very attractive plea offer—one year in the Somerset Federal Correctional Institute, a minimum-security facility with more amenities than my gym, or at least the version of my gym that I could recall. I hadn't stepped foot into it in five years.

Cray took it.

Despite that most lawyers would be pleased with the outcome under these circumstances, I wasn't able to shake that case. It was six months after Marsha had walked out on me. I wasn't myself. I was lost. I was lonely. I had lost my fight. I am confident that if I had a do-over with Cray's case now, I would have found a way to save that young man. That case continued to haunt me. It would intrude into my memory at the oddest times, often during Sunday church service. When Walt called and needed representation for another member of his family, Cray's mother, I felt that my prayers had been answered for an opportunity to redeem myself.

So, when Rollins Bishop spouted off about the deal offered from Rick Watson, I must have come across as a madman. The prosecution had a weak case; we had a solid defense. Rick Watson knew it, thus the plea.

Rollins wasn't even impressed by the discovery of Brandy Chastain and her story. He presented the solicitor's likely rebuttal—*a middleman picked up Josh during a bus stop and drove him to Harper's Corner where Josh fed a tall tale to a naïve and gullible bimbo to establish an alibi.* I cringed at Rollins' characterization of Brandy as a "bimbo." But, then again, we saw everything through a different lens.

Rollins and I were at a stalemate. I decided to withhold the new information gleaned from interviewing Nancy Nichols—the answering machine message she overheard from Charles to Alice about the Jessamin Island code change. Rollins would find holes in that as well. I was starting to believe he would readily dismiss any corroborating evidence obtained by me, the Beaufort solo practitioner. In fact, he was going to strongly advise Charles to take the deal. I wholeheartedly believed in Savannah's and Charles' innocence. I wanted to take the case to a jury. Of course, I had to present the plea to Savannah. If she decided to accept the offer, it was her decision to make.

Interestingly, at the conclusion of the meeting, Elliott Gray asked to speak to me. I hadn't heard the man even mumble one word throughout all our meetings. He was like a human tape recorder, diligently documenting every word spoken. He asked if I would accompany him the following day to visit Charles.

"Charles needs to hear your assessment of the solicitor's evidence and the witnesses for the defense," he said.

And the kicker, Elliott Gray told me that he believed my theory. In fact, he had communicated it to Rollins Bishop weeks ago. Rollins had told him to "save it for your next novel."

"Thanks for telling me that," I said. "It's nice to have reinforcement from someone with your experience. Savannah's mother believes it too. These ruthless sons of bitches started a war when they killed Josh Abbott. And I'm not going to just roll over with some damn plea. I am ready to fight. I am going to win."

Apparently, Charles Walker liked what he heard. He said that if Savannah rejected the plea, he would reject it too. However, he wanted me to represent him at trial. With his freedom and reputation on the line, he didn't want an attorney who wasn't behind him wholly and unconditionally.

For a businessman, I had to give Charles Walker credit. Juries were perceptive. If Rollins Bishop wasn't totally committed to the defense, the jury would see right through him.

Savannah rejected the plea outright, like I thought she would. I was ready to fight. And, this time, I wasn't going to let the Abbotts down. Or Charles Walker.

Chapter Seventy-Four

Solicitor Rick Watson

Primary Day was several weeks away. I had rarely faced any formidable opponent in my twenty years as solicitor, and almost never in a primary. To make matters worse, my opponent, Vic Jenkins, had a personal ax to grind. Vic had recently entered a plea on behalf of his brother for drug trafficking. Initially, he flatly rejected my plea offer. But, as the trial approached, Vic got cold feet.

"Your brother has a rap sheet a page long," I argued. "With his record, the jury won't believe anything he says," as I handed the printout of previous arrests. "He will be viewed as a hard-core criminal. If convicted, his sentence will be five times longer than what I am offering."

Admittedly, the evidence was sketchy. Vic argued that it had been planted, but I had no control over the facts. Facts are delivered to me by our sheriff's department. I have to play the hand I am dealt.

I thought when William Wilson left for Kentucky that the number of rotten hands dealt would cease. For those of us on the inside, it was common knowledge that Wilson pushed the envelope when it came to constitutional searches and seizures. His security was more important than "the scumbags' rights." Wilson justified his sleezy procedures, saying that he put himself in harm's way every time he responded to a call.

I hate to admit that my strongest weapon as a trial lawyer was the fear of the unknown. I frequently used it to my advantage, especially when I had a weak case.

"You can take my plea to the bank. A jury's decision is as unpredictable as death. Do you really want to place your client's future in the hands of twelve people who you don't know? Jurors present the greatest uncertainty within our judicial system. Trusting them with your life is like playing Russian Roulette."

I had a list of scare tactics a mile-long, all intended to convince a defendant into accepting a plea. My conviction percentage would be much lower had these cases gone to trial.

Vic's campaign agenda was clear. He intended to exploit my record to demonstrate the incompetence of Rick Watson and his entire staff, and their reckless squandering of taxpayer money. His slogans were everywhere: *A Vote for Vic is inVesting in a Safer Community. "Vic for conVICtions based on eVidence, and Vic for Value.*

Everywhere I seemed to turn, I was surrounded by his campaign propaganda and all those highlighted Vs and Vics. His signs seemed to be spreading like wildfire. They were popping up everywhere. Hell, there were several yard signs on my street. I was more than curious where his campaign contributions originated. Who was financing this assault?

Local reporters had obviously noticed this onslaught. Several articles regurgitating Vic's message had already appeared in the local newspaper and on the coveted front page, no less.

Over the last twenty years, I could count on one hand where I was even mentioned in any article and never on the front page. Jessamin Island, Beaufort, Port Royal, and all the surrounding communities were tourist havens. They didn't produce sensational or bizarre cases. But the Walker case was in a league of its own. Every local news network had requested cameras in the courtroom for the March trial. I was basically going to be on trial along with Charles Walker and Savannah Abbott. The press would dissect my every move from my opening statement to my examinations of each witness.

I could see the caricatures of me now in the paper. I was not immune to the jokes about my physical appearance. My hair was *a colossal comb-over, a badly frayed rug*. My eyebrows were capable of *mopping a floor* or *flossing teeth*. I even overheard one of my loyal staff members laughing about my *ear hair comb-over*.

Years before the rapid demise of my hair was replaced with the wild growth of ear hair and wiry eyebrows, I had been teased about my large head. In middle school, on hot days, the joke was to stand beside me because I would provide some shade. My nickname "Shade" stuck, even throughout high school. Yep, I was going to be a courtroom artist's dream.

This case was about more than the fate of Charles Walker and Savannah Abbott. It would determine my destiny. The influence and respect that I currently held was only due to my title as solicitor. I was quite aware that my position was the only reason that Tina, my new girlfriend, even looked twice at me. There was really no other explanation why a middle-aged, balding man with an oversized head and hair growing out of his ears would otherwise stand a chance with Tina. She was cute, had a knockout figure, and was fifteen years my junior. More was at stake with this trial than just a win or loss on my record.

Hopefully, Rollins Bishop would take the plea. However, with Earl, not a chance in hell. He was undefeated in battles with me in the courtroom. So, my strategy was to present a very attractive plea offer to Rollins outside of the presence of Earl Dixson. I knew the only chance I had with Earl was if the Atlanta big wig was calling the shots.

My strategy backfired. Not only was Rollins Bishop not calling the shots, he was either fired or a strategic decision was made to have only one attorney at the defense table. I understood that strategy because I had counted on the opposite. I knew that the presence of multiple attorneys would flaunt Mr. Walker's wealth. When only Earl Dixson showed up to represent both defendants, I knew I was in trouble.

PART XIII

Chapter Seventy-Five

Earl Dixson

I have tried hundreds of cases, but I was experiencing flashbacks of my first one—sweaty palms, a pit in my stomach, a racing pulse, and the rash that started on my chest and spread like wildfire up my neck. Back then, the emotions were triggered by inexperience, insecurity, a fierce desire to serve my clients' interests, and a passion to win. The intervening years brought experience and with experience, my insecurities dissipated. The pretrial side effects vanished and were forgotten until now. This morning—the morning of the first day of *The State v. Charles Steven Walker and Savannah Hart Abbott,* I was greeting the day with my head over the toilet and a violent, splotching rash that was not only on my chest and neck but also now spreading up my face.

Before today, my focus had been solely on impressing the jury with my arguments. I had never considered my appearance---what the jury may think of my out-of-date suit, tie, or scuffed loafers. But now, in addition to my A-game, I wanted to look my best. I wanted to impress Hannah Anne.

I ripped off the plastic dry-cleaning bag from my new suit and starched, white, button-down shirt. With my shaky hands, I knotted my new tie, a Christmas present from Hannah Anne. My anxiety briefly subsided when putting on my socks—matching socks, also a Christmas gift from my girlfriend. She assumed that I was color-blind, the reason behind my monotone attire and mismatched socks.

We both laughed after opening that present. And it had been a hearty, contagious laugh, bringing tears to our eyes. Though it was a funny gift, I attributed our belly laughter to our respective defense mechanisms—a release from the heavy sadness that accompanied spending the holidays without Savannah.

I felt responsible for this predicament. The judge who had presided over the bail hearing was newly elected. I had yet to appear before him. I was no longer intimidated by a judge's imposing black robe or lofty position behind the elevated bench, especially one wet behind the ears. I knew they weren't infallible. I knew their professional weaknesses and their personal struggles. After all, they and their families were human too. What neither cocky Rollins Bishop nor I had anticipated was the packed courtroom and media coverage for the bail hearing.

Chief Deputy Barbee testified that the day preceding the bail hearing, one of his officers overheard Savannah Abbott bragging that she was "getting the hell out of dodge on a private plane with her boyfriend." The green judge sustained my hearsay objection—the appropriate witness should have been the officer who heard the conversation, not Chief Deputy Barbee. Although the judge agreed with me, he obviously was influenced.

It didn't help matters that Rick Watson argued that Charles Walker had the resources to flee the country. "They are both flight risks," he said. "I will expedite the trial date but strongly oppose any bail."

I should have demanded that Rollins keep his mouth shut and let me do the talking. In response to the solicitor's offer to expedite the trial, he jumped to his feet.

"A substantial bail posting will eliminate any risk of flight," he proffered.

Of course, it was no secret that Charles Walker had significant assets, so Rollins Bishop's argument fell on deaf ears. Bail was denied.

When I learned that The Honorable Samuel B. Cobb would be the presiding trial judge, I assured Hannah Anne that we would get a fair shake, unlike the bail hearing before the "spineless man of straw," as she referred to the judge. I refrained from telling her that our trial judge was another sign of divine intervention—that Savannah had a guardian angel watching over her. Locating Brandy Chastain, the convenience store clerk in Harper's Corner, North Carolina, had been the first sign.

I knew things about Judge Sam Cobb that no one else did. I knew where he had grown up and that his middle initial stood for Baxby, his mother's maiden name. I had forgotten or never knew who had referred the scared and inexperienced young lawyer to me. What I'll never forget was his panicked message on my office answering machine: "My family needs help. You come highly recommended. My uncle, Charlie Baxby, has been arrested for aiding and abetting prostitution. If you haven't heard of him, he's a state senator. You could say he has a few enemies. He's been framed. Please call me back as soon as possible."

Like most evenings, I was working late. I certainly had heard of Charlie Baxby. He was a renegade. His fire-and-brimstone orations in the state Senate could have been from behind a church pulpit. He was a civil rights activist who had no fear. He was constantly on a warpath against the Walhollow County Sheriff's Department and its ignorance of probable cause, use of excessive force, and targeting "Badhollow," the department's characterization of the lower-income sections of the city.

Walhollow County was the westernmost county in the state and also the poorest. No one paid attention to the tirades from the "hick from Walhollow." He was merely seeking attention, trying to garner free publicity for his aspirations for a higher political office. It would take me four and half hours to drive there from Beaufort, but I hopped in the car that night and met Sam at an all-night diner. He began to talk about his uncle.

"Uncle Charlie drives down Main Street, past downtown to the seedy side of the city. He's been doing it for as long as I can remember. It's common knowledge that he pulls over when he sees a lady loitering on a corner. Uncle Charlie rolls down his window, hands them whatever cash is on him, and offers words of encouragement. Most of the time, my Aunt Ethel is with him. However, the first time she witnessed my uncle's generosity, I happened to be with them too. He asked Aunt Ethel if she had any cash. She told him that all she had was 20 bucks. 'Why in the world do you need cash?' she asked him. 'You'll see,' Uncle Charlie said. He then pulled up to the curb and handed a woman the $20 bill. Aunt Ethel screamed at him and said he'd gone crazy. 'That woman is not homeless, she's a prostitute,' she told him. He said, 'I'm well aware of that, Ethel.' She said, 'Charlie, I know you mean well with that bleedin' heart of yours, but those women are no better than the corruption you try to get rid of in the sheriff's department!' My uncle just shook his head, and I'll never forget what he said 'til the day I die. He said, 'These women are lost; they don't see a different path. They need someone to believe in them. They need to find hope for a better way.'"

During our third cup of coffee, I started believing the young man. His uncle was the reason he had entered law school. He had paid his nephew's tuition. "There needs to be at least one honest lawyer around," he told Sam. Then Sam said pleadingly, "I've only been practicing three years. I don't have the experience to handle a case this hot. I need your help."

"Uncle Charlie's arrest was made by his primary target in the police force—the same one who followed him on numerous occasions in an unmarked car. Uncle Charlie used to laugh about it. 'You are playing with fire, Charlie,' my Aunt Ethel cautioned, to which Uncle Charlie would respond, 'What's he going to do, arrest me?' But the day she wasn't with him, that's exactly what happened. My uncle is innocent," he said, choking up.

Though the clothes on my back were all I had, I stayed a week in Walhollow County. It only took five days to gather evidence of a scam carried out by the arresting officer. After Charlie Baxby drove away from the women on the street corner, the officer got a kick out of pocketing Charlie Baxby's cash in exchange for not charging them with prostitution. One recounted that the officer handcuffed her, placed her in the squad car, sat beside her in the backseat, and placed her hand on his zipper. "You can keep ol' Charlie's $55 if I get a $55 service." She spit on him. He took the cash, drove a mile farther down the road, and dumped her.

Had I stayed longer in Walhollow County, I suspected that I would have learned so much more. But, I didn't need more time. Fearful of the publicity from my findings only after five days, the charges against Charlie Baxby were quickly dropped. Samuel Baxby Cobb, now one of the longest tenured circuit judges, would never forget it.

Chapter Seventy-Six

Earl Dixson

After Rollins Bishop strongly advised Charles Walker to accept the plea, Charles canned him. I no longer had to tolerate Rollins' pompous showboating, but the burden I was carrying was overwhelming. Nevertheless, when I entered the courtroom, I regained my focus. At my core, I was an introvert, but somehow, this environment transformed me. I felt more at home here than in my own house. I related to the men and women in the juror's box. I had more in common with them than with my inherited client, Charles Walker.

With the bailiff's announcement of "All rise," the Honorable Samuel Baxby Cobb entered the courtroom. No one had ever made the connection between the judge and his uncle, especially this far east. When Sam was first elected to the bench, I wondered if he would recuse himself when my cases were scheduled for trial. I wasn't going to raise the potential conflict of interest because it would expose his secret. And, I certainly wasn't going to take advantage of our history. But, there was no better man to be presiding over the Walker and Abbott case. This judge had experienced police corruption in a personal way.

When the bailiff announced, "This court is now in session," adrenaline shot through my body and took me to a different place. Along with the solicitor, Rick Watson, I starred in the opening act, a stage on which I excelled. It was game on.

Ladies and Gentlemen of the Jury, my name is Rick Watson. I am the Solicitor of Thurmond County. I will be presenting the case against Charles Steven Walker and Savannah Hart Abbott. The evidence will clearly and unequivocally show that the defendants conspired to murder Alice Walker, the wife of defendant, Charles Walker. Why? Mr. Walker and Ms. Abbott were having an affair, and they had the perfect hit man. Ms. Abbott's husband, Joshua Abbott, is a convicted felon. Joshua Abbott had just been released from federal prison in Kentucky after serving time for cultivating and distributing narcotics. Upon his release, he traveled to Jessamin Island where he was to murder Alice Walker, who was spending time in the couple's vacation home. Thankfully, the scheme failed. Alice Walker's life was spared. Charles Walker and Savannah Abbott should be punished severely, not only for plotting a murder but also for using a vulnerable, desperate, and troubled man. This man was so tormented about his decisions that he took his own life. Charles Walker and Savannah Abbott have Joshua Abbott's blood on their hands and, but for a little luck, they would have Alice Walker's blood on their hands too. I appreciate your service and your attention to the facts that will be presented in this case. May justice prevail.

Good morning. I'm Earl Dixson. I represent the defendants, Charles Walker and Savannah Abbott. Like Mr. Watson, I appreciate your service and trust that justice will prevail. It is people like you—everyday, hardworking citizens—who will be able to understand this case. You have the proper perspective to understand the damage to our community when corruption and power infiltrate and prevail in our justice system. Here, the corrupt individuals are people whose job it is to protect us. I know that's a hard pill to swallow. We need to have faith in our justice system. We need to have faith in our law enforcement officials. For all these systems to maintain integrity, those who make up the core of these invaluable structures must be held accountable just like you and I would be held accountable if we committed a crime. Accountability is especially essential for the leaders in our prison system. I have faith in each of you. I know you will listen to the witnesses and thoughtfully consider the evidence. I am confident you will conclude that Charles Walker and Savannah Abbott had no part in this botched plot. Am I going to argue there was no plot? Absolutely not. The evidence will prove that there was a plot, but the conspirators were Alice Walker and her father, William Wilson. William Wilson is the warden of the prison where Joshua Abbott was incarcerated and later released. As Solicitor Watson conveyed, Joshua Abbott is the deceased husband of the defendant, Savannah Abbott. Despite Mr. Abbott's imprisonment, the couple had a happy marriage. Defendant Charles Walker's marriage, however, is not a happy one to say the least. But, it isn't Charles Walker who is having an affair. The evidence will demonstrate that it is Alice Walker who is cheating, and with not one, but numerous lovers. Alice Walker desperately wants out of her marriage. Alice Walker wants unfettered access to Charles Walker's holdings and their bank accounts. On top of wanting Charles Walker out of the picture, Alice Walker wants his reputation ruined. She wants him to rot in jail. Her father was more than willing to provide the means to carry out her wishes. His motivation goes beyond just helping his daughter. The evidence will prove that Alice Walker's father has significant financial issues. He stood to gain if Charles Walker was out of the way, and his daughter had complete access to his assets. William Wilson and Alice Wilson Walker are the guilty parties, not Savannah Abbott and Charles Walker. Thank you again for your service in this case.

Judge Cobb announced a fifteen-minute recess. In all my trials before him, he had never taken a break so early in a trial, much less right after the opening arguments. I wondered if his uncle's case was coming back to mind. I hoped that it was.

Chapter Seventy-Seven

Earl Dixson

When Judge Cobb reentered the courtroom, he instructed the solicitor and me to approach the bench. I was more than curious as I stepped around the defense counsel table and walked toward the judge.

"Gentleman, as you know, the media coverage of this case is significant, more so than I anticipated. I am not going to permit any grandstanding, and if you raise an objection, you better have a solid basis."

I knew Judge Cobb's remarks were directed to the solicitor. He was notorious for such tactics.

"Mr. Watson, please call your first witness," Judge Cobb announced, as we made our way back to our respective corners.

"Thank you, Your Honor. The prosecution calls Ronald Griffin."

The diminutive guard known as "Shorty" from the Kentucky federal prison placed his hand on the Bible and swore to tell the truth, the whole truth, and nothing but the truth.

"Mr. Griffin, what is your position?" as the solicitor began his direct examination.

"I am a guard at the Kentucky Federal Penitentiary. Been there for ten years," Griffin responded.

"As a guard at the Kentucky prison, did you know inmate Joshua Carter Abbott?"

"Yes, sir. I did. I was in charge of his release on parole."

"By 'in charge,' do you mean in charge of arranging his transportation from the prison?"

"Yes, sir."

"And from the prison to what location?"

"Wherever he tells me he is going."

"Where did Joshua Abbott tell you that he was going?"

"To Beaufort, South Carolina. He said he had some things to settle with his ex-wife."

I jumped to my feet.

"Objection," I said, emphatically. "There is absolutely no evidence of this statement, and it is contrary to the facts. It's one thing to permit communications between the deceased and Mr. Griffin about otherwise verifiable information but quite another for statements that only Josh Abbott, who is deceased, can confirm."

"I'll permit it," Judge Cobb said, overruling my objection. "As you know, Mr. Dixson, the dead-man statute doesn't apply in criminal cases. You will have sufficient opportunity to present your evidence to the contrary."

"Thank you, Your Honor," the solicitor said, attempting to suppress a smile. "So, Mr. Griffin, did you transport Joshua Abbott to Beaufort, South Carolina?"

"No, I took him to the bus station. He got on a bus to Beaufort. He was to immediately check in with his probation officer who would then verify this contact to me."

"Did you ever receive that verification?"

"No. Thomas Phillips, I mean, Joshua Abbott, never attempted any contact with his probation officer."

"What is the procedure when you don't receive verification?"

"I inform my warden. Our protocol is to issue an APB, but the warden makes the call when to do that."

"And do you know whether that was done in this case?"

"Yes, that's how we located him."

"Where was he located?"

"He had checked into a hotel on Jessamin Island in South Carolina. The Thurmond County Sheriff's Department contacted me after his arrest. They told me he was in possession of crack cocaine, a significant amount of cash, and what appeared to be documents instructing a hit."

"Thank you, Mr. Griffin."

"Mr. Dixson, do you have any questions for Mr. Griffin?" Judge Cobb inquired.

"Yes, Your Honor. Mr. Griffin, I represent Charles Walker and Savannah Abbott. Have you ever met either of these individuals?"

"No, I have not."

"Savannah Abbott is the wife of Joshua Abbott. Did you contact Mrs. Abbott and inform her that her husband was being released on parole?"

"No. It is our practice to ask the prisoner who we should contact. Mr. Abbott did not instruct us to call anyone."

"You testified that you drove Joshua Abbott to the bus station and that he boarded a bus for Beaufort, South Carolina. Is that correct?"

"Yes, it is correct."

"How do you know that Joshua Abbott boarded a bus to that location?"

"Well, because I purchased the bus ticket, handed him the ticket, and saw him board the bus."

"Did you wait for the bus to leave the station?"

"Yes, I sure did."

"There is no doubt in your mind that Joshua Abbott was on the bus when it left on its route?"

"That's correct. That's part of my job—to verify that the inmate connects with the specified transportation."

"By inmate, I assume you are referring to Joshua Abbott, who had been released by your facility?"

"Yep, that's right."

"Your Honor, I would like to present into evidence the scheduled bus route testified to by Mr. Griffin."

"Any objection?" Judge Cobb asked, directing his question to Rick Watson.

"None, Your Honor," Watson responded, after examining the bus schedule.

"I have no further questions, at this time," I said.

"Mr. Watson, call your next witness," Judge Cobb instructed, as Shorty Griffin exited the witness stand.

"The prosecution calls Chief Deputy Jimmy Barbee of the Thurmond County Sheriff's Department," Rick Watson announced.

Officer Barbee made his way to the stand, dressed in his crisp police uniform. He wore it well. The starched shirt snugly outlined his fit physique. He strutted to the stand like a peacock. I suppressed a chuckle at my thoughts. My girlfriend's "Hannah-isms" were rubbing off on me. I noted that a couple of the female jurors were particularly engaged. I hoped that Hannah Anne was watching carefully and taking good notes, as I had requested.

The background questions by Rick Watson established that Jimmy Wayne Barbee, the Chief Deputy in the Thurmond County Sheriff's Department, was the officer who arrested Joshua Abbott at the Jessamin Island Breezeway for possession of crack cocaine with intent to distribute and conspiracy to commit murder.

"What led you to the room occupied by Joshua Abbott?" Rick Watson, continued.

"The department received a call about drug trafficking in the vicinity of the Jessamin Island Breezeway. Upon my arrival, the desk clerk communicated odd behavior from one of the guests. The guest checked in under the name Thomas Phillips," Deputy Barbee recited. "I later learned Thomas Phillips was an alias used by Joshua Abbott. I proceeded to his room for a knock and talk. Based upon the clerk's statement, I suspected this guest may have observed suspicious activity or was engaged himself in said activity. When he opened his door, he was holding a beer, and I observed several empty beer bottles on the floor. His eyes were visibly glassy, indicative of narcotic use. He exhibited disorderly conduct, defiance, and was belligerent. I observed an open duffle bag. When I requested inspection of the bag, he began cursing and reached around his back. Thinking he may in possession of a concealed weapon, I restrained him. I seized the duffle bag and discovered that it contained a large amount of crack cocaine."

"What led you to believe Joshua Abbott was involved in a murder conspiracy?"

"In addition to the narcotics identified in the duffle bag, there were several sketches and photographs inside of the bag."

"Can you describe the sketches and photographs?"

"Yes, sir. There were several photographs of a woman, which we later identified as Alice Walker, the defendant's wife. There were also photographs of a house, which we learned was defendant Charles Walker's home located on Jessamin Island. The sketches contained the home's address, Alice Walker's estimated arrival and departure times, and detailed methods of access into the home."

"Your Honor, I would like these photographs and sketches, marked as Exhibits A–E," Solicitor Watson said, handing the proposed exhibits to Judge Cobb.

"Chief Deputy Barbee, can you read for the jury the notes on the sketches marked as Exhibit A?"

"Option #1 is the back door. The entry is hidden from the neighbors. The key to the back door is in the rock (see photo). Option #2 is the front door. It has a keyless entry with a digital combination lock. The code is 6290 ##. The # must be entered 2x. The door will unlock after entering the code," Deputy Barbee read.

"Did you confirm that the code did in fact open the front door?"

"Yes, sir. After entry of the code on the instructions, the door unlocked."

"When did you learn of Joshua Abbott's death?"

"After his arrest, as I mentioned, he was so strung out that we secured him in a cell to sleep it off. When I went to question him the next day, he had hung himself—made a noose with his belt. Like I said, he was strung out when I picked him up. I was going to question him the next morning."

"Is this standard procedure within the department?"

"Yes, sir. The department has received several complaints of mistreatment in attempting to question a defendant while under the influence. While we disagree with the allegations of mistreatment, we are transparent and take these complaints seriously. So, we implemented new policies. Our procedure protects both the department and the suspect."

"Thank you, Deputy Barbee. I have no further questions, Your Honor."

"Mr. Dixson, do you have any questions for the witness," Judge Cobb asked me.

"I certainly do, Your Honor," I said, as I approached the stiff, uniformed officer.

"Why do you refer to the instructions on Exhibit A as containing 'sketches'?" I asked, knowing that Deputy Barbee had been coached to use language from the letter Savannah had sent to Josh in prison.

"I don't understand your point," Chief Deputy Barbee responded, though he was taken off guard with my initial question. I saw him squirm in his seat. I hoped that the jury made this observation as well. And, I hoped Hannah Anne was watching them carefully and noting any reaction.

"'Sketch,' as defined by *Merriam-Webster Dictionary*, is a 'rough drawing representing the chief features of an object or scene and often made as a preliminary study.' You just testified that the hit instructions contained photographs and sketches. Would you say that the typed instructions on Exhibit A are drawings?"

"In my line of work, I don't have time to consult a dictionary at a crime scene. The evidence speaks for itself."

"Indeed, it does, but Deputy Barbee, words are important, especially when describing a crime scene and evidence obtained from a hotel room without a search warrant. I will ask you the question differently. Did the alleged hit instructions comprising Exhibits A–E contain any hand-drawn pictures?"

"No, just sketches," Barbee answered, sticking to the rehearsed testimony.

"Your Honor, I would like to submit the definition of the word 'sketch' from the *Merriam-Webster's Dictionary* into evidence."

"Watson? Any objection?" Judge Cobb asked the solicitor.

"Other than relevance, Your Honor. As the experienced deputy testified, he doesn't consult a dictionary at a crime scene. The evidence speaks for itself."

I knew that Watson was going to introduce the letter Savannah had mailed to Josh at some point during his case, likely during the examination of Warden William Wilson. Watson had provided a copy of the letter to Rollins Bishop when he laid out the case against Charles and Savannah—the letter that supposedly contained the hit instructions. Her letter enclosed sketches. Of course, we knew that what she enclosed were Cray's cartoons. But her letter wasn't clear. In her letter, she had written, "*Do you have any updates on your parole? I am enclosing some sketches. I am also enclosing some photos. I will explain them further when we talk.*" Describing the hit instructions as "sketches" was calculated and important to the prosecution. I had hoped to introduce Charles' conference speech and the use of Cray's drawings. That evidence would substantiate the truth—that Savannah didn't send hit instructions to Josh through the mail but copies of her son's contributions to Charles Walker's presentation. However, due to the last-minute change in Charles' topic for the conference, the cartoons about digitalization weren't applicable, and Charles didn't use them. I had to come up with a different angle.

"Watson is correct. The exhibits marked into evidence don't contain any reference to a 'sketch.' The jury shall disregard use of the word 'sketch' and refer to Exhibits A–E for what they are. I am not going to allow your exhibit, Mr. Dixson."

Judge Cobb knew as well as I did that asking a jury to disregard something they had already heard was asking someone to unsee something, or as Hannah Anne would say, "un-ring a bell." At least, that is what I was counting on.

"Chief Deputy Barbee, you testified that you have been with the Thurmond County Sheriff's Department for twelve years. When did you obtain the status as Chief Deputy of the department?"

"Ten years ago."

"So, let me get this straight, you were with the department for only two years before being named Chief Deputy?"

"That's correct. Guess I impressed my superiors," he said, turning toward the jury box.

I noticed one female juror snickering.

"Well, I'm glad you brought that up. When you joined the Thurmond County Sheriff's Department, who were your superiors?"

"My first year, Rodney Turner was Sheriff. Then, my second year, William Wilson."

"Do you know where either Mr. Turner or Mr. Wilson are today?"

"I've heard that Rodney Turner is off the grid somewhere fishing. William Wilson left the department for Kentucky. I believe he is still there."

"Do you know why William Wilson left for Kentucky?"

"I believe for a new job."

"Chief Deputy Barbee, are you aware that William Wilson is currently the warden of the Kentucky Federal Penitentiary?"

"I recall he was moving over to the feds—I mean a federal facility."

"The man you arrested, Joshua Abbott, wasn't he an inmate in the Kentucky Federal Penitentiary?"

"I believe he was, yes."

"Believe? You aren't certain? As Chief Deputy, would you not have knowledge of the APB issued for Joshua Abbott?"

"The man arrested at the Jessamin Island Breezeway had checked in under the name of Thomas Phillips. We didn't connect the APB for Joshua Abbott to Thomas Phillips until later," the Chief Deputy quipped.

"I will restate my previous question. Did you know that Joshua Abbott had been an inmate at your former boss' prison?"

"Like I said, not until after he had been arrested did we connect Joshua Abbott to Thomas Phillips."

"Is it your common practice to knock on doors of hotel guests without a search warrant?"

"It's our department's duty to keep our community safe. We received a tip about suspicious activity at the Jessamin Island Breezeway, where Joshua Abbott checked in. Drug trafficking is common in this vicinity. I thought that I should check it out. I interviewed the desk clerk. He communicated that a recent guest paid with cash, was extremely jumpy, and was carefully monitoring the parking lot."

"Is it your common practice to respond to reports of suspicious drug activity without backup or another officer present in high-risk areas?"

"Sir, we are strapped as it is. If a call is received and no one is nearby, we go it alone. The public's safety takes precedence over our own."

"Did you know that William Wilson's daughter, Alice Walker, is the alleged victim in this case?"

"Objection." Watson said. "I don't see how the target of a hit can be characterized as an 'alleged' victim," Watson objected a bit too dramatically.

"Dixson, rephrase the question," Judge Cobb said.

"Deputy Barbee, did you know that William Wilson's daughter is Alice Walker?"

"I don't know Alice Walker."

"Alice Walker, the wife of Charles Walker, the defendant?"

"Like I said, I don't know Alice Walker. I didn't know William Wilson's children."

"Alice Wilson Walker. Again sir, did you know that the hit instructions that you testified was in the duffle bag discovered at the Jessamin Island Breezeway, now marked as Exhibits A–E, was for the daughter of William Wilson, your former boss?"

"Not at the time, no."

"I see that was a tough question for you to answer so I will move on. Option #2 of the alleged hit instructions that you read described a digital lock. Are you familiar with these types of locks?"

"Yes, they are common on Jessamin Island due to the vacation rental market. There have been a number of thefts over the years when renters forget to return traditional keys. And, in some instances, keys have been reproduced. Since the replacement of keys with these digital locks, the number of thefts that we respond to on Jessamin Island has been greatly reduced."

"Understood. So, these types of codes, I assume, can be changed after every renter fairly easily?"

"Yes, that is my understanding, but a rental agency could answer that question."

"Did you verify that the code in the instructions on Exhibit A in fact worked?"

"Yes, like a charm. The hit instructions were precise and worked perfectly."

"Did you investigate when the rental agency last changed the Walker's digital code?"

"No."

"But I believe you testified that these codes are common at rental homes on Jessamin Island and more secure than keys."

"That's correct."

"For these codes to provide more security than keys, I would assume that they must be changed often."

"Well, I don't know about that. Again, a question for a rental agency."

"Did you also verify the location of the hidden key to the back door?"

"Key? I don't understand."

"Yes, the key noted in Option #1 of the hit instructions?"

"Uh. Oh yes, I sure did."

"So, you located the key hidden in the rock shown in the photograph, now marked as Exhibit B, and verified that it unlocked the back door?"

"Yes."

"Can you describe the key?"

"Describe it? It was a key, like any other key," the deputy said, smugly.

"Like every other key? So, there was nothing different about this key?"

The deputy looked at Rick Watson with an expression like what is he getting at here? Rick Watson seemed as confused as the witness.

"It was a key," the deputy answered.

"Chief Deputy Barbee, was Josh Abbott armed?"

"Like I said, he reached around in the direction of his back like he was going to pull a weapon, but no, he was not armed."

"Did you find a gun or any other weapon in his room?"

"No."

"One last question. I realize that it was many years ago, but how soon after William Wilson became the sheriff were you promoted to CHIEF deputy?" I asked, emphasizing his rapid ascent to chief, hoping the jury picked up on my exaggeration of his title.

"Well, I had worked with Mr. Wilson since my first day on the force, so he was familiar with my reputation and work ethic."

"Yes, I'm certain he was. Please answer the question."

"I recall that it wasn't too long after Mr. Wilson was elected sheriff that I became his chief deputy."

"Wasn't too long? What does that mean? One hour, one day, one week, one month?"

"Like you said, it was a long time ago. I really can't recall, but I'm sure someone in the department has records."

"Well, guess what? I have the records. Seems you were promoted to the position of Chief Deputy the day after William Wilson became sheriff. Your Honor, I submit records from the city budget's office reflecting the rank and pay for the sheriff's department during the years in question. These records have been authenticated by the budget office, Your Honor."

"Watson, any objection?" Judge Cobb asked the solicitor.

"I object again to the relevance of this entire line of questioning; but since Your Honor is permitting the questioning, I don't object to the authenticity of the document."

"After apprehending Joshua Abbott, you testified that you secured him in a cell to sleep off his condition. Can you explain your actions in securing him?"

"Like I said, he was extremely strung out and basically passed out on his bed. We locked the cell. He was secure and alone."

"Your steps to ensure his security didn't include removing his belt?"

"I guess hindsight is 20/20, now isn't it?" the deputy snarled.

I thought I detected a chink in his armor.

"So, your answer to the question is no, that you didn't remove his belt?"

"Correct."

Now was not the time to introduce the inventory of Joshua Abbott's belongings when he entered the Kentucky Federal Penitentiary. When he was apprehended, he was wearing his standard farming clothes—khaki coveralls with no belt. Brandy Chastain could corroborate that fact.

"I don't have any further questions for Chief Deputy Barbee."

Barbee strategically placed his peaked cap under his arm displaying the Chief Deputy emblem, I thought, as he strutted by the jurors' box.

Thankfully, Judge Cobb interrupted the gazes from several of the female jurors when he announced the recess for lunch.

Chapter Seventy-Eight

Earl Dixson

Phyliss Ramseur was the first witness after the recess, and I planned to have fun with her. The jurors needed to be alert for my examination, in lieu of a nap after a big lunch. Due to the media circus, Judge Cobb was reluctant to allow the jurors to leave the courthouse, so he was having lunch brought in. That worried me because I knew Sam's favorite spot was the Italian staple across the street from the courthouse.

If I didn't know Sam's roots were by way of Walhollow County, based on his food preferences, I'd sworn he had Italian in his blood. For the life of me, I couldn't understand how he didn't gain one hundred pounds when his circuit court rotation brought him to Thurmond County. I had joined him on numerous occasions at Fratelli's. For lunch, he always ordered the baked meatballs or sausage and peppers from the Starter Menu saving the heavier entrée selections for dinner. His favorites were the eggplant parmigiana with spinach risotto, chicken piccata with fettucine alfredo, or its signature dish, Sammy G's lasagna. During one of those meals together, I learned that Walhollow didn't have any Italian restaurants. The only thing close to Italian cuisine the judge had experienced growing up was canned Chef Boyardee spaghetti and pepperoni TombStone frozen pizzas. After his first tastes of authentic Italian cuisine, he was hooked.

My hunches were confirmed when the jury returned and Juror #9, Lamar Edwards, was still using the extra-long toothpick provided in the ceramic breadstick by the cashier counter. I surmised Juror #9 had overindulged in the complimentary watermelon rind pickles, pub cheese with saltines, celery sticks and carrot sticks with the restaurant's homemade version of 1000 Island Dressing.

Rick Watson would likely put them to sleep before my planned assassination of the tart waffle, what Hannah Anne called the bank administrative assistant who had been gunning for Savannah's job. I had to suppress my chuckle at Hannah Anne's appearance in the men's room minutes earlier. That woman was feisty, sassy, fearless, and sexy. She had brought me more joy in the past several months than I had experienced in a lifetime. And, I had fallen in love.

"The prosecution calls Phyllis Ramseur," Rick Watson said, snapping me back to reality.

As Phyllis Ramseur was making her way from the gallery to the witness stand, I caught Hannah Anne's eye as she looked up from her note taking. She winked at me. I had participated in hundreds of trials in my career and never needed validation from anyone. But, this time it was different.

"Ms. Ramseur, what is your occupation?" Watson asked the new witness.

"I am the executive assistant to Joe Blake, the vice president of Palmetto State Bank. Been with him from day one when he was just a loan officer. As he moved up the ranks, I moved with him," Ms. Ramseur said, proudly.

She seemed quite sure of herself.

"How many years have you been at the bank?"

"Twenty years."

"Do you know the defendant, Charles Walker?"

"Why, yes, I know him very well. My office is on the executive floor. My office is actually closer to Mr. Walker's than Joe's, I mean Mr. Blake's."

"Given your long tenure with the bank and as the assistant to the vice president, I presume that you have knowledge of bank procedures."

"Yes, sir. I sure do."

"I presume that you also know the executives on a personal level."

"Yes, sir. Very well, as a matter of fact. We spend a lot of time together. We are like a family. You know the good and the bad, so to speak."

"What is your opinion of Charles Walker?"

"Obviously, he is very good at what he does. He is our president. He works hard, is very detail oriented, and strict when it comes to following protocol, rules, and the bank's procedures."

"Before I ask more about the bank procedures, what are your impressions of Mr. Walker's personal life?"

"Mr. Walker is a very private person. He doesn't discuss personal matters, but you know over the years, you hear things, see things, and pick up on things. It's no secret. I mean you can pretty much ask anyone on our floor. It is common knowledge that he and his wife don't have a good marriage."

"Can you provide any facts to support your statement?"

"Yes, sir. I sure can. When his assistant left, I answered his phone, and his wife didn't call not once. I found that odd because Mr. Blake talks to his wife several times a day. And he doesn't have any photos of his wife in his office, just his daughter, Tara, who died recently in a car accident," Phyllis Ramseur said, shaking her head. "We were all very sad, of course, but after Tara's death, this may sound kind of crass, but some of us took bets on how long it would be before the Walkers separated."

I had grounds for objecting, but all of Phyllis' speculations played to my advantage. I anticipated more gossip from this witness. The more she testified, the more she would come across as the office busybody. Any objection would be construed that I was attempting to gag her to suppress evidence of an affair between Savannah and Charles. So, I let her blab away.

"Other than the lack of calls from his wife and no photos of her, is there anything else?"

"You mean what I actually know? 'Cause there are lots of rumors."

"Yes, stick to your direct knowledge."

"OK. There was this conference where Mr. Walker was speaking. The conference was at the Ritz Carlton on Amelia Island. All of his accommodations were paid for by the conference. I was in constant communication with the organizers. Before Tara died, the whole family was going. I reserved a two-bedroom suite as he instructed. The suite I reserved had one king bed, and the second bedroom had one queen. They just had one child, so I thought that should be fine," Ms. Ramseur speculated. "Later, one of the conference organizers called to confirm a change for two queens in the master bedroom. I didn't request the change. I learned that Mr. Walker had called the hotel directly. I mean that was part of my job to handle the details. Like I said, he is a private person. I guess he didn't want me to know that he and his wife slept in separate beds."

"Did you learn anything else while working for Mr. Walker?"

"Yes. Well, at that same conference—the one at the Ritz Carlton—he had spa packages comped. I ask him several times if I should coordinate with Mrs. Walker about scheduling a service. I mean who wouldn't want a free spa service at the Ritz? He said that wasn't necessary. I learned that Savannah Abbott went to the conference with him instead and was using the complimentary spa treatment," Phyllis Ramseur's words dripped with envy.

"Did you ever observe any improper behavior between Mr. Walker and Mrs. Abbott?"

"It was obvious to all of us that he really liked her. He never talked to his previous assistant like he did to Savannah. And, Mr. Walker has this open-door policy. If any of the administrative employees went into his office, we had to leave the door open. I don't think Savannah had been there a week when she was in his office with the door shut. No one could believe it! And when she went with him to the conference, well, we were all convinced then that something was going on. No assistant has ever been needed at a conference."

"I bet a bank the size of Palmetto State Bank has lots of rules and procedures to follow, am I correct?"

"More than you can imagine."

"Are you familiar with steps taken in the hiring of administrative assistants?"

"Yes. When you complete the application, you have to sign a consent for a drug test and a criminal background check. Mr. Walker is highly selective about who has access to the executive floor."

"Do you know if Mrs. Abbott complied with those requirements?"

"Yes, I do know. Her background check was fine, but we learned that both her son and husband were in prison."

"Was it unusual for Charles Walker to extend on offer of employment under those circumstances?"

"Yes, sir. It sure was. Prior to Savannah's hiring, I encouraged one of my friends from church to apply for an opening. The position was mail clerk. She was way overqualified, but I told her she could work her way up. I felt terrible when she didn't get the job. I overheard Mr. Walker tell Joe, I mean, Mr. Blake, that 'The entire family has to represent our culture. There is no room for error.' I learned that her husband had a minor shoplifting charge, which was bogus and eventually thrown out, but that was why she didn't get the job."

"Is there anything that you learned about the hiring of Savannah Abbott?"

"Yes. Charles Walker shredded the background checks on Josh Abbott, Savannah's husband, and on her son, Cray Abbott."

"Ms. Ramseur, how do you know this?"

"Any mail coming to a bank officer is opened, the date received is stamped on the document, and a printout of the items are summarized and attached to a sealed folder—all for security and legal reasons. When I was helping out with Mr. Walker's work while he was interviewing assistants, I delivered this folder to him. I noticed that one of the listed items was criminal background checks," Phyllis Ramseur continued. "Another one of my jobs is to remove the trash bin that contains confidential material and put it through the shredder. When I went to retrieve Mr. Walker's bin, there was a shredded document with the other papers. I found it extremely odd that of all the confidential papers in the bin, one was already shredded. Well, it wasn't completely shredded. I noticed that it was a police report or something like that and I saw the information about Savannah's husband and son," Phyllis admitted.

"I understand. What did you think when you heard that Ms. Abbott was hired?"

"I thought Charles Walker had broken his own rules, which would have been a first for sure. Then, when I met Savannah, I couldn't help but think that he must have a crush on her. She is quite attractive."

I thought Phyllis' jealousy was clearly evident, and I hoped the jury saw it.

"While Mr. Walker and Ms. Abbott were at the conference together at the Ritz, did anything unusual happen back in the office?"

"Why, yes, sir. It sure did," Phyllis exclaimed. "An officer from the Thurmond County Sheriff's Department showed up looking for Ms. Abbott. I tried calling Ms. Abbott's hotel room but there was no answer. I then tried to contact Mr. Walker. I called his cell at least fifteen times, but he didn't answer. I must add that in my experience, this was very strange. Mr. Walker always has his cell and is very prompt in returning calls."

"Did you leave any messages when you placed the calls?"

"Yes, sir. I sure did. I left a message that it was urgent that I speak to him—that a police officer was there to speak to Savannah. It seemed very serious."

"Did you ever speak to Mr. Walker?"

"Yes, sir. I sure did, that is, when he finally called me back. He said to have the officer call him. After the officer talked to him, I heard him report to someone that they were both at the hotel."

"No further questions."

"Your witness, Mr. Dixson," Judge Cobb announced.

Was it my imagination, or was the judge attempting to suppress a smile? Like me, he had observed many witnesses over the years, and he had presided over numerous trials with me. I couldn't help but think that he knew that I was going to have some fun with Ms. Ramseur.

"Ms. Ramseur, how do you know that Savannah Abbott used a free spa treatment at the Ritz Carlton as you testified?"

"Well, I knew the conference planners had offered them to Mr. Walker because I handled his initial reservations."

"So, you made a spa reservation for Ms. Abbott?"

"No, I did not."

"I'll repeat my question. How do you know for a fact that Savannah Abbott used a free spa treatment?"

"Well, when I learned that Savannah was at the conference, I was just a little curious. I called the Ritz to inquire about the spa reservations, and they confirmed that Savannah was coming in later that morning for a treatment."

"How do you know that Ms. Abbott didn't pay for her treatment?"

"Well, I verified that it was part of Mr. Walker's conference package—you know, what they said would be comped."

"Ms. Ramseur, you testified that Charles Walker had shredded the information on Ms. Abbott's son and husband. Is that correct?"

"Yes, it is."

"I'm having a little difficulty here understanding how one can read a shredded document. Your Honor, I would like to present Charles Walker's shredder into evidence. The serial numbers on this equipment have been verified by the bank as well as the shredder utilized by Ms. Ramseur."

"Any objection, Watson?"

Solicitor Watson was in a sticky situation. He knew that I wouldn't fabricate any evidence and if he made a big deal out of a shredder, it could backfire on him.

"No objections at all, Your Honor, other than relevance. The relevant fact here is that Mr. Walker shredded the criminal records."

I took the shredder from Charles Walker's office and plugged in the machine and handed Ms. Ramseur copies of the criminal records that had been provided by Watson to Rollins Bishop. Watson couldn't very well object to records, especially after the judge's initial warning of baseless objections. After all, Watson provided them to the defense and opened the door to this evidence in his questioning of his witness.

"I'll let you do the honors, Ms. Ramseur. From your testimony, you obviously know how to use a shredder."

She looked at Rick Watson then looked at the judge as if to say, I don't have to really do this, do I? Watson was no help. He pretending to be taking notes on his legal pad.

"Go ahead, Ms. Ramseur," Judge Cobb instructed.

After the shredder finished slicing and dicing the records into the plastic bin underneath, I reached in for effect, grabbing a fistful of the small pieces, letting them fall back into the bin.

"It must have taken you hours to piece these jiblets together." Watson surely could have objected but he kept his head down and stayed in his seat. "Your Honor, I would like this bin presented into evidence for the jury's viewing."

"So, Ms. Ramseur, let me see if I understand your testimony. In addition to calling the spa, you went through the confidential trash of the bank president, read a shredded document, and contacted the conference hotel to inquire into who was using the complimentary spa treatments? What other things have you done that would fall into the category of snooping?"

"Objection," Watson said.

"Sustained," Judge Cobb said. "Dixson, rephrase your question."

"I'll move on. Ms. Ramseur, do you receive annual reviews from your employer?"

"Yes, I do," but it was if the wind had been let out of her sails. Her confident tone and body language had taken a dramatic turn. "I have always received excellent scores on the quality of my work," she said meekly.

"Are you given copies of your reviews?"

"Yes."

"Your Honor, I would like to have Ms. Ramseur's reviews for the past five years marked as exhibits and entered into evidence. These have been authenticated by the Human Resources Department of Palmetto State Bank."

She had to know where this was going.

"Ms. Ramseur, isn't it true that your scores under the headings Leadership Qualities and Trustworthiness are the lowest possible.

She cleared her throat.

"Well, I can explain," she attempted.

"I appreciate that, but the form is self-explanatory, or as the solicitor would argue, the document speaks for itself. The explanations are provided here: You are referred to as a 'pot stirrer,' 'drama queen,' 'gossip,' 'busybody,' and 'manipulative.' That you 'lack discretion.' Isn't that what the document says?"

I was hoping that the jury was picking up on what I saw—the air had completely gone out of her balloon.

"Obviously, some of the women are jealous of my position and have said some negative things about me. You know when you work in a competitive environment, it's not all that surprising. There are many who are gunning for my position."

"Ms. Ramseur, did you apply for the open position as the assistant to Charles Walker?"

"Yes, I did. I mean I was the most qualified."

"And isn't it true that Mr. Walker didn't consider you for the job?"

"Well, I don't know about that, but I wasn't interviewed for the position, if that's what you mean.

"Isn't it true that you were upset about not being considered?"

"Not really. I love working for Mr. Blake."

"Ms. Ramseur, are you jealous of Mrs. Abbott?"

"No, I would never be jealous of someone whose husband and child were in prison."

"I'm sure you were quite pleased to obtain that confidential information."

"Objection!" Watson boomed.

"Dixson, is there a question?" Judge Cobb asked, matter-of-factly.

"No. I have nothing further for this witness."

"We'll take a fifteen-minute recess before proceeding with the last witnesses for the day," Judge Cobb announced.

Chapter Seventy-Nine

Earl Dixson

During the break, I headed to the restroom. The last witness of the day was Warden William Wilson. I needed to keep my emotions in check, but I was afraid that I wouldn't be able to keep a cool head at the sight of him. All I wanted to do was strangle the man. I turned on the faucet and began splashing water on my face. As Hannah Anne said, William Wilson was "lower than a snake's belly in a wagon rut." His contemptible antics had ruined so many lives over the years.

I jumped when I heard the door open. I didn't want Rick Watson or anyone on his team to think I was anything but confident with how things were going so far. But, it wasn't anyone from the prosecution's side. I was shocked to see Hannah Anne.

"Hannah Anne, this is the men's room."

"Well, I know that. I just had to tell you how proud I am of you. You sure put that awful Phyllis in her place. She's the cream of the crap, and the crap of the cream! But you showed her; bless her heart. You were fabulous," as she grabbed my cheeks and planted a big kiss on my lips. Then, she turned and scurried out.

I grabbed several paper towels from the automatic dispenser to dry my face. Hannah Anne was in and out of the restroom so quickly, she didn't even comment on the water dripping from my face. But, she was exactly what I had needed. I was grinning from ear to ear and headed back into the courtroom relaxed and with renewed confidence.

My pulse remained steady even when Rick Watson called Warden William Wilson to the stand.

"Please state your name and position."

"William Alan Wilson. I am the warden of the Kentucky Federal Penitentiary."

"Was Joshua Carter Abbott a prisoner in your facility?"

"Yes, he was."

"Your Honor, I would like to introduce into evidence a letter that the defendant Savannah Abbott sent to Josh Abbott while he was incarcerated at the Kentucky Federal Penitentiary."

He handed the letter to Judge Cobb.

"Any objections, Mr. Dixson?"

"None whatsoever, Your Honor," I said.

Watson was feeling quite smug with the introduction of this letter since Deputy Barbee's testimony described the hit instructions that he observed in Josh's duffle bag as "sketches."

"Warden Wilson, I am going to hand you what is marked as Prosecution Exhibit F. Will you read this to the jury, sir?"

Warden Wilson reached into his suit pocket and retrieved his glasses and studied the exhibit. Smooth, I thought—like this was the first time he had viewed the letter.

"Dear Josh,

Things are going well here. Thank you again for your understanding why I had to leave. I realized I should have taken this step earlier. Mom is happy that I am back home.

Do you have any updates on your parole? I am enclosing some sketches. I am also enclosing some photos. I will explain them further when we talk. I trust that you receive everything.

Savannah"

The warden removed his glasses, looked down and began shaking his head.

"Do you need a minute, sir?" Watson asked.

"Yes, please," Wilson said, taking a few deep breaths.

Talk about grandstanding! Admittedly, Wilson appeared distraught after reading the letter. If he ever decided to leave the prison system, he may be able to make in Hollywood, I thought.

Judge Cobb wasn't having any of this.

"Watson, if you have further questions for this witness, let's move on."

"Warden Wilson, do you know what the sketches and photographs were that Mrs. Abbott enclosed in her letter?"

"Well, I do now. She enclosed hit instructions for my daughter!"

"Your Honor, may I approach the witness for his review of Exhibits A–E?"

Judge Cobb motioned his approval to Watson.

"Warden Wilson, I am handing you sketches and photographs previously marked as Exhibits A–E."

"Objection, Your Honor," I said, calmly. "We covered this ground previously about the hit instructions being referred to as sketches. As Solicitor Watson argued this morning, the typed instructions speak for themselves."

"Sustained. The jury shall disregard the characterization of the documents as sketches."

"I'll rephrase the question. Warden Wilson, were these exhibits the enclosures in Mrs. Abbott's letter to your inmate Josh Abbott?"

Wilson put his glasses back on, flipped through the exhibits, and again, began shaking his head.

"Yes, they were," he responded, removing his glasses and wiping his eye. I wanted to clap and yell, "Wonderful performance," but that would definitely fall into the category of grandstanding.

"Warden Wilson, were you aware that Mr. Abbott obtained photographs and sketches of a hit while in your prison?"

I didn't need to object again. Judge Cobb took care of it.

"Watson, as you have advocated, the documents speak for themselves. I will once again instruct the jury to disregard the characterization as sketches. And, I am instructing you to do the same."

"I'll rephrase. Warden Wilson, were you aware of these enclosures in Ms. Abbott's letter to your prisoner?"

"Of course not. That would have been grounds for revocation of Mr. Abbott's parole."

"Is mail coming into the prison reviewed prior to distribution?"

"Yes, it is."

"Can you explain why instructions for a hit were not intercepted?"

"We receive all types of items that are prohibited from drugs to guns. So, sketches and photographs of a house wouldn't raise suspicion. It was common knowledge that Mr. Abbott was going through a divorce. Maybe they thought it was related to a property settlement or something."

"Objection," I said. "Again, there is absolutely no evidence that Josh and Savannah Abbott were separated, separating, or had any trouble in their marriage," I said. "I move to strike that uncorroborated statement."

"Sustained," Judge Cobb ruled. "The jury shall disregard any comments about the state of the Abbott's marriage from this witness," Judge Cobb instructed.

"Warden Wilson, had you learned of Mr. Abbott's arrest following his release on probation?"

"Yes, very unfortunate."

"Prior to your position as the warden of the Kentucky federal prison, what was your previous job?"

"I was the sheriff of Thurmond County."

"Do you know Jimmy Wayne Barbee, the current chief deputy?"

"Of course, I do. He was with the department when I was there. He was the best officer we had. I have had success throughout my career because I have a knack for spotting talent. I promoted him to be my chief deputy."

"Do you recall how long Mr. Barbee was with the department before his promotion?"

"Not exactly but if my recollection is correct, it wasn't long. I'm not one to play games; I call 'em like I see 'em. If someone has talent, I do my best to reward them."

"Did you authorize the APB on Joshua Abbott?"

"Yes, sir. I did.

"Why was that?" Watson asked, knowing the answer to this rehearsed testimony.

"Our protocol is that an inmate released on parole must contact their assigned probation officer. Depending on the circumstances, such as travel, we use discretion before we initiate an APB. After confirmation that Joshua Abbott's bus had arrived in Beaufort, South Carolina, we waited for three hours before initiating the APB for him—more than sufficient time in my opinion."

"Were you surprised that Joshua Abbott failed to comply with the conditions of his release?"

"Surprised? No. I say that because I deal with worse every day. Sir, I am a like a babysitter to folks with criminal minds. Most of whom are very smart. I mean Joshua Abbott had been cultivating and distributing narcotics for years before he was caught."

"Objection," I raised. "Your Honor there is absolutely no evidence that Joshua Abbott distributed narcotics."

"Ladies and gentlemen of the jury, you are to disregard Mr. Wilson's last statement. Mr. Wilson, please answer with only facts," Judge Cobb said, forcefully.

"Warden Wilson, did you trust Josh Abbott?"

"I learned a long time ago that when you begin to trust anyone, you will get burned. Joshua Abbott met our rules for release pure and simple."

"No further questions," the solicitor concluded.

"Your witness," Judge Cobb said to me quickly. He didn't even bother to ask me if I had questions for the warden.

"Mr. Wilson, are you in financial trouble?" as I cut straight to the chase in my cross-examination.

"Objection, Your Honor. What is the relevance here?" Watson interrupted.

"Judge, my line of questioning directly supports our defense."

"I'll permit a limited inquiry," Judge Cobb said. "You may answer the question."

"I assume you are referring to my recent divorce. My line of work puts a strain on a marriage. But to answer your question, no, I am not in financial trouble, simply a temporary cash flow blip due to a property settlement. Anyone that has gone through a divorce certainly understands the predicament."

"Mr. Wilson, when is the last time you visited your daughter at her home in Beaufort?"

"I came down right after I heard that she was lucky to be alive."

"And prior to that, when was your last visit?"

"It would have been for the funeral for my granddaughter—several months ago."

"Isn't it true that you didn't even attend your granddaughter's funeral, that you left after the wake at the Walker's home?

"I recall that my trip was cut short due to my job."

"Or was it due to an argument with Charles Walker over money?"

"I answered the question."

"Isn't it true that while attending the wake for your granddaughter, you asked your son-in-law for a substantial sum of money to pay off loans that had been called by Community Bank & Trust, your bank, and you got angry and left when Mr. Walker declined to bail you out?"

"Objection," interjected Watson.

Watson's tone sounded like a question. Like he didn't know what to expect. Clearly, his witness hadn't disclosed his financial troubles to the solicitor.

"Overruled," Judge Cobb responded.

"Your Honor, I offer into evidence the letter that Mr. Wilson received from Community Bank & Trust two weeks before attending his granddaughter's wake," I resumed.

"Like I said, merely a cash flow problem. I have been banking at Community Bank & Trust since I moved to Kentucky. I was part of their ribbon-cutting ceremony. It was a computer glitch due to new management, that's all. I take care of my business."

"Speaking of taking care of your business, do you recall the case *Duggins v. Thurmond County Sheriff's Department*?"

"Objection, Your Honor!" Watson said, strongly.

"On what grounds, Watson?" Judge Cobb asked, peering over his readers.

"Relevance, Your Honor. A previous civil lawsuit is completely irrelevant to this case."

"Overruled, but Dixson, if you are going somewhere with this, you'd better get there quickly," Judge Cobb cautioned. I surmised that Sam's warning was to placate Rick Watson. I knew that he would give me a rather long leash.

"Mr. Wilson, do you recall the case *Leroy Duggins v. William Wilson and the Thurmond County Sheriff's Department*?" I asked again, using the situation to repeat my question.

I hoped at least one juror would take notes, Google the case, and read all about it. It wasn't every day that a sheriff was sued personally along with his department. But, a young, aggressive reporter had picked up on the evidentiary flaws and other shenanigans within the Thurmond County Sheriff's Department and highlighted the reasons in an exposé. The article was titled *Leroy Duggins v. William Wilson and the Thurmond County Sheriff's Department:* "Enforcement? Entrapment? We'll Never Know."

I reminded Wilson that the case involved excessive force and allegations of planted evidence. It was resolved by a confidential settlement.

"Goes with the job. I don't have to tell you that there are lots of hungry lawyers out there."

"I guess hunger would also explain the criminal cases thrown out of court. Do you recall how many cases were tossed due to unlawful searches during your term as sheriff?"

"Objection," Watson offered up meekly.

Was I wearing down the solicitor? His objection was raised rather dispassionately. Watson should have known not to base his case on evidence produced by Wilson's former right-hand man. Between Chief Deputy Barbee and the former sheriff, many of Watson's cases had imploded when their rotten tactics came to light. Watson knew where I was going and that it wasn't going to be pretty.

"I'll allow it," Judge Cobb said. "Answer the question, sir."

"It's easy for people like you to look at things in a vacuum. I am proud of my record of successful prosecutions during my tenure. Of course, you would focus on the ones where there were technicalities."

"By technicalities, do you mean an individual's constitutional rights?"

"I mean when lawyers like yourself put criminals back on the street."

"Mr. Wilson, in the matters where, as you said, criminals were put back on the street, you and one other officer were consistently involved. Do you recall that officer?"

"No, I handled hundreds of cases and worked with numerous officers."

"Your Honor, I offer into evidence the Orders of Dismissal due to a range of evidentiary abuses where William Wilson and Jimmy Barbee were the arresting officers. I have no further questions."

"We will recess for the day," Judge Cobb announced.

Chapter Eighty

Hannah Anne Hart

The only trials I had experienced were those from Elliott Gray's books. I had never watched lawyer shows on TV; in fact, I rarely watched any TV. I guess I was a genuine bookworm, the name I had been called since elementary school. If my daughter's freedom wasn't in the balance, I would have enjoyed all the theatrics taking place in the courtroom.

I was captivated by the jurors, the judge, and of course, Earl. I even was enthralled by the solicitor, the bailiff, and the stenographer. I had missed my calling, I thought. I could have been an attorney-at-law, a good one. That chance had long passed. I never could have managed four years of college, three years of law school, and the grind of a law practice as a single parent. Now wasn't the time or place to think about the what-ifs and what-fors. I had a job to do.

Earl's instructions to me were to carefully observe each juror, their reactions to testimony, their body language, their attentiveness, and their note-taking. I was to take my own notes as well. Earl gave me a legal pad to record my observations.

Juror #9, Lamar Edwards, an electrician, who could have been anywhere from 55–65, looked like he had lived a hard life. It was unfair of me to pigeonhole this man. But, I couldn't help but think he was a hard worker who, at quitting time, likely tried to forget the day with a twelve-pack of beer or a fifth of hard liquor. He was primarily stone-faced but seemed to become animated during the testimony of the bad guys, including the prison guard, the Thurmond chief deputy, and warden of the Kentucky Federal Pen. I thought he was in our corner until William Wilson said that if you begin to trust the prisoners, you will get burned. At that, he began nodding his head in agreement. I put a question mark for Juror #9.

Juror #5, Brenda Sanders, owned a beauty shop. When blabbermouth Phyllis was talking about Savannah, I couldn't judge Brenda's reaction. Was she disgusted by or did she approve of Phyllis' meddling, going through the confidential trash and calling the Ritz about the spa treatment? During that testimony, she was nodding her head back and forth. However, when Phyllis said she could never be jealous of Savannah—someone whose husband and child were in prison—I thought she was going to leap out of her seat with an "amen sister." I placed an asterisk beside Juror #5. Brenda was for the prosecution, I logged.

Juror #1, Rosemarie Cox, was an executive assistant to the regional manager of the state's utility conglomerate. She seemed to be enamored with that crooked deputy, Jimmy Barbee. Couldn't she see that he was all brawn and no brain? But I started changing my mind about her during Earl's questioning of Phyllis, the bank busybody. When Earl asked about her evaluation scores, Rosemarie Cox took notes furiously. I bet she had experienced the likes of a Phyllis in her job. And Rosemarie was cute and petite. She likely was the target of office gossip as well because she hadn't allowed her figure to go to seed like Juror #5 and Phyllis. I logged her as a "strong maybe" for us.

I had jotted down my impressions of all twelve jurors. A few were keeping their cards close to their vests like good poker players. But Earl had said that we only need to convince one. My conservative assessment was that we had at least five on our side, but this was just day one.

I had been so focused on my assignment that I hadn't seen Bo enter the courtroom. When he approached me during the recess, after I had returned from the men's room, I felt faint. My mind raced with questions, but front and center was whether he had been by the house? Had he noticed the signs that another man had been there and sleeping in my room, no less? Some of Earl's clothes were in my closet. His toothbrush, shaving kit, and Old Spice deodorant were in my bathroom. Our breakfast dishes were still in the sink. One of my questions was answered in a flash.

"I started to call and let you know that I would be here for the trial," Bo said. "But I didn't think you would believe me, and I didn't want to add to your stress. I'm sorry for the way I left but had some things I needed to tie up. I just got here.

How about I pick up dinner for us? I want to hear about how it's going so far. And, I have lots of news for you."

I should have said I had plans because I did. Earl was coming over after he checked on things back at his office and finished preparing for Day 2. Last week when his trial preparation consumed his time, I told him I understood if we needed to take a break during the trial. I didn't want to create any distractions. He had dismissed my offer quickly and said that he had never been happier, more at peace. He said that my presence energized him and reignited a passion that he hadn't felt since he first hung his shingle. He needed me with him now more than ever. Then, he said it, "I love you. I am in love with you, Hannah Anne."

This was the first time he had said those words. That night, our lovemaking reached another peak. I was all in. I had fallen in love with him too. I felt loved, cared for, protected, and safe.

What was I going to do now?

Chapter Eighty-One

Walt Benton

Before returning to Beaufort for the trial, I traveled back to my home in Duck, North Carolina. Maudie returned to Kentucky. We were in different places in our lives. I was retired. She was busy running a farm and helping with the new distillery. Though we talked several times a day, I wondered if the calls would become fewer and farther between or cease altogether.

Maudie urged me to visit, but I didn't want to step foot on the Abbott Tobacco Farm. It was the place that took both the love of my life and my son from me. Maybe I just needed more time, but deep down, I knew I never would recover from the pain and resentment that boiled inside me at the mention of that farm.

I received weekly updates from Earl. Weeks ago, he had slipped that he and Hannah Anne had a good strategy session over dinner. I was relieved that Hannah Anne had company, particularly since Bo had bolted again. After fielding several of Earl's questions about Hannah Anne, I suspected his interest was more than just discussing the case.

When I retained Earl, I disclosed that Savannah's father wasn't in the picture and that he had abandoned his family many years ago. Then, after Bo and Hannah Anne accompanied me on a visit to meet with him, Earl's inquiries seemed more than just background information about his new client's parents.

After numerous compliments about Hannah Anne's intuitiveness, her initiative, and her spunk, Earl asked if Savannah's parents had reconciled. He definitely was interested in Hannah Anne. And I couldn't blame him. I knew he was lonely. And she had always been attractive but had grown more confident and spirited in recent years.

When I first met my son's future mother-in-law, Hannah Anne looked more like an older sister to Savannah than her mother. She had the same bronze skin that didn't need a drop of makeup, the same blonde hair, and the same lean figure. She was shorter than Savannah and, at that time, lacked Savannah's luster. I thought that Savannah's height and magnetic charm had to come from her father's side. Her eyes sparkled. They exuded an innocence and yet a wildness. They were the bluest blue I had ever seen. Hannah Anne's eyes were dull and lifeless.

Now, knowing Hannah Anne's history, I knew her eyes must have reflected her inner sorrow. Her years as a single parent had been hard. But, those years hadn't hardened her. To the contrary, they had blessed her with a bold toughness and an intolerance for anything other than complete honesty—an authenticity bestowed upon survivors, if you will.

During my weekly telephone status briefings with Earl, he mentioned other outings with Hannah Anne Hart, including a trip to Harper's Corner. It had been a most productive getaway "for the case," he had emphasized. But I surmised that the excitement in his voice was likely due to more than just the discovery of a convenience store clerk named Brandy. After my return to Beaufort for the trial, I met with Earl in person, and his attraction was obvious, or as Hannah Anne would say "as plain as the nose on one's face."

More than the new spring in Earl's step, it was his appearance that confirmed my suspicions. His hair was actually combed and possibly sported some hair product. He was clean-shaven. His shirt and pants were crisply pressed, and he looked quite dapper. I detected a hint of cologne. It was as if he had undergone a makeover.

When I spotted Bo Hart in the courtroom, I thought now was not the time for a love triangle. I imagined that Hannah Anne may be in a pickle and weathering a whirlwind of emotions. Earl was to begin presenting our witnesses the following day. Earl needed to stay focused. The last thing we needed was for him to get dumped. So, I offered Bo a place to stay.

I had rented a house on the river for the duration of the trial. Although it was the first time I had seen Maudie since our reconciliation of sorts, I owed it to Hannah

Anne. After all, when Bo had jumped ship again, I encouraged her to move on and to start living in the present instead of the past. But, her present and past were now colliding at a most inopportune time.

Thankfully, Bo didn't resist my invitation, as it was more of a subtle command. He should have given Hannah Anne fair warning before just showing up again. We were dealing with enough anxiety.

Earl's spirits didn't seem rocked by Bo's presence. In fact, Day 2 of the trial, he remained even-keeled and collected, but there was a tangible difference in his temperament. I wondered if he had stayed at Hannah Anne's the previous night. I thought he was marking his territory in and out of the courtroom.

Earl called the first defense witness to the stand—Harry Gibson, the Walker's go-to handyman for the Jessamin cottage. Harry testified that he received a voicemail message from Charles Walker asking about the new door code and the location of the hide-a-key. Harry testified that Alice Walker had not contacted him for any maintenance work. He wasn't aware that she had gone to the cottage during the week in question. He also testified that the key to the back door was on his key ring and not hidden. The Walkers never used the home, and with renters there all the time, he thought it was careless to leave a key in a rock that was obviously fake. Earl asked him how he could distinguish the Walker's key from all his other clients'.

"It's easy," he said, and he detached a large silver ring from his belt with what appeared to hold a hundred keys. "This one's theirs," he continued, holding up a key.

"Can you describe that key for the jury, Mr. Gibson?"

"Whatcha mean? It's a key."

"Explain how it differs from all the others on your key ring."

"Can't you see it? It's a hammer design. You can get 'em at the hardware store. Alice asked me to have two of 'em made—one to hide in the rock outside and the other for someone in Beaufort who helps with the pool."

Under Watson's cross-examination, Harry admitted that Charles could have been feigning ignorance about the location of the hide-a-key and could have easily replaced one, one without a hammer design. He could have been setting Harry up as a witness in his favor.

"I guess anythang's possible," Harry Gibson said, exasperated. But it was it was the way he looked at Charles Walker after he said it. I hoped I wasn't imagining things, but if I were on the jury, my impression of Harry Gibson was that Watson had convinced him of the prosecution's theory.

Earl then called Betsy Collins, a real estate agent with Jessamin Beach Rentals. Betsy managed vacation rentals for Tara's Cove. Through Betsy, Earl established that Alice Walker had removed Tara's Cove from the rental market the week of her alleged attempted hit because Charles wanted to have some maintenance done. Betsy further testified that when Charles called her to check on the rental status of the house, he was oblivious to the fact that Tara's Cove was off the rental market. Further, Betsy testified that the access code had been changed recently at the Walker's home and that an email had been sent to Alice Walker with the new code on the day the code was changed. Betsy authenticated the email that the rental agency sent to Alice Walker. Earl entered the email into evidence.

Watson's cross-examination strategy with Harry Gibson and Betsy Collins was identical—Charles could have been pretending not to know about the code change, setting her up as a witness in his defense.

On re-direct, Earl masterfully laid out the time frame with Betsy Gibson, establishing that the email notification of the code change was sent to Alice on a date after Savannah's letter to Josh containing the sketches and photos. Based on the date, it was impossible that the letter included the not-yet-established new door code. The warden had testified that the alleged hit instructions included the code in question. Earl had done an excellent job, I thought, in discounting that the sketches referred to in Savannah's letter were the hit instructions claimed by the prosecution.

Betsy had been an excellent witness. As good as she was, Brandy Chastain, the convenience store clerk in Harper's Corner, North Carolina, was the smoking gun.

Brandy testified that a very handsome man stopped for gas and asked for directions to the local post office. He was driving a large, black pickup truck. Brandy thought the man looked familiar. She was convinced that he was famous, maybe a movie star, professional athlete, or singer. She was curious, and she asked him lots of questions. She learned that he was in a hurry to get to South Carolina to his wife but had to make a stop on Jessamin Island first. She learned that this traveler's real name was Josh Abbott, not Thomas Phillips, the name used for the trip. She testified that Josh wanted to mail his son a letter. She led him to the post office, saw him go inside with a letter, and saw that he didn't have the letter when he returned. She verified the date, which matched the postmark.

Watson's attempts to discredit her testimony imploded when she showed the picture that she had taken of Josh Abbott on her phone the day he was supposedly on a bus to Beaufort.

Earl Dixson was on fire. I couldn't help but wonder if he had seen Bo, and his alpha male instincts had kicked into high gear. Whatever it was, I was glad he was on our side.

On Day 3, Earl Dixson fried Alice Walker. His private investigator had obtained numerous photos of her with various suitors. She attempted explanations with each picture. Earl saved the most incriminating ones for last. Alice Walker was silent when a blown-up photo was displayed on the large screen and captured a clear shot of her and a man parked outside a hotel. They apparently couldn't wait to get inside before beginning their sexual interlude. She stared coldly at the picture of Norris Nichols from her doorway with his hands under her shirt when it was shown to the jury.

"Charles treated me like crap," she blurted. "I was like an indentured servant. After Tara's death, I needed comforting. That's all."

Earl's last witness for the day was Nancy Nichols, the best friend of Tara Walker. Nancy relayed a message that she heard on the Walker's answering machine— Charles Walker's voice asking his wife for the code to the Jessamin Island cottage around the time that the alleged hit was to have occurred.

Though Earl said the past three days had been good for the defense, it was too early to begin celebrating. "Jurors are less predictable than a pop-up storm in August," he said.

Earl hoped that his next two witnesses, Cray and Wayman Ritchie, the guard at Cray's prison, would further discredit the hit instructions supposedly sent to Josh. They both were going to testify that Hannah Anne communicated

Savannah's request for cartoon sketches for a presentation by her boss at a banking conference. If all went according to plan, Earl didn't think it would be necessary for either Charles or Savannah to testify.

Chapter Eighty-Two

Earl Dixson

Hannah Anne wouldn't let up about calling her as a witness.

"I mean I was the one who took Savannah's notes into the prison, showed them to Wayman, read them to Cray, and actually saw the cartoons," she argued. "And I am the ONLY one who can testify about that beady-eyed Fig Newton interrogating me about the details of the conference. It's clear now he was passing that information on to Josh's warden. I would love to give that Rick Watson an earful about his preposterous case. What I'd really like to do is tell him to take a long walk off a short pier!"

I was concerned that if I called Hannah Anne as a witness, I wouldn't be able to keep her on task. No, strike that; it was more than concern. I knew for a fact I would lose all control of her. No doubt, she would veer off in a number of different directions. If I interrupted her to get her back on track, the jury would think I was trying to hide something. Other than her testimony about Cray's cartoons, I didn't see where she could be helpful. Moreover, she would be viewed as extremely biased. And, Rick Watson would make her spitting mad when he established that she couldn't prove what Savannah had mailed to Josh. She seemed to accept my reasons to keep her at bay.

Cray's testimony should be enough to establish that his grandmother had communicated a request from Savannah about her boss' presentation on digitalization in the banking industry. He could discuss the evidence of his grandmother's visit and the summary of the assigned topic on her notes—notes that Guard Wayman Ritchie reviewed and approved.

Cray would also testify that he received a letter from his father postmarked from Harper's Corner, North Carolina. Earl hoped that Judge Cobb would permit the letter into evidence. Even if the judge excluded the letter, the critical evidence was that a letter was mailed from Harper's Corner to Cray, just as Brandy had testified. And Brandy had also testified that Josh was driving a black truck. The videotape from the post office corroborated her story, and the time the letter was mailed. Why would the Kentucky Federal Pen officials lie about observing Josh Abbott board a bus to Beaufort unless they were setting him up?

While Brandy Chastain had been uncovered by my tenacity and sheer doggedness to chase every possible angle, Wayman Ritchie was another story. Sometimes, you just get lucky. Wayman's original testimony was solely to corroborate Cray's testimony to describe the finished cartoon sketches and give his opinion of Cray's artistic ability. I also hoped that the judge would allow Wayman's opinion of Cray's character.

I anticipated that Watson would try to discredit Cray's credibility on cross-examination because he was a convicted felon. If he opened that door, I was prepared to blow it wide open with the facts surrounding Cray's arrest. That would be the only way for me to get those facts in front of the jury. Though Judge Cobb had been lenient in his evidentiary rulings, there was the risk that he wouldn't permit it. He could view it as irrelevant to our case and too prejudicial. Judge Cobb could reason that Cray's conviction wasn't the subject of the trial. He could also find that the note Josh had slipped Walt detailing the circumstances of Cray's setup couldn't be authenticated.

I knew Rick Watson was suffering in the polls with all the daggers thrown at him by his opponent in the upcoming primary. Vic Jenkins was on his own mission against the corruption in the sheriff's department. And our solicitor knew Vic's assaults were true. From my past cases with Watson, he had admitted as much every time I kicked his ass in court.

I had failed the Abbotts before but not this time. The plea that I obtained for Cray had been eating at me. I should have fought harder for him then. But, as they say, timing is everything. And with the additional information Wayman reluctantly shared with me, the time was ripe for a heart-to-heart with Solicitor Rick Watson.

Chapter Eighty-Three

Solicitor Rick Watson

Vic's attack on my record was catching on. The press sensed the swing and was beginning to ride the wave. I was getting eaten alive by the news coverage of the first three days of the trial. I was seeing firsthand how public perception was manipulated. I definitely had a target on my back.

The headlines in the local newspaper included: "The Case Against Charles Walker is Shallower Than a Kiddie Pool" and "The Solicitor Wears An Empty Suit." Then yesterday's editorial, "Washed Up Watson," detailed the testimony about the hit instructions containing a code that wasn't even known to the accused. "How did the prosecution miss such a critical fact?" the writer chastised.

I had never won a case against Earl Dixson. Juries are unpredictable, but he definitely had the momentum heading into our last day. So, I was extremely curious why he had wanted to meet. Earl was solid, honest, and a straight shooter, but I couldn't help but think that he was trying to throw me a curveball. This meeting might be intended to distract me from my much-needed preparations for the last day of testimony and closing arguments.

I knew from experience that Earl was fiercely loyal to his clients. He built his cases with precision, slowly laying the groundwork for the crescendo at the end. Was his proposal really in my best interest or just a ruse to free his clients? Could he really be sympathetic to my position, as he claimed?

Earl's synopsis of the evidence was accurate. My theory had holes big enough to drive a truck through. I wanted to defend myself, reminding him that it wasn't my theory per se. William Wilson and Chief Deputy Barbee had concocted the theory, and they agreed to testify under oath to support it. It sounded like an open and shut case other than why Josh Abbott would accept a hit job proposed by a purported ex-wife. But in the number of drug crimes I had been involved with over the years, I had witnessed the extreme actions taken by addicts for cash. The facts I had been presented were that Josh and his son, Cray, were both in prison for drug-related offenses. Warden Wilson believed there was a larger distribution network. So, I came to believe that Savannah Abbott could have used her estranged husband to knock off her boss' wife. Who knows? Savannah may have told Josh that in addition to the large sum of cash he would be paid, it could serve him well to get on the banker's good side—in case he ever needed a loan to help subsidize the farming operations. However, now it appeared that Josh and Savannah were not estranged. More so, the marriage didn't even seem to be on the rocks, incarceration or not.

The letter from Josh Abbott to his father, a decorated Marine, detailing the facts associated with the arrest of his son, Cray, had me doubting the Abbott men's involvement in drugs at all. Plus, Cray Abbott appeared squeaky clean during his tenure at Somerset. When I saw Cray's name on the defense witness list, I thought I could expose a nick in Earl's armor. What was he thinking putting a convicted felon on the witness stand? I thought I would be able to eat Cray Abbott alive on cross-examination. But, my interview of Wayman Ritchie, one of the Somerset guards, only established that Cray Abbott was one of the most popular and gifted inmates. Even my go-to, Franklin Newton, didn't have anything on the young man. In the past, if a proposed witness had served time in Somerset, I could always count on Franklin to provide some dirt to annihilate their credibility.

I was more than second-guessing my case. Worse, Earl forecast a firestorm would occur if Judge Cobb allowed the letter into evidence. I could feel Vic Jenkins' drool dripping down my neck. Earl made it clear, "If Judge Cobb denies admissibility of the letter, I am not stopping there. I intend to begin a campaign to highlight the corruption by William Wilson in Kentucky. I will also prove the corruption has infected the Thurmond County Sheriff's Department with Wilson's protégé, Chief Deputy Jimmy Barbee."

I had a lot to figure out. I attempted to set aside my personal objectives—re-election, title, power, and my girlfriend. If Judge Cobb permitted the evidence Earl had just recited to me, I had more repercussions than a courtroom loss. Vic

Jenkins would strangle me with it. It was exactly the type of evidence that he needed to re-open his brother's case. His brother was serving five years. The only reason that his brother's case hadn't kept me up at night was because Vic's brother was a bad apple. Our city was safer with him in the slammer whether he was innocent this last time or not.

I was not only leaning toward dismissing the case but also on pressuring William Wilson to use his connections to release Cray Abbott. He was approaching the end of his sentence, and I believed Earl that the young man had been setup along with his father. What is worse, I was starting to believe that Josh Abbott hadn't hung himself. This had William Wilson's and Jimmy Barbee's fingerprints all over it.

I poured a stiff scotch. Though it was close to midnight, I called Earl. The charges against Charles Walker and Savannah Abbott would be dropped on the condition that Earl would silently participate in a joint press conference where I would announce that new evidence had been uncovered that clearly exonerated Charles Walker and Savannah Abbott. Earl would decline to answer any questions or rehash any of the evidence. Earl was on board with my proposal.

My next call was to William Wilson. That man was crooked to the bone. I took pleasure in communicating that Earl Dixson was getting ready to re-open the case against Cray Abbott and that it wasn't looking good for him. My advice— find a way to release that boy as soon as possible.

Chapter Eighty-Four

Earl Dixson

After hanging up with Rick Watson, I jumped in my car and drove as fast as I could to tell Hannah Anne the news.

I stopped by the 24-hour Piggly Wiggly en route and grabbed the most expensive bottle of champagne the grocery store carried. This moment was worthy of a celebration despite the late hour, worthy of interrupting Hannah Anne's rigid bedtime routine where she typically was fast asleep by 10:00 p.m. The woman slept like a rock, until 1:00 a.m. when she would toss and turn until 3:00 a.m., before becoming comatose again until 6:00 sharp. She was mortified when I acknowledged her nightly habit. She apologized for keeping me from getting a good night's sleep. But, I had gotten used to it. Now, I even slept through her 1:00-3:00 a.m. fidgety sleeplessness. I smiled just thinking about sneaking in with my key and waking her to share this incredible news. It was only about ten minutes before her 1:00 a.m. wake-up time anyway.

My giddiness took an abrupt, 180-degree turn when I saw a car in the driveway. I realized then that I didn't know the make or model of Bo's car. I tried to push away that possibility. It had to be some family member who had arrived for the last day of trial, although she hadn't mentioned anyone. And, in retrospect, she hadn't objected to my request to be alone tonight to collect my thoughts, prepare my remaining examinations, and work on my closing argument.

As my headlights shone on the license plate of the large truck, the Texas license plate kicked me in the gut. Then the decal on the back of the car bore the words: DRILLER'S LIFE.

No doubt, this was Bo's car. Hannah Anne's bedroom light was out, as well as every light in the house. On the way home, I tossed the bottle of unopened champagne out the window.

Chapter Eighty-Five

Hannah Anne Hart

I understood why Earl needed his space tonight. Even though he never lost his cool, I could tell he was on edge. He needed time to prepare for the last day of trial. He carried the weight of the world on his shoulders with all his clients, but if he'd said it once, he said it a thousand times—this trial was different. The defendant was Savannah, my daughter. I did have the greatest faith in him, just not in the jury.

I had watched the jurors intently every day, but my impression of whose side they were on changed daily. I wasn't cut out for reading a jury. I overanalyzed every note jotted down, every furrow of a brow, and every nod of a head. For this reason, my head was swimming. Earl had given me one assignment, and I felt like I had let him down. When he questioned me nightly, I realized that my strong opinion after the first day had become a jumbled mess as each day passed. I simply had no idea what they were thinking.

Of all nights, this was not the night to be alone. I was out of sorts and shaking like a leaf. My daughter's freedom would be decided tomorrow, and Bo was back in town. He said that the reason he left Beaufort was to tie things up—that he had lots of news. I was getting ahead of myself thinking that after all this time, he may be coming home to stay.

I poured an Abbott Farm bourbon on the rocks and went to the porch swing. As the burn of the bourbon was kicking in, the memories of our family did as well. Our time together was short-lived but good. No, the time was more than good; it had been magical.

There was a coolness in the air that was rare for Beaufort. I went inside to grab a blanket and more bourbon. I jumped out of my skin when I heard the door opening.

"Earl?"

"No. It's Bo."

When he saw the stunned look on my face, he said, "Sorry, I knocked several times, but you didn't answer."

"I was out on the porch. I just came in for a blanket."

"I should have called before popping over. I wanted to check on you because I'm a nervous wreck."

"I am too. I am having bourbon on the porch. Want to join me?"

"Would love to."

I poured Bo a bourbon and wrapped up in the blanket on the swing.

"Climate change must be a real thing. I don't ever remember it getting this cold. Care to share that blanket?" he asked.

"You're not so tough after all," I said, as I patted the seat beside me on the swing.

We swung for a while, sipping our bourbon. Bo finally broke the silence.

"So, what do you think?" he asked.

"Well, after the first day, I thought we had at least five on our side. But, then after the second day, I crossed two of those off but added a different juror. Then, I just started second-guessing myself with all of them. I always thought I had good instincts but, honestly, I have no idea."

"I know Savannah is innocent. But I also know that things don't always turn out like they should. I'm a living example of that. Will you ever be able to forgive me?"

"Oh, Bo. You had to find your own way. You always provided for us."

"I tried. I really did. And I thought about both of you a lot. I'm sorry I left like I did. Both times. The first time I was an immature coward, pure and simple. This last time, I had some things to wrap up. I left because I knew I was coming back— and this time, to stay. I didn't tell you because I knew you wouldn't believe me. And, I don't blame you. But I am back. And I am not going anywhere, Hannah Anne. You are still my wife. This is still our house. I want to come home."

Bo took my glass of bourbon from my hand and placed it on the table. He put both his hands on my cheeks and looked me in the eyes.

"I love you. I have never stopped loving you."

He leaned in to kiss me, and I felt like I was in quicksand. I had waited for this moment for forty years. I had cried myself to sleep so many nights. I had more dreams than I could count of Bo coming home, running to me, kissing me wildly, lifting me into his arms, and carrying me to bed. My dreams had always stopped there. I would wake up and try to go back to sleep. I wanted the dreams to pick up where they left off.

But this was no dream. His kiss was real. I felt like that infatuated schoolgirl many, many years ago who couldn't believe when Bo Hart had even noticed I was in the room, much less wanted to make out with me. A thousand things were racing through my head. Before I could process my emotions, he stood up, grabbed my hand, and led me into the house in the direction of my bedroom. Our bedroom.

When we entered the room, a wave of clarity washed over me. In all of her books, I couldn't recall a time where Jacqueline Summers had ever analyzed a man's kiss. Before Earl Dixson, the only man I had ever kissed was Bo Hart. Clearly, I didn't qualify as an expert in the field. But the differences were significant, and I couldn't help but think that they were also revealing.

Bo's lips were hard and tight, his mouth stiff like it was barely open. He retreated quickly. Earl's lips were soft and tender. His mouth was inviting and embracing. Earl lingered. Earl's kiss was exactly the type I had envisioned as a teenager when practicing on my pillow and mirror.

What a fool I have been, I thought. I had fantasized about Bo for so long. I had created a far different version of our romance than had ever existed. My short time with Earl had opened my eyes to lots of things. Most importantly, our relationship embodied a wholeness, a completeness, an inner peace that comes from the security of a faithful companion. Earl loved me with a full heart.

I turned Bo around and led him back toward the porch.

"I want my bourbon. And, we need to talk."

Chapter Eighty-Six

Earl Dixson

I couldn't remember the last time I had cried. Apparently, I was way overdue for a good one because the floodgates opened. Between my sobs, I began contemplating my life. I had dedicated it to my clients. Along the way, I had neglected relationships. I either had forgotten or never experienced deep passion. I was an emotionless zombie until Hannah Anne came into my life.

When my wife of twenty-five years walked out the door, I didn't even shed a tear. Now, I had fallen hard, too hard, for Hannah Anne. I had ignored my lawyerly analytics and listened to my heart. I believed her when she said she was over Bo. I should have known better. Her infatuation with him was clearly alive and kicking the first time we met in my office. It was impossible to miss the way she had gazed at him.

When Walt informed me that Bo had up and left again, why did I think I stood a chance? There was just something about Hannah Anne that made me roll the dice for once in my life. I decided to take a risk and go for it.

I should be celebrating tonight. I had secured freedom for Charles Walker, Savannah, and Cray. Deep down, I knew that justice wasn't complete. William Wilson and Alice Walker should be prosecuted for their horrific charade. But, I had agreed to keep my mouth shut. The evidence against William Wilson and Alice Walker would be sealed in return for the dismissals and Cray Abbott's discharge. I didn't want to know the details of how they would pull off Cray's release, but Rick Watson assured me that William Wilson's associations would make it happen. Would I have agreed to such a plan if Hannah Anne hadn't been in the picture? Had I permitted my infatuation with her to color my judgment?

I needed to focus on the result. But my head hurt, and my heart ached. I didn't sleep a wink and was startled when my alarm woke me up at 6:00 a.m. I didn't have to be at the courthouse until 9:00. Rick Watson and I were jointly meeting with Judge Cobb to reveal that the solicitor's office was dropping the charges. The trial was over.

It had been a long time since I had the luxury of a leisurely morning. I had time to read the newspaper with a cup of coffee, prepare a hot breakfast, and take a long shower. But, I didn't have the energy to get out of bed. I stared at the clock until 7:00 and then forced myself to get a grip. I was acting like a lovesick teenager.

The hot shower snapped me back to reality. I closed my eyes as I enjoyed the massage option on the expensive showerhead Marsha had installed. I had never taken the time to mess with the spray alternatives. I smiled thinking about this unknown asset that I had retained in the divorce. I made a mental note that I needed to upgrade my water heater, as the hot water turned warm and then cold (of course, the rare time when I let myself linger in the shower). I shut off the invigorating shower massage and grabbed a towel. I thought I was imagining the smell of bacon and fresh coffee permeating through the house. I wrapped the towel around my waist and followed the aroma into the kitchen.

"Thought you needed a good breakfast for today," Hannah Anne said, as I entered the kitchen. "And, I missed you last night."

"I came by to share some news but saw that you had a guest."

"Yes, I did. Bo thought I may need the company. So, what's the news?"

Now was not the time to cross-examine her about what that meant, although I wanted an explanation about when Bo had returned to town or, more importantly, why his car was still there after midnight.

"Rick Watson and I are meeting with Judge Cobb this morning. Watson is dropping the charges. It's over Hannah Anne."

She screamed and ran into my arms. She began kissing me exuberantly. I had never made out in my kitchen before. My towel dropped to the floor.

"How about breakfast in bed?" she asked.

I wondered if we would make it out of the kitchen.

"Have I ever told you what a wonderful kisser you are?" Hannah Anne asked, leading me to the bedroom and shutting the door.

PART XIV

Chapter Eighty-Seven

The Opening

The evening was doubly exciting. It was the Grand Opening of the Joshua Abbott Center for Lowcountry Arts. And, Elliott Gray was kicking off a book tour for his newest novel, *Hired Hit on Jessamin Island*.

Charles Walker, the host of the event, had always been an avid supporter of the arts and decided it was time that Beaufort had a place to showcase the works of the talented artists in the Lowcountry. He not only conceived the idea but also financed the project. He wanted to honor Josh's memory. Then, Elliott Gray stepped up and privately committed an undisclosed percentage from his new book sales. "After all," he said, "Charles' story was the inspiration." There were already a record number of pre-release sales for the much-awaited new novel.

Since his release from the Somerset Federal Correctional Institute, Cray Abbott had been consumed with the new facility. Charles requested his input from the planning stages to the final design and displays. Cray met extensively with the architects and the interior design team. Cray visited galleries and met with numerous local artists. After the construction was complete, Charles was underwhelmed with the stale and cold entrance. He wanted it "to sing."

Charles commissioned Cray to paint a large mural to encompass the entryway. Cray suggested a dedication to the Lowcountry birds. Charles loved it.

A rookery filled with white egrets covered one entire wall. With Savannah's approval, Cray mixed the remainder of Josh's ashes into the paint for the trees. The detail was magnificent. The other walls burst with painted buntings, oystercatchers, terns, blue herons, and sandpipers—all Savannah's favorite creatures.

The opening was highly anticipated and with the inclusion of Elliott Gray, the draw extended beyond Beaufort County. A record crowd was expected. In addition to all the author's fans, it was a reunion of sorts—a gathering of souls that the Abbott journey had introduced, united, and reunited.

Walt and Maude returned from a Caribbean vacation and were glowing more than usual with their bronze tans. Maude's sister, Hazel, and her family made the trek from Manteo. Vincent Ellis, the long-time business attorney for Charles Walker, accompanied Rollins Bishop, who was overheard taking credit for developing the strategy and obtaining the evidence that sealed the victory.

Charles Walker, who was never one for social events, seemed to enjoy the spotlight. He was in rare form. Perhaps the striking convenience store clerk from North Carolina was part of the reason. It seemed that Charles was never too far from her.

At Charles' request, Earl had contacted Brandy and extended an invitation. She politely declined; she couldn't afford to take time away from her three jobs. And there was a gnawing remorse. She didn't think she could bear to look Savannah in the eyes. Charles persisted with a plane ticket, accommodations, and expenses. Earl relayed that both families were so grateful. Without her, the outcome may have been very different.

"Neither Savannah nor Hannah Anne know the details you told me about you and Josh," Earl said. "Don't beat yourself up about it. They both believe you are an angel, a divine intervention. They are glad Josh felt comfortable sharing with you the information crucial to cracking our case. You can trust me. No one else needs to know; no one else will ever know."

Hannah Anne, Savannah, and Cray accompanied the real hero of the night, Earl Dixson. Other than Rick Watson, no one knew the additional information disclosed by Cray's former guard, Wayman Ritchie, who was also in attendance. Wayman was not attending as a guest but as an employee. He had been hired as the head of security for the Joshua Abbott Center for Lowcountry Arts.

When Wayman was first introduced to Cray Abbott, his opportunity for career advancement was within the prison system. Never in his wildest dreams could he have imagined being the head honcho of a beautiful building that housed expensive artwork. It was the polar opposite of a prison.

The night before he was scheduled to testify, Wayman recounted to Earl Dixson new information. When Cray started his sentence, Wayman had been approached by his boss, Franklin "Fig" Newton, with a new assignment. If successful, Fig promised him a substantial reward. Fig assured Wayman that he had the Somerset warden's ear. Wayman naively thought that any reward could include a raise, a better schedule, or even an administrative position. He wanted to impress his boss.

"A new inmate, Cray Abbott, is involved in a massive drug distribution ring led by his father, an inmate in the Kentucky pen," Fig reported. "You are tasked to watch Cray Abbott carefully. You are to intercept and review every piece of mail addressed to him. Befriend the boy—unearth his story; discover his weaknesses and uncover any dirt on his family."

Wayman tried every trick in the book with Cray Abbott. But, the kid rejected every ploy. With Cray's move into Shipping and Receiving, where all the illegal goods found their way into the prison, Wayman was sure that Cray would succumb to temptation. Cray would witness first-hand the money that could be made under "The Donald's" operation.

Fig Newton grew impatient with Wayman's inability to produce even one iota of anything crooked, much less criminal, against Cray Abbott. Wayman had seen and heard a lot within the prison walls. He believed that all of the allegations about the Abbotts were misplaced. The Cray Abbott that he had observed wouldn't knowingly be involved in drug trafficking. And, his grandmother, Hannah Anne Hart, was nothing but honest-to-goodness.

When Fig Newton questioned Wayman extensively about the papers that he permitted Ms. Hart to "slip to Cray," Wayman became suspicious, not of Cray or his grandmother, but his boss. Ms. Hart's words kept echoing in his head, "Cray Abbott would give you the shirt off his back, he wouldn't hurt a flea, and he has never even run a red light. I hope you're looking out for him, Wayman."

Franklin Newton relieved Wayman of his duties with Cray Abbott because of the notes he allowed Ms. Hart to bring into the prison. At Ms. Hart's next visit, she would be greeted by Newton instead. Wayman believed that his boss was making much more of the notes that sweet Ms. Hart brought with her. He picked up on other things as well. He overheard Bull tell Cray during a tattoo session about Newton vacationing with Bull's cohorts. Earl learned that before his new job at the Somerset Correctional Institute, Wayman's boss, Franklin Newton, had been employed by the Thurmond County Sheriff's Department.

Wayman liked Hannah Anne Hart, and he liked Cray Abbott. He wanted Earl Dixson to know that he would testify about the sketches and Cray's character. "But let's keep the other information to ourselves. I have a mother to support, and I need my job," he politely requested of Earl.

Now, Wayman was standing with Savannah, Brandy Chastain, and his new boss, Charles Walker. Savannah was educating them about all the Lowcountry birds reflected in the mural. Many of these birds were also now permanently emblazoned on inmates at the Somerset Federal Correctional Institute. Their conversation was interrupted by Hannah Anne who appeared with a tray filled with glasses of Abbott Farm Single Barrel Bourbon.

"I'd like to make a toast," she said. "To Cray—he beautifully captured his father's favorite bird and the rookery, Savannah's special place with Josh. Josh will live forever within these walls."

Everyone took a sip of the Kentucky bourbon.

"And here's to Earl Dixson," Hannah Anne continued, "to whom we are eternally grateful. You have given us freedom—freedom to live and freedom to love."

Earl tried to maintain good spirits. It was an evening worthy of celebration. Hannah Anne was by his side. She had disclosed their relationship to Bo. She was in love and committed to Earl.

Despite the celebratory spirit, Earl couldn't shake the call from Rick Watson earlier that day. The Solicitor's Office was issuing a press release stating that no suspects had been identified for the hired hit on Alice Walker. The county wasn't expending any additional resources on the investigation. The case was officially closed. When Earl inquired into the investigation of Josh Abbott's purported suicide while in jail, Watson informed him that he had attempted to follow up with Benji Webb, the former cellmate of Josh Abbott. The solicitor wanted to confirm the alleged conversations between Josh and Benji about Josh's suicidal thoughts, which were supposedly overheard by the Kentucky prison guards.

Unfortunately, Benji died in a single-car accident the day that he was released on parole, so he couldn't be interviewed.

At the end of the evening, Earl pulled Charles aside and delivered the news that the case was officially closed. Charles didn't need an investigation to know that his now ex-wife and ex-father-in-law orchestrated the murder-for-hire plot. His father-in-law's old crony, Jimmy Barbee, had planted the evidence in Josh's motel room, he was sure. Likewise, he knew that Josh Abbott didn't hang himself. Josh was murdered. Josh's former prison mate's car accident probably wasn't an accident either. Josh and Benji knew too much. They were successful hits ordered by Warden William Wilson. It was reprehensible that he wouldn't spend the rest of his life behind bars for these crimes. But, at least, the rest of this tragedy was righted—that, he could live with.

Though it was not justice, Josh Abbott, as a sacrificial lamb, delivered forgiveness and joy among these previously broken families. Savannah and Cray were back in Beaufort. Walt and Maude were reunited. Hannah Anne met the love of her life, Earl Dixson, and could finally forgive Bo Hart, who reconciled with his daughter. Charles Walker escaped his miserable marriage and was embracing his life and his community.

Joshua Carter Abbott's tender-hearted spirit would forever encircle all of them. And, they would feel his presence with every sighting of a Lowcountry bird.

Acknowledgements

To my three sons, Andy, Walt, and Peter...you are my proudest accomplishments in life. Somehow, I survived your shenanigans, so guess what? Payback is another book for you to promote!

And to my Wake Forest sisters who are enthusiastically pushing me along on this new journey: Becky, Ginny, Jane, Laura, Lisa, Pam, and Sylvia...Raise What? And to my real sisters, Denise Sherman, Amy Perko, and Melanie Caudron—if I started to express all the amazing things you do, it would make this book too long!

Thanks again to the incomparable Erica Levy Photography.

There are not enough (unedited) words to express my appreciation and admiration to the talented women on my editing team: Rachael Cox, Susan Lower, and Laura Cavagnaro. And, what can I say to Christos Angelidakis, my cover designer, except ypérochos!

Made in the USA
Columbia, SC
25 June 2022